W9-BJU-271

PRAISE FOR ISLAND 731

"Robinson (Secondworld) puts his distinctive mark on Michael Crichton territory with this terrifying present-day riff on The Island of Dr. Moreau. Action and scientific explanation are appropriately proportioned, making this one of the best Jurassic Park successors."
— Publisher's Weekly - Starred Review

"Take a traditional haunted-house tale and throw in a little Island of Dr. Moreau and a touch of Clash of the Titans, and you wind up with this scary and grotesque novel. Robinson, a skilled blender of the thriller and horror genres, has another winner on his hands."
— Booklist

"[Island 731's] premise is reminiscent of H.G. Wells' The Island of Dr. Moreau, but the author adds a World War II back story...vivisection, genetic engineering, Black Ops, animal husbandry and mayhem. This is the stuff that comic books, video games and successful genre franchises are made of."
— Kirkus Reviews

"A book full of adventure and suspense that shows 'science' in a whole new horrific light. This is one creepy tale that will keep you up all night! And it is so well written you will think twice before taking a vacation to any so-called 'Island Paradise!'"
— Suspense Magazine

PRAISE FOR SECONDWORLD

"A brisk thriller with neatly timed action sequences, snappy dialogue and the ultimate sympathetic figure in a badly burned little girl with a fighting spirit... The Nazis are determined to have the last gruesome laugh in this efficient doomsday thriller."
— Kirkus Reviews

"Relentless pacing and numerous plot twists drive this compelling stand-alone from Robinson... Thriller fans and apocalyptic fiction aficionados alike will find this audaciously plotted novel enormously satisfying."
— Publisher's Weekly

"A harrowing, edge of your seat thriller told by a master storyteller, Jeremy Robinson's Secondworld is an amazing, globetrotting tale that will truly leave you breathless."
— Richard Doestch, bestselling author of THE THIEVES OF LEGEND

PRAISE FOR THE JACK SIGLER THRILLERS

THRESHOLD

ALSO BY JEREMY ROBINSON

The Jack Sigler Novels

Prime
Pulse
Instinct
Threshold
Ragnarok
Omega
Savage

The Chesspocalypse Novellas

Callsign: King
Callsign: Queen
Callsign: Rook
Callsign: King – Underworld
Callsign: Bishop
Callsign: Knight
Callsign: Deep Blue
Callsign: King – Blackout

The Jack Sigler Continuum Series

Guardian

Standalone Novels

The Didymus Contingency
Raising The Past
Beneath
Antarktos Rising
Kronos
Xom-B

Jenna Flood Thrillers

Flood Rising

Secondworld Novels

SecondWorld
Nazi Hunter: Atlantis

The Antarktos Saga

The Last Hunter – Descent
The Last Hunter – Pursuit
The Last Hunter – Ascent
The Last Hunter – Lament
The Last Hunter – Onslaught
The Last Hunter – Collected Edition

Nemesis Novels

Island 731
Project Nemesis
Project Maigo

Horror (Writing as Jeremy Bishop)

Torment
The Sentinel
The Raven
Refuge

Short Story Collections

Insomnia

ALSO BY SEAN ELLIS

Jack Sigler/Chess Team

Callsign: King
Callsign: King - Underworld
Callsign: King - Blackout
Prime
Savage

The Nick Kismet Adventures

The Shroud of Heaven
Into the Black
The Devil You Know
Fortune Favors

The Adventures of Dodge Dalton

In the Shadow of Falcon's Wings
At the Outpost of Fate
On the High Road to Oblivion

Jenna Flood Thrillers

Flood Rising

Novels

Ascendant
Magic Mirror
Wargod (with Steven Savile)
Hell Ship (with David Wood)

Secret Agent X

The Sea Wraiths
The Scar
Masterpiece of Vengeance

FLOOD RISING

A Jenna Flood Thriller

JEREMY ROBINSON
WITH SEAN ELLIS

BREAKNECK MEDIA

*To Cheryl Dalton, for bringing the
readers and authors together*

FLOOD RISING

"The best way to predict the future is to create it."

~Peter Drucker

FLIGHT

ONE

Jenna Flood realized two things in the time it took the black numbers on the silver, liquid crystal display to tick between 55 and 54: she was looking at a bomb and she had less than a minute to live.

49...

48...

Jenna took a step back. Her flip-flops slapped against the soles of her feet, the only noise she could hear over the sound of blood roaring in her ears. She wasted the precious seconds wavering in indecision.

Listen to your gut, her father was fond of saying, *but make up your own damn mind.*

He seemed to always have sage one-liners ready, like some ancient wise man. His first name was actually Nathan, but everyone called him 'Noah.' Noah Flood. Despite the funny looks he got when people first heard the name, Jenna thought it actually pleased him to be nicknamed for the world's most famous mariner. He had been Noah to her since she could talk—not Dad or Daddy.

Jenna's ability to separate gut instinct from thoughtful rationale was not as finely tuned as Noah's, which was almost certainly the very point he was trying to make. A visceral gut reaction could alert a person to very real dangers, which was a possibility for an adolescent girl in South Florida. The human body had only two responses to those instinctive warning signals: fight or flight.

Her gut told her to flee. There wasn't time for any kind of rational approach to this problem. Not for her. But her father...

"Noah!" Her voice sounded shrill in her ears. "Noah! There's a bomb in here!"

45...

44...

She opened her mouth to shout again, but glimpsed movement on the deck outside. Noah, slid down from the bridge, hands on the rails of the ladder, feet never touching the rungs. He landed on the deck and burst through the cabin door. She waited for him to laugh and admit to a prank, or to chide her for mistaking some harmless piece of equipment for a bomb, but he did neither. Instead, he pushed her aside with a brusqueness she had seen him use only once before, just a week earlier. She had seen a different side of him that day, and it had been so anomalous that she never expected to see it again. Yet, here it was again.

Caught off-balance she started to stumble, but his hand clasped her forearm, steadying her. Then he pulled her behind him, dragging her toward the upper deck's door.

She craned her head around and caught one last glimpse of the timer counting down—

39...

38...

—before Noah jerked her away. As she followed, she continued the countdown in her head, muttering under her breath. "Thirty-seven alligators, thirty-six alligators..."

What will happen when it gets to zero?

With her mind's eye, she looked past the numbers on the simple kitchen timer, and saw the rest of it. Several plastic-wrapped blocks of something that looked almost like cheddar cheese, lined the bottom of a sixteen-quart Igloo cooler that someone had left under the table in the small but well-appointed salon. Her gaze had been drawn to it immediately. The lunch-box sized cooler looked completely out of place in the cabin. The galley had not one but two fully functional refrigerators, one of them stocked with a variety of beer and soft-drinks. Clients never brought along coolers, and they certainly never left anything behind.

If she hadn't been curious about what was inside it, or had just been delayed a minute longer out on the deck... *What would have happened?*

What was *going* to happen?

The yellow packets had to be some kind of plastic explosives—C4 or Semtex—that was what they called it in the movies. There were three bricks, each at least as big as a pound of butter. *Three pounds of plastique*, Jenna wondered, *is that a lot?*

She thought it must be. Evidently Noah did, too.

"Thirty-four alligators. Thirty-three alligators..."

Her father would know. He had a habit of correcting action movies, commenting on magazine capacities, overpressure waves and how to treat stab wounds. But how did Noah Flood, a fifty-something year old, charter boat operator, know about things like overpressure waves and how many rounds a semi-automatic pistol ought to have?

As Noah opened the door and started through, Jenna heard a sound like a hammer striking the bulkhead above the doorframe. Noah ducked back, uttering a rare profanity, and he peered through the tinted glass windows.

"What's wrong?"

"Sniper," Noah said. "Probably up on the roof of the bait shop. He can't see us in here, but if we try to leave..." He shook his head. "He'll keep us pinned down here until the bomb takes care of us."

Thirty alligators. Twenty-nine. "A sniper? What's going on? Who is doing this?"

Even as she said it, Jenna knew it was a stupid question. Well, maybe not stupid, but definitely the wrong time to ask. Still, it was going to take longer than twenty-seven alligators to wrap her head around the idea that someone was trying to blow them up. That was something so far outside her experience, the only way her fifteen-year old brain—even as sharp and quick as it was—could begin to grasp it all was to begin with *why?*

Noah had his hands on his hips in that familiar *what am I going to do now* pose that usually made her smile. He figured out a lot of problems in that pose, and she knew that somehow, he was going to figure this out, too. Of course, it usually took him a little longer than twenty-five seconds.

"Can we just throw it overboard?" she asked.

He usually hated it when she offered suggestions, especially since she was so often right. This time, instead of shushing her, he just shook his head. "Not with that sniper out there. That's why he's here. We don't get to leave and neither does the bomb."

Twenty-one alligators. Twenty alligators.

Noah darted back to the cooler and peered inside it, cocking his head sideways. "I don't see a jiggle switch," he muttered, then looked over his shoulder at her. "Get in the head."

"*What?*"

"Sometimes, these things come with an anti-tamper trigger." Noah's voice was eerily calm. "If I try to move it, it could explode. The walls of the toilet might shield you enough to survive."

When she did not move right away, he stopped being calm. "Jenna! Move!"

She jerked into motion and ran to the aft head, sliding the pocket door open just enough to squeeze inside. Despite his warning, she peeked out to watch what he was doing.

Jiggle switch? Anti-tamper trigger? How does he know that? As she thought about this, she realized she'd lost the count. *How much time left? Maybe fifteen seconds?*

Noah swung the lid of the cooler closed, then moving with excruciating caution, picked it up by the handle. Careful to avoid jarring or tilting it, he turned and headed forward, into the master stateroom. He disappeared inside, then emerged a moment later, moving much more quickly.

Jenna thought he was going to join her, but instead he turned into the galley. When he stepped out again, he carried four 2.5-gallon water jugs, two in each hand. Still moving at a jog, he returned to the stateroom. When he came out again, he was empty-handed and running toward the small toilet compartment. Without saying a word, he pushed inside and pulled her down, covering her with his body.

"Noah," she whispered, though there was no reason to. "*Who is doing this?*"

She no longer thought of it as a stupid question. In fact, it was the only thing that mattered now. In about seven seconds, she was probably going to die. There wasn't anything she or Noah could do about it. All that was left was to answer that one burning question: why?

Who wanted them dead?

Five alligators... four alligators...

Noah didn't answer. "Cover your head," he said, much louder than her whisper. "Keep your mouth open." He opened his mouth in a wide O, and when she tried to emulate him, her ears popped and her jaw hurt.

Two... one...

Zero.

Nothing?

Did I mess up the count? Maybe it's not—

TWO

6:32 p.m.

Jenna had been helping Noah run trips on weekends and during breaks from school nearly all her life. They were partners as much as they were family, and often she thought of him more as a mentor than a father. He was not an absentee breadwinner, like the parents of so many of her friends at school. He was always there, including her in everything, teaching and molding her at every opportunity. The *Kilimanjaro,* Noah's forty-eight foot Uniflite Yacht Fisherman, was as much a second school for her as it was his place of business, and of course, it was the place they both called home.

The gleaming white fiberglass craft was a comfortable, if not exactly traditional home. The centrally located cabin contained a spacious salon that served as both dining room and galley. In addition to the forward Master Stateroom, which Noah maintained for the use of guests on overnight trips, there were two smaller staterooms, one for him and one for Jenna. When not cruising through the waves, propelled by twin 410 horsepower engines, Jenna often passed idle afternoons on the forward deck, soaking in the sun. There was also plenty of room to hang out and relax on the aft deck, or on the bridge above the cabin, where she often went to watch the picturesque sunsets.

The complete absence of any kind of familial resemblance between her and Noah was also a factor in defining their relationship. Noah was five-ten, average height for a man and solidly built. All his life, so he claimed, people told him that he looked like a young Ernest Hemingway—young being a relative term as Noah was in his early fifties, which seemed positively ancient to Jenna. Perhaps because of the perceived likeness, Noah had chosen to emulate the literary icon by leaving the rest of the world behind and retiring to the Keys to raise his daughter and spend the rest of his life 'chasing that big fish.'

Jenna on the other hand was tall—she already stood nose to nose with Noah—and willowy. Nature had seen fit to let her skip over the body-awkwardness of early adolescence. With long straight chestnut brown hair that looked black when wet, but in a certain light, glowed almost red, and with dark brown eyes, she was often told that she looked exotic. People sometimes asked 'What was your mother?' She understood that they meant nothing offensive by the question, but it was a hard thing to answer.

What was she? *Alive.* What is she now? *Not alive.* Jenna didn't know much more than that. Not her name. Her face. Or something as basic as her nationality.

Noah had no pictures of the woman and almost never spoke of her. When her mother did come up in conversation, she was always 'your mother.' It was the one topic of conversation Noah refused to indulge. Jenna never detected a hint of lingering grief in his tone, but she imagined that they must have been deeply in love. There was no other way to explain his refusal to share memories of the woman with her only daughter. Jenna often daydreamed about her mother, but all she really knew was that the woman must have looked a lot like her, because Jenna looked nothing like her father.

Jenna wondered why thoughts of her mother, of family and the familiarity of home, had popped into her head at a moment like this. Maybe it was her version of that old cliché about a person's life flashing before her eyes before she died.

As the world around her screamed, shook and burned, Jenna wondered if, at long last, she was going to meet her mother.

THREE

6:33 p.m.

The world moved in slow motion. Jenna's senses, hyper-acute with adrenaline and anticipation, dissected every excruciating detail. The fiberglass wall bulged inward. A deep soul-crushing thump pushed through her body. The air in the small compartment flashed blast furnace hot.

Is this what it feels like to die?

Then even her heightened awareness could not keep up with the overload of stimuli that followed. Everything went dark. She felt herself turned upside-down. Shocking coolness replaced the intense heat as the Gulf of Mexico poured in around her.

There was a grunt of exertion and then light flooded in. Noah had wrestled the sprung door out of the way. With her first glimpse of the aftermath, Jenna wondered if she had been transported to some kind of parallel universe where everything was familiar but nothing was where it ought to be. She lay on a bulkhead, with the deck sloping away beside her and the molded plastic commode somehow protruding out above her head, blue chemically-treated water sloshing out.

We're sinking.

That was only partly true. As Noah cleared the opening, Jenna saw that the world outside the head had likewise undergone a profound reality shift. Instead of the warm and welcoming wood-paneled salon with tinted windows affording an almost unrestricted view of the marina, there was only torn fiberglass, dangling hoses, wires and dark water.

"Move it!" Noah shouted.

Jenna shook off her sense of dislocation and pulled herself through the surreal three-dimensional maze. It was like trying to escape from a carnival funhouse. Nothing was what it seemed or where she expected it, and the only way to stave off vertigo was to close her eyes and keep moving. She felt Noah's hand close on her biceps, pulling her the rest of the way through.

Outside, the situation was no less disorienting. Aft, the mostly intact deck was canted upward, like a ramp leading nowhere. Most of the superstructure—the top of the cabin and everything that had extended up above it—was gone, ripped out by the roots. The hulls of the vessels in neighboring slips—the *First Attempt* and the *Martha*

Ann—rose up on either side, looking none the worse for wear. The sight of the two completely intact boats hit Jenna like a cold slap of reality. The only home she had even known was in ruins all around her, and the rest of the world would just keep going on like nothing had happened.

The forward end of the *Kilimanjaro* was completely gone past the galley, split apart like a mailbox vandalized by a delinquent with a cherry bomb. What was left of the front end was settling quickly into the harbor. Whatever Noah had done with the bomb in the last few seconds before the timer ran out had focused most of the blast energy out the front end. His quick thinking had saved their lives.

Jenna started to crawl up toward the still dry aft deck, but Noah pulled her back. "Not that way. The sniper is still out there. We have to make him think we're dead."

"We're going to be in about three seconds," Jenna replied, and in her head, an involuntary countdown started. Three alligators...two...

"We'll swim out." He pointed into the dark water below. Jenna didn't look where he was pointing though. Her gaze was fixed on the enormous gash that stretched across his forehead, streaming blood down into his eyes. "Jenna, focus. You have to follow me. Keep your head down. Don't let him see you. Do you understand?" He shook her arm. "Jenna, do you understand?"

She nodded.

"If we get separated, for any reason, go to Mercy."

"Separated?"

"Time to go." Without further explanation, Noah let go of her arm and half-slid, half-crawled down the tilted deck until he was in the water. She saw how he kept himself pressed flat against the floor, staying low to avoid detection. His movements seemed automatic, like second nature.

Who are you? she thought, but the question felt wrong. She knew who he was, at that moment. Who he'd been for a long time. *The real question is, who did you used to be?*

Jenna put the mystery out of her thoughts and did her best to imitate him. She splashed into the water beside him, and then, at his signal, she took a deep breath and plunged her head under the surface.

The water stung her eyes. It was full of diesel fuel and battery acid and who knew how many other chemicals leaking from the ruined yacht, but below was the lukewarm salty soup of the Gulf. She saw Noah swimming through the green murk, diving down deep into the shadows beneath the *First Attempt*'s keel. She twisted her body around, and kicked after him. She looked back just once and saw the remains of the *Kilimanjaro*, slowly sinking toward the bottom of the harbor.

Noah angled his body upward and surfaced under the wooden pier that ran alongside the *First Attempt*. Jenna came up right next to him and slowly exhaled. She could hold her breath for two full minutes, so the short swim had hardly been a warm-up.

Rays of sunlight slipped through the gaps between the boards overhead and cast surreal stripes across Noah's craggy, blood-streaked visage. For a moment Jenna felt as if she was looking at a stranger.

"Stay here," he said.

He took a deep breath and arched his body in preparation to dive, but Jenna caught hold of his arm before he could slip beneath the water again. "Where are you going?"

"Emergency services are probably on their way. He'll have to bug out soon."

He? Noah was talking about the sniper on the roof of the bait shop, but Jenna failed to see how that was any kind of answer. "So let him."

He offered a smile that was both patient and very, very cold. "Someone just tried to kill us, Jenna girl. I'd like to know who that someone is, wouldn't you?"

Jenna was surprised to find herself in agreement. For the first time since discovering the bomb, her instincts were telling her that it was time, not to flee, but to fight. When Noah plunged beneath the water once more, she was right behind him.

FOUR

6:35 p.m.

Jenna edged out from under the pier just far enough to peek up at the sloping sheet metal roof of the imposing structure that looked down on the marina. She and Noah had always called it 'the bait shop,' but it was several different businesses under one roof: the marina offices, a general store, several tour operators and a few gift shops and restaurants. Movement drew Jenna's eyes. Someone was on the roof, just beyond the peak. A man wearing a tropical print shirt. She couldn't make out his features, but she recognized the shirt.

"It's Ken," she whispered. Ken Soebel had been one of their clients for the day's fishing trip.

Noah gave her a dark look. "I told you to stay put."

She didn't respond. Her thoughts were occupied with the question of how she'd spent the last eight hours in close-quarters with someone who had been planning to kill them, and had not sensed a threat from the man. Not even a hint. *So much for listening to my gut.*

"Do you think he's working for Carlos?" she asked.

Carlos Villegas, a Cuban-American thug who had, along with his brother, come aboard the *Kilimanjaro* one week before, for a day of SCUBA diving on the reefs near Dry Tortugas. He had in fact been interested in recruiting Noah to smuggle drugs across the Gulf of Mexico. Carlos's brother, Raul, had been interested in something else: her. The situation had escalated to the point of a violent confrontation, and Jenna had seen a very different side of her father.

Afterward, Noah had told her that they would not speak of it again, but Jenna's instincts—her gut—told her the brothers would want payback for bruises to both their bodies and their egos. Who else could possibly want to hurt them?

Noah shook his head, but whether it was an answer or from frustration, she couldn't tell. "What else do you see?"

She looked up again, but there was no sign of Ken. "He's gone."

"Damn it." Without further explanation, Noah broke from the cover of the pier and heaved himself up out of the water and onto the wooden deck. He moved so quickly that Jenna didn't have time to ask what he was doing. She let out a reflexive gasp as she realized that he was now in the open, exposed to the sniper, but then just as quickly realized that the sniper—Ken—had gone and was not coming back.

Noah must have realized that, too.

Jenna pushed off one of the upright pilings and swam out from under the floating dock. The wooden platform was only about two feet above her, but for a moment, it seemed unreachably high. The section of dock that ran along the mooring slips was lower, closer to the water's surface, but swimming back would have put her further from her goal, requiring her to waste time she didn't have. She tried to recall how Noah had surmounted this obstacle. Her father had made it look almost effortless.

She reached up as high as she could and then kicked furiously, like a dolphin trying to launch out of the water. The maneuver got her up high enough to grasp the edge of the dock with her fingertips, but that was as far as she got. She hung there, straining to pull herself up, but at the same time feeling the wood slipping away beneath her fingers.

Jenna kicked again, pulling herself up with all her strength, and before she knew it, she was rising, the dock chest-high. She kept kicking, her feet now merely splashing water, and she wriggled forward until she felt the edge of the platform biting into the exposed skin of her abdomen. Her customary uniform—a bikini with an oversized blue Conch Republic T-shirt, knotted at the waist—was the perfect attire for a day-trip aboard the boat, but for life-and-death struggles and clambering around on creosote treated docks, not so much. Her flip-flops were gone. She had kicked them off during the swim. Now her bare toes could find no purchase on the algae-slick pilings. With a final thrust of her legs, she propelled herself forward and rolled onto the dock.

For a moment, she could only lay there, savoring the small victory, but then she glimpsed Noah, sprinting up the ramp that connected the moorage to the boardwalk in front of the bait shop. Getting out of the water was step one. She still had more steps to take, though she hadn't really figured out what they were, aside from *follow Noah*. She sprang to her feet and took off running after him.

A slowly dissipating black cloud hung above the marina, and a foul smell, like burning tires, filled the air. Gawkers lined the docks, gazing in astonishment at the debris-strewn hole in the water where *Kilimanjaro* had been just a few minutes before. She saw a few people that she recognized—faces only, boat operators and residents that she passed every day but had never exchanged words with—and heard them muttering names: Flood, *Kilimanjaro*, Jenna.

She didn't stop. Noah disappeared around the corner of the building. Jenna, sprinting all out, reached the same spot just a few seconds later.

There was a parking area at the northwest end of the structure, but the rest of the space on the leeward side of the bait shop was reserved for long-term parking, storage of trailers and boats undergoing repair. The lot was isolated, with no one to witness what Jenna now beheld.

Noah and Ken were fighting.

It was a close, brutal struggle. It was nothing like the fights in those movies with fists and feet flying, nor even like the sparring she did in the *dojo*, where she trained religiously, two-hour sessions, three days a week. The two men grappled, at times hardly moving at all, each trying to unbalance the other or find some weakness to exploit. Their movements were sinuous, understated, but then Noah's opponent, evidently spotting some opening, let go with his left hand and drew back for a punch.

Jenna realized that she had come to a complete standstill, partly in amazement at what she was seeing, and partly because she didn't know what to do.

She saw a ladder, propped against the side of the tall building, and beside it, a long rectangular case, big enough to hold a guitar. *Or a rifle*, she realized.

Noah must have surprised the would-be assassin as he descended the ladder. Not the man she knew as her father, but the Noah Flood she didn't really know at all: the decisive man who had overpowered Carlos and Raul Villegas a week before, and who had just a few minutes ago known how to shield Jenna from a bomb blast...

What was he thinking? What did he hope to accomplish by charging headlong into combat with a killer?

Whatever the answer, Noah seemed to know what he was doing. Instead of trying to block or dodge the punch, Noah leaned into it, catching the fist on his forehead. There was a spray of blood as Ken's fist made contact with the still weeping gash above Noah's eyes. Noah didn't seem to notice. He let go with both hands and reached up to trap Ken's wrist. Faster than her eye could follow, he flipped his entire body around and pulled Ken to the ground, trapping his opponent's arm with both hands and legs. Jenna heard a crack as cartilage and ligaments separated, and Ken's grunts of exertion became a low howl of agony.

Something moved just beyond the struggling men, and Jenna glimpsed another man running toward them. It took her a moment to recognize him. It was Zack Horne, the other client who had been with Ken during the fishing trip. The friendly expression he'd worn throughout the day was gone, replaced by a hard grim mask. He was looking right at her.

Jenna saw him raise a hand, as if to point in her direction, but instead of an extended fingertip, she saw something dark...and then a tiny flash.

Something cracked against the wall beside her, throwing out a puff of dust and splinters, and Jenna's mind went into overdrive.

A gun. He's shooting at me.

She ducked back, behind the corner, removing herself from Zack's line of sight, but her instincts weren't telling her to flee.

Listen to your gut, Noah always said, *but make up your own damn mind.*

Your gut reaction to a threat will be to either run away, as fast as you can, or to blow through it head on, which, he had added with a trace of sarcasm, *is probably what you will do because you're a teenager and you think you're invincible. But a lot of times, those are the worst choices you could make. You might make a bad situation even worse, or you might miss out on an opportunity.*

Opportunity for what?

She couldn't believe that Noah had been talking about threats like this—or had he?—but she had taken the advice to heart. Her instincts were saying that she should stand her ground and fight these men who seemed intent on killing her. She had to help Noah, but she had to let her mind guide her now, rather than her primal urges.

Zack had a gun, a pistol. She hadn't heard a report, which meant he had a silencer, which also meant none of the gawkers on the other side of the bait shop would hear the shooting and come running.

It's not a silencer, damn it, Noah would say whenever someone in a movie called it that. *It's a suppressor. It's just a fancy muffler, like on a car.* Noah would then go on to complain about how pistols weren't very accurate beyond about twenty-five yards, or how most of the ones the movie stars used didn't have much stopping power.

That information did not seem particularly helpful right now. Even if it didn't kill her, she wasn't keen on letting even one bullet find her. But there was something else Noah always said. *Run away from a knife, but run toward a gun.*

She had pressed him for an explanation on that one.

A bullet can run faster than you can. If someone is trying to shoot you, the only way to stop them is to take their gun away. You get close to them, move faster than they can track you, and you'll take away their only advantage.

How do you know these things? she would ask, and he would just smile and wave a dismissive hand.

How *did* he know those things?

She crouched at the corner, holding her breath and listening. Over the grunts of Noah's battle with Ken, she heard the thump of footsteps.

Wait for it.

Get close.

Remove the advantage.

Zack appeared, gun extended, looking down the side of the building, as if expecting to see her at the far corner. He realized his mistake and glanced down, the gun moving toward her with a slowness that was merely a trick of her senses.

Jenna exploded out of her crouch. She threw her left arm out in a rising block that kept the muzzle of the weapon from finding her, and drove her right fist up, into his exposed throat. Zack staggered back, the gun falling from his fingers, hands clutching protectively at his throat. Jenna however, was just getting started. She drew both hands to her hips and then planted a front-kick into Zack's sternum. Despite the fact that he outweighed her by a good hundred pounds, when her heel connected, he flew back and went sprawling. Jenna kept her balance and moved gracefully forward, as if this were nothing more than one of her karate *katas*.

Zack recovered more quickly than she expected, scrambling to his feet and matching her ready stance, and for a fleeting instant, her resolve faltered. Her many years of martial arts training had, without her even realizing it, accustomed her to the idea that sparring matches ended with such a decisive attack. Even though her body knew what to do, her head had, if only momentarily, let her forget that this was a life-or-death struggle.

A bestial growl interrupted whatever was about to happen, and both Zack and she turned to see Noah give Ken's head a violent twist. Ken's struggles ceased and his body went completely limp in Noah's grasp.

The sound of vertebrae being wrenched apart sent a chill through Jenna. Ken was dead. It was as if she could see the life evaporating out of him. She had never seen a person die before, never seen a person killed.

Killed.

Noah just *killed* someone.

Zack gaped in disbelief for a moment. As Noah shoved the lifeless body of his partner away, Zack turned and ran.

Jenna stood rooted in place, her impulse to fight replaced by a numb paralysis. Noah was suddenly standing before her, sweeping her into his arms—the same arms that had just broken Ken's neck...

She heard Noah's voice, felt his breath on her neck. "Are you okay?"

Am I? "Yes."

She meant it, too. The initial shock of what she had just witnessed was ebbing, and in its place, was an unexpected swell of pride.

They tried to kill us. We fought back.

We won.

They were still standing there, Jenna enfolded in Noah's protective embrace, when the first Monroe County sheriff's deputies arrived.

FIVE

6:38 p.m.

"Let me handle this," Noah whispered in Jenna's ear. He relaxed his embrace, but only enough to allow him to turn and face the two men in black uniforms who were striding toward them.

One of the approaching deputies spotted Ken's motionless corpse and reacted instantly, drawing his service pistol and thrusting it toward them. His partner did the same.

Jenna started—more guns, pointed at her—but Noah held her fast. He raised his hands slowly, and she did the same. She could see the fear and confusion in the deputies' faces. They had no idea what was going on, but had been trained to meet any perceived threat with open aggression. The news was full of stories about people killed by law enforcement officers who overreacted.

That would be just perfect, she thought. *Survive the killers, and then get killed by cops.*

"Move away from her," shouted one of the deputies.

"He's my dad." The words were out before she could even think.

"Jenna, it's okay." He took a slow step to the side, and raised his hands even higher. "Just do what they say. We didn't do anything wrong, but they don't know that."

"On your knees," ordered the same officer, while his younger partner yelled, "Face down. Grab the pavement."

The conflicting orders, sprinkled with a dose of tough cop cliché, would have been comical if not for the guns. Jenna decided face down was better than knees and complied, even though she was pretty sure the command was meant for Noah. In the corner of her eye, she saw him getting down as well.

She looked past the two deputies, past the flashing red and blue lights on their white patrol car, to see more emergency vehicles pulling into the main parking area—a fire truck, an ambulance and Key West police officers. She had been a spectator to such a response before, but had never been at the focal point. It was surreal, but oddly comforting; this was how things got back to normal. The police came, and when they left, you picked up and went on with your lives.

Except she knew that was not going to happen. The boat—their home—had been destroyed. People were trying to kill them, and there was no reason to think they would stop after one attempt.

Zack was still out there, probably only a few blocks away. He was the bad guy, the one that should be face down and grabbing pavement. Jenna wondered if she ought to tell the deputies about him. She rolled her head to the side and was about to whisper that question to Noah when she caught a glimpse of another vehicle rolling up, a black SUV with no lights or identifying marks.

Two men got out. They wore blue windbreakers, and looked enough alike that they might have been brothers. The most obvious differences were cosmetic. One had a military buzz cut while the other had a neatly trimmed if somewhat pedestrian mall-salon hairstyle. They looked exactly like action-movie detectives, and Jenna wasn't at all surprised when one of them waved a badge case at the deputies. "Federal agents. Stand down."

What happened next wasn't exactly what Jenna expected. The deputies did not lower their guns or start grumbling about jurisdiction. Instead, they turned their guns on the new arrivals.

"Keep your hands where I can see them," shouted the senior of the two. He glanced quickly at his partner and added. "Jimmy, secure the suspects. I got this."

The agents seemed momentarily taken aback by the reception, but did as instructed, raising their hands and doing nothing that might provoke a violent response. Jimmy, the younger deputy, circled around Noah and Jenna, his aim never wavering.

The agent who had flashed his badge seemed to grasp that the deputies weren't going to simply stand aside. "Deputy, please. We're all on the same side here, but you need to stand down."

When the uniformed officer didn't respond, the agent continued, "Check my credentials if you must, but we have to get these people out of here. They're in immediate danger."

These people, thought Jenna. *He's talking about us. But how could he know that we're in danger, when we only just figured it out ourselves five minutes ago?*

The deputy lowered his pistol and waved the agent forward. The man with the buzz cut stepped up and held his badge up again for closer inspection. From where she lay, Jenna could make out the gold shield topped with an eagle.

"FBI," mused the deputy. He glanced from the identification card to the agent and back again, then took a step back, his posture wary but no longer quite as assertive. "Special Agent Cray, you need to take this up the chain. Our job right now is to secure this scene until the detectives get here, so I suggest you get back in your car and sit tight."

Agent Cray did not look pleased by the deputy's reticence, but as he pocketed his badge, he gestured again in Jenna's direction. "Can we at least get them someplace where they'll be less exposed?"

The older deputy glanced back, uncertainty giving way to resignation. "Jimmy, pat 'em down. Make sure they're not carrying. Then we'll put them in the patrol car." He looked back to the agents. "That work for you?"

"I'd prefer my vehicle," said Cray. "They aren't suspects, deputy. They're material witnesses, and I'd like to keep anyone from seeing them."

Jenna looked back and saw the younger deputy holster his weapon and approach Noah as cautiously as he might a sleeping alligator. "You packing? Got any blades or anything sharp on you?"

It seemed like a ridiculous question to Jenna. Noah was wearing board shorts and a white T-shirt with the *Kilimanjaro Expeditions* logo, both garments soaked and clinging to his skin. Even if he had owned a weapon—which he did not—there was nowhere for him to hide it on his person.

But instead of answering in the negative, Noah spoke in a low voice, barely loud enough for Jenna to hear. "Deputy, listen to me. Those men are not federal agents. You absolutely must not let them put my daughter in their vehicle."

"Right," replied Jimmy, making no effort to conceal the exchange. "They're not feds. I'll just take your word for that."

Not federal agents? Jenna was still trying to make sense of Noah's claim when she saw the older deputy glance back at them, his face creased with concern and indecision. There was nothing indecisive, however, about Cray's reaction. With startling swiftness, he brushed back his windbreaker, drew a pistol from a holster clipped to his belt, and fired at point blank range into the deputy's chest.

A gun appeared in the hands of the second agent, even as the report from Cray's weapon reached Jenna's ears. Jimmy, in the act of kneeling to frisk Noah, was caught off balance and stumbled as the second agent fired in his direction. Noah rolled sideways, getting closer to Jenna, and shouted something. Jimmy recovered from his fall, and from a kneeling position, tried to unholster his pistol. More shots sounded—Cray and the other agent firing together. Jimmy fell again.

A hand clapped down on Jenna's shoulder. It was Noah, his face just inches from hers. "Run!"

Jenna felt stuck in place, caught in the flypaper of too many things happening all at once, but Noah broke her from the inertia with a shove that rolled her onto her side. She saw him lift up on hands and knees, his back to the agents, his body in between her and their weapons.

"Run!" he shouted again.

Something warm and wet sprayed across Jenna's face. She blinked and twitched her head involuntarily, and when she opened her eyes she saw...

"No!"

The scream came unbidden. Noah's T-shirt, just below the silk-screened silhouette of the *Kilimanjaro*, was stained bright red.

Noah was grimacing, but his eyes never left her. "Run," he repeated, but this time it was only a whisper.

Behind him, the agents had stopped shooting and were moving forward, guns still out. The one named Cray locked stares with her. "We're not going to hurt you," he promised. "But you have to come with us."

Jenna ran.

SIX

6:41 p.m.

Flight.

It wasn't what her gut was telling her to do, not with Noah's blood drying on her face.

As she sprinted along the side of the bait shop, Jenna heard Cray shouting after her, repeating his assertion that he intended no harm to her. She had no reason to believe him, but if he was telling the truth, she might be able to get close enough to fight.

But Noah had told her to run.

Not federal agents...must not let them put my daughter in their vehicle.

The realization almost stopped her in her tracks. She could almost get her head wrapped around the idea that Carlos Villegas was trying to kill them, but how did the rest of it fit?

She was missing something, something that Noah had figured out before he...

Jenna refused to let herself finish that thought. Noah had told her to run, and that's what she was going to do. She rounded the corner and kept running.

The boardwalk that connected the marina to the bait shop was crowded with firefighters, deputies and curious spectators. She considered running to one of the deputies, or trying to lose herself in the crowd, but she rejected the idea. The bogus agents had not hesitated to use violence against law enforcement officials, and she didn't think they'd let the danger to innocent bystanders stop them either. Noah had told her to run, but he hadn't told her where.

Yes he did.

If we get separated, for any reason, go to Mercy.

Jenna veered away from the ramp leading down to the dock and vaulted onto the handrail that ran the length of the boardwalk. It was about twenty feet to the water below, which did not seem very far, until she was looking down at it. Her momentum overcame any uncertainty, and as the oily surface rushed up, she straightened her body and brought her hands together ahead of her. She felt a warm slap, and then the murky green enfolded her.

She turned her palms out and arched her back, leveling out, swimming parallel to the surface without rising. As the water absorbed the initial energy of the dive, she continued propelling herself forward in a graceful underwater breaststroke until she reached the shadows beneath the nearest pier.

There was no sign of pursuit, but she stayed where she was, peering up at the blurry outline of the bait shop and the barely visible figures moving in front of it. The water felt soothing against her skin, and the simple act of holding her breath forced her to remain calm, when she felt like screaming.

Go to Mercy.

She turned and swam deeper into the darkness below the moorage. A splash warbled through the water, and her gaze was drawn to the shattered remains of the *Kilimanjaro* resting on the harbor floor more than thirty feet below her. Figures were moving through the water above the wreck: a pair of rescue divers checking for survivors inside.

With their masks, the divers would have no trouble spotting her if she got too close. She thought about the two deputies and the two men who had claimed to be agents, and decided it was better to avoid being seen.

She had to get out of the marina unnoticed, and the only way to do that was to stay in the water, swim out of the marina and make for one of the island's beaches. It would be a long swim, but the real challenge would be avoiding detection. She would have to swim near the surface to breathe, and that would put her in view of anyone watching from the bait shop, including the killers who knew that she was in the water.

I could swim underwater, she thought. The SCUBA equipment in the *Kilimanjaro*'s aft locker had probably survived the explosion, but with rescue divers crawling all over the wreck, there was no way to reach it.

Then it occurred to her that there were other places to get diving gear.

The idea of stealing from one of her neighbors was so foreign to Jenna that, for a few seconds, she could almost believe that a little cartoon devil on her shoulder had whispered it into her head.

I could never do that. Noah would kill me for even considering...

The thought slipped away, not because of the grief that it might unleash, but because she knew she had it completely wrong. Stealing someone's dive gear to get out of this mess was exactly the kind of thing Noah *would* want her to do—not the Noah she thought she knew, but the man who seemed to know all about how to survive a bomb blast and how to kill a man with his bare hands. The Noah who could sense danger, told her to run and gave his life to make sure she got away.

A spasm in her chest reminded her why she needed a self-contained underwater breathing apparatus, and she slowly rose to the surface to fill her lungs, staying close to the hull of one of the parked boats and well out of anyone's line of sight. Just as quickly, she dove back down, staying beneath the dock where no one would see her.

At least half of the boats in the marina had dive gear, but even with the distraction, Jenna didn't think she could make it aboard any of them unnoticed. She had a different destination in mind.

She swam the length of the pier, coming up for air twice. When she reached the end of the long dock, she swam down until she felt the urge to pop her ears, deep enough she reckoned, for the water to hide her from surface view. She leap-frogged to the next row of boats. From the end of the second pier, she could make out a converted houseboat at the far edge of the harbor, and the weathered, hand-painted sign with the familiar red and white 'diver down' flag. It had yellow letters that read: *Dive 'n' Moore SCUBA Shop.*

John Moore's dive shop was a regular stop for Noah and many of the other charter operators on their way out into the Gulf. It was a last chance to rent equipment and a place to pick up tourists eager to put their freshly minted PADI certifications to real world use. There would be plenty of gear in John's storeroom, and with the attention of nearly everyone else in the marina fixed on the emergency response, the odds were good that she could slip in and out without attracting any notice.

She made the crossing to the pier where the dive shop was permanently moored. She lingered just below the houseboat's deck for a moment, checking to ensure that no one could see her, then pulled herself up and out of the water, before crawling close to the exterior wall.

So far, so good.

The main entrance to the dive shop was situated on the side that faced out toward the marina, but there was a second, private door that opened closer to the pier. From the corner of the structure, Jenna could see the door and the long dock that led back toward the bait shop. There were a dozen people scattered along the dock, all staring across the harbor at the unfolding drama. To reach the door, she would have to risk being spotted, but given the distance, it was doubtful that any of them would recognize her, much less realize what she was doing.

She took a calming breath and stepped out into the open, taking confident but measured steps to avoid looking conspicuous. She stopped at the door, cast a sidelong glance in the direction of the spectators, and then grasped the doorknob.

Unlocked.

She let her breath out in a sigh of relief, then eased the door open a few inches and looked inside. It occurred to her, too late to do anything about it, that the door might be equipped with an electronic signal or even something as low-tech as a bell, but the only sound she heard was the faint rasp of the door's weatherstrip brushing the threshold.

The back door let open to a small sales floor adorned with racks of sundry dive accessories, wet-suits, T-shirts and other souvenirs. She had an unrestricted view of the interior, all the way through to the open front entrance. Off to one side was a counter, and behind it, an open door that led, she assumed, to the storeroom where the more valuable equipment was kept. The shop appeared deserted. John was probably just outside, watching, along with everyone else.

She pulled the door shut and darted to the end of the counter, crouching behind it. She crouch-walked until she was at the door to the back room. She edged around the doorpost, saw that the coast was clear, and then slipped through.

During her swim, she had compiled a mental shopping list, the bare minimum of equipment she would need to swim out of the marina and reach her next destination: mask, snorkel, fins, buoyancy compensator, twenty-pound belt, regulator and a filled gas cylinder. She wouldn't be swimming very deep, no need to worry about decompression sickness. A twelve-liter bottle would more than suffice.

The back room was well organized, and she was quickly able to locate the first few items on her list. She stuffed her selections into a nylon mesh carrying bag, and then moved to a row of bright yellow tanks, lined up with near-military precision. Each one had a paper tag wired to the K-valve fitting, which noted the date it had been filled and the internal pressure measured in bars. She took the closest one and cradled it in her arms.

The squeak of a loose floorboard caused her to look up, but the warning came too late. Her eyes met the weathered visage of John Moore, the dive shop proprietor. He stood warily in the doorway, and then, overcoming his initial surprise, he started toward her.

SEVEN

6:53 p.m.

"Just what the hell do you think you're doing?"

Jenna froze. It was an instinctive response, and in the back of her mind, she heard Noah chastising her for not being more aware of her surroundings, not being in control of her reactions.

Freezing, she knew, was just another way of fleeing a situation, mentally at least, and hoping that things would get better. Usually, they didn't. Freezing up was a way of surrendering control, letting luck and circumstances guide the outcome rather than a conscious decision.

Your gut reaction to a threat will be to either run away, Noah had told her, *or to blow through it head on, which is what you would do because you're a teenager and you think you're invincible.*

Run away?

John was between her and the exit. Nowhere to go.

Blow through?

Yes, she could do that. She could swing the SCUBA bottle at him, knock him down and then run... No, that would defeat the purpose of coming here.

Throw the tank at him, and then when he's distracted, go on the attack, just as she had with Zack. A couple of punches to the jaw... Maybe hit the sweet spot and knock him out on the first try...or a kick to the solar plexus.

I can take him.

The very idea of attacking this man, not a killer with a gun but one of her neighbors, kept her rooted in place.

But a lot of times, Noah had continued, *those are the worst choices you could make. You might make a bad situation even worse, or you might miss out on a real opportunity.*

Most people are an open book. Watch a stranger for a few minutes and you'll know everything there is to know about them—their body language, the way they move their eyes when they talk.

Jenna had exchanged pleasantries with the shop's grizzled namesake, but not much more. He was the epitome of a crusty old beach bum: mid-sixties, a full head of white hair, skin bronzed and eyes faintly yellowed from too many years of staring at the sun-dazzled water. She didn't know if he recognized her. The only thing she saw in his eyes was the fear of what might happen next.

Opportunity.

She shifted her posture, trying to mimic his alert stance, then slowly, visibly relaxed. Her spine straightened, her neck stretched, making her appear taller, more confident. She smiled.

"John!" She said his name like he was an old friend she hadn't seen in years.

Uncertainty flashed across his face. She saw his eyes flicker upward, ever so slightly, as he searched his memory, trying to find the right connection to her.

"Hi, John," she said again, repeating his name, reinforcing the familiarity. "Where do you want me to put this stuff?"

"What?" His eyes were moving wildly now, the biological equivalent of a computer hard-drive spinning to access data scattered across dozens of file locations.

Shape his perceptions, she told herself, *control the finished product.* When Noah had first taught her these techniques, she had been doubtful regarding their effectiveness. It seemed like something right out of the Jedi Knights' handbook. Surely, real people couldn't be that malleable. But thereafter, she had become acutely aware of how often people were easily tricked.

"For the trip out to the reef, John. Remember?"

"Ummm..."

I'm losing him, she thought. *These aren't the droids you're looking for.*

She mimicked his pose again, narrowed her eyelids, and used the small muscles of her eyes to change her focus and dilate her pupils without releasing his stare. It was a hypnotist's trick, but she had no idea if she was doing it right, much less if it even worked at all.

"John, did he forget to tell you?" Her voice was lower now, almost seductively soft, but full of sympathy and commiseration. She made a conscious effort to avoid using any other name but his own. If she mentioned Noah, it might trigger a memory cascade that would connect her to the destroyed boat, and the spell would be broken.

"Do you want me to call him, John? I'll bet he can get this cleared up in a jiffy." *Jiffy* was a good friendly word. "Or we can take care of it when we get back? That's probably what we should do."

A smile, confused but nonetheless friendly, finally split his craggy face. "Ah, sure. That'll be fine."

"Thank you, so much."

He nodded, but then the uncertainty started to creep back into his expression. *Don't let him think about it.* "I could use a hand getting this stuff outside."

"What?" John seemed to snap back into the moment. "Oh, sure thing, Miss...?"

She took a quick step forward and let the cylinder roll toward him. His reflexes took over and his arms came up to catch it. She scooped up the mesh bag containing the rest of the equipment she had gathered, then stepped around him, moving slowly to hold his gaze as he turned. She stayed close, backing toward the rear door. She made small talk about his wares, asked vague technical questions about diving to keep his mind occupied, and step-by-glacial step, got him to the back door.

She set the bag down and reached out for the filled tank. "I've got that one. Can you get the other one?"

"The other?"

"Yep. Thanks. Oh, I guess I'll need a manifold, too."

"Oh, sure thing." He seemed almost reluctant to turn away, to let go of her stare. Truth be told, she was a little worried about that, too. How long would the spell last?

"I'll be right here," she said, with as much innocence as she could muster. "Just grab another bottle and a manifold."

With an audible sigh, John ducked back through the door. As soon as he was gone, Jenna pitched the cylinder over the side, and then, with the mesh bag in hand, she jumped in after it.

EIGHT

7:29 p.m.

NO PERSONS UNDER 21 ALLOWED

Jenna stared at the notice, mounted just to the right of the weather-beaten wooden door. Just below it was another sign that declared: NO SHOES, NO SHIRT, NO SERVICE.

At least I've got a shirt, she thought, as she gave the door a push and went inside. The space beyond was dark, or seemed that way after fifteen minutes of walking into the setting sun. She waited until her eyes adjusted.

She had exited the harbor, underwater and undetected, and headed north, staying in the channel that ran along the eastern side of the island until her tank was about half-empty. Then she ditched everything but the mask, snorkel and fins, and paddled up onto shore. With dry land underfoot, she had discarded the rest of the gear and headed west across the island.

A teen-aged girl walking barefoot down the street was not that unusual a sight—not in a place like Key Weird anyway. Once she got her bearings, she had stayed off the main thoroughfares, weaving down cross streets and through neighborhoods of trailer homes. Although she had lived on the island all her life, she had found herself experiencing it from a completely new perspective. Everything seemed different at a walking pace, familiar but at the same time foreign. The strangeness of her surroundings compounded the mental and physical exhaustion she now felt.

She didn't want to run anymore. She was tired of running. Noah was dead. She hadn't completely processed what that meant. She knew that eventually she would feel pain and loss, but right now she felt only anger: anger at the men who had blown up their boat and shot Noah, and anger at herself for running when what she really wanted was to fight. And since she couldn't do that, she just felt tired.

The stuffy air inside the bar smelled of bleach and fry oil, undercut with a hint of stale beer. Country music drifted through the air, but it wasn't loud enough to drown out the audio from two different television sets mounted to a wall behind the bar, one displaying a baseball game, the other tuned to an all-news network. Jenna studied the latter for a moment, curious to see if the events at the marina had made the news, but the commentators were discussing an international crisis—something about a bio-terrorism attack in China...or had it come from China? On any other day, Jenna would have been fascinated by the subject. While other girls she knew wanted to be famous singers or sports stars—or to just marry rich husbands, she hoped to become an epidemiologist at the Centers for Disease Control and Prevention. Today, she scarcely noticed the bio-attack story.

The sunspots in her vision continued to recede, and after a few more seconds, she could make out human shapes. Two men stood over the pool table that dominated one end of the establishment. It took a moment longer for her to realize that they were looking at her. She turned away from their watchful stares, and moved toward the bar. Two of the stools were occupied, the patrons hunched over their drinks, their backs to Jenna.

"Jenna, honey, what are you doing here?"

Jenna felt the last of her weariness slip away at the sound of the voice. "Mercy!"

Thirty-six year old Mercedes Reyes was the sole proprietor of *Ex Isle*, a not-quite disreputable, out of the way, dive bar, frequented by local regulars and ignored by the island's transient vacationing population. She was also Noah Flood's girlfriend, or at least Jenna assumed she was.

The exact nature of the relationship between her father and Mercy was difficult to pin down. They didn't live together and their very independent lives meant that they didn't spend much time with each other. Mercy was almost twenty years younger than Noah, making him literally old enough to be her father. She was also more than twenty years Jenna's senior, old enough to be Jenna's mother. Given the striking resemblance between them, a similarity which only seemed to increase as Jenna approached maturity, the question of whether they were actually related had come up more than once. Both Noah and Mercy insisted that they met for the first time when Jenna was three years old. The obvious explanation, that Noah was attracted to Mercy for the very reason that she resembled Jenna's mother, would have made sense if not for the somewhat cool nature of their relationship. They were certainly friends, but they seemed to be in no great hurry to have a more intimate connection. Either that, or they were just very discreet about what they did have.

Jenna had always been of two minds about that. Because he was the most important person in her life, she felt both jealous and protective of her father. Sometimes she wanted him all for herself, and sometimes she wanted him to find someone to make him happy. Jenna thought of Mercy as both mother and big sister, and that, too, was problematic. There was no sense in upsetting the status quo with romance.

Now, all those considerations were moot.

"Mercy, I... Noah..." The words refused to form. If she said it out loud, that would make it all true. She had put her grief into a box and buried it deep. Her sole focus had been getting away, running, reaching Mercy, just like Noah told her to do.

Mercy's face creased with concern. "Jenna, honey, what's wrong?"

She tried again. The words didn't come. The tears did.

Mercy, unbidden, folded her arms around Jenna, hugging her tight.

Stop it!

The thought was so sudden, so violent, that Jenna jerked away from Mercy's embrace. She blinked furiously at the tears, embarrassed at the display of weakness, but that was not why she had pulled back.

Noah's instructions to seek out Mercy had been specific: *if we get separated...* Mercy's bar was to have been a place to rendezvous, not a refuge. But how was Mercy going to help? She would call 911—what else could she do?—and that would almost certainly bring Cray and his partner right to her doorstep.

She couldn't put Mercy in danger. She couldn't let herself be put in danger.

So what am I supposed to do?

What would Noah do?

That was a question she no longer felt she knew the answer to, but she knew one thing: *He wouldn't put Mercy in danger.*

"I'm sorry," she said, blinking away the tears. "I shouldn't have come here."

NINE

7:33 p.m.

As she crossed the parking lot, Jenna quickened her pace, moving with a determined stride that none-too-subtly telegraphed the message: *Leave me alone.* Mercy, standing at the entrance, called out to her but didn't follow.

Jenna felt a profound, but short-lived sense of relief. She had protected Mercy and probably herself as well, but in so doing, had wiped clean the slate of options. She was on her own now, and the men who had tried to kill her were still out there. There was nowhere else she could go, no one she could trust to save her...

You've got to stop thinking that way, she told herself. *Noah didn't raise you to let other people solve your problems.*

"So I'm just supposed to take on these killers myself?" she muttered.

If it comes to that. Flight or fight. You either run away, or you take the fight to them. You stood up to Zack, and he had a gun. You are not powerless. Trust your gut, but make up your own damn mind.

Her gut told her to fight, but who was she supposed to be fighting?

"Who wants me dead?"

She had thought that perhaps the bomb attack was the work of the Villegas brothers, wanting revenge for what had happened a week before.

Noah was very careful about which clients he would let her interact with, especially now that his little girl was becoming a very attractive young woman, but he would always introduce her to clients as a way of testing her people-reading skills. When he introduced Carlos and Raul Villegas, a pair of young Cuban-American entrepreneurs who, if their claims were to be believed, operated a successful night club in Key West, her keen senses went on high alert.

She could tell, at a glance, that Raul was the younger brother. He looked younger, with an athletic physique, a clear unlined face and a full head of jet black hair, but it was the less obvious clues that spoke to Jenna. Raul was cocky, with a strutting attention-seeking demeanor that was textbook younger sibling behavior. She noted his clandestine glances to see if older brother Carlos was watching him, but she couldn't tell whether Raul was looking for his older brother's approval, or trying to assert his independence. She also caught him looking at her, not leering openly, but letting his eyes flick up and down her body.

His attention had made her uncomfortable enough to loosen the knot in her T-shirt hem and tug it down to her thighs.

Carlos was very different. Handsome but not in a youthful way. He had a fake but practiced smile and eyes that never seemed to move. He made her wary. Noah had warned her about people like this, men who were well-versed in the art of manipulating others to get what they wanted—hucksters and pick-up artists who used their charisma to exploit people. Carlos hadn't even looked at her.

She had retreated to the *Kilimanjaro*'s bridge and later, when Noah had joined her and asked for her impressions of them, she had expressed her opinion in the most succinct terms. "They're both creeps."

"It's actually much worse than that," Noah told her. "Carlos Villegas has been making the rounds of charter operators, looking for someone to run errands for him."

Jenna was intelligent enough to know what that meant. The Villegas brothers were small-time drug traffickers who were looking to find new ways to bring product across the Gulf. "You knew that, and you still let them come on board?"

"Today, they are just clients, out for a dive. Their money is as good as anyone else's. Don't worry. I'm not going to become a smuggler."

Only now did she recall that his answer, and his evident willingness to even associate with men like the Villegas brothers, had bothered her. Subsequent events had caused her to forget all about that.

It had happened just as they were preparing to weigh anchor and head back to port. Carlos had approached Noah and tried to strike up what he must have thought would be a casual conversation as a way to make his pitch. Jenna had been eavesdropping from the relative isolation of the bridge, curious to hear how Noah would shoot him down, when to her astonishment, Raul had appeared on the ladder.

"Is this where you've been hiding, *chica*?" Without waiting for an invitation, he climbed up onto the elevated deck and then leaned back against the control console as if he had every right to be there.

Jenna had felt herself go cold. It was, she realized now, the first time she had ever truly felt the fight or flight response. She wanted to scream for help, to run down to the lower deck and take shelter behind Noah, but she had resisted the urge. This was one of those opportunities Noah had talked about, a chance to put what she had learned to use in real life. And besides, other than sneaking up on her, what bad thing had Raul done? Nothing. Yet.

His smile had been genuine, but his eyes had betrayed him. Jenna noticed how he had kept glancing to his left, mentally constructing the fiction he would use to win her over. "You should come down and party with us."

"I don't think my father would like that."

She had stressed the word 'father' hoping that would be enough to discourage him, and almost immediately saw that it would not. He had smiled like they were old friends who skirted parental rules on a regular basis. Co-conspirators. "You always do what daddy says?"

"It's a small boat."

He had licked his lips and eased forward. "Aww, c'mon baby. Don't play hard to get."

He wants me to call for help, to be scared. What will shut him down?

She had forced herself to relax, leaned against the console beside him, mimicking his posture, and had looked him in the eye. "Raul, I'm not playing hard to get."

There was a glimmer of triumph in his eyes, and she had wondered for a moment if she had misjudged him. Desperately, she had searched her repertoire of techniques. "Do you have a sister, Raul? Or is Carlos your only family?"

The triumphant look had faded. He had looked away, and she'd known that she had found the right pressure point, perhaps more than one.

"No. No sister. I have a younger brother in Cuba."

"Oh? What's his name? How old is he?"

She had sensed a shift in his demeanor. His narcissism was ebbing. He no longer felt compelled to conquer her, to possess her. His lust was gradually changing into something more like the protective love of a brother for a sister.

Suddenly, Noah had charged up the ladder. "What the hell is going on here?"

Before Jenna had been able to answer, Noah had slammed a fist into Raul's abdomen. Raul had curled around the blow like a worm on a fishhook. Noah had grabbed him by the neck and propelled him away from Jenna, pitching him off the elevated platform. Raul had thudded, senseless, onto the deck below.

Noah had turned to Jenna, and in a voice that still chilled her, said simply. "Stay here."

Jenna had complied, but her insatiable curiosity had driven her once more to spy on what was happening below. She saw Noah pull Carlos close and whisper something in his ear. A moment later, both of the Villegas brothers had gone into the water, willingly it seemed, and had begun swimming toward nearby Long Key.

When Noah had joined her on the bridge, he'd said, "We won't speak of this."

And they didn't.

To the best of her knowledge, no complaints were registered with local law enforcement or maritime authorities. If they had wanted to, the Villegas brothers could have sued Noah or tried to get his charter privileges revoked, but doing so would have exposed them to further investigation that might have revealed their illegal activities. Yet, they had not seemed the sort to simply let it go.

Somehow though, the idea that the Villegas brothers were behind the bomb attack just didn't fit. It was too complex, too sophisticated. They were small-time thugs, more likely to lie in wait with a baseball bat. If she had read them correctly, they were the sort of men who preferred to deal with their enemies personally.

There were other pieces that didn't fit. Who were the men posing as FBI agents? Why had they been interested in her?

Suddenly, she saw what she had been missing, the one thread woven throughout all of the unconnected dots, the one thing that was constant in every instance. It still made no sense to her, but the connection was there.

The sound of a vehicle approaching from behind drew Jenna out of her musings. She moved to the edge of the street to give it room to pass, and then turned to make sure that she was clear. Her heart fell as she recognized the weather-beaten Ford F-150 pickup that pulled up beside her.

Mercedes Reyes leaned across the seat and spoke to her through the open passenger window. "Jenna, get in."

There was an unusual gravity to her tone, and despite her reservations, Jenna found herself opening the door and climbing into the cab. She settled into the seat but refused to meet Mercy's stare. There was a long uncomfortable silence, filled only by the gentle chug of the idling engine.

"Are you just going to sit here?" Jenna finally asked.

"I tried to call Noah," Mercy said. "No answer. So I called the marina. They wouldn't pick up either." She laid a hand on Jenna's forearm. "What's going on?"

Jenna felt her resistance eroding. Mercy's touch seemed to uncork the bottle into which she had placed her weariness and grief. Mercy had the uncanny ability to read her like a book, sometimes even better than her own father.

"I don't know." *Don't tell her. You'll only put her in danger.* She met Mercy's gaze. "What are you doing here? You need to get back to the bar."

"We're closed for the rest of the day. I would have been here sooner, but it took a couple of minutes to roust everyone."

"You didn't need to do that."

Mercy squeezed her arm. "Talk to me. I can tell something is seriously wrong. Let me help."

"You really want to help?" Jenna drew in a breath. "Then tell me this. Who in the hell is my father?"

TEN

7:37 p.m.

Mercy stared at Jenna for a few seconds then turned her eyes forward and let off the brake. "I'm not going to insult your intelligence," she said, with a low controlled tone, "by acting like I have no idea what you're talking about."

"So it's true. Noah has some kind of secret life?"

Mercy pursed her lips together. "Jenna, please tell me what's happened. Is Noah all right?"

"Noah's dead." It was like ripping off a Band-Aid. She braced herself for a tide of emotion but it didn't arrive. Perhaps it was too soon, the event too fresh in her mind to truly be perceived as a loss, but Jenna thought it might also have something to do with the sudden realization that her father seemed more like a stranger to her now.

"How?"

Jenna stared at Mercy, surprised at the coolness of her reaction. *This isn't a surprise to her at all.* "Somebody blew up the boat. We got away, but afterward, two FBI guys showed up. Only Noah said they weren't really FBI. One of them shot him. I ran."

"Are you all right? Were you hurt?"

"I'm fine."

"Tell me everything. Start at the beginning."

Jenna did, only realizing after she started recounting the events of the last hour that Mercy had deftly avoided answering *her* question. As she described the arrival of the bogus FBI agents— or rather *allegedly* bogus, since she had only Noah's say-so—she seized the opportunity to shift the conversation back. "Noah told the deputy that they weren't really federal agents. How would he know that?"

Mercy just shook her head and kept driving. Jenna recognized their surroundings. They had circled around and were in the neighborhood where Mercy lived, just a couple of blocks from the bar.

"What happened then?"

"Then? Then they shot him, and I ran like hell." She curtailed the story there and tried again. "He told the deputy not to let them put me in their car. Me. Somehow, he knew they were there for me. How did he know that? *What* is going on?"

Mercy pulled off the street and parked in front of her single-wide mobile home. Jenna thought of the trailer as her own second home. During the school year, when Noah was out on the water, she would come here after school to await his return. She had spent endless hours here, watching television, playing games, doing homework. Now that the boat was in ruins, it was the only home she had left, and that thought filled her with dread. Right now, she didn't need the false comfort of the familiar. She needed to know why her life had been thrown into chaos.

"What are we doing here?"

"I don't have all the answers. But I might know where to start looking. But first, you need some clothes. And I have to get a couple things."

She got out, and Jenna followed her up the steps. Mercy waited until they were both inside, the door firmly closed behind them, to start talking. "Noah never talked much about his past. I take it he never told you much, either?"

Jenna had never thought about it, but it was true. Noah had always been accessible, always teaching her, eager to listen and advise, yet he had never really told her much about his life before her. He had retired to the Keys, but retired from what?

"You can always spot the phonies," Mercy went on. "They talk big, especially after a couple of beers. The real ones never talk at all."

"Real what?"

Mercy shrugged. "Soldiers. Spies. Special Forces guys. I'm not sure which Noah is."

Jenna felt an impulsive urge to deny the suggestion but stopped herself. It made too much sense not to be true.

Mercy didn't elaborate, but instead went to a pile of unfolded clothes on the living room couch. She pulled out a pair of jeans and a T-shirt and tossed them to Jenna, then she headed into the bedroom.

As Jenna pulled the jeans on over her still-damp swimsuit, she mulled over Mercy's speculative comment, and was astonished at how perfectly it filled in all the little gaps and answered the niggling but easily dismissed questions. How better to explain Noah's knowledge of weapons, his quick reaction to the bomb, his ability to recognize the FBI agents as impostors, his lethal hand-to-hand combat skills?

"If you're right," she called out, "then is this some kind of..." She searched for the right word, and she found it in the jargon of movie spies. "Blowback? Some old enemy from Noah's past coming after him?"

Mercy reappeared, carrying a pair of beat-up deck shoes and a large brown string-tie envelope. She dropped the shoes on the floor beside Jenna then began unwinding the thread that secured the envelope. Jenna did not fail to notice one other object Mercy had retrieved from the bedroom.

"You have a gun?" She was surprised by the fact that this didn't surprise her. After everything that had happened and Mercy's revelation about Noah's history, the fact that one of her closest friends owned a firearm was merely a curiosity.

Mercy's hand momentarily fell to the butt of the weapon, a matte-black semi-automatic pistol in a holster clipped to the waistband of her jeans. "Yeah."

"Cool." Jenna stripped off her sodden T-shirt and replaced it with the dry one Mercy had given her, then sat to tie the shoes. "What's in the envelope?"

"I don't know. Noah gave it to me for safekeeping years ago. I assumed it was important papers: the title for the boat, insurance policies, stuff like that. Things that he would need if the boat was ever..." She trailed off, and then dumped the contents onto the coffee table. "Maybe there's something in here that will tell us a little more about him."

There were several smaller envelopes, each marked with bold black letters drawn in Noah's familiar all-capital, block-print style. Jenna's gaze was drawn to one that had just three numbers. Nine-one-one. "In case of emergency?"

Mercy nodded. "I think this qualifies."

Jenna tore it open. Inside was a strip of paper with a string of numbers.

25.321304 -80.557173 (-80)

She took a moment to absorb the digits, letting her abnormal memory file them away for later with perfect clarity. Like people with eidetic memories, she could recall images, sounds and objects with high precision. The difference was that normal eidetic memories faded after a few minutes. Any information Jenna focused on stayed with her forever. She also learned quickly, intuiting things that usually required instruction or training, recalling bits and pieces of casually remembered details suddenly made relevant by a new challenge.

"Great," Mercy muttered. "In case of emergency, do math."

Jenna shook her head. "These are navigational coordinates. At least the first two sets of numbers are. Twenty-five north latitude, eighty west longitude. That's in the Glades, somewhere south of Miami."

"I'm impressed."

"I live on a boat." She winced even as the words were uttered—*Not anymore, I don't*—but she shrugged it off. "I better know how to read map coordinates."

Mercy dug out her phone and began swiping the virtual buttons on the screen, and Jenna found herself craning her head around for a look. Although the *Kilimanjaro* had been outfitted with a variety of electronic devices, some necessary for navigation, others for the comfort of passengers, Noah had never upgraded to the latest generation of smart phones. When Jenna had asked him for one, he had mumbled something about becoming too dependent on technology. Noah himself avoided technology, and refused to even own a personal computer. The administrative side of his charter service had been handled by an outside agency, freeing him of the need to own a computer or maintain any kind of personal presence in the digital world. At the time, she had written it off as a lame excuse, but now it occurred to her that his anti-technology tendencies might have been motivated by a desire to reduce his exposure to potential enemies.

But they found him anyway.

Before Jenna could put these concerns into words, Mercy said, "You're right. It's just outside Homestead. Looks like the middle of nowhere." She tapped the screen again. "Why would—"

"We should go there," Jenna said, rising and tucking the strip of paper into a pocket. "Now."

Mercy stared back at her, lips moving as if to form a question or perhaps an excuse, but then she nodded. "Okay. It'll be midnight before we can get there, but we can grab a hotel room and head there first thing in the morning."

Jenna was grateful that Mercy seemed to understand her urgency. She turned for the door, threw it open and nearly collided with the man that was ascending the steps.

It was Zack, and in the frozen instant that followed, Jenna saw that he had found a new gun.

ELEVEN

7:52 p.m.

Jenna leaped back through the doorway and slammed the door closed behind her. She reached out for the deadbolt knob, but before she could twist it, the aluminum door shuddered, struck from the outside. For a fleeting moment, Jenna thought Zack was pounding on it with his fists, but that didn't explain the holes, each as big around as her index finger, that were suddenly erupting with tufts of fiberglass insulation. Then she felt something burning along her left biceps.

She threw herself flat as bullets continued to punch through the door, passing right through the space where she had been a moment before.

Mercy overcame her astonishment and dragged her pistol from its holster. She seemed to be moving with exaggerated slowness, but Jenna knew this was merely a trick of her own heightened awareness. Mercy got the pistol up, holding it, Jenna saw, in what Noah had once told her was a *Weaver's stance.* One leg was behind the other, body turned sideways, lined up directly behind the gun, right hand pushing the weapon out, left hand cupped around it and pulling back for stability.

Fire jetted from the muzzle of the pistol. The report was painfully loud in the enclosed confines of the trailer, and Jenna felt the heat of the round passing through the air above her. Mercy yelled something. Jenna's ears rang, and she couldn't make out the words, but the accompanying nod in the direction of the back door was easily enough understood. *Let's go!*

"Not that way," Jenna shouted. If Zack had managed to replace his lost gun, maybe he had replaced his dead partner. Someone might be covering the back, or worse, the door might be wired with explosives, just as the boat had been. She headed for the bedroom. "This way."

As she swept into Mercy's bedroom—the room where she most often had hung out, laying on Mercy's bed, with its dark green comforter, watching Mercy's forty-two inch, plasma-screen television—it occurred to Jenna that the people trying to kill her had now taken away her only remaining home. True, Mercy's trailer had not been physically destroyed—not yet, anyway—but its sanctity had been breached. It would never again be that place of refuge. They had taken that from her forever.

That realization made it easier to wrap her arms around the television set and heave it through the enormous bay window that looked out from the end of the trailer. Pain throbbed in her arm, a reminder that she'd been struck by something when Zack had shot through the door. She glanced down to inspect the injury site. She did not think she had been hit by a bullet, but something had scraped across the outside of her arm. It hurt, but appeared superficial: a stripe of raw flesh, slowly oozing sweat-like beads of blood.

Mercy came in just as the glass exploded outward. If the destruction bothered her, she gave no indication. Her attention, and the business end of her gun, were both fixed on the front door as she backed into the bedroom.

Jenna scooped up the plush comforter and threw it over the windowsill, knocking jagged shards of broken glass out of the way. "Come on!"

Once again, she didn't wait to see if Mercy would follow, but clambered over the windowsill and lowered herself down. Twilight had fallen over the island, turning the surrounding homes into surreal, shadowy blocks silhouetted against a purple sky. She looked back up and saw Mercy peering down.

"Come on!" she urged again.

There was a loud bang behind Mercy as the front door burst inward. The impact that had forced it open shook the whole trailer and gave Mercy the impetus she needed to make the leap. Jenna put out a hand to steady her as she landed, and then both of them were running for the truck. There was no sign of Zack or anyone else, but Jenna didn't doubt he would soon discover their escape route and move to cut them off. She headed straight to the passenger door, got in, then locked it and hunched down out of direct view. Mercy slid in behind the wheel and fumbled with the key.

"Give me the gun," Jenna whispered.

"What?"

"You can't drive and shoot at the same time."

Mercy's face, barely visible in the darkness, drew into a frown. "Do you know how to use it?"

"I'm a quick learner."

Mercy gave a weary sigh then handed it over, careful to keep the business end pointed away from either of them. As Jenna curled her hand around the gun, which was much heavier than she expected, Mercy said, "Do not touch the trigger, or do anything else unless I tell you to, okay?"

Jenna nodded. Mercy slotted the key into the ignition. The engine roared to life after just a second, and then she threw the truck into reverse and stomped on the gas pedal. There was a roar of spinning wheels, and a scattering of loose gravel shot out ahead of the pickup as it lurched backward into the street. Mercy hit the brake.

Jenna heard the mechanical thump of the transmission shifting into 'drive,' but her attention was fixed on a dark shape about fifty yards behind them. It was a parked car that definitely had not been there when they had arrived only a few minutes earlier. As if to confirm her suspicions, the car's headlights flared.

Zack *had* brought some friends along.

Mercy accelerated a little less dramatically, but in a few seconds the truck was cruising down the street well in excess of the posted residential speed limit. The twin headlights behind them halted their advance right in front of Mercy's trailer, stopping only long enough for Zack to climb inside. Mercy turned a corner, and the car was lost from view. Just a few seconds later, Jenna saw the sweep of its headlights again, and she knew the pursuit was only just beginning.

She felt the truck slowing, and she whipped her head around to see what was happening in front of them. Mercy hit the brakes, slowing as she approached an empty intersection. "What are you doing?" Her voice was more frantic than she intended.

"Stop sign," replied Mercy, but even as she said it, she seemed to grasp the foolishness of the automatic reaction, and accelerated again. "Sorry. This is a new experience for me."

"Me too." Jenna wondered if the same could be said for the men in the car. Probably not. In a situation like this, experience would count for a lot. She searched her memory, trying to recall all of Noah's little critiques of the action movies they had watched together. "Turn off your lights."

"What?"

"It will be harder for them to spot us if they can't see our tail lights."

"And harder for us to see where we're going."

Nevertheless, Mercy reached down and turned a switch. The dashboard went black. The road ahead of them was much harder to see, but the overhead streetlights cast enough illumination for Mercy to stay on the paved surface.

They passed dozens of trailer homes and a few other, more permanent-looking structures, and Jenna recognized where they were. "Take the next right."

Mercy looked at Jenna, her expression unreadable in the darkness, then steered in the indicated direction. "Where are we headed?"

"For the moment, I just want to lose these guys." It was such an absurd thing to say that Jenna had to suppress an urge to laugh aloud.

"And then what?"

"Homestead. That's where Noah wanted us to go."

"So we need to get to the highway without them realizing that's where we're going." Mercy looked back to the road ahead. "Okay, I think I can manage that."

Encouraged, Jenna craned her head around. She saw the pursuing car's lights come into view at the intersection, about a hundred yards behind them. Mercy took another turn, back into the maze of neighborhood streets. She sped up, the engine revving as she pushed the gas pedal too hard, but then just as quickly, she slowed and took another turn. Jenna, who had never experienced the least bit of seasickness, felt her stomach begin to churn with the rapid maneuvers. She faced straight ahead, closing her eyes until the sensation passed.

When she opened them again, she recognized where they were. She saw familiar buildings: the boatworks, a Baptist church, a Tom Thumb convenience store. Mercy had her headlights on again, and maintained a steady thirty to forty mile-per-hour pace. In a few more blocks, they would reach the Overseas Highway that linked the Keys to the mainland. She risked a glance back, but instead of seeing just one set of headlights, she saw several, as well as the receding taillights of vehicles moving in the opposite direction. It was impossible to distinguish makes and models, but Jenna knew their pursuers would be facing a similar challenge.

Mercy pulled up to the stoplight at the highway intersection and made a rolling stop before taking the turn. She accelerated quickly, though evidently not quickly enough. An eastbound car traveling in the same lane caught up to them, let out a long irritated honk and swerved around them as if they were standing still. Mercy's only reaction was to keep driving, and soon they were just a few car lengths behind the irate motorist, cruising down the tree-lined causeway toward Boca Chica Key.

"Were those the men that killed Noah?" Mercy asked, breaking the long silence.

"I'm not sure. I recognized one of them, Zack, one of the guys who put the bomb on the boat. So, I guess he would have to be, right? Unless all of Noah's old enemies picked today to show up and settle..." She turned to face Mercy again. "This doesn't make any sense. If this was just about getting revenge on Noah, why come after me...us?"

"Us?"

"They went to your place. They didn't follow me there, so they must have been looking for you."

Mercy shook her head but didn't take her eyes off the road. "I'm listed as Noah's primary emergency contact. They might have assumed that you would come to me."

Jenna processed that with a frown. "Well, even if that's true, it doesn't explain why they are coming after *me*. They already got Noah." She paused, recalling again her father's reaction to the men posing as federal agents. *I'm still missing something.*

"This guy's coming up fast." Mercy said, squinting into the rear-view mirror.

Jenna looked back again and saw the headlights of a car, coming up fast in the inside lane. In a matter of seconds, it pulled alongside the pickup and then, at least from Jenna's perspective vanished.

"Where did he go?"

"He's pacing me." Mercy tapped the brakes a little and the car pulled ahead for a moment. Jenna leaned forward, trying to get a look in through the car's passenger side window, but all she could see was the reflection of the pickup's headlights on the glass. The car was a mid-sized sedan, a newer Dodge model, with a conspicuous sticker on the bumper from a car rental agency. Zack and Ken had claimed to be tourists, on vacation. They might have had a rental. Jenna hadn't been able to see the car that had been waiting outside Mercy's trailer, so there was no way to know if this was it...but it *could* be.

The Dodge abruptly fell back, disappearing once more into Jenna's blind spot. She leaned closer to Mercy, trying to follow its movements, and saw it easing back further still, its front end almost perfectly even with the truck's rear tires.

Jenna saw what was about to happen like a premonition. "Brakes. Now!"

Mercy reacted without question, but in the fraction of a second it took her to translate Jenna's cry into action, the sedan made its move. Just as Mercy was tapping the brake pedal, the sedan swerved sharply to the right and its front bumper crunched into the pickup.

The rear end of the pickup slewed wildly as, first the impact knocked it off course, and then as Mercy frantically compensated by trying to steer away. The Ford was too heavy to be shoved off the road by the smaller sedan, but the suddenness of the attack and the reflexive nature of Mercy's response sent the vehicle careening toward the edge of the road. She managed to straighten it, but not before the right side struck the guardrail. The truck slid along its length with a shriek of tearing metal and a shower of sparks. The sedan rebounded away, weaving back and forth across both lanes ahead of the pickup, as its driver likewise fought to restore control. Mercy wrestled the truck back onto the road, but seemed uncertain about what to do next.

"Go!" Jenna shouted.

Mercy hesitated. "What about them?"

"They won't try that again," Jenna replied, unsure of how to explain what had just happened. "They're outmatched and they know it."

The driver of the sedan had attempted to do what Noah had once called a 'pin.' He would always complain about the way car chases were presented in movies, where the driver of the pursuing vehicle would ram their prey from behind. He would then explain that the way to force a car to stop was by pulling alongside and turning into its back tires. If done correctly, the impact would spin the fleeing vehicle around, stalling its engine as the sudden change in direction and the car's own momentum created reverse compression in the motor. Jenna had recognized, almost too late, that the driver of the sedan was attempting exactly that. If Mercy had not started to brake when she did, they would have been dead on the road.

The sedan straightened out and then pulled away, but Jenna's fleeting hopes that they might be leaving the scene were dashed when she saw their brake lights flash. A figure leaned out the passenger side window and looked back, one hand extended. It was Zack.

"Gun!" Mercy shouted.

Jenna felt the pickup decelerating again. "No. Charge them!"

Mercy was incredulous. "What?"

"Run them off the road."

A small flash appeared at the end of Zack's extended hand and something cracked loudly against the windshield. Jenna ducked, but the glass remained intact. A quarter-sized divot had been gouged in the windshield, almost perfectly in line with Mercy's head.

Jenna was thrown forward as Mercy stomped on the brakes.

"No," she protested. "You can't stop."

"They're shooting at us," Mercy challenged, her normally cool tone replaced by strident hysteria.

"And you're going to make it impossible for them to miss." Jenna fought to keep her own voice calm. "The only way to survive this is to take them out. Keep your head down, but don't back off."

Mercy held her gaze for a moment, eyes squinted. "You sure you don't have a secret life you want to tell me about, too?"

There was another crack, another round striking the windshield, closer to center this time. A ragged crack appeared, connecting the two impact sites. Jenna knew she hadn't convinced Mercy. If she wasn't going to go on the offensive, the only option was to make a U-turn and flee back to Stock Island. Before she could articulate this alternative however, Mercy punched the accelerator, and they lurched forward.

"Maybe you should give them something else to think about," Mercy said, her body bent forward so that she appeared to be peeking over the steering wheel.

Jenna blinked uncomprehending. Mercy glanced at her with a wry smile, her emotions back under control. "Shoot them."

Jenna looked down at the pistol, all but forgotten, in her hand. She had never fired a gun in her life, and she wondered now why she had bothered to ask Mercy for it. With a shake of her head, she steeled her nerve and then rolled down the window.

The pickup closed the gap, but as they got to within fifty yards, the sedan's brake lights went out and the car started pulling away. Mercy jiggled the wheel back and forth, causing the pickup to veer from one side of the road to the other.

"Better use both hands," Mercy advised. "Don't drop it, and for God's sake, don't fall out."

Or get shot, Jenna added silently.

She leaned against the doorframe, both arms extended, with the pistol braced in her hands the way she'd seen Mercy do back at the trailer. A blast of air hit her full in the face as she looked down the length of her arms, not sure exactly how to sight the weapon. She slid a finger into the trigger guard.

"Is there a safety?" she yelled. It seemed like the right question.

"No safety. Just point and shoot."

Jenna tried to imagine an invisible line traveling down her arm, past the gun and ending where she wanted the bullet to go— not at Zack who was still hanging out of the sedan's window, trying to line up a shot of his own, but at a target that she felt sure she could hit: the sedan's back window.

She pulled the trigger and felt something move under her fingertip. A piece of plastic protruded from the metal lever like a secondary trigger, but at her touch, it slid back into a recess, flush with the trigger itself. Then the trigger itself started to move, but slowly, as if resisting her. She applied more pressure and suddenly felt the pistol jerk, like a firecracker going off in her hands.

Jenna gave a yelp of surprise, and despite Mercy's warning, almost let her grip relax. *So that's what it feels like,* she thought. *Okay, I can do this.*

The sedan swerved as her bullet smacked into the rear window, the tempered glass instantly turning opaque with countless fractures. She saw Zack pull back inside, and for a moment she dared to hope that her bullet had been enough to send their attackers packing.

Abruptly, two fist-sized holes appeared in the sedan's glazed rear window, broadening out as the car's occupants began clearing away the glass fragments. Jenna saw two men framed in the opening, and just as she was starting to line up for another shot, she saw them thrust their own guns out through the opening.

She squeezed the trigger, but at the same instant the two gunmen fired. A hailstorm of bullets slammed into the pickup, and Jenna's world transformed into chaos.

TWELVE

8:10 p.m.

The windshield exploded inward. Splinters of glass, driven by the wind, stabbed into Jenna. She barely noticed, because in that same moment, the truck yawed, veering to the right, but also tilting like an out of control carnival ride. She tried to find Mercy, but her body refused to cooperate. She felt herself being pushed and pulled in different directions, shaken like a captured gazelle in the mouth of a lion. She was dimly aware that the truck was no longer traveling in a straight line along the flat road surface, but corkscrewing, twisting through the air, and then she was flying free.

The sensation was like nothing she'd ever felt before. It was strangely exhilarating and a welcome relief from the punishment of being thrown about the hard metal cage of the pickup's cab, but it happened so fast that before she could understand what was happening, it was over.

She slapped against something, a hard surface, only it wasn't a surface exactly. She felt something like the sting of a belly-flop dive into a pool, which as it turned out was almost correct. Warm water engulfed her, flooding into her open mouth, choking her. A reflexive spasm of gagging brought her out of her daze, but for a few moments, she was nothing more than a thrashing, coughing animal, in the grip of a primal panic.

A cool breeze on her face calmed her by degrees, but her mind still raced to comprehend everything that had just happened.

She looked around, grasping at last that she was floating in the warm waters of the Boca Chica Channel. She saw lights off in the distance, and as she turned her head, she found the elevated hump of the highway, ten feet away. It loomed above her like a great wave about to crash down and sweep her to oblivion. Then she spied a flaw in the dark horizon. A light cut through the night, illuminating a patch of water fifty yards out to sea. It took her a moment to recognize it as a single headlight, shining out from an overturned vehicle that had broken through the guardrail, and was now perched precariously at the edge of the road.

She clutched at her last clear memory: leaning out the window of the pickup...the shots from the men in the sedan.

The pickup had rolled, and Jenna had been thrown clear. She owed her life to the fluke of luck that had catapulted her into the water. She might just as easily have been crushed under the somersaulting vehicle or thrown onto the hard pavement, which would have flayed her raw and pulverized her bones.

Mercy!

Jenna recalled the horrible sound of the bullets striking the truck. Had Mercy been hit or had she just swerved in a misguided effort to avoid that fate?

Mercy was probably still in the truck, injured or dying.

Maybe already dead.

Anger and grief surged within Jenna. First Noah, now Mercy. The killers had taken everything from her now.

No, not everything. You're still alive.

With a start, Jenna realized that the killers were not done with her. They would almost certainly check the wrecked truck, and when they discovered she was not in it, they would realize where she had gone.

I have to get away from here, she thought, but then another inner voice countered: *And go where?*

She turned back to the lights she had spotted off in the distance. Boca Chica Key lay off to her right, perhaps a mile away. In the other direction, a little closer, was Stock Island.

Going to Boca would put her that much closer to her ultimate destination on the mainland.

But what would she do once she got there? Hitching a ride was just too risky. If the killers didn't spot her walking along the roadside, the cops almost certainly would, and chances were good that they were already looking for her. She might be able to stow away in someone's car or truck. That was less risky, but there was no guarantee that it would get her where she needed to go.

Steal a car?

She felt a twinge of dismay at even considering that possibility, but she couldn't dismiss it out of hand. As with the theft of the SCUBA gear, extreme circumstances justified extreme actions. She tabled her moral reservations, and considered the practical aspects of such a course. She had a learner's permit, and she was pretty confident behind the wheel. She didn't have the first clue about how to break into a car or hotwire it, but she was pretty sure that it wasn't the kind of thing that could be learned through trial and error. Noah had always scoffed at how easy they made it look in movies. No, if she was going to boost a car, she would need to find one that came with keys. *A valet parking lot maybe?*

She shook her head, dismissing that idea as well. The Overseas Highway was more than a hundred miles long. Even if she could steal a car, she'd never reach Miami without being caught. So what did that leave?

If she went back to Stock Island, she would be moving further away from her goal, but there were a few more options that way. She knew people there: school friends, teachers, some of Noah's acquaintances.

She glanced up at the truck, wondering again whether Mercy was trapped inside, dying, or maybe already dead. Was that the fate that awaited anyone who helped her?

Suddenly, Jenna thought of someone else who might be able to help her. It was a crazy idea, crazier even than stealing a car, but the more she thought about it, the more certain she was that it would work.

She rolled over in the water, and as quietly as she could, she began swimming back toward Stock Island.

THIRTEEN

Key West, Florida USA
9:38 p.m.

When she had heard the words 'night club,' Jenna had envisioned a glitzy, neon-bright industrial exterior, pulsing with a deafening bass backbeat, and a crowd of young over-dressed socialites queued up behind a velvet rope. In hindsight, she should have known better. This was kitschy, touristy Key West, not Miami. The place looked like a standard Key West home, a pastel pink Bahamian conch house, single-story, built on wooden piers so air could circulate underneath. The only indications that it was anything but a residence were its location on historic Duval Street, an area zoned for commercial use, and the hand painted sign that read: *The Conch Club—Members Only.* The only neon around was a sign in the window with the words: *ATM inside.* There was no line waiting to enter. The entire block seemed sedate, as if people were making an effort to avoid being seen in the vicinity. As Jenna stared at the old house, she wondered if she had made a mistake in coming here.

It had seemed like a good idea an hour before, floating in the Boca Chica Channel, hunted, sore, exhausted, hungry, and worst of all, completely alone.

Who am I kidding? she thought. *This is a terrible idea.*

She realized now that the actual destination had not been as important as the simple fact of having a goal. Something to work toward.

The first few minutes of the swim had been a Herculean ordeal. The simple act of stretching her arms out to swim had awakened pains and aches unlike anything she had ever experienced. The sting of dozens of tiny cuts crisscrossed her arms and face. She had wondered if she was bleeding. The blood could have attracted a ravenous tiger shark or bull shark. Or both. The minutes had passed and the pain gradually had subsided into a more tolerable throb, but the ache in her temples had grown, along with a gnawing hunger in her belly.

She hadn't attempted to swim all the way back to Stock Island, but instead came up amid the trees that lined the side of the road closer to the island. Hidden by the trees, she had made her way back to the island and then kept going, following the Heritage Trail, which ran parallel to the Overseas Highway, until she had reached the address that she recalled from the registration paperwork the Villegas brothers had signed, when they had come aboard the *Kilimanjaro* the previous week. The information was just another bit of information in the filing cabinet of her perfect memories.

Now that the goal was finally in sight, she was filled with dread for what would happen next. Even worse was the sinking feeling that all her efforts had not brought her any closer to the answers she craved. She took a deep calming breath, headed up the steps and opened the door.

She stepped into a small unfurnished foyer. There was a cash machine in one corner, a window that looked a little like the check-in desk of a rundown hotel and a closed door. On the other side of the counter, an elderly gray-haired woman—Jenna thought she looked old enough to be Noah's grandmother—played mahjong on a computer.

The woman started to speak, but when she got a look at Jenna, whatever she had been about to say was forgotten.

Jenna stood there, unable to speak. She had been mentally preparing for a different sort of gate-keeper, maybe a beefy steroid-infused bouncer or a hostess wearing a leather dominatrix outfit. She shook her head to clear away the hesitation. "I need to speak to Raul."

She saw the flicker of recognition in Granny's eyes. *Well, at least I've got the right place.* Then the woman's face twisted into a matronly look of concern. "Oh, sweetie. You can't be here."

Jenna kept her expression neutral, but puffed up her chest a little, leaning forward. "Raul."

The old woman squinted behind her glasses, as if questioning her original appraisal, then reached down and pressed the button on an intercom box. "Someone here to see you, Raul."

There was a brief pause and then a tinny voice issued from the speaker. "Send him back."

The woman glanced at Jenna again, the anxious look back on her wrinkled face. *She really wants me to leave. Maybe I should go while I still can.* Jenna pointed down and mouthed the words: "Out here."

Granny nodded to her then pushed the button again. "It's not a 'he,' and I think maybe you should come out front." As she lifted her finger, the woman gave Jenna a sad, resigned look, as if to say 'I tried to warn you.'

Yes you did, she thought. *But I'm going to play this through to the end.*

The door opened and Raul Villegas stepped out. He was wearing a white linen suit over a lavender silk shirt, opened to just above his sternum, revealing the thick gold chain around his neck. There was an easy-going smile plastered on his face, which vanished in an instant when his eyes found Jenna.

She took a deep breath and then turned away, heading for the door. She had rehearsed this encounter dozens of times during her long walk. It was imperative to control every aspect of the scene, and the first step was moving Raul away from his home turf. Equally important, she had to make sure that she had an escape route if things went sour. She paused on the front porch, waiting to see if he would follow.

He did.

Raul exited the house, glowering. "You," he said in a low, threatening voice. His body was tense, a coiled spring full of unpredictable energy.

Take control, she told herself. *Keep him off balance.* "I need your help," she said quickly, forestalling the accusations that she knew would come.

She turned to face him, positioning herself under the porch light so that it would illuminate her scrapes and bruises. She saw his eyes move, and knew that he had seen them. His mouth opened, but before he could say anything, she continued.

"I ran away, Raul. You saw how violent he is." She held his gaze, tightening the muscles of her eyelids so that her eyes would not betray the fiction in her words. The ability to detect falsehood was instinctive, even in those untrained in the techniques she was now attempting to use.

Raul's indignation seeped away. "He did that to you?"

She nodded, but did not elaborate. The lie would be all the more convincing if she let Raul's imagination fill in the details. "I can't go to any of my friends. You're the only person that can help me."

His eyes began moving, and Jenna recalled Noah's words. *Most people are an open book.* She had no difficulty reading his thoughts. Raul was calculating how he would turn her vulnerability to his advantage. He would invite her inside, get her somewhere isolated, comfort her with words, a touch, maybe offer her a drink, and then he would take her. She knew this was a dangerous game, but it was a game she could win.

"Do you need some money?" he asked.

That surprised her. "Money?"

"Isn't that why you came here?" A faint smile played across his lips.

She shook her head. "No. Maybe. I don't know. I just need to get out of here."

I'm losing him, she thought. *Get back on track. Control the scene.* She glanced at the street, gauging the distance to the nearest well-lit storefront where she might be able to find refuge.

His expression was becoming more confident. "Oh, sure baby. I can help you with that."

With an effort, she stilled her racing heart and met his gaze again, reminding herself to mimic his stance. "I shouldn't have bothered you, Raul. I thought you might be able to drive me to Miami, but I have no right to ask."

There, she thought. *The seed is planted.* Without breaking her stare, she turned her body away from his, as if preparing to leave.

"Hey baby, don't run off. Of course I can take you to Miami. First thing in the morning. And you can crash here if you want. Or come back to my place."

"No. I have to go tonight. Right now, before he realizes I'm gone." *It's not working*, she realized. *It was a stupid idea. Time to go.*

In the moment she looked away, preparing to step off the porch, she felt a hand close around her arm. The grip was firm, and it sent a throb of pain through the wound she'd sustained when Zack had shot through Mercy's door. She jerked away.

"Wait," Raul implored, drawing his hand back and holding it up in a disarming gesture. "I can help you. I'll take you."

Jenna studied his face again. He was doing his best to project sympathy, but his eyes could not hide a predatory gleam. *You knew this might happen*, she told herself. *You knew you would be playing with fire.* She took another deep breath and managed a grateful smile. "Thank you."

"I'll go grab my keys. Meet me around back."

As she watched him leave, Jenna felt no sense of victory. The most dangerous part of the game, she knew, was yet to come.

FOURTEEN

10:01 p.m.

Any sense of physical relief Jenna might have felt at sitting in the plush seats of Raul Villegas's 2006 Corvette was squashed by the stress of maintaining her façade of innocent helplessness and hiding the sheer terror she felt. She was ignoring a sacrosanct command that had been drilled into her head by Noah, Mercy, her teachers and innumerable public service announcements: don't ever get in a stranger's car. But Raul Villegas wasn't actually a stranger. With a stranger, there was the possibility that the ride was merely an altruistic gesture. She tried, with limited success, to comfort herself with the knowledge that there would be no surprises where Raul was concerned.

When Raul had turned the key in the ignition of the red sports car, the upbeat rhythms of Caribbean music assaulted Jenna. He moved to turn the volume knob, but Jenna waved him off. "I love this music. Turn it up."

Any louder, and the stereo system would become a sonic weapon, but the strident music made casual conversation impossible. She endured the pulsing beat and managed to bob her aching head in time with the relentless rhythm of the congas. Raul stared at her sidelong and smiled, then put the car in gear.

With Raul's attention occupied by the drive, Jenna finally allowed herself to relax a little. She figured at some point Raul would try to make a move on her, but if she played him right, he would wait until they reached Miami, where she would find a way to give him the slip. She could not ignore the possibility that he might pull off on some deserted side road and try to take what he wanted by force. If it came to that, she would be ready to do whatever it took to stop him.

What she was not prepared for was the snarled traffic on the Overseas Highway leading out of Stock Island. Jenna silently berated herself for not taking it into consideration. The only road to Miami led right past the place where the pickup had overturned. The emergency response was going to take time. She tried not to think of the incident in terms more specific than that, but it wasn't easy.

As the Corvette slowed and stopped, taking its place at the end of the long line of brake lights, Jenna considered jumping out and abandoning this dangerous game. But the traffic jam was a grim reminder that Raul was the least of her enemies. Noah's last message—what she had come to think of as his 'fire alarm'—had directed her to Homestead. She felt sure that reaching the coordinates he had left behind was the only way to end this ongoing threat. Or at least get answers.

The music went silent. Jenna opened her eyes to see Raul staring at her, his expression more bemused than lascivious. "So what are you going to do in Miami?"

She gave a careful shrug. "Whatever I have to."

He nodded. "What are you, nineteen?"

It took all her willpower not to laugh aloud. He knew damn well that she was jail bait, and probably assumed she would be flattered at any suggestion otherwise. "Something like that," she replied. The line advanced a couple of car lengths, then it ground to a halt again.

"I thought so," he continued in the same smooth voice. "I've got a friend who runs a modeling agency in South Beach. You're going to need money to get started, am I right?"

She considered the question carefully. What response would satisfy Raul, keep him on her side? "A modeling agency?" she said with a tone of awe. "That's so cool. But I'm not pretty enough to be a model."

"Oh, baby, who told you that? Your old man, I bet. You made the right decision getting away from him. He's *muy loco*, understand?"

She bit the inside of her cheek to conceal her emotions. *It's just a game*, she told herself, and then a flash of inspiration hit her. "Hey, so, tell me something. Last week, just before he—my father— kicked you off the boat, he said something to you."

Raul's eager expression darkened at the memory. He turned his eyes forward, staring into the red glare of brake lights. Jenna sensed a return to the smoldering anger that had initially greeted her. "What did he say?" she pressed.

Raul grimaced. "Like I said, *loco*. He told Carlos that if he ever saw us again, if we ever tried to get some payback, he'd kill us both and then go after our family."

The threat was so unlike Noah that Jenna had to fight back the urge to accuse Raul of lying, and yet, if she had learned anything in the last few hours, it was that she really didn't know anything about her father. It was the reason she had asked the question in the first place. "I thought you said your family is still in Cuba."

She winced even as she heard herself speak. It was the wrong thing to say, and if she wasn't more careful, he would see right through her.

Raul did not seem to notice, however. Anger had loosened his tongue. "He knew about them. Knew their names. He said if anything ever happened to him..." He glanced over, concern creasing his forehead. "Or to you, that he would have his people hunt them down and feed them to the sharks."

That definitely did not sound like her father. If true, it explained why Noah had not been more concerned about the possibility that the Villegas brothers might seek retribution for his insult.

His people? What did that mean? What was Noah involved in that gave him 'people' who can go to Cuba and assassinate someone?

Then another thought occurred to her. What if Noah's fire alarm was nothing more than a kill order on the Villegas family?

Her gut told her it had to be more than that. If Noah did indeed have 'people,' then the fire alarm was her best chance of finding them, and maybe turning the tables on whomever it was that wanted her dead.

"Don't worry," she heard herself saying. "He'll never figure out that I came to you."

"Hey, I ain't afraid of that old man."

She decided silence was the best answer. Maybe fear of Noah's reprisal would make him think twice about making any kind of move on her. The lapse in conversation lasted for nearly a mile. In the distance, Jenna could see the flashing lights of emergency vehicles at the very spot where Mercy's truck had rolled. She wondered if Mercy was still there, still trapped in the truck or maybe wrapped around a tree on the roadside.

She glanced at the clock on the radio display. It was late. She figured it had taken her an hour and a half to get to Raul's club from Mercy's trailer, and maybe another thirty minutes had passed since then. More than enough time for the firefighters to pull Mercy out of the truck and get her to a hospital. Mercy was alive, she had to be. The traffic snarl was just the cops doing what they did, measuring the skid marks and taking pictures. No doubt, someone had noticed the bullet holes in the truck. That would make it a crime scene.

For the first time since starting back toward Key West, Jenna found herself wondering what had become of Zack and the other men in the sedan, and she settled a little lower into the Corvette's passenger seat.

Raul evidently noticed. "You worried the cops might see you?"

"Is it that obvious?" she lied.

"Just be cool," Raul advised. "Don't give them a reason to give you a second look."

She heard an undercurrent of anxiety in his voice, and she realized he was just as concerned as she was, albeit for very different reasons. This might well be her last chance to bail out and turn herself over to the authorities.

Her thoughts drifted back to the last time she had seen flashing emergency lights, sheriff's deputies and firefighters responding to the explosion at the marina. She remembered the two men claiming to be FBI agents who had gunned down the deputies...and Noah. Would they be here, too? The killers had the resources to insinuate themselves into the investigation. They might even now be searching for her.

Somehow, being with Raul seemed a lot safer than trusting the authorities to protect her.

"I can do cool," she replied, giving him a reassuring nod.

As they inched closer to the flashing lights, Jenna saw vehicles in the right lane merging into the left ahead of them, shunted aside by a line of guttering orange flares and hastily deployed traffic cones. Raul followed the lead of the car that pushed in front of him, veering to the extreme left edge of the highway. The Corvette was not made for such low speeds, and the delicate job of accelerating and clutching kept his attention fully occupied as they rolled past the crash scene. Jenna risked a casual glance off to the right. She saw the battered Ford pickup resting on the deck of a flatbed tow truck. It was surrounded by men in uniform. She looked back at Raul. Just like that, they were through. The road opened up to two lanes, and motorists charged ahead like racehorses out of the gate.

"See?" Raul said cheerily, letting the Corvette do what it did best. "Stay cool, and there's no problem."

"No problem," echoed Jenna, wishing that she could believe it.

FIFTEEN

Sugarloaf Key, Florida, USA
11:37 p.m.

Jenna awoke with a start, dismayed that she had so easily surrendered to the seductive embrace of sleep. A person was never more vulnerable than when they were sleeping, and she had let her guard down with a potential enemy seated right next to her.

She straightened and looked down to see if her clothes had been disturbed—there was no indication that they had—and then glanced over at Raul. He smiled back at her.

She looked away from his unnerving gaze and out the window. The Corvette moved slowly, no longer on the highway. The constant rate of speed and the persistent thrum of the engine had lulled her to sleep. The change in speed as they exited the highway, had woken her.

"Why did you turn off?" The question burst from her, revealing her trepidation.

"Gotta gas up," he replied, but she saw his eyes flicker ever so slightly.

He's lying. Jenna felt a chill pass through her, but forced a nod. "Maybe we could get something to eat. I'm starving."

He grunted and returned his attention to the road.

Jenna stared through the windshield looking for some hint of where they were, but the road ahead was featureless. They could be anywhere, but she was pretty sure there wouldn't be a gas station on this remote tree-lined stretch of asphalt.

She glanced down at the door lever. The Corvette was barely crawling forward, maybe twenty miles an hour. A leap from the car would cost her only a few more bruises, but what then? Run?

Running was looking like a pretty good option.

She forced herself to relax as she mentally rehearsed her escape. She would have to release the catch on her seatbelt. She might be able to do that without Raul noticing, but the dashboard indicator would give her away. The door had electronic locks. She recalled that they had automatically engaged when the car had gotten up to speed earlier. If she tried the handle first and the door didn't open, that too would reveal her intentions and give Raul time to take action.

She would have to synchronize her actions perfectly. *Seatbelt with my left hand, the lock with my right.*

The engine revved suddenly, but only because Raul had depressed the clutch and shifted to neutral. The abruptness of the move caused Jenna to falter and miss the perfect moment to initiate her plan. But her curiosity overrode her urge to flee. She looked forward and saw a metal fence on either side of the roadway. A man swung a gate open to admit them.

Jenna glimpsed the man's face in the headlights.

It was Carlos Villegas.

She reacted instantly, stabbing a finger at the lock button, but even as she grazed it, something slammed into her chest, driving the wind from her lungs and knocking her back into the seat. As she gasped for air, she felt Raul's hand at her waist, groping for the seat belt, sliding along its length to find the catch so he could hold it secure.

"Nice try, baby," he said, his voice a smooth and dangerous croon.

"What...?" She couldn't find the breath to finish the question.

"Good news, *chica*. You know that job I told you about? It's all yours. You're going to love it." He swung his gaze around to the figure that now stood just outside the window.

Carlos looked in and gave Jenna a cursory glance. "Well, well. The captain's daughter. Nicely done, *hermanito*."

"I thought you'd like. She just walked right up and gave herself to me. Couldn't believe it."

"You're sure this isn't a setup?"

"Look at her, *hermano*. She's all beat up. Her old man did that, like I told you. She's for real."

In some distant recess of her mind, Jenna heard the deep sense of satisfaction in Raul's voice as he savored his older brother's praise. That was about the only thing that made sense to her.

How did I miss this?

"Take her out to the plane," Carlos continued. "I'll get the gate."

As the elder Villegas brother stepped back, Raul turned to Jenna. "I don't want to mess up that pretty face of yours, but if you so much as breathe wrong, I'll knock your teeth down your throat. Got it?"

She nodded, and he let go of the seatbelt.

She spoke, "Raul, what—"

He held up his hand, fingers curled into a fist, and shook it in front of her face. "Shut up."

She nodded again. He lowered his hand to the gearshift lever, and worked it into position. The Corvette rolled forward again. Jenna saw a long stretch of pavement cutting across their path. A runway lined with small civilian aircraft.

She forced herself to go limp. Maybe if she appeared compliant, the brothers would relax their vigilance just enough for her to break away.

She had misjudged Raul, underestimated him. Somehow, he had gotten word to his brother. A phone call or text message, probably sent when he had gone inside the club for his keys. She didn't see another car. Carlos must have leapfrogged them, flying from Key West while they were stuck in traffic. While she had been congratulating herself on her ability to manipulate Raul, she had let the Villegas brothers draw her deeper into their web.

Lesson learned, she told herself. *Don't underestimate them again.*

Her first mistake had been believing that Raul wanted her for himself. There was something more going on here. She recalled his earlier line about a modeling agency, and his quip about having a 'job' for her. *I don't want to mess up that pretty face of yours*, he had said.

She shuddered as the picture resolved.

Noah had misjudged the Villegas brothers as well. They weren't drug dealers, or if they were, it was just one of the criminal enterprises they were running out of *The Conch Club*. Jenna understood now why the little old lady behind the counter had urged her to get away while she could. She wondered how many girls her own age were imprisoned behind the doors of that unassuming house. Of course the brothers wouldn't dare put her to work there. She might be recognized. No, they would take her somewhere else. Somewhere out of the country. Then they could sell her, like livestock.

Raul stopped in front of a twin-engine plane at the end of the line. It was a relatively small craft with low slung wings protruding from the bottom of the fuselage. Jenna didn't know the make or model, but it looked like the kind of aircraft used by island-hopper charter companies.

And smugglers.

"Stay put," Raul warned, thrusting a finger under her nose for emphasis.

Jenna put on her best deer-in-the-headlights look, and to all appearances, she cowered in the seat. Raul stared at her a moment longer, then seemingly satisfied that he had broken her spirit, he opened his door and got out. Jenna watched through hooded eyes as he circled around the front end of the Corvette. He approached her door and used the remote on his key fob to disengage the lock. Then he reached for the handle.

Jenna's movements were swift but sure. In the instant that her door started to open, she dropped a hand to the seat-belt buckle and depressed the button. Then, with the same smooth motion, she pivoted and planted both feet on the door panel, thrusting out as if trying to jump sideways across the interior of the car.

The door slammed into Raul and sent him sprawling backward. Jenna used the same energy to propel herself through the open driver's side door. A moment later, she scrambled to her feet and sprinted down the tarmac.

The Corvette's lights shone a good fifty yards down the runway. Beyond that expanding cone of illumination, the landing strip was shrouded in darkness. She ran toward the unknown, but she knew whatever awaited her had to be better than what she was leaving behind.

She could hear someone chasing after her, the rapid footfalls just out of sync with her own, but she did not look back. The hard tarmac gave way to soft grass on sandy soil. Almost too late, she saw that the grassy area ended at the perimeter fence they had passed through earlier. She caught herself before slamming headlong into the barrier. Then she quickly laced her fingers through the diamond-shaped mesh and climbed, as if it were a rope ladder to freedom.

When she reached the crest, she realized that the top of the fence was adorned with a long coil of razor wire. The thought of getting ripped up by the barbs stopped her only for a second—what were a few scrapes compared to being sold as a sex-slave—but the moment was enough for Raul to catch her. She felt something clamp around her ankle, and then she was ripped away from the fence and thrown to the ground.

SIXTEEN

11:47 p.m.

Sand cushioned Jenna's fall, but before she could even begin thinking about what to do, she felt a weight settle onto her chest. In the faint glow of the starlight, she could see the silhouetted form of her attacker sitting astride her chest, pinning her body and left arm beneath his straddled legs.

Noah's voice flashed through her mind, an ancient movie commentary that seemed grossly inappropriate at the time, but came to her now as welcome knowledge. *Three good punches to the kidneys will put a man down and make him piss blood for a week.*

Her free hand sprang to action before the memory faded. She struck hard and fast, delivering two solid punches to Raul's back, just below the ribs, sending a pulse of pressure through the kidneys. Raul shouted in pain. "Bitch!" He caught her arm before the third punch could connect.

She struggled to buck him off, but the effort ended with a blow to the side of her head that nearly knocked her senseless. There was a flash of blue across her vision, like the inside of a lightning bolt. Her ears rang, and the taste of blood filled her mouth.

She knew she could not stop fighting. To give up was to surrender the rest of her life to a fate that seemed like the stuff of bad dreams.

I'd rather die than let them put me on that plane.

The thought of dying snapped her out of her despair. Maybe she had misjudged the brothers, but they were still just a couple of small-time thugs. Jenna had survived more than one attempt on her life this night, from people a lot tougher and a lot smarter than Carlos and Raul, and she was not about to let these assholes stop her from figuring out who was after her and why.

As the ringing in her ears relented, she realized that Raul was almost face to face with her, shouting threats and obscenities, showering her face with spittle.

"Okay!" she shouted, or rather tried to. Blood and saliva had gathered at the back of her throat, and when she opened her mouth, it triggered her gag reflex. She turned her head, spat and then tried again. "Okay. I give up."

Like hell I do.

Raul seemed to hit the pause button on his rage. "I warned you what would happen."

"I know you did. I'm sorry." It was another lie, but she didn't care if he believed it or not. What mattered was his reaction to what came next. "I didn't tell you the truth about Noah. About my father."

"You think I care about that?"

"You should," she said, choking on another mouthful of blood. Her tongue probed the inside of one cheek where Raul's blow had shredded it against her teeth. "He's dead."

All the fight went out of Raul, but he did not move, did not release her. "Dead?"

"Someone killed him. Some very bad, very connected people, and they're after me now. That's why I came to you." Jenna paused, partly to let the words sink in, and partly because she wasn't sure exactly how to play this wild card.

The pressure at her chest abruptly vanished, but before she could think about trying to turn it to her advantage, Raul knotted his hand in her hair and hauled her erect. A whimper of pain escaped her lips, the motion aggravating all of her injuries all at once. He yanked her forward, striding away. She had no choice but to follow, jogging to keep up, a dog on a leash.

She had run much further than she realized. The Corvette's headlamps were just pinpricks of light, far down the landing strip, a beacon guiding them onward. The trek was an excruciating ordeal. Raul kept tugging the handful of hair in his fist. But Jenna used the time to concentrate on what she would say next. If she got this wrong, she would have very few options left, and all of them were of a very final nature.

I won't die without knowing why Noah was killed, she promised herself.

Carlos met them halfway, and even in the darkness, Jenna could see the laughter in his eyes. "This one's a tiger. She almost got away from you, *hermanito*."

"Maybe I need to tame her," Raul answered. His words were clipped, his breathing rapid, whether from the exertion of the chase or from anticipation, Jenna could not say.

"Better not," Carlos answered. "She's worth a lot more if she's still got her cherry." He pushed his face close to Jenna. "How 'bout it, girl? You still a virgin?"

Jenna almost spat in his cold, calculating face, but stopped herself. Angry people were easy to manipulate but only if the anger wasn't directed at the person trying to do the manipulating.

"She says her old man is dead," Raul intoned. "Someone offed him."

"Yeah? Damn, all of a sudden it's like Christmas. I'll send a 'thank you' card to whoever did it."

"You don't want to mess with the people who did it," Jenna managed to say. She hoped she had judged the brothers correctly. A taunt like that might very well push them away from the thing she planned to use as bait.

"Oh?" Carlos made a clucking noise. "The captain made some very bad friends, did he? I'll bet he wishes he'd done business with us instead."

"They're looking for me now," Jenna went on. "They think I can lead them to their money."

Jenna thought it sounded contrived, but maybe that was because she knew it was a falsehood. *Or is it?* Suddenly, she wasn't sure anymore. What if Mercy had gotten it wrong? Maybe Noah had been involved in something illegal? Maybe the attack on the boat had been some kind of organized crime vendetta? The fact that she could not easily dismiss the notion ate at Jenna's resolve like a cancer. *I have to know the truth. I have to get to Noah's fire alarm.*

Carlos had heard only one word, and he repeated it almost breathlessly. "Money?"

She let the seed of the idea germinate in silence as she allowed herself to be drawn closer to the shining headlights. What she needed to do next would work better if she could see their faces, though she was in no hurry to get closer to the waiting airplane. When she could finally look her tormentors in the eyes, she elaborated. "A lot of money. Noah hid it somewhere in the 'Glades."

Carlos gestured for Raul to release Jenna, and then he gripped her arms and held her so he could study her face. She realized that he was using the same lie detecting techniques she had—reading eye movements to detect intention and duplicity—and she made a willful effort to control her reactions. The look of fear came easily enough. Then she tapped into the possibilities of what Noah might have concealed in Homestead, making her fabrication feel authentic, even to herself.

"How much?"

Jenna shrugged. "I don't know. A lot, I guess. Enough to kill for." She looked up as if hit by a lightning bolt of inspiration. "I'll take you to it, if you let me go."

Carlos shook his head. "Why don't you just tell me where it is? If it's there, then maybe we can make a deal."

His eyes did not betray the lie she knew he was telling. He had no intention of letting her go. Nevertheless, she smiled as if she believed him. "I can't tell you exactly how to get there. I'd have to show you. But it's all yours if you want it. Just promise to let me go."

Raul was shaking his head, looking at the screen of his smart-phone. He held it up, revealing a news report about shots being fired at the marina. "This is messed up, *hermano*. Her story is legit. Someone killed the old guy because of it. That's heat we don't need."

Carlos ignored his brother. "The Everglades. That's pretty vague. Narrow it down for me."

"If you promise to let me go." Jenna needed him to believe that she was desperate enough to trust his word.

"I don't make promises like that, little girl. But I promise that if you're screwing with me, you're going to wish we'd just stuck to the plan and sold your ass. Now, where in the 'Glades?"

"Near Homestead." She let her lip quiver a little, as if she wanted to say more but knew better. Carlos snapped his fingers in a 'tell me more' gesture, but she just shook her head.

He stared at her a moment longer, then turned to Raul. "Get your car off the runway."

It took Jenna a moment to comprehend the significance of this. "We're flying?"

"We can be at Homestead in less than an hour by air," Carlos replied. He didn't seem irritated by the question, but when he grabbed her arm and pulled her toward the airplane, his forcefulness silenced her. He shoved her onto the plane's wing and opened the door that lay just above it. "Get in."

She complied, squirming through the opening into the claustrophobic confines of the cabin. It was her first time in any kind of aircraft. She had expected it to be more spacious, but then she could not have imagined that her first flight would be under these circumstances. As she settled into a seat just behind the cockpit, she surveyed every detail of her environment like a general studying a battlefield in anticipation of a fight. As a last resort, she was prepared to crash the plane by attacking the pilot—presumably Carlos—on take-off or landing.

She thought she might even survive.

Jenna wondered why the brothers had been looking for charter boats to make smuggling runs for them if they had a plane and knew how to fly it. Maybe they were trying to distribute the risk?

Carlos waited outside until Raul returned, then both brothers climbed inside. Carlos got into the cockpit and fiddled with various instruments. Raul took a seat across from Jenna, his eyes never leaving her.

So much for the kamikaze plan, she thought. Her chances would probably be better once they reached Homestead. It would be easier for her to create an opportunity to escape in the unfamiliar territory of the Everglades, especially since she would be leading the way.

As the engines roared to life, it occurred to her that, when they did get to Homestead, she would have only one chance to turn the tables on her captors. She had about sixty minutes to figure out just how she was going to do that.

SEVENTEEN

Homestead, Florida, USA
Sunday, 1:04 a.m.

The hour passed quickly. When the distant lights of Miami came into view, the small plane descended toward a dimly lit area in the foreground that could only be Homestead. The ride had been rougher than Jenna expected, but none of her expectations were based on any kind of prior experience. She had imagined that flying would feel smooth compared to other forms of travel, but the air, much like the water upon which she had spent most of her life, was full of invisible currents and pockets of turbulence that rocked the small plane. It was enough to fill her with nausea, exacerbating the roiling of her empty stomach and intensifying the headache that had taken root during her long walk to Key West. She wanted to close her eyes and seek refuge in sleep, but even if her body had been able to do so under such conditions, she knew that dozing off could be a fatal mistake.

The shaking grew worse as the plane descended through the layers of the lower atmosphere. Outside the window, Jenna saw the buildings and streets of Homestead grow larger until it seemed that they would set down right in the middle of traffic. Then a ribbon of asphalt appeared beneath them and a moment later, the fuselage shook with the impact of touchdown. Jenna squeezed the armrests, holding on for dear life. All thoughts of how she would escape the Villegas brothers were forgotten as she envisioned the plane coming apart around her, exploding in a fireball.

She sighed with relief as the aircraft settled onto its wheels and slowed, trading the rough chaos of thin air for smooth but unyielding terra firma.

Raul laughed at her. Jenna considered flipping him the bird, but decided that would be a bad idea for several reasons, the first being that she'd have to let go of the armrests.

They taxied for several minutes before pulling to a stop alongside a row of similar aircraft. Jenna looked in vain for ground crew or other personnel that she might be able to call out to if the chance presented itself, but the airport looked deserted.

Carlos extracted himself from the cockpit and threw open the door. After the unexpected cool temperature in the plane's interior, the hot, humid, tropical air was yet another physical assault on Jenna's frayed nerves.

Pull it together, she urged herself.

"I'm hungry," she said, aware of how pathetic she sounded.

"Tell you what, *chica*," Raul answered. "After you take us to daddy's stash, I'll buy you a great big steak dinner."

The thought of eating steak—greasy, salty, dripping with bloody juices—nearly made her retch. "Actually, not that hungry after all," she murmured.

Carlos ignored the exchange and led them down the tarmac, around a building to a nearly empty parking lot. As they approached a generic looking sedan with a rental sticker on the rear bumper, Carlos took out a phone and began tapping the screen. After a few minutes, the sedan's locks clicked open.

"How did you do that?" Jenna asked, curious in spite of everything else.

"I've got the app" he said, waggling the phone in Jenna's direction. "No more waiting in lines or filling out papers. No business hours."

She had been wondering how they would proceed once arriving at Homestead. Hiring a taxi or renting a car might have given her yet another opportunity to seek help or slip away, but Carlos had avoided all human contact by ordering the rental car online and having it delivered to the airport, keys inside, to be unlocked remotely when he entered a confirmation code.

Carlos directed his brother to take the wheel, then opened the rear door for Jenna, sliding inside next to her. "Where to now?"

Jenna tried to remember the brief glimpse she'd caught of the map displayed on Mercy's cell phone. "It's south of the city."

"What's the address?" Carlos's tone was impatient.

"There's no address. It's out in boonies. You know, it would be a lot easier to do this in daylight."

"I'm sure it would. For your sake, I hope you can show us how to get there in the dark."

She clamped her mouth shut. Daylight would have been preferable for a very different reason, but if the map was any indicator, the area where they were going was so remote that she doubted they would see anyone else even at high noon.

"I'll need your phone."

He laughed. "You think I'm stupid, little girl?"

"I need your phone's GPS to find the exact spot."

He considered this. "Just tell me the GPS location. I'll put it in."

"If you want the money, we do this my way." The confidence in her voice wasn't just an act, and she wondered from where she'd gotten her wellspring of fortitude. *Noah*, she decided. From watching his example and from listening when he spoke.

Probably his genes, too. Is grit an inheritable trait?

Jenna braced herself for the expected reprisal, but Carlos surprised her by holding out his phone. When she reached for it, he whispered, "You try to call someone or send a text, and I will hurt you."

She nodded and took the phone. Although Noah had never let her own one, she had used Mercy's phone many times, as well as occasionally borrowing them from her classmates. She brought up the phone's search program and typed in the coordinates from memory.

25.321304 -80.557173

The search returned a variety of options. She spotted 'maps,' but as her finger hovered above the screen, she quickly scanned the other search results.

Interesting.

The list was replaced by a close-up satellite projection of the area. She saw a road leading to it, but if her suspicions about the place were correct, there would be no vehicle access. With two fingers, she zoomed out until the outskirts of Homestead were visible, a patchwork of neat green and tan rectangles sitting above the featureless brown of the Everglades. She found the airport at the edge of the city, and then she memorized the route they would need to follow to reach their final destination.

She handed the phone back to Carlos without making any effort to erase the search. It didn't matter if he knew the coordinates now. Her brief look at the search results had revealed something very unique about their destination. There hadn't been much really, just links to web pages, with only the title and a few words of description for each, but it was enough for her to finally make sense of the bizarre coordinates, and the last set of numbers Noah had written down.

Jenna felt as if there was now a light at the end of the tunnel. For the first time since Raul had revealed his treachery, the advantage was hers.

EIGHTEEN

The Everglades, Florida, USA
1:31 a.m.

Jenna watched Carlos's face as he contemplated the gate blocking their path. "It's about six miles down that road," she said. "Sure you don't want to come back and try this during the day?"

He gave her a patronizing smile, leaned forward and whispered something in Raul's ear. The younger brother reached under his jacket and took out a pistol. He waggled it under Jenna's nose. "Oh, look! We brought the key, *chica*."

She stared at the weapon, more angry than surprised. She hadn't realized that the brothers were carrying guns, though in hindsight, she thought she should have expected it. *No matter*, she thought. *A lot of people with guns have failed to kill me tonight. It doesn't change what I have to do.*

Raul got out and walked up to the barrier. He looked around, as if making sure that they were as alone as they seemed to be, then aimed the gun and pulled the trigger. The loud report sent a pressure wave rippling through the interior of the car. They were well away from inhabited areas, so there was little chance of the shot being heard. Even if it was, the locals might assume that it was one of their good ol' boy neighbors out poaching. The broken padlock fell to the ground at Raul's feet. He kicked it out of the way, then swung the gate open and returned to the car.

A concrete road waited beyond the gate. It was wide enough to allow two vehicles to pass, but encroaching vegetation had shrunk the passable space down to one lane. Raul steered the rental car down the middle, proceeding slowly to avoid storm debris and other obstacles. More than once, Jenna glimpsed movement in the shadows, as large animals ducked away from the headlights. Intersecting roads hinted at human activity, but most were overgrown. Jenna knew from her brief glimpse of the satellite map that these roads led to empty lots and abandoned buildings.

"How much farther?" Carlos asked after about fifteen minutes.

"I'll tell you when we get there," Jenna retorted, but then to avoid any repercussions, added, "It shouldn't be much further. The road goes straight for a while, then makes a hard left turn. Just follow the pavement."

They arrived at the turn less than a minute later. It was the first significant deviation from the straight line they had been following since leaving the main highway. A dilapidated concrete building stood at the corner, and Raul slowed the car. "Is that it?"

Jenna stared at the half-ruined structure for a moment. She didn't actually need to take the brothers to the exact place indicated by Noah's coordinates. She just needed a place where she could slip free of their control and escape. On the other hand, if she had to run, she might not get another chance to retrieve Noah's fire alarm.

"No," she said. "That's not it. Keep going."

A mile and a half later, she saw another building, a sheet-metal structure, several stories high, with a large square opening, like a garage door, at the southern end. "That's the place."

Raul pulled to a stop fifty feet from the opening. He shut off the engine, but left the lights on, illuminating the interior and revealing another identical opening on the opposite side.

Carlos stared at her for several seconds, as if searching for some hint of treachery. "Your old man put the money in there?"

She nodded. "This is the place."

Carlos got out and then motioned for Jenna to do the same. "All right, little girl. It's show time. Lead the way."

Jenna complied, careful not to seem too eager or too reluctant, though in truth, she felt a lot of both. She wanted to see what Noah had left behind, to learn the truth about her father, and perhaps discover why someone wanted him—and her—dead. She was also anxious about the imminent showdown with the Villegas brothers. She didn't know exactly how it was going to play out, and that scared her a little. It was also exhilarating. She felt like a volcano, desperate to erupt before the pressure blew her apart.

The headlights illuminated the area closest to the large door, leaving the rest shrouded in darkness. Carlos and Raul both used their cell phones as flashlights, casting the beams into the shadowy corners. There was debris on the floor, and pieces of metal and construction material was scattered everywhere, but the building was mostly an empty shell.

"What is this?" Raul asked, shining his light up at the cavernous ceiling. There were holes in the roof, where sheets of metal had been torn away. "An airplane hangar?"

Jenna did not know if it was a rhetorical question, but she decided to treat it as one. She saw no benefit in revealing what she knew about this place. When she had entered the coordinates into Carlos's phone, one of the search results had triggered a memory about an obscure bit of South Florida history that she had learned and never forgotten.

In the early 1960s, as America and the Soviet Union raced to conquer space, a company called Aerojet had spent $150 million to build a solid-fuel rocket testing facility in the Everglades, just outside Homestead. But NASA decided to use liquid-fueled rockets in the Apollo program, and that, along with a waning interest in the Space Race—once Neil Armstrong planted the Stars and Stripes on lunar soil—had resulted in Aerojet closing the plant before the decade's end. They abandoned it entirely, leaving the derelict structures, many still filled with specialized equipment for producing and testing solid rocket fuel, like the ruins and relics of a forgotten civilization. One particular relic that was mentioned in news reports and documentaries about the Aerojet facility, was the AJ 260-2 rocket motor body, which had been used to test the fuel mixtures.

The rocket motor, one of the largest of its kind ever, was too large to move by truck or train. A canal had been dug so that the rocket could be floated to the facility on a barge, where it was lowered into the silo with a crane. The silo had to be open to the air for test fires, but covered the rest of the time, so the engineers had designed the enormous shed to be movable. The rocket motor was just a metal cylinder—a fuel tank without any hardware to create ignition. For the tests, it had to first be filled with the rubbery, solid rocket fuel, and then fitted with a cone-shaped rocket nozzle, placed atop the motor, so that its explosive energy would blast into the sky. According to one documentary Jenna had watched, the glow of the third and final test in 1967 had been visible from Key West. At sixty feet in length and more than twenty feet in diameter, it was too large to be removed from the site, so for more than forty-five years, it had sat idle in this enormous structure, or more precisely, under it. The rocket motor still rested in a silo, covered over with plates of welded metal, directly beneath where Jenna now walked.

It was not the rocket motor that had captured Jenna's attention, though. It was the silo. Fifty feet wide. One hundred-eighty feet *deep*. It was the only place anywhere near the coordinates Noah had left where the third number in the message made any sense.

25.321304 -80.557173 (-80)

'Minus eighty' had to mean eighty feet *down*. Noah had left his fire alarm in the silo, probably somewhere under the rocket motor.

Carlos gave Jenna a look that was both impatient and suspicious. "Well?"

Jenna stomped a foot on the floor. The metal plate beneath her made a hollow sound, and the vibration made her captor jump back in surprise. "It's under here."

"Under?" He turned his light onto the welded plates, and his inspection showed where many of them had rusted completely through.

Jenna inched closer to the walls where the floor was bare concrete. The metal plates were covering the silo opening, and if Noah had left something eighty feet below, then there had to be access. Her eagerness to discover exactly what it was her father had hidden overrode her anxiety regarding her present situation. Freeing herself from Carlos and Raul was still high on her list of priorities, but figuring out who was trying to kill her—who *did* kill Noah—was still at the top of that list.

She crept around the floor's edge, skirting the metal plates and inspecting the seams of each to see if all of them had been welded shut. After five minutes, she came upon a section that was covered by a thick metal grate. She peeked through and could just make out a large cylindrical object. She knelt, threaded her fingers through the grate and tried to lift. It gave just enough for her to know that it wasn't welded in place, but it was too heavy for her to lift alone.

"Help me," she called out, and when neither brother moved to assist her, she added, "Do you want the money or not?"

Raul looked to his brother as if checking for permission, and then moved to help Jenna. Like her, he attempted to lift the grate up, but even with their combined strength, it refused to yield.

Carlos regarded Jenna suspiciously. "That thing hasn't been moved in years, little girl. I think you're jerking us around."

Jenna was inclined to agree with the first assertion. Unfortunately, it didn't support her claim that Noah had recently hidden money here. But she felt certain that this was the place. "Just help us lift it. Or better yet, find something we can use as a lever." She glanced around the debris strewn floor, looking for something sturdy enough to fit the bill.

"Raul," Carlos said, his tone still dubious. "Get a tire iron from the car."

The younger brother moved off without question, leaving Carlos and Jenna alone. Jenna measured the distance between herself and him, calculating her odds of taking him on one-on-one. He was bigger but she had years of training in unarmed combat, and she would have the element of surprise on her side. He had a gun, but as Noah had often told her, people with guns had a tendency to put too much faith in them. If she charged, he might waste precious seconds trying to draw the gun and aim it, time in which she would be able to close the distance and punch him in the throat.

But not quite enough time, she thought. Carlos, consciously or not, had kept a good stand-off distance. That was another thing Noah always complained about when watching action movies. When someone—a cop maybe—held a prisoner at gunpoint, they would always get right up in their face. It was dramatic as hell, but Noah always scoffed and talked about how easy it would be to disarm the gunman in that situation.

It was funny how all those little things Noah had said and done over the years, things which she had never thought twice about, now made sense. All that time, Noah had been teaching her, passing along his accumulated wisdom, preparing her for...

For this?

He must have known a threat like this might someday materialize, and while he had chosen not to reveal the truth about himself to her, he had taken steps to ensure that she would be prepared. He had trained her, mind and body, to deal with whatever happened. That was why, even though her muscles ached, her empty stomach rumbled and her head throbbed, she did not feel afraid.

Raul came back with a short lug wrench, tipped with a chisel point at one end for popping off hubcaps. It was not long enough to provide much leverage, but Raul was able to work it into a seam and managed to lift the grate and jam the pry bar under it.

"See," Jenna said, pointing triumphantly.

Carlos looked unimpressed, but joined in. The three of them succeeded in pushing the grate aside a full eighteen inches. He then shone his light down into the hole. Jenna looked in and saw the smooth concrete walls that curved in either direction to form a wide circle, and at the center of the circle, the enormous white cylinder of the rocket motor. A line of hooplike protrusions— curved pieces of rebar, each about the size of a horseshoe—were set in the concrete wall at one-foot intervals, forming an access ladder.

She was itching to descend into the silo, to seek out its hidden depths and whatever it was that Noah had left here, but she waited for Carlos to give her the go-ahead. She did not want to let either of them go down the ladder, but neither did she want to seem too eager to do so herself. If either one of them did decide to explore the silo, she decided that would be her cue to strike.

"Okay, little girl," Carlos said, gesturing at the opening. "This is your show. Go get it."

NINETEEN

2:03 a.m.

Jenna dropped onto the floor, swung her legs out into empty space, and twisted around until she felt a steel rung underfoot. She tested it. After forty-five years of exposure to the tropical Everglades air, the steel could have been as rusted as the metal plates covering the silo. The first rung felt solid underfoot. She stepped down to the next and tested it the same way. Just as she was about to take the step that would plunge her into the darkness below, she raised her eyes to Carlos.

"I'm going to need a light."

He frowned then looked at his phone for a moment before handing it over. "No bars out here, so don't bother trying to call for help."

In truth, the idea had not even occurred to her. "I just need to see what I'm doing."

She turned the bright LED down into the depths of the silo. Far below her feet, at the base of the rocket, was a platform made of the same metal grating. The distance seemed about right for Noah's 'minus eighty.' She slipped the phone into the back pocket of her jeans and started down again.

The round mouth of the silo, dimly lit to begin with, shrank to a spot that glowed about as brightly as the luminescent numbers on a wristwatch—enough to be seen, but not enough to illuminate anything. She didn't need light for the descent, though. She could see everything in her mind's eye, and she knew exactly where she was in relation to the platform. She had, without even thinking about it, calculated the number of rungs. She ticked them off in her head as she went down, testing each hold before trusting it with her weight. After several minutes, she reached a foot out behind her to find the platform.

She was less certain about its stability, but there were no creaks or groans. With one hand on a rung, she lowered her other foot down and stood there for a moment.

"Okay, Noah. I'm here," she murmured. "What am I supposed to do now?"

She took out the phone. It had timed out and gone dark, but she found the button to wake it up and was gratified to see that there was no password lock. That would come in handy if she needed to use the phone after...

First things first.

She used the screen's brightness to survey the area. The rocket motor was just behind her, its rounded end perched atop a solid concrete pedestal at the center of the metal grating. The silo continued down into the shadowy unknown, but Jenna knew that what she wanted would be found right here. She waved the light around, painting the area into her mental image but also looking for anything that seemed out of place.

She focused on recesses and niches hidden in shadow. Noah would not have left his cache out in the open. As inaccessible as the silo's bottom was, there was nothing to stop a thrill-seeking urban explorer from making the descent. Noah would have recognized that possibility. After a few moments of searching, she spied something just above the inverted dome of the rocket motor.

It was a metal box, about the size of the aluminum lunch-boxes that some of her schoolmates carried. Most kids who brought lunch from home used collapsible insulated bags, but a few liked the kitschy appeal of having a metal box painted with images from cartoon shows. *My Little Pony. Hello Kitty.* Things she had never been interested in. This box was an undecorated gun-metal gray. She rapped her knuckles on it. Solid as a bank vault. She held the light closer and saw where the box had been spot-welded to the rocket. She also saw that it was secured with a three-digit roller combination lock.

It was suddenly all very real now. Noah had been here, standing right where she now stood.

When did he do this? It had to have been many years ago, probably on a day when she was in school and there were no charters on the schedule. She recalled that, among his many tools for boat maintenance, Noah had a miniature acetylene blow torch. He sometimes used it to braze pieces of copper tubing. He would have used the torch to cut through the grate above, and then made the same descent she had. It would have taken only a few minutes to weld the box in place.

"Okay," she said aloud, as if speaking to her father's ghost. "What's the magic number?" She cycled through birthdays: hers, Mercy's and Noah's late November birthday. A four-digit combo was out. *What else?*

He had left it with Mercy. Could it be an important date that only the two of them shared? If that was the case, her only option would be a brute force attack, trying successive combinations until she finally hit on the correct one. If she started at all zeros and the number was in the 900s it would take her close to an hour. *It might not even be a date.*

Think. Noah wanted the right person to open this if the need arose. He left precise coordinates so it could be found in case of emergency...

"Duh!" She quickly set the combination to 9-1-1 and heard an internal mechanism click. The box opened to reveal a small leather-bound notebook inside a large Ziploc bag, and nothing else.

Jenna opened the bag and then the book. She thumbed through it, instantly recognizing Noah's precise printed letters. It was a journal. She didn't read any of it. There would be time for that later.

The book was too large to fit in a pocket, so she put it back in the bag, stuffed it into the waistband of her jeans at the small of her back and covered it with her T-shirt. She drew a deep breath and mentally centered herself, putting her dojo habits to use in the real world. She moved to the steel rungs and began climbing.

The ascent went quickly, partly because she did not take the time to test her footholds, but also because the impending confrontation, like the last day of summer vacation, was something she dreaded. It was the exact opposite of the old saying about watched pots never boiling.

She maintained her calm focus by counting down the rungs. When she got to fifteen, she could see the faces of her tormentors, silhouetted in the ambient light, staring down at her. When she got to eight, Carlos called out.

"Unless you've got a wad of ten thousand dollar bills in your pocket," he said in a low menacing tone, "I think I'm about to be very disappointed."

She climbed a couple of rungs higher before giving the answer she had mentally rehearsed. "The money isn't here. It's in a bank account. Cayman Islands." She thought that sounded pretty plausible. "My dad hid the account number here. I've got it now."

Carlos did not look convinced. "Give it to me."

She reached into a pocket and found the strip of paper on which Noah had written the coordinates for the silo. It was still damp from her plunge into Boca Chica Channel but she succeeded in taking it out intact. She waved it for Carlos to see. Then, she took another step and held it up like an offering.

Carlos reached out to snatch the paper from her fingers, but as he did, she let go of it and encircled his wrist with her hand. His face registered surprise, but she only caught a glimpse as she yanked down hard on his arm.

As he started to fall toward her, she let go and pressed herself flat against the smooth concrete wall. There was a tug of friction as his body slid past hers, but she held on tightly, and an instant later, Carlos was gone.

TWENTY

2:24 a.m.

Jenna exploded out of the silo like a missile, leaping toward the stunned figure of Raul. He was too far away to be pulled in. She knew that trick wouldn't work twice, but she had something different planned for the younger Villegas brother.

She landed on the iron-clad floor, coiling like a rattler getting ready to strike, and then she unleashed all her energy in a kick aimed at Raul's head. Even as she moved, she saw him struggling to draw his gun, just as she thought he would. She corrected her aim at the last moment, striking his right shoulder. Raul spun around, unbalanced. The pistol flew from his hand.

Jenna did not stop. She had committed to this course of action the moment she had started climbing out of the silo. She would not stop. Not to catch her breath. Not to assess the results of her attack. Not until Raul was...

Dead?

Yeah, dead.

She felt no guilt about that. She had already sent Carlos to Hell, and that didn't bother her at all. She felt about as much remorse for Carlos as she would for a roach ground beneath her heel. Truth be told, it was a rush. It was like she'd been given an invitation to a secret and very exclusive club. Noah had been in that club. Something told her that Ken was not the first man he had killed. Noah might not have wanted her to join the ranks of killers, but he'd prepared her for it, perhaps knowing this initiation might be unavoidable.

I'm a killer now. I passed the test, and I'm ready to do it again. Raul, your brother's holding the door for you.

She advanced, throwing a pair of mid-body punches that rocked Raul back again. With each strike she shouted her *kiai*, using the sound to focus her energy and intimidate the man. Despite the attack, he stayed on his feet. She might have been able to punch through boards and bricks, but Raul was probably twice her weight, and flesh yielded whereas planks and cinder blocks cracked. Punches, she realized, weren't going to do the trick. She took another step forward and with another shout, spun into a roundhouse kick, aimed low to sweep him off his feet.

Her foot struck his calf, a few inches below where she had aimed, and she rebounded away, struggling to recover her balance and irritated with herself for missing. It wasn't the worst thing that could have happened, but it did erase any advantage her surprise attack had given her.

Raul snarled at her. She could see in his eyes that he was now little more than an enraged animal. His fury would allow him to tap into reserves of near-superhuman strength. If he got close enough to grab hold of her, she might not be able to break free. She took a step back, forcing herself to stay calm and focused.

He charged but she stepped aside, whirling around to deliver a powerful blow to his already pummeled kidney. It was enough to knock him off his feet. He went sprawling on the metal plates that covered the silo. A few feet to the left and he would have plunged into the hole.

Jenna didn't think he would be fooled into such a reckless advance a second time. She backed away, glancing around for a weapon. She didn't know where the gun had gone but the tire iron lay just a couple steps away. As she reached for it, Raul scrambled back to his feet and charged again.

A math problem flashed through her head: *R is moving toward J at 15 m.p.h. J is trying to reach a tire iron 5 feet away. Will J reach the tire iron before R kills her?*

It was a chance she couldn't take, and at the last instant, she veered off. Raul had indeed learned his lesson, and he pulled up short, facing her, taunting her with curses and threats, reverting to some kind of primal threat display. "Me cago en la madre que te parió! Think you're tough, chica?" He motioned to his body. "Think you can take this?" He spat at her. "You're nothing but a puta. A scared little puta."

She ignored his empty words and paid attention to what his eyes were saying. He took a step toward her, and she matched him, backing up as she settled into a ready stance. He took another step, and then his eyes darted to the side. She knew what would come next. When he lunged, she shouted a *kiai* and aimed her fist at an imaginary spot six inches behind his chin.

The punch connected solidly. Raul's jaw broke with an audible crack. Yet, even as his head snapped back, his flailing hands caught her T-shirt. When he staggered away, she was pulled off balance.

Then his arms were around her, pinning her own arms against her body, crushing her in a bear hug. For a moment, they were locked in a crazy dance, Jenna trying to squirm free and stay on her feet, Raul simply trying to stop her from doing either. Then, they crashed down to the concrete floor.

The collision sent a flare of pain through Jenna's body, but she ignored it and focused on the much more immediate peril. Her *sensei* had taught her some grappling, just enough to know that strength and size were not always the deciding factor in a wrestling match. But if Raul squeezed the breath out of her, she would not be able to put up much of a fight. She twisted, squirming to get her hands free of his embrace. He doubled his efforts, squeezing tighter.

In a flash of inspiration, she drove her forehead into Raul's chin. There was a bright flash in her field of vision, but the sound of grinding bones filled her head. The broken pieces of Raul's lower jaw smashed together, followed by a howl of pain. His hold loosened, just enough. She ripped her arms free of his grasp and wrapped them around his skull.

She felt him pounding his fists against her back. The blows were painful but not precise enough to do any real damage. She answered his fury with her own, wrenching her body back and forth, as if trying to rip his head off. In a way, that was exactly what she was trying to do. She remembered how Noah had broken Ken's neck. Could she do that?

After just a few moments, she knew that she couldn't. Maybe there was some special technique, but what she was doing wasn't it. She felt Raul moving beneath her, rolling over and struggling to rise. If he succeeded, she would have almost no leverage against him. He was too strong, and she was too light. She squeezed and shook him again, but to no avail. She just wasn't strong enough...

Maybe my arms aren't strong enough, but I've got other muscles.

The same intuitive guidance that had prompted her to head butt him now gave her a different set of instructions. She dropped her grip onto his shoulders and then pushed down, launching herself straight up like a child playing leapfrog. The move got her high enough to swing one leg over Raul's shoulder, and a moment later, she had his neck caught in a scissors hold between her thighs. With a shout that was like the mother of all *kiais*, she twisted her entire body—and Raul's head with it—completely around.

The sound of snapping vertebrae vibrated through her body. When his body went rag-doll slack beneath her, she knew it was over.

The fight ended somewhat anticlimactically, with Raul collapsing beneath her, his death throes slamming her onto the hard floor. She disentangled herself quickly, scrambling away from him like he was on fire.

She lay there for a moment, panting. The fight had taxed her, but her breathlessness owed more to a sense of victory. She had won.

Her moment of triumph ended when she felt a hand close over her arm. She jerked in surprise and found herself staring into the bloody visage of Carlos Villegas.

Impossible. It was an eighty foot fall. He couldn't have survived.

She jerked free. He made no effort to hold on to her, and as she crabbed backward, she saw why.

He had somehow survived and crawled back up out of the silo. But survival was a relative term. The fall had broken him, literally. Although she had recognized him, his face was misshapen, stretched over a skull that was no longer in one piece. Blood streamed from his ears and eyes. His limbs were also deformed. The hand that had grasped her appeared to be the only one of his extremities still functioning. She still could not fathom how he had pulled himself back up, but he had no strength left with which to menace her.

He didn't need strength, though.

As she backed away, he reached his good hand down to his shattered body, and when she saw it again, he was holding his gun.

Jenna felt herself go numb. Carlos had been in no condition to fight her, not like Raul had, but she had instinctively retreated from him, creating the standoff distance that would allow him to shoot her before she could reverse course.

I have to try, she thought. *Maybe he'll—*

The report made her jump, but there was no pain, no sensation at all. It didn't seem possible that he could have missed. When he slumped forward and didn't move again, she realized that Carlos had not fired his gun.

The shot had come from behind her.

She turned slowly and saw a tall figure silhouetted in the still blazing headlights of the rental car, one arm outstretched, holding a gun. Jenna's rescuer lowered the gun and took a step forward, then gestured at the two bodies on the floor. "You've been busy."

Though the face was still obscured by shadow, Jenna instantly recognized the voice and bolted forward, shouting, "Mercy!"

TWENTY-ONE

2:34 a.m.

Unlike Jenna, Mercedes Reyes had been wearing her seatbelt when her pickup lost control and started corkscrewing down the Overseas Highway. Aside from being shaken up like the marble in a can of spray paint, Mercy had come away from the accident with nothing more serious than a few aches and bruises.

"I think they almost crashed, too," Mercy said. "When my head stopped spinning, they were gone. I looked for you for a while, but then the police showed up."

"I'm surprised they let you go. Aren't you like a material witness or something?"

"I may not have actually hung around to answer their questions." Mercy ducked her head guiltily. "You said that the bad guys might be connected with the police. I couldn't take the chance. Someone gave me a ride as far as Marathon, and from there I was able to get some wheels and come here."

"Because you knew this is where I would go."

Mercy's expression became grave. "No, honey. I came here because I thought you were dead. If I had known you were out there, I wouldn't have left. I came here because it was what Noah told us to do."

Jenna felt chastened. She had done exactly the same thing, albeit by a much more dangerous route. "Good thing you got here when you did."

Mercy nodded. She explained how she had walked into the building just in time to see Carlos aim his pistol at Jenna. Her own gun had been lost during the wreck, but she had found Raul's discarded weapon on the floor and had not hesitated. Jenna had a lot more questions, and she suspected that Mercy did, too, but those could wait. There was only one thing that really mattered now. "So, did you find it? What Noah left?"

Jenna felt for the journal tucked into her pants, but it was gone. She looked around, panic building, but quickly found it on the floor, still safe inside the Ziploc bag. She picked it up and moved forward until she was bathed in the glow of the car's headlights. She opened the Ziploc, pulled out the journal and let the bag fall to the ground.

"Are you sure you don't want to wait?" Mercy nodded toward the pair of corpses. "Maybe go somewhere that's a little more...I don't know...*not* here?"

Jenna shook her head. "After everything I've been through to get here, I just want to know the truth." She opened to the first page.

If you're reading this, then you'd better put it back where you found it, right now. Seriously.

She could almost hear Noah's slightly gruff voice as she read the words. It triggered an unexpected surge of emotion.

Or I suppose it could mean that something very bad has happened. It's okay. Don't worry about me. I came to terms with my mortality a long time ago, and now I'm off to find the answer to life's greatest mystery.

But that bad thing I mentioned? Well, that's a problem, isn't it? Mercy? If it's you reading this, and I hope to hell it is, there's just one thing I want you to do. Get Jenna and take her to Miami. When you get there, look up a guy named Bill Cort. I wish I could say he's an old friend, but that wouldn't quite be the truth. If you get the time to read the rest of this book, you'll understand what that means. And you'll probably have a better idea of why this is all happening.

Below that was an address, but it had been crossed out and an arrow pointed to the margin where a different address had been written in.

Mercy read over her shoulder. "Next stop: Miami?"

Jenna blinked back tears and swallowed. "I want to read the rest of it. I have to know what was so important that it got him killed."

She turned the page and read aloud. "November sixteenth, nineteen ninety-nine..."

STORM

TWENTY-TWO

November 16, 1999
10:35 p.m. (local time)

They appeared as barely visible specks—particles of black debris in the blue-white froth of the storm-tossed surf. There was a lot of flotsam in the water, most of it washed into the sea by the floods that resulted from the torrential rain of Hurricane Lenny, but unlike most of the litter, these black shapes moved under their own power.

Swimming was the wrong word for what they were doing. The six neoprene-clad men were engaged in a life or death struggle with the relentlessly turbulent surf. They were all strong swimmers—strong men—but these were extraordinary conditions that taxed their individual abilities to the limit. One man won his freedom, and turned to help the nearest of his comrades. These two helped the next, and in short order, all six were on the beach, above the reach of even the largest breakers. Though exhausted from the epic battle against nature, none of the men showed the least sign of fatigue. They organized into a wedge formation behind the point man and made for the relative cover of the nearby tree line. Their footprints would be gone by morning, and there was little chance of anyone happening upon the marks in the sand before they were erased by the driving rain. No one was foolish enough to be out here in the middle of the storm. No one but these six.

And one other.

A red light flashed out from the trees, went dark, then flashed again. This signal kept repeating, the intervals random and irregular, like a train-crossing signal with a stutter, until the point man spotted it. He flashed a return signal with his red-hooded Mini-MagLite and adjusted course, homing in on the flashing light. As he neared the margin of the beach, a stout form, also clad in black neoprene, stepped out to greet them.

"You find the strangest things on the beach after a big blow," he said in a booming voice. He had been waiting here for more than an hour, and he knew that there was no one around to overhear their exchange. As the men gathered around, he lowered his tone just a little, but still had to yell to be heard over the lashing rain. "Any problems?"

"Problems?" the leader of the six-man element replied. "You mean aside from the kind of problems that come with having to swim a mile-and-a-half through open water on the edge of a hurricane? Whose brilliant idea was this, anyway?"

The seventh man regarded the leader with patient but critical eyes. "The mission was handed down from the DO, but using the storm to cover our movements was *my* brilliant idea." He emphasized the last three words, but he did not mean it as an admission of culpability. Operators—he knew their preferred term was *shooters*—tended to whine a lot about little details at the beginning of a mission. The complaints were usually just a way of working out the jitters. That was fine with him, but they needed to know that he was not going to be a very sympathetic listener. There was work to do.

"Officially, we are Action Team Storm, and my designation is Storm God. That was *not* my brilliant idea, in case you're wondering. I'd rather you just call me 'Papa.' Everyone does." Papa allowed a moment for the shooters to introduce themselves with their preferred operational callsigns. There was Driver, the leader; Rodent, the demolitions man; Van Gogh, the designated marksman who along with his spotter, Loco, formed a sniper team; Mutant, the team medic; and Billy Boy, who ran communications.

"The objective is a small compound right up there." Papa pointed to a spot on the bluff, high above them, but it was too dark to see any manmade structures. "It's about a five klick walk to get there."

The shooters knew all this, but their initial briefing had been presented by an agency analyst, down from Langley, who despite being familiar with satellite photos of the facility, had no real world experience with the target. Papa produced a laminated satellite map and shone his red light onto it. He kept it tilted so that the rain would run off. "Concrete construction to withstand the weather, but there's been a lot of erosion over the years. The place was originally supposed to be a resort hotel, but it's been repurposed for special research."

"Special research?" Driver asked. "I don't like the sound of that. Can you be a little more specific?"

"Actually, I can't." The question was a valid one, but Papa did not care for Driver's tone. Sometimes, the gripes were nerves, but sometimes they revealed a deep-seated resentment of the way military special operations were routinely co-opted by civilian intelligence agencies. That most definitely was not okay with Papa. "All I can say is that the research being conducted in the facility poses no immediate danger to us, but does have strategic threat potential."

In truth, Papa was not sure about that last part. The intel was spotty at best, but it was a better answer than the standard 'need-to-know' line.

"On site security works four shifts of three on duty at any given time. Probably a dozen, but no more than fifteen in all."

None of the shooters offered comment on the size of the security force they would be going up against, so Papa went on. "There's a sentry post here." He tapped a spot on the map. "And the other two guard the gate, which is hardly ever used. They'll be buttoned up tight tonight.

"Civilian personnel numbers no more than twenty. Scientists and support staff. Most of the work is done in the east wing of the old hotel building." His finger continued to move about the map. "Living quarters are in west wing. That's where we'll be doing most of our work tonight. You all have your cards?"

Each of the shooters had been issued a short deck of laminated cards, the size and shape of regular playing cards, with photos of key targets believed to be at the facility. Although destroying the facility and everyone in it was the primary objective, if any of the researchers survived, there was always a chance that the project could be reconstituted, probably somewhere a lot harder to reach. Driver nodded, answering for the rest of the team.

"Our job is simple and dirty. If you see them, kill them. No exceptions."

Papa watched for a reaction—a flinch, a look of distaste, or perhaps worse, a gleam of hungry psychotic anticipation—but he saw nothing. These men were professionals. They knew that they were just a policy tool—a sword—and like any weapon or tool, they bore none of the responsibility for how they were wielded from afar by politicians and bureaucrats. The job was the job. They did it and then they went home. If they were lucky, the memories of the violence done would quickly fade.

Even the most dedicated and capable soldiers were sometimes haunted by the ghosts of the men they had killed in open combat. Unlike regular soldiers, spec ops shooters sometimes had to carry out assassinations, killing unsuspecting, and often unarmed, targets from a distance. Usually—not always, but usually—there was a very good reason why those targets needed to be taken out, but part of the job description was that you didn't second guess the chain of command. The toughest part of the shooter's job was the balancing act: keeping humanity in check long enough to get the job done, without being driven crazy by the ghosts or turning into a sociopath.

Not everyone succeeded.

"If you see them and they're already dead," he continued, "check to see if the face matches one of your cards. Bring me a royal flush, and I'll buy a keg for your team room." When that did not immediately elicit the laughter he had hoped for, Papa decided to wrap it up. "Any questions?"

There were none. Papa inclined his head. "Driver, it's your show."

As the team leader began assigning individual tasks to the other men, the one called Billy Boy approached Papa and handed him a small, black, waterproof bag. Inside, Papa found a set of A/N PVS-7B night vision goggles, a short-range radio with headset, and a Skorpion vz 61 7.65 millimeter submachine pistol, outfitted with a suppressor. He gave the Czech manufactured weapon a cursory inspection. Its collapsible wire stock was folded over in the stored position, so it was only a little bigger than an ordinary semi-automatic pistol.

With a cyclic rate of 900 rounds per minute, the Skorpion was not the subtlest of weapons, but it had the advantage of being extremely generic. Like a lot of weapons from former Soviet-bloc nations, there were so many of them on the black market that they were virtually untraceable. When the storm passed and the damage was discovered, there would be nothing to directly point the finger back to the Agency. There would be suspicions, of course, but no meaningful physical evidence.

Papa fitted the night vision goggles over his head and turned them on. After a moment, the world was rendered in a hazy green. Raindrops scattered the ambient light, giving the impression of static, but it was a big improvement over what he had been able to see before. He snugged the radio headset into place, and then waited for the team to finish their preparations. When Driver called for a radio check, he dutifully keyed the mic and said, "This is Papa, roger, out."

"Move out," Driver did not transmit this message, but spoke in his normal voice. "Papa, stick with me."

Papa nodded and fell into step alongside the team leader. His job was to observe, and if something unexpected happened, advise. He was content to do the former in silence. Billy Boy trailed behind them, while the rest of the team split off in pairs, carrying out their respective pieces of the mission.

It took about an hour and a half for them to hike through the forest and up to the storm battered bluff where the converted resort sat perched above the sea. Driver signaled for a halt at the edge of the woods, and then he keyed his radio. "This is Driver. Report."

"Vincent, here." Vincent was Van Gogh. It was a sort of nickname within a nickname. Papa assumed that the moniker derived from his 'artistic' talents—only instead of paint, his medium was lead. Van Gogh and Loco had gone ahead and were now somewhere in a tree looking over the concrete fence that surrounded the compound. "We're in position. Waiting for go."

Another voice sounded in Papa's ears. "This is Rodent. Charges set. Waiting for go, over."

Rodent and Mutant were concealed near the main gate. At the 'go' signal, they would detonate small, shaped charges to breach the gate, then sweep in and take out the guards stationed just beyond.

"Stand by." Driver turned to Papa. "Any last words of wisdom?"

Papa hefted his Skorpion and signaled his readiness with a nod. He followed Driver and Billy Boy to within sight of the gate. Mutant and Rodent were starkly visible in the green monochrome display, but Papa knew that to the unaided eye, they would be indistinguishable.

"Prepare to execute," Driver said, "Counting down... three... two... one... go!"

TWENTY-THREE

November 17, 1999
12:26 a.m. (local time)

Rodent held up an M57 trigger device and started pumping it in his fist. On the second squeeze there was a muted thump at the gate—the sound was no louder than a door slamming—and then both men were moving. More noises followed, none as loud as the shaped charge that had blown out the gate's lock. Then there were voices, Van Gogh first, then Mutant, reporting that the targets were down.

"Roger," Driver answered. "We're coming in. Vincent, maintain overwatch while we set the charges."

Papa followed the others into the compound, but remained at the gate, scanning the grounds for any sign of activity, while the four-man element went about their deadly business. The compound was dark, the power out, but whether that was because of the storm, or because of rationing, Papa could not say. If anyone had heard the sound of the breaching charges, they had chosen not to investigate.

It took the team five minutes to set demolition charges around the outside of the old hotel building, but the job was only half done. To bring the structure down, they would need to go inside and place explosives on load-bearing walls. It would take only a few charges, but placing them would be the most dangerous part of the mission. Driver lined up his men at the front door and they all filed inside.

Papa held his breath. For a long time there was no sound but the howl of the wind and the steady beat of the rain. Then he heard a squawk of static and Mutant's voice over the radio. "Contact. Tango down."

Driver's voice answered, "Sitrep, over."

Papa inferred that the men had split up, moving to different points through the building to accomplish the objective faster.

"Ah, Driver, I think I need you to take a look at this." There was a strange, high pitched noise in the background.

An alarm? That wasn't likely. It cut out as soon as the transmission ended, so it clearly wasn't loud enough to rouse the entire complex.

Papa's brow furrowed behind the night vision goggles. He keyed his mic. "Mutant, this is Papa. What's the situation? Did you locate one of the key targets?"

"Not exactly, Papa. Actually, maybe you should get in here and tell us what to do."

"On my way." As he hastened across the courtyard and entered the building, Papa could not help but speculate on the nature of the discovery that had so bewildered the shooters. He could only assume that it was something to do with the mysterious research being conducted at the facility. What that was, he had no idea. Special operators were trained to deal with a broad range of nuclear, biological and chemical agents. It would take something extraordinary to confound these hardened shooters.

Once inside, he could hear the wailing noise again. It seemed unbelievably loud, and he wondered how it was possible that the residents of the building had not been roused by the clamor. Hefting the Skorpion to meet any attack, he fixed the source of the sound—it came from the east wing, the research section—and he closed in on it.

"Papa here," he whispered into his mic. "Coming your way. Don't shoot me."

He rounded a corner and found himself in a large room, what might once have been a conference hall or a small lobby. In the green display of his night vision device, he saw the four shooters in black neoprene, looking like shadows, arrayed around a motionless form on the floor. He recalled that Mutant had reported contact and a kill just prior to whatever it was that had brought the mission, quite literally, to a screeching halt. His gut twisted with dread as he realized what the sound was. One more step brought him to Driver's side.

The body on the floor belonged to a woman. She was older, perhaps in her mid-fifties, heavy set, with salt-and-pepper hair done up in a matronly bun. It looked like she had caught two rounds. One was centered just above her ample bosom, the other had gone through her left eye. Papa knew without checking that she was not one of the special targets, just support staff, an unlucky hired hand.

Probably a nurse, he thought, shifting his gaze to the squalling bundle pressed against her chest.

"Is somebody going to shut that thing up?" Rodent growled.

Papa glanced at him. Despite his justifiable anxiety about the noise, the shooter made no move to do what he had just proposed. None of the men moved, and the infant in the dead woman's arms continued to scream.

Mutant's first shot—the bullet that had probably stopped the woman's heart—had missed the baby by scant inches. It had probably been a reflex shot. The orders to kill everyone had been explicit, so positive target identification wasn't a concern. Even so, the shooter probably wouldn't have taken the shot had he known she carried a child.

Mutant looked to Driver. "What do we do, boss?"

"You know the answer," the team leader replied, and he turned to Papa. "No exceptions, right?"

Papa let out his breath. No exceptions meant no exceptions, but if there were ever to be an exception, this would be it.

"One thing at a time," he muttered, and knelt beside the dead woman. He slipped the child free of the lifeless arms, and raised it awkwardly to his shoulder. The screaming seemed to intensify.

"Shhhh," he whispered, patting the baby's back and gently shaking it up and down. He had never married, never spent any time with children, but this was what people did in movies, so it was worth a shot. He continued patting and crooning for a few seconds, and miraculously, the baby quieted. "Okay," he said in a low whisper. "Charlie Mike, boys. Finish setting the charges so we can get out of here."

The three subordinate team members moved off, but Driver lingered. When the others were out of earshot, he asked, "What are you going to do?"

Papa continued to rock back and forth, still crooning softly, as he pondered the answer. There was no wiggle room in the orders. They weren't supposed to leave anyone alive. *Anyone.* This unexpected development changed nothing. It was just a fluke that the woman had brought the child down to the research level. If they had been upstairs sleeping, none of the team would have even known about the child.

It wasn't as if he needed to kill the child himself. He could simply leave it behind. When the explosives brought the building down, it would die exactly as it would have had they not known about it.

The problem was, they did know about it.

War was hell. Every shooter knew that. Even the most precise surgical strike carried the possibility for collateral damage—a nice polite term that meant dead women and children who had nothing at all to do with the targeted hostile forces. But it was a lot harder to pull the trigger or call in the air strike when looking one of those innocents in the eye. Papa knew of several instances where operators—men just like the shooters of Action Team Storm—had been captured or killed after their observation posts were discovered by local children. Hardened steely-eyed killers had sacrificed themselves, rather than kill innocents in cold blood to keep their presence a secret.

He looked at Driver. "Uncle Sam doesn't pay you boys to kill babies. Or to live with the baggage that comes afterward."

Driver seemed to grow lighter as the burden was removed from his shoulders, but he was still a professional. "What about the orders?"

Papa looked down at the child in his arms. Its cheek was pressed against his shoulder and it had dozed off. *It,* he thought. He didn't even know if the infant was a boy or a girl, but it certainly wasn't just an 'it.'

There was only one answer to Driver's question. "You let me worry about that," he said, and turned away.

Ten minutes later, he rendezvoused with the four shooters at the designated rally point a kilometer from the compound. There had been no further encounters, and the rest of the demolition charges had been set without incident.

Even though he could not see their eyes behind their goggles, Papa could feel them looking at him as he walked up.

"What did you...?" Driver let the question hang, as if he feared that saying it aloud might give him nightmares for the rest of his life.

"I took care of it," Papa assured him. His tone was neutral, as it had to be. The orders were, after all, very clear. There could be no survivors. "Blow it."

Driver hesitated, but only for a moment. He held up a radio transmitter and pressed the send button.

There was no flash of light, only a resounding thump that shook the ground under their feet. A thousand meters away, the former hotel building imploded and collapsed into a heap of shattered concrete. A moment later, there was another noise, a sustained roar this time, as waterlogged ground broke loose and slid down the bluff, crashing into the sea below.

It was possible—unlikely, but possible—that some of the residents might still be alive, trapped in the rubble, but the storm and the remoteness of the location ensured that their survival would only be a temporary condition. The local authorities might not even bother to investigate the wreckage, but would write it off as a natural occurrence—one more storm-born disaster.

"Mission accomplished," Papa murmured. Normally, this declaration would have been greeted with cheers of triumph and satisfaction at a job well done, but the reaction of the team was somber and subdued, and Papa knew why. All of them were thinking about the child. Perhaps they would find at least some comfort in never really knowing for a certainty what fate had befallen the child.

He spoke, more to fill the awkward silence, than to see the night's activities concluded. "Well, gentleman, this is where we part company."

"You're not leaving with us?" Driver asked.

Papa shook his head. "I'll make my own way home."

Driver seemed poised to inquire about this, but then he thought better of it. He keyed his mic. "Vincent, Loco, meet us on the beach. We've got a boat to catch."

After the shooters melted into the forest, Papa hiked to a place where he could look down on the beach. He could see the newly reconfigured landscape. A tumble of mud, trees and the broken remains of the old resort, piled up at the base of the cliff, directly below a scallop-shaped divot in the bluff. He stayed there for a long time, until he saw six dark shapes cross the sandy margin and enter the tumultuous surf. Somewhere out in the darkness, an American submarine waited to receive the shooters. Their main objective complete, all that remained was the journey home.

When he could no longer see them at all, Papa turned away. He envied the shooters. Their ordeal was nearly over. His was just beginning.

FIGHT

TWENTY-FOUR

The Everglades, Florida, USA
Sunday, 2:58 a.m.

Jenna stared at the journal, not moving, barely breathing. None of what she had endured—not the explosion, the repeated attempts on her life, the crash or the brutal fight that had ended with her killing a man—had hit her as hard as the revelation contained in Noah's journal.

That baby was me. He took me from the arms of that dead woman.

"I was three months old," she whispered. Yet, even that was something of which she could no longer be certain. Her birthday was just another fiction, invented by the man that had called himself her father.

He killed my parents, abducted me and raised me as his own daughter. It's all a lie.

"Jenna?"

She felt Mercy's hand on her arm, a concerned but tentative touch. Mercy had read every word.

"He's not my father," Jenna whispered, the revelation weakening her knees and pulling tears into her eyes. "He never was." She remained standing only because of Mercy's steadying grip. "Jenna's probably not even my real name..." She looked Mercy in the eyes. "Did you know?"

"No. I had no idea. But, honey..." Mercy faltered. "This doesn't change how he felt about you."

Jenna felt rage building in her chest. "How can you say that? He *kidnapped* me."

"Jenna, you know that's not what happened. He saved your life."

"Saved? He destroyed my life." Yet, even as she said it, part of her knew it wasn't true. Nathan Flood, wasn't Noah's real name any more than 'Papa' had been or Noah was now. Mercy had been right. Noah was some kind of special government operative. Probably CIA. He'd been sent to destroy a secret research base. Had been ordered to kill everyone, not realizing that 'everyone' included an infant girl. Unable, perhaps unwilling, to carry out such a cold-blooded execution, he had instead concocted a way to save the baby's life, spiriting her away from the island, and then dropping out of sight. He had led a fictitious life as a widowed charter-boat skipper raising his daughter all alone.

In her heart, she saw it for what it was: an act of mercy. But an unforgivable act of mercy, if there was such a thing. His sudden attack of conscience hadn't prevented him from murdering everyone else in that compound. The nurse that had been holding her. Her real parents. Had they been sleeping upstairs when Noah had taken their daughter away and hid her in the forest?

She now understood why Noah never permitted her to ask about her mother, why he had actually preferred that she call him Noah instead of Daddy, Father or, God forbid, Papa.

She was so angry that she almost missed the absence of the one thing she had been looking for—an explanation for why someone was trying to kill her.

She wiped a forearm across her eyes and cleared her throat. "We need to talk to this Cort guy."

Mercy nodded slowly.

Jenna looked back at the silo. She could almost feel the residue of Noah's presence there, but now every memory she had of him was different. She banished the thoughts as she had banished her tears. People were probably still trying to kill her, and that was something with which she had to deal. The mystery of her own past would have to take a backseat, though her intuition told her that Bill Cort might know a thing or two about that, as well.

She ventured out onto the metal plates and knelt beside the lifeless sack of meat that had once been Carlos Villegas. She wondered if she should say something—*good riddance* or *enjoy your stay in Hell*—but what was the point? Instead, she contented herself with a single acquisition: his pistol.

It was different than Mercy's gun, the one she had lost in the wreck. It was a semi-automatic, but bigger and noticeably heavier, made completely of metal, and lacking the unusual split-trigger mechanism. As she inspected it, Mercy walked over and put her hands on it without attempting to take it away.

"This is the safety," she said, touching a swivel catch at the back end. She indicated a little red dot. "When you see red, it means it's ready to fire."

Jenna nodded, and then carefully worked the safety until the red dot was covered up. She had a lot more questions but this was neither the time nor the place. She stood and made a silent promise to do some more Internet research at her next opportunity. "Let's get out of here."

Without another look back, they headed for the exit. As they passed the Villegas brothers' car, high beams still blazing, Mercy opened the door and leaned inside. Jenna saw another car parked behind it—Mercy's car. A moment later, the headlights went out and the only remaining source of light was the car's dim overhead dome light. Mercy closed the door and the light faded away, plunging them into darkness.

But not total darkness. Although the sky was overcast, blotting out the stars, a silvery blob marked the location of a waxing gibbous moon. To the northwest, there was a faint yellow glow, like distant city lights.

Jenna's eyebrows came together in a frown. Homestead lay to the northeast, and was surely too far away to appear so bright.

The glow grew brighter. Jenna felt her guts knot with dread. "Mercy. Someone's coming."

TWENTY-FIVE

3:10 a.m.

Mercy peered out across the dark landscape. "Did they—" She jerked her head back toward the building and the Villegas brothers still inside, "—call some friends?"

Jenna shook her head. "I don't think so. Doesn't seem like their style. But it doesn't matter. We can't let anyone find us here."

"There's only the one road leading out."

Jenna focused on the problem. They were in the middle of the Everglades—alligator country—and the paved, dry road was the only safe route to freedom. If even a fraction of the things she'd heard about the vast marsh were true, attempting a cross-country journey, on foot and in the dark, was suicidal. *Okay*, she thought. *What are the other options?*

None. They had to drive out. It was the only way. But to do so, they would have to get past the approaching car without being seen.

"Mercy, start your car but keep the lights off. Pull around behind the shed, where they won't see you, and wait for me there."

"What are you going to do?"

"No time to explain." Jenna wheeled around and ran for the other car.

She opened the door and slid behind the wheel, feeling the press of the journal and Carlos's cell phone in her pocket. She laid the gun on her lap and turned the key. The engine came to life, the dashboard lights dimming as the partially drained battery tried to supply the power needed to turn the motor over, but then it caught and a low murmur filled Jenna's ears. She located the switch for the headlights and turned them on, flipping on the high beams. Light filled the interior of the building once more, revealing the debris-strewn floor and the carcasses of her tormentors. She put her foot on the brake, exactly as she had learned in the Driver's Ed class Noah had made her take, and shifted into 'drive'. She let up on the brake, allowed the car to roll forward through the opening and then stopped.

That was as far as she needed to go. She shifted back into 'park' and got out, leaving the lights on and the door open. As she moved back out of the building, she checked to make sure she still had the journal and the gun, and then she ran through the darkness toward the edge of the building, where Mercy was still moving her car out of sight.

Jenna turned the corner of the building and gestured for Mercy to hurry. The approaching glow was much brighter now. She figured they had only a few seconds left before the unknown visitor rounded the corner for the final approach to the silo building.

"Is this good?" Mercy called.

Jenna nodded. "Keep it running but no lights."

"Aren't you going to get in?"

Jenna knew that was what she should do, but her curiosity about the identity of the visitor overpowered her logic. It might be a late-night thrillseeker or some kids coming out to party at the abandoned rocket facility. It might be a cop, investigating the open gate, perhaps responding to reports of activity on the closed road.

That would be bad, but Jenna's real concern was that it might be something even worse. She remained at the edge of the structure, the gun gripped tightly in her hand, her thumb hovering above the safety catch, and she watched as the headlights appeared.

They came fast. So fast that Jenna felt certain, even without being able to see for herself, that her worst suspicions were about to be confirmed. In a matter of seconds, the car arrived in the parking area and pulled in behind Carlos's rental. She couldn't make out any details about the vehicle itself, but when the doors were thrown open, three men got out. As they ran into the building, she recognized them.

Zack and company. How did they find us here?

The answer came to her almost as quickly as the question. *Not us. They followed Mercy.*

She ran back to the car and opened the door. The dome light came on, but she was pretty sure it wouldn't be visible to the driver in the other car.

As soon as she was in with the door closed, she turned to Mercy. "Do you still have your phone?"

"Sure." Mercy held up the device. "I don't think you'll get a signal out here."

Jenna took it and hurled it out the window.

Mercy let out a gasp. "Hey!"

"They tracked you here." Jenna didn't offer any further explanation, and Mercy didn't argue, but now she wore an apologetic expression. "They're inside. If we're lucky, they won't be able to see us in the dark, and it will be a few minutes before they realize we're not here anymore."

Mercy put the car in gear and let it roll forward. "And if we're not lucky?"

Jenna shrugged. "Drive like hell?"

"That worked so well last time," Mercy grumbled. She steered wide, swinging as far out into the darkness as she dared, careful not to touch the brakes, lest a flare of red light give them away.

Jenna's attention flickered between the nearly impenetrable darkness ahead and the bright square of illumination that was the building's entrance. There was movement within, and Jenna strained her ears, listening for shouts of alarm that might indicate they had been spotted. A moment later they were past the parked cars and headed down the faintly visible stripe of white that was the concrete road. Jenna looked back, watching for some sign of pursuit, but it appeared that their stealthy escape had worked.

"Faster," Jenna urged.

"I'm going faster than I can see already," Mercy retorted through gritted teeth.

Jenna pursed her lips and kept watch through the rear window. Not that there was anything to see. The building had been swallowed up by the night.

Suddenly the world lit up red. Mercy had tapped the brakes, just enough to make the northward turn without losing control. Jenna let it pass without comment, but as the red glow vanished, she saw a warmer yellow light in the distance directly behind them, and her heart sank.

"They're coming."

TWENTY-SIX

3:16 a.m.

Mercy kept the lights off even though it meant sacrificing speed for stealth. Jenna took out Carlos's phone and searched through the history until she found the map she had used earlier to find the Aerojet facility. She had memorized it upon her first inspection, but her attention had been focused on navigating to the silo building.

"There's a side road coming up on the right," she said.

"I won't be able to see it."

Jenna eyed the little dot on the screen that monitored their progress. "Couple more seconds. I'll tell you when."

Mercy let off on the gas and peered into the darkness along the roadside. Jenna saw the faint gap in the foliage. "There. Turn now."

Mercy wheeled the car onto the siding. There was a crunch of snapping twigs as the left front tire rolled through the brush, but Mercy corrected and found the pavement once more. On the display screen, the little dot was centered on the line that marked the road, and in a matter of just a few seconds, they were halfway to the cluster of squares that marked the derelict Aerojet buildings.

"Stop here."

Mercy did, and the brake lights flashed again behind them, but she quickly shifted into 'park' and shut off the car. Jenna leaned her head out the window and found the bright glow that marked the advancing vehicle. It was close enough that she began to wonder if the men in the car might have seen them turn off. She unconsciously squeezed the gun in her hand and held her breath as the light grew closer, closer...

The car passed without slowing.

Jenna let out her breath in a long sigh, but she had to be sure the ruse had worked. She threw open the door and got out, looking over the car's roof until she found the glow again, moving away in a northward direction. While it was impossible to judge their speed, she figured it would take the men about ten minutes to reach the highway, if they drove at a reasonable speed. If they threw caution to the wind, they could probably do it in three.

Something about the receding glow changed. It dimmed for a few seconds, and then returned, brighter than before.

Jenna's breath caught again. They were coming back. She was sure of it. But why? Had one of them seen the car? A lucky guess? She glanced down at the phone, wondering if they were tracking its GPS locator, as they had done with Mercy's. It seemed impossible that they could have identified Carlos so quickly or known that she now had his phone, but if there was even a chance that the phone was leading the killers to them, it would have to go.

She studied the map again, committing every detail to memory. About a mile ahead, the road intersected a canal, but there was an access road that ran alongside the waterway. There would probably be another gate at the end of that road, but it looked like their only option. She cocked her arm, preparing to hurl the phone away, but then stopped.

Over the tick of the rental car's cooling engine and the low cacophony of insect noise, she heard a persistent whirring sound that reminded her of a leaf-blower or a small outboard motor. She tried to isolate the sound, but it did not change when she turned her head. It sounded distant, yet everywhere. She looked up at the night sky, seeing nothing, but detecting the sound's source.

With widening eyes, Jenna realized what the sound was and why the men in the car had turned back. She rejoined Mercy.

"We have to go," she said. "They're tracking us with a drone."

"A drone?" Mercy was incredulous.

"Go!"

Jenna's mind raced. She knew nothing about surveillance drones beyond the fact of their existence. She had seen them in the sky a few times during charter trips. Various government agencies used them to patrol the Gulf, looking for drug smugglers. Noah had pointed them out to her—UAVs, unmanned aerial vehicles, that's the technical name for them—but none of his lessons had included what to do in the event that a drone was stalking her.

There was one obvious detail, though. The people chasing her were pulling out all the stops. She thought again about the FBI agents. Noah had claimed they were bogus, but what if he was wrong? What if the people chasing her, who had killed Noah, really were government operatives? It made a sick kind of sense. Noah had disobeyed orders by saving her life. He had gone rogue. That was the expression they used in those movies. Off the reservation. Under the radar.

All of the above?

Somehow, he had ended up back on the radar, and so had she.

How can I hide from the government?

Mercy had started the car, but they weren't moving. "Which way?"

"Straight," Jenna replied, but it sounded like a question in her ears. "Go straight," she repeated, trying to think about the next move. "Might as well use the lights. They can see us anyway."

They can see us.

The drone probably had night-vision capabilities. Was it armed? Was it locking on to them with one of those missiles that sounded like the name of heavy metal band...Stinger or Hellfire...something like that?

She shook her head. If that was an option for them, they would have already used it. No, the UAV was just an eye in the sky. The real danger was from Zack and his team. They had to get someplace where the killers couldn't reach them.

She looked at the map again, not searching for a specific route this time, but trying to download every detail into her brain. The satellite image showed an astonishing degree of detail, but the image wasn't a perfect reference. For one thing, the data was a couple of years old. The cars that were visible, parked on driveways, or captured while moving down the remote roads, were long gone now. Other details might have changed as well. The entire area had been transformed by the opening of a canal designed to restore the freshwater balance of the Everglades.

"Dead end," Mercy said.

Jenna looked up. There was a low earthen bank ahead. It was a dike to hold back the canal during the rainy season. If the map was accurate, the access road ran along the top of the earthworks. "Drive onto the dike," she said, trying to inject a tone of certainty into her voice. "Then turn left."

They slowed, but in the headlight beams, Jenna saw the ruts of old tire tracks leading up onto the dike. She had made the right call. Mercy eased the car up the bank, and for a few seconds, the headlights shone into the sky like a searchlight. They leveled out and Jenna could see the black ribbon of the canal passing in front of them. Mercy steered left as instructed, and found the road Jenna had promised.

The canal hooked to the northwest a few hundred yards later. Jenna saw on the map that it would bring them back to the highway, just a little way from the gated road leading into the abandoned complex. The men hunting them would know this, too. It would be the perfect place to set a trap.

She searched the map for some alternative route, something to confound the expectations of the hunters and fool the watchful eye of the drone. She settled on a swatch of green with a road that ended in a bulb-shaped parking area. A little blue dot indicated that there were photos and more information associated with the spot, so she tapped on it. "That might work."

She zoomed out and mentally plotted the route they would have to take. It was only a couple of miles away, but it lay on the other side of the canal.

"Do you trust me?"

Mercy glanced over at her. "Of course I..." The automatic response faltered, replaced by suspicion and dread. "Why?"

In a perfectly calm voice, Jenna told her. "I want you to drive into the canal."

TWENTY-SEVEN

3:26 a.m.

There really wasn't time to explain, but Jenna knew she had to give Mercy something to support her leap of faith.

"We have to get to the other side of the canal," Jenna said. "Best way to do that is to drive into it, and swim for it."

"*Best* way?" Mercy countered. "I can think of a lot of better—"

"Mercy, we have to do this. *Now*."

To her credit, Mercy didn't balk. She cranked the wheel to the right and punched the gas pedal. The engine revved, and the front end of the car dropped with a violent crunch. The surge carried the vehicle forward, scraping across the edge of the bank until gravity took over. The car tilted down and plunged into the water below.

On any other day, Jenna might have been disoriented by the chaotic upheaval, but after everything she had gone through, the splashdown was about as exciting as a cheap, carnival kiddie ride. Her only reaction to the tepid water rushing in through the open window was to hold the phone above her head to keep it dry. Noah's journal was going to get soaked. She had mixed feelings about that. There might still be a few more answers within its pages, but she wasn't sure she could handle any more revelations about her past. And Noah's answers seemed to lead only to more questions.

With the water level rising up around her, she stuck her head and upper body out the window and pushed off, swimming free as the car settled further down the sloping bank.

"Jenna?"

"I'm here," she called, and she swam toward the sound of Mercy's voice. The only light was a murky glow rising from the bottom of the canal: the car's headlights shining into the muddy water. "Swim for the other side."

She tried not to think about what else might be in the water. There were a lot of things in the 'Glades that could kill a person, ranging from alligators and snakes to microscopic bacteria and viruses carried by mosquitoes. The canal was only about as wide as a two lane road and took all of ten seconds to cross, but getting out was a little trickier. The earthen bank slipped out from under her, dropping her back into the water. On her third attempt, her fingers wrapped around a tuft of Sawgrass. She used it to haul herself onto dry land, ignoring the dull pain caused by the plant's serrated leaves, which tore into her skin. As soon as she reached the top of the bank, she located Mercy and helped her climb over the slick bank.

"Come on," she urged, eyeing the rising light across the canal. Their pursuers were closing in. She didn't think they would attempt to follow. With the drone keeping watch, they could afford the long detour required to reach the other side of the canal. Still, she wasn't going to underestimate them.

Jenna had chosen this spot for the crossing for a very specific reason—a road intersected the canal here. Even without a car, a road was critical to her plan. She searched the darkness until she found the turn off, and then beckoned Mercy to follow.

Her goal lay a mile away, a fifteen minute walk at a brisk pace, but Jenna wasn't sure they had fifteen minutes. So she ran. At first, the pain of her many superficial injuries, compounded by the gnawing emptiness in her gut and the throbbing pain of a persistent headache, made the run feel like an exercise in self-torture. But the situation's urgency got her through the first few steps, and after that, she settled into an almost mindless rhythm, dissociated from the pain. Mercy kept up, and after a few minutes, Jenna stopped looking back.

The road led through a wooded area, deepening the darkness, but also providing some concealment from the drone still buzzing above. Not that they needed to hide. Jenna's plan relied more on what they would do once they reached their destination and less on concealment.

She slowed to a trot and checked their progress with the GPS dot on the map. Her eyes had adjusted to the darkness, and the phone display was painfully bright. She cupped a hand over it to shield the light, both from her own eyes and from the drone, and she squinted at the map.

"We're almost there," she announced. "There's a turn-off just ahead."

"A turn-off to what?" Mercy asked. There was a hint of irritation in her voice. She had followed Jenna this far without question or complaint, but seemed to be reaching her limit for acts of blind faith.

Jenna stalled a few moments longer until the promised turn-off appeared. There was a gate across the drive, a metal beam designed to block vehicle access. No one in their right mind would be traipsing around out here on foot after business hours. As if to emphasize this fact, a low throaty roar—like the sound of someone trying to start a chainsaw—issued from the darkness. Jenna could make out the silhouette of a large sign, just off to the side of the road, and although she couldn't make out the words or pictures painted on it, she knew that it held the answer to Mercy's question.

"Gator Station," she said, clambering over the gate.

"As in 'alligator?'" Mercy had heard the unseen creature's bellow and her annoyance deepened.

"It's one of those tourist places," Jenna said. "Don't worry. Gators are usually timid. They'll run away from us."

"So now you're an expert on alligators?" Mercy stood, unmoving, on the other side of the gate.

Jenna did not consider herself an expert, but you couldn't get through the Florida public school system without doing at least one or two reports on the apex reptilian predator. "They'll leave us alone if we stay on the road."

She hoped that was true. The place was a tourist park after all, and while that didn't necessarily mean that the creatures were domesticated, she was pretty sure that there would be safety measures in place to prevent the animals from having free run of the park.

Mercy gave a sigh and was just starting to climb over the gate when a different noise disrupted the quiet. The sharp zipping sound came from behind Mercy and passed by Jenna's head, making her flinch. It was followed by a soft, muffled cough.

She spun away from the gate. There was not a doubt in her mind that someone had just shot at them, someone close by, using a suppressed weapon. The noise repeated as Mercy dropped down next to her. The round pinged off the gate.

"Run!"

Mercy needed no further urging. They both sprinted into the alligator park. Over the sound of their footsteps, it was impossible to tell whether more shots followed.

As she ran, Noah's old advice replayed in Jenna's head—*run toward a gun*—and she felt anger supersede her impulse for self-preservation. Part of it was the memory of the man that she now knew was not her father, not in the sense that mattered. But mostly it was anger at having to flee. Again. She was tired of running. She wanted to turn and fight.

To do so would be suicidal, she knew. One or more of the men hunting her had followed on foot.

They probably have night vision goggles, Jenna thought, *just like Noah and his team had used.*

Don't think about that, she told herself. *Focus on surviving. You can't fight if you're dead.*

Her hand found the pistol still tucked in her waistband. It had been immersed during the swim in the canal and she wondered if it would still fire. Probably, but until she could see a target, there was no point in wasting bullets.

A square silhouette rose up out of the darkness and then another. She had seen the buildings on the map. Gator Station. Trying to reconcile what she was seeing—what she could barely see—with her mental map, while running from a gunman, was a lot more difficult than she had anticipated. She recalled that there was a path around the buildings toward an enormous pond, which the satellite photograph revealed was brimming with alligators.

She veered in that direction, barely able to make out the path until she was right on top of it. The phone had a built in light that could be used as a camera flash or a flashlight, but using it would be a dead giveaway—literally—even if the men hunting her didn't have night vision. And if they did...

If they did, then maybe there was a way to level the playing field. Without slowing, she took out the phone and turned it on. The screen display flared brightly, but she held it close to her body, hiding its illumination until she could activate the camera.

She stopped, turned and with the phone held high in her left hand, she thumbed the camera button.

Even though she wasn't looking directly at it, the flash seemed to light up the world. The path and the trees appeared before her, and right in the center of the scene was a tall figure, caught in mid-stride, a pistol in one hand and a futuristic looking goggle covering one of his eyes. The image vanished as quickly as it had appeared, and when the darkness returned, it seemed even blacker than before.

There was an odd scuffling sound behind her and a snarled curse. Amplified by the night vision device, the flash must have seemed as bright as an atomic bomb blast. Blinding the man, however, was only the first part of Jenna's plan. She aimed the pistol at the spot where the man had been, thumbed off the safety, and pulled the trigger.

TWENTY-EIGHT

3:41 a.m.

The report was deafening. The pistol bucked wildly in her hand, and she almost dropped it. In her haste, she had forgotten about bracing against the recoil. It seemed unlikely that the shot had found its mark, but the show of resistance might give the killer a moment's pause.

"A little warning next time," Mercy said.

"Sorry." Jenna could barely hear Mercy over the ringing in her ears, and she didn't know if her muttered apology was audible. Yet, she also knew that if another opportunity presented itself, she wouldn't waste time keeping Mercy in the loop.

She turned back, using the phone's screen to briefly illuminate the way ahead. The path continued alongside a building and split, with one branch leading to a small wooden grandstand and the other turning onto a long wooden platform that extended out over the alligator pond. Jenna found Mercy's arm and pointed her toward the latter. As Mercy charged out onto the platform, Jenna ducked into the seating area and faced the path again.

She stood in a textbook Weaver's stance, the pistol gripped firmly in her right hand and braced with her left. She waited for the man to make his approach. The lingering effects of the loud report faded with each passing second. When she held her breath, she could make out the sound of Mercy's footsteps on the platform and the more guttural noise of alligators bellowing in the pond.

She let out her breath slowly, quietly, and drew in another.

There was soft squishing sound, the noise of wet shoes on the path. The sound repeated, louder and closer. She homed in on the noise like a bat using sonar to pinpoint a mosquito.

"Jenna?"

Jenna gasped at the sound of Mercy's voice, a low hiss from the darkness, and pointed the gun away. She had almost pulled the trigger, almost shot her friend.

Even as the horrifying image of Mercy, dead at her own hands, flashed through her mind, Jenna heard the squishing sound again, closer still, much closer than Mercy's voice had been. The man was there, right in front of her.

She brought the pistol up again and fired. This time, the gun barely moved. The bright muzzle flash illuminated the man for just an instant, and Jenna saw the surprise on his face as he jerked back, surrounded by red mist. She fired again and saw him go down.

In the stillness that followed, she felt the same rush she had experienced after her battle with Raul, a sense of power and victory. She had fought back. She had killed. And now she knew that she could do it again.

She kept the gun at the ready, but risked dropping her left hand to the pocket where she had stashed the phone. In the screen's glow, she could see the unmoving form. He lay on his back beside the wooden railing where the paths diverged. A ragged wound on the man's left cheek dribbled blood. The rest of his face was obscured by something that looked like a small camcorder. The lens end extended out from his right eye. The apparatus, which she assumed was his night vision device, was held in place by a web of straps that encircled his head.

She approached tentatively and knelt beside him. She laid the gun on the ground, freeing her hand, and then grasped the monocular. The straps were tight, and her first attempt to pull it loose caused the man's head to tilt back and forth, a grim reminder that she was looting a corpse, but it also revealed a chin strap, secured with a plastic buckle. The strap was damp with warm blood. She fought back her revulsion and squeezed the clasp until it popped free. The head harness came away, and the monocular fell to the ground with a muted thump.

As she reached for it, a hand shot up and grasped her shirt front. The attack was so unexpected that the man—not quite so dead as he appeared—got his other hand up before she could move. In an instant, both his hands were around her throat.

She clutched at the gripping hands, trying to break the chokehold, even as she threw herself back. Both actions, fueled by a cold spike of adrenaline that raced through her nervous system, were in vain. The man's grip was like iron, his body an anchor that held her fast. The momentary failure snapped her out of panic mode. She had the skills to escape, but they were useless if she let the primitive part of her brain take over.

She willed herself to stop fighting the choking hands. To let go. Hands free, she clapped her cupped palms against either side of the man's head. The action elicited a howl of rage, but the man's grip tightened. Jenna felt her thoughts go fuzzy. She struck him again, feeling the solid contact of her punches against the man's face, the hard unyielding skull just below the surface.

This isn't working, she thought, almost frantic, and she knew why. The animal brain was still telling her to oppose strength with strength, but that was a battle she could not win. This man, injured though he was, was stronger, heavier and unlike Raul, he had almost certainly received formal combat training. *You know how to get out of this.*

She did. She threw her right arm up, and felt the immediate pressure as her collar bone squeezed the grasping hand even tighter. Then, she rolled to the right. The man's hand, pinched tight by her upraised arm, was forced to bend at the wrist and his grip faltered. She was free.

Almost free.

As she gasped for breath, it occurred to Jenna a moment too late that she ought to follow up with a counter-attack. She drove out with her elbow, but the man twisted away. She landed only a glancing blow that deflected off his rib cage. Then her elbow struck the ground. The impact sent an electric jolt through her arm from shoulder to fingertips.

Then he was on her, driving his full weight into her like a football lineman charging into the scrimmage. She tried to twist away, but she was too slow by a heartbeat. He slammed into her, driving her back into the wooden rail with such force that Jenna heard something snap. The breath was driven from her lungs, and an almost paralyzing pain radiated from the point of impact. But the noise had not been the sound of her bones breaking. It was the rail.

The crack of splintering wood, the shriek of nails being torn out of two-by-fours and an underlying chorus of bestial hisses from just a few feet below, merged to form a discordant symphony. Restless alligators thrashed through the water before her, crowding together in anticipation of a meal. Then, with a stomach churning lurch, the rail gave way and she fell.

TWENTY-NINE

3:55 a.m.

Jenna flailed for something to stop her fall, but the only thing within reach was the body of her assailant, and he, too, was falling. Then, as abruptly as it had begun, the fall stopped. The damaged rail had given beneath their combined weight, but had not collapsed entirely. It sagged over the alligator pond, groaning as the nails slowly lost the battle to hold the structure together.

The jolt of the sudden stop sent another lance of pain through Jenna's body, but the hissing and snapping of reptilian jaws scant inches below her was a wonderful anesthetic. Her attacker pushed hard against her. She couldn't tell if he was attempting to shove her the rest of the way over or simply trying to recover himself. Ultimately, the result was the same. The rail lurched and dropped another foot.

Jenna clutched at her assailant. If she was going in, he was, too. Her body was slanted down, as if she was hanging by her knees from the monkey bars on a playground. She could feel solid ground pressing into the back of her thighs. Too much of her weight was already hanging out over the edge. When the rail gave way, there would be nothing to hold her back.

Something struck the rail beside her head, sending a tremor through the wood. She heard another hiss and splash. One of the gators had made a grab for her, missing by inches. The impact was the last straw for the railing. With one last tortured squeal, the nails pulled free, and the barrier dropped, along with the two bodies sprawled atop it.

Jenna's attacker scrabbled in vain for a handhold. She felt him scrape past her and then heard a splash and a howl of denial that was abruptly silenced amid a tumult of growls, snapping jaws and the distinctive sound of bones cracking.

Jenna however, didn't fall. She could still feel the ground beneath her legs, but there was something else there, too. A weight was pressing down on her feet, holding her in place. Then she was pulled, dragged back up onto terra firma.

"Mercy?" she croaked, her throat still on fire from her assailant's chokehold.

"I've got you," came the reply. Mercy's voice was taut with effort, but to Jenna it was the most beautiful sound in the world. She reached out and felt a hand close over her own, hauling her away from the precipice.

Jenna savored the feel of solid ground beneath her body, and she even welcomed the throb of pain from injuries old and new. Hurt was a lot better than dead. For a few seconds, they both just lay there, panting from the exertion.

Finally, Mercy spoke again. "So, was that what you had in mind?"

Jenna almost laughed, but the quip reminded her that this minor victory would count for nothing if they didn't keep moving. "Not quite," she replied, rolling over and rising to her hands and knees. She had lost both the gun and the phone in the struggle, but her groping hands found the former and something else as well: the man's night vision device.

She turned it over in her hands, feeling the hard lens at one end and the soft rubber eye cup at the other, and held it up to her eye. Nothing. She continued exploring its exterior until she found a small knob. She twisted it, felt it turn and click, and then there was a flash of green as the device turned on, and the world lit up like the dawn.

That's more like it, she thought, as she settled the straps over her head and locked the monocular into place. It was heavier than she expected, but the discomfort was a small price to pay for the ability to see in the darkness. Jenna got to her feet. Her first few steps were halting. The green display played havoc with her depth perception, but she found that her unaided eye, even though virtually night blind, still helped her see the world in three dimensions.

She turned back to Mercy who was gazing up at her, pupils fully dilated and shining like little white buttons. "We can't stay here."

As if to underscore the statement, the display grew almost painfully bright as an artificial light source appeared from somewhere down the path that had brought them here.

"Damn it." She hauled Mercy to her feet. "I thought we'd have more time. Come on."

"Where...?" Mercy didn't seem to know how to finish the question.

Jenna steered her back onto the wooden platform that crossed the alligator pond. With the night vision device, she could see everything in stark detail. A writhing mass of alligators was entangled with the collapsed rail section, biting and snapping at each other as they fought over what remained of the man she had shot.

She looked away and focused on what lay at the far end of the platform. Beyond the alligator pool, the platform descended to a wooden dock that ran the length of a narrow canal. A flat bottomed metal boat with something that looked like an enormous fan mounted at its aft end was moored to the dock.

"That," Jenna said, pointing to the airboat, "is what I had in mind."

THIRTY

4:06 a.m.

Mercy squinted at the airboat. "Do you know how to drive one of these?"

It was the first time Jenna had ever laid eyes on one of the Everglades' famous flat-bottomed watercraft, but she had grown up on a boat, and she was confident that she could figure it out. She quickly identified the steering lever, a mechanical arm that controlled a set of louvered vanes behind the fan—push the lever and vanes would direct the flow of air one way, pull and they'd go the other. The engine that turned the huge fan was no more complicated than an outboard motor, and it took just a few seconds for her to prime the fuel line and start it up.

She had known about the boat because she had seen it on the satellite map. She had also seen the network of deep canals that marked the designated routes of the rides. The picture was a couple of years old, but she was sure the boat would be there. Airboat rides through wild gator country were all part of the day's fun at Gator Station.

"Cast off," Jenna called out, settling into the pilot's chair on an upraised platform in front of the idling engine. The seat was equipped with a safety belt. Given her inexperience, it seemed prudent to use it. "Then sit down and hang on!"

Mercy unwound the rope that held the boat in place, and stepped aboard, shoving off with one foot. As soon as she was seated, Jenna engaged the fan. The engine itself wasn't much louder than a car's motor, but the rush of air being pulled through the spinning blades sounded like a Category Four hurricane. As the craft began to pick up speed, it felt like one, too.

Jenna quickly got the hang of using the rudder lever to change course, and in moments they had left the Gator Station complex behind and were racing through the marsh. The boat drew only a few inches of water, and skimmed over the surface, almost hydroplaning, effortlessly floating over patches of grass and reeds. She resisted the urge to go full throttle—any faster and the slightest bump might launch the boat into the air.

Her memory of the satellite map was of little use here, where the landscape changed almost as quickly as the weather. But her newly acquired night vision monocular allowed her to navigate around sunken tree boughs and other obstacles that might have stopped the nimble airboat.

After a few minutes, the initial thrill and novelty of the experience wore off, and Jenna remembered the reason she had chosen this form of travel. She glanced over one shoulder, peering through the blurry disc of the spinning fan blades, looking for any sign of pursuit. What she saw made her let off the throttle. The boat coasted forward a few yards until it scraped to a halt atop a patch of reeds.

"What's wrong?" Mercy asked, evidently sensing Jenna's sudden anxiety.

Jenna unbuckled her belt and stood up. She turned a slow circle, scanning the horizon. In every direction as far as she could see, the landscape was a flat, featureless tableau, randomly dotted with clumps of vegetation and a few trees. "It all looks the same."

Mercy tried to peer into the darkness, but without light, she had even less with which to judge their position than Jenna did. "Can't you use the GPS on your phone?"

"I lost it." She hadn't been able to find the phone again after the narrow escape from the alligator pond. It had probably fallen in.

"Well...if we keep going in a straight line, we're bound to come across something familiar, right?"

"If we *can* go in a straight line."

Maintaining a linear course would be almost impossible in the airboat. They would have to steer around large obstacles, and without anything to use as a handrail, there would be no way to make sure that they got back on the same azimuth. The wind and irregularities in the surface might also alter their course without her even realizing it. Minor changes could add up, causing them to meander in circles until their fuel ran out.

Jenna turned her eyes skyward, searching for some celestial clue. The overcast sky hid the stars, and the sun would not appear in the east for a few more hours. The moon, though mostly hidden behind the clouds, gave enough light that she could fix its location, but the moon was not as reliable a navigation aid, especially not when moving at high speed.

There was also the unanswered question of where exactly she wanted to go next. The boat could take them almost anywhere—to the outskirts of Homestead, or even to the coast. If she kept the moon at her back, that would take her in a generally eastward direction. That would put her closer to Miami, and closer to Bill Cort, the man who might be able to tell her the truth about her parents and explain why people were trying to kill her.

East it is.

She sat down, strapped in and pulled the lever back. The boat swung around in what she hoped was the right direction. As it did, she spied movement off to her left. It was just a spot, probably a mile away, but because it was taller than anything else in the landscape, it was readily visible and readily identifiable.

Another airboat.

While there was no way to make out its occupants, the fact that it was running without lights was proof enough that the hunters had not given up.

Jenna pressed the throttle pedal and held the rudder stick on course. She was going as fast as she dared, and for the men in the other boat to have even a chance of catching her, they would have to run at a dangerously high speed. Unfortunately, the men hunting them didn't need to catch them on the water. All they had to do was follow and stay close. When Jenna and Mercy made landfall, the men would be only a couple of minutes behind.

Not much time to escape, but maybe enough to set an ambush.

Movement, straight ahead and just above the horizon, caught her attention. Not another boat, but something moving above the marsh, flying. There was no mistaking the profile—a solid body in the middle, thinner wings stretching out to either side. It was an aircraft, but much smaller than the Villegas brothers' plane.

The drone, she thought. But why was it flying so low? The whole point of the UAV was discreet surveillance. It almost seemed like the remote operator didn't care if she spotted it. As it got closer, cruising just a few feet above the surface, right in the boat's path, she realized the action was intentional. She was *meant* to see it.

With each passing second, it became more and more evident that the UAV was not going to veer off or ascend. It was on a collision course.

It's a bluff, she thought. *They wouldn't destroy a million dollar drone just to kill me, would they?*

Because she wasn't sure, Jenna let off the throttle and steered right. The boat's forward momentum kept it moving forward. Instead of carving a precise turn, the boat slid forward and started to spin. Jenna momentarily forgot about the game of chicken with the drone. She eased off the rudder and nudged the accelerator, regaining control. At that instant, the unmanned aircraft shot past, its wing tip clearing the airboat's fan by mere inches. There was a strident whine as the drone's propeller noise reached a climax and then was drowned out by the boat's engine.

"What was that?" Mercy shouted.

"The drone just buzzed us." Jenna saw that the aircraft was climbing back into the sky and circling around for another run. She knew why, too. Dodging the drone had cost her several seconds, and the pursuing airboat was now much closer.

She wondered how many men were aboard. Three men had gotten out back at the rocket facility and a fourth had stayed in the car. Subtract the one she had fought with at the alligator pond...three, then? Three trained killers against Mercy and herself. "Do you still have that gun?"

Mercy's expression knotted with sudden anxiety, but she held up the pistol. "Why?"

Two guns. Not nearly enough to tip the balance in their favor. Besides, as she had learned from the encounter at the alligator pond, sometimes it took a lot more than a single bullet to kill a man. Still, if she did not do something, and soon, the situation would be the same, only their enemies would dictate the terms.

"Get down," Jenna said, bringing the boat around until the bow pointed toward the approaching watercraft. "Find something to hide behind if you can."

"What?" Anxiety transformed into panic.

"We have to take the fight to them," Jenna explained, with more patience than she felt. "Go on the offensive. Otherwise, they'll just run us down."

"And just how are we supposed—" Mercy stopped herself in mid-sentence and then continued in a more subdued voice. "I hope you have some kind of plan."

Jenna did not have a plan, and did not think she could come up with much of one in the thirty seconds it would take for them to close the gap with the other boat. Her only solace was that the killers didn't know that she didn't have a plan.

Run toward a gun. That wisdom had served her well thus far, but always in a literal sense. Now she was going to test it at something a bit faster than running speed.

The distance shrank faster than expected. The boats moved at least as fast as cars on a highway. She could make out the dark outlines of the other boat's occupants, one man in the pilot's chair—she thought it might be Zack—the other two hanging onto the passenger seats. All three wore monocular night-vision devices like her own. All three watched her approach with rapt anticipation.

When she was close enough that she could see the look of alarm on the pilot's face—definitely Zack—Jenna steered to the right, as if to avoid the imminent collision. One of the passengers raised his pistol and started tracking her with the muzzle, anticipating the moment when the two boats would pass.

With just fifty feet separating them, Jenna abruptly steered back to the left, once more on a collision course. Zack reacted just as she hoped he would: instinctively.

Jenna was no expert with the airboat, but her uncanny ability to learn any new skill—physical or mental—had given her a sense of familiarity with how the craft would respond to even the slightest variations of speed and direction. She was still learning, but she was learning a lot faster than the men in the other boat. When she changed course, steering right toward them, Zack jerked his steering lever.

The other boat slewed sideways, out of control, and one of the gunmen was catapulted from his seat like a guided missile. Jenna ducked as the hurtling body sailed through the air toward her. There was a resonant gong as his body hit the fan's protective wire covering, following by a strident rapid-fire chattering as the bent metal screen struck the whirling blades. The entire boat shook with the impact. A second impact rattled beneath Jenna as the two boats scraped past each other. Amid the chaos, Jenna heard several reports, and she caught a glimpse of Mercy hunched down behind one of the seats, firing into the other boat at almost point blank range.

Then, just as quickly as it had arrived, the collision was behind her, and the two boats moved apart. Her boat hadn't sustained any structural damage, though something was rattling against the fan blades like a playing card in the spokes of a bicycle. The noise was an assault on the senses but there was nothing she could do about it. She ground her teeth and steered into a broad turn. Mercy remained crouched down behind a seat back, unhurt.

There was no sign of the man that had been ejected from the boat. He'd been stunned or perhaps even killed by the impact.

Either way, the marsh had already claimed him. Zack was just beginning a sluggish turn, and Jenna wondered if one or more of Mercy's shots had found its mark.

But the battle was not over. She had scored a small victory but if she didn't press her advantage, she would lose it. She lined up the bow of the little airboat, and opened the throttle once more. The clamor of the fan blades beating against the bent piece of the wire screen reached a fever pitch, climaxing with an eruption of noise and another vibration that shook the entire boat, and then the noise vanished. Jenna glanced back and saw that a portion of the wire screen had broken free, exposing the whirring propeller blades just a couple of feet behind her head.

She felt the boat starting to drift left, and realized that one of the steering louvers behind the fan had been damaged. She tried to correct by turning against the drift, but no matter which way she turned it, the bent vane pushed the boat in the opposite direction. But she did not ease off the throttle. She knew from experience that speed had a way of smoothing out rough seas. She worked the rudder back and forth, keeping the boat on a more or less straight course, and charged the other boat once more.

She couldn't tell if either man was wounded, but both were preparing for another open water joust. The passenger was concealed behind a seat. Zack did his best to hunker down in place, presenting as small a target as possible. Jenna doubted the men would fall for the same trick, but her experience with sparring had taught her the importance of the feint. She would make them *think* they knew what she was going to do. Then she would do something else. What exactly, she was still trying to work out. Part of her wanted to just ram the other boat, driving over the top of the two killers. While that would be very satisfying, it would also destroy both boats and leave them stranded in the middle of the swamp.

Zack seemed to divine her intent, and as she closed with him, he accelerated, pushing the boat so hard that Jenna thought she could actually see it starting to float above the water's surface. The move caught her by surprise, and she barely had time to steer away. Mercy attempted to shoot them, but a fusillade of return fire forced her down. Jenna ducked as bullets smacked into hard surfaces all around her.

That none of the rounds hit her was not quite the miracle it seemed. The shots were not well-aimed and seemed to serve no other purpose than to keep Mercy from returning accurate fire. The boat drew near before Jenna could take any other action, and then, just as it was about to pass, almost close enough to touch, a large moving shape filled the display of her night vision device.

In the instant it took for her brain to process what she was seeing, the man had made the leap to her boat and was on her, driving the naked blade of a knife at her throat.

THIRTY-ONE

4:26 a.m.

Jenna's body reacted faster than her brain. She threw her hands up to block the knife attack, catching the man's forearm, and thrust both feet out for leverage. Her right foot was still on the throttle, and she unthinkingly jammed it down, sending a surge of power to the fan. The sudden acceleration did more to save her from the slash than her flagging strength. The man fell forward against her, his arm folding at the elbow, the blade's lethal trajectory interrupted.

The man pushed away from her but kept one hand planted against her shoulder, pinning her in place as he wrenched free of her grip and drew back for another thrust.

Run away from a knife. Yeah, right.

It wasn't very big—just a folding pocket knife, the blade not even three inches long—but as it flashed toward her, it looked like a sword from *The Lord of the Rings* movies. Jenna knew, with a sick certainty, that even if she survived this, she was going to get cut.

She got her hands up and caught the man's arm once more. His superior strength began to overwhelm her defense. Her efforts barely slowed his thrust, but she managed to twist to the side as the blade rammed forward.

Something tugged at her left arm, preventing her from moving any further, and her entire arm, from shoulder to fingertips, swelled with what felt like an injection of liquid fire. A cry slipped past her lips, but with the pain came a strange clarity, as if time had slowed to a crawl. She saw the look of consternation on her assailant's face. He wasn't looking at her. His attention was on the knife buried to the hilt in Jenna's left biceps—almost exactly the same spot where she had earlier caught a grazing bullet. The blade pierced her arm and pinned her to the seat back. She could see the rise and fall of his chest and feel his breath on her face. His eyes broadcast his intentions as he grasped the knife hilt, gathering his strength to pull it free like Excalibur from the stone.

No you don't, Jenna thought, as she brought her knees up into man's chest.

The blow, coupled with the sudden deceleration as Jenna's foot came off the pedal, staggered him back. He recovered quickly and launched himself at her again.

Jenna jammed her foot down on the pedal and the engine revved again. As the boat lurched forward, she tried to pull back on the steering lever, but nothing happened. Her arm, still nailed in place by the blade, refused to grip the control handle. The man rocked with the sudden acceleration, but he kept his balance and took a menacing step toward her.

Something about his stance triggered a memory—or rather a muscle memory—and Jenna reacted exactly as she had learned in the *dojo*. She got her free hand up and grabbed a handful of the man's shirt. She pulled him forward, adding her energy to his own, and brought her knee up hard.

Although he probably outweighed her by a hundred pounds, his momentum made him seem fifty pounds lighter. He flew past her, arms flailing. An unseen force seized hold of him, tearing him out of her grasp.

Even though she could not see what was happening behind her, Jenna knew with sickening certainty that the man had been pulled into the exposed propeller. There was a wet grinding noise as the fan blades pureed flesh and bones. The engine whined in protest for a moment, struggling against the sudden workload, and then idled down to an almost peaceful rumble.

Jenna forced the vision of the man's grisly demise from her thoughts. She felt weak, stretched to her limits, almost numb with pain, but the battle was not over. Zack was out there, and the fight would not end until one of them was dead.

She saw Mercy, rising cautiously from her place of concealment, straining to find Jenna in the darkness. "Jenna? Are you okay?"

Jenna refused to admit the truth aloud but she didn't have the strength to lie. With her free hand, she found the hilt of the knife that held her fixed in place like a bug on a pin. The blade had pierced the meaty part of her arm but had missed the bone. Blood oozed from the wound. She knew that removing a penetrating object from a puncture wound could cause a fatal hemorrhage, but under the circumstances, it was a risk she felt she had to take. She gripped the hilt and pulled, triggering a throb of agony, but the knife refused to budge. After a few seconds of struggling, she gave up and turned her attention back to the more immediate threat.

Reaching across her body, she worked the steering lever with her right hand, and brought the boat around until she found Zack's boat. She was surprised to see that he wasn't coming around to face her but was motoring away, as if fleeing a battlefield. For a fleeting moment, Jenna wondered if the demise of his comrades had broken his will to fight. Then she spied movement above him, and grasped the reason for his retreat.

The drone dropped out of the sky, swooping toward them like a hunting raptor. Jenna stared at it, almost hypnotized by its graceful motion.

Mercy made her way back to the pilot's chair. "You're hurt."

Jenna barely heard. Her mind wrestled with this new tactic. When the UAV had buzzed them before, she had assumed it was to block their escape and give Zack and the others a chance to catch up. *So why...?*

The answer came in a premonition. Even though her first impulse was to reject it as unbelievable, there could be no other explanation. In some distant control room, a decision had been made: destroy Jenna Flood, no matter the cost.

"They're going to kamikaze the drone."

Mercy stared back as if she'd spoken in a foreign language. Jenna tore her gaze from the approaching aircraft and looked into Mercy's eyes. "You have to jump."

"Jump?"

There was no time to explain, and if there had been, Mercy probably would have refused. So Jenna did the only thing she could think of to end the discussion: she gave Mercy a shove that sent the woman pitching backward into the marsh. When Mercy hit the water, Jenna opened the throttle wide and the boat shot forward.

She had to fight to maintain a straight line at first, and as the airboat picked up speed, she wondered what sort of thoughts were going through the drone operator's head, watching her struggle to stay on a collision course. Kamikazes both.

She wanted to believe there was a method to her madness. That by accelerating toward the drone, doing something so totally insane and unpredictable, she might...

She shook her head. Maybe there was no rationale. No motivation but her soul-deep weariness. Or perhaps the simple desire to see the relentless pursuit ended on her own terms.

As the drone descended and the boat raced across the water's surface to meet it, she felt as if she was watching a video played frame-by-frame, complete with range distances and graphs of trajectories. She saw exactly where the collision would occur, where the drone's nose would strike the boat. If she slowed down and cut power at the last second, would the UAV fall short and crash into the marsh? No, it was leveling out. If the operator was as skilled as she thought he must be, he would stay about three feet above the water—the level of her knees. She had no doubt that the crash, when it came, would kill her. Slowing down would only delay that outcome by a millisecond.

There might be time to steer away. As she considered the possibility, she realized that she didn't want to die after all, but evasive maneuvers wouldn't solve anything. She couldn't keep dodging the drone forever.

There was only one course of action that had any hope of survival.

Fight.

She stabbed the throttle pedal down. The boat rocketed forward so fast that the wind buffeted her face, forcing her to squeeze her unaided eye shut. The effect on her depth perception was immediate, but she had already worked out the distances and the angles. All she needed to do now was stay the course.

Without Mercy's additional weight, the boat seemed to float above the water, and then, it began to do so quite literally. The shape of the flat hull, turned up at the bow so that it could roll over the tall grass unimpeded, was not all that different from an airplane wing. As air piled up beneath its curvature, the boat did what airfoils do at high speed—it started to fly.

THIRTY-TWO

4:37 a.m.

The boat lifted free of the water, and Jenna dared to believe it might simply float up into the sky like Santa's sleigh or ET on Elliot's bicycle.

The illusion was short-lived.

In the instant that the front end started to rise, the tremendous weight of the engine pulled the rear of the airboat down. The craft flipped up, like a hat blown off in a windstorm. Jenna's stomach lurched, and a throb of pain radiated through her arm as her body tried to fold itself over. The boat went almost vertical, the bow pointing at the sky. The fan chopped at the water but was unable to overcome the force of gravity. The boat rolled backward, caught in the struggle between the forces of inertia and aerodynamics. It might have continued flipping end-over-end, pinwheeling across the Everglades, but before that could happen, the drone arrived.

There were too many variables to predict an outcome with any degree of certainty, but a lot of what happened was as she had hoped. She had thought the boat might lift off, if she pushed it hard enough. She had believed her best chance of surviving a collision with the drone was to use the boat as a shield/battering ram. In both respects, her desperate plan was a success. The small victory was lost on Jenna amid the chaos that followed.

The drone struck low, almost exactly level with the engine block, and tore the boat in half. The shockwave stunned Jenna, but even worse was the heat flash, more intense than the *Kilimanjaro's* explosive end. The airboat's rapid disintegration and immediate plunge into the marsh saved Jenna's life from the flames.

Awareness returned in a series of disconnected sensory inputs. Warm water splashed against her face. A distant engine hummed, rising in pitch as it drew close. A faint light glowed in the otherwise all-consuming darkness.

She blinked the water out of her eyes and tried to move. A mistake, she quickly realized. Not only was every muscle of her body stiff and aching, but something held her immobile. The night vision monocular still hung from the strap around her head, but the crash had knocked it askew. When she tried to reposition it, she discovered two things: the electronic display was dark, and only her right arm seemed to be working. When she tried to lift her left arm, a dull throb reminded her that there was a knife blade skewering her biceps.

Working one-handed, she unclipped the chinstrap buckle and let the useless monocular fall away. Her left eye had adjusted to the darkness well enough that she could make out silhouettes against the overcast sky, but in her right eye she saw only a uniform red haze, as if she had stared too long into a bright light. In a way, that was exactly what she had done. The night vision device was essentially a tiny television monitor positioned half an inch from the eyeball.

The engine noise grew louder. The outline of an approaching airboat emerged in the distance. As her mental reboot continued, she recalled that Zack, the man who had been stalking her and trying to kill her for the last several hours, was on that boat. She tried to move again, and was again denied. This time however, she was able to grasp the cause of her immobility. In addition to the knife stuck through her arm, she was held tight by a strap of nylon across her hips. It was the safety belt attached to the pilot's chair. The boat had been destroyed in the crash with the UAV, but the seat had been torn loose from its mount and deposited upright in the marsh, with Jenna still safely buckled in.

The boat went silent and coasted to a stop beside her. She felt its wake lapping against her chest, and heard a splash as someone jumped into the water.

Warning bells sounded in her head, urging her to release the seat belt and crawl away to safety, but she willed herself to remain motionless. She couldn't possibly outrun the killer, but maybe...

The silhouette of a man appeared before her. In the diffuse silvery light of the cloud-shrouded moon, she could just make out the black protrusion of a night vision monocular against the pale skin of Zack's face.

"Damn," he whispered, shaking his head. He extended his arm, and Jenna knew, without seeing, that there was a gun in his hand. "I guess they were right about you. You *are* dangerous."

"Why?" Her question was a barely audible whisper. What she really wanted to know was *who?* Who was right about her? Who had ordered her death? But she didn't have the strength to articulate that request.

Zack leaned forward. "You don't even know what you are," he said, and Jenna thought he sounded a little sad.

She wondered if Zack and the men with him had felt the same kind of moral reservations about their assignment that Noah and his assault team had felt all those years ago. "I'm...just...a kid."

"Yeah, right. A kid who just killed three of my friends."

"Just...defending myself."

"Is that right? Pretty damn good at it, too, aren't you? You're every bit as dangerous as they said you were." He straightened and aimed the gun. "Look, for what it's worth, I have to do this, but that doesn't mean I enjoy it."

Jenna muttered something barely audible even to her own ears.

"What's that?"

She repeated the words, but this time, her broken whisper was even softer. Zack leaned forward, turning his head to hear her final confession.

Just as Jenna hoped he would.

Her right hand, which had been snaking across her body toward her wounded arm, now grasped the knife hilt in an ice-pick grip and wrenched it loose with a volcanic eruption of strength.

There was a burst of pain and an even greater sense of relief, as the offending piece of metal was removed from her aggrieved flesh. She ignored both and focused everything into driving the knife point into Zack's eye.

There was a wet hiss as the blade sank into the orb, and just the slightest bit of resistance as it punched through the sphenoid bone at the back of his eye socket, penetrating into gray matter.

Zack howled, all thoughts of finishing his assignment forgotten, as Jenna drove the knife deeper, twisting the blade until both the cries and the thrashing ceased. Zack's dead weight collapsed into the marsh, tearing the knife from her grasp.

Jenna stared at the place where Zack had stood a moment before, feeling the adrenaline drain away, and whispered, "I said, 'It gets easier.'"

THIRTY-THREE

4:44 a.m.

She sat there for several minutes, drifting in and out of consciousness, trying to find the willpower to move. She could see the abandoned airboat, just a few feet away, and that she wouldn't survive without it.

Just need to rest a minute, she told herself. *One minute more, and then I'll move.*

A minute came and went, and she did not move. Then another.

You don't even know what you are.

What had Zack meant by that? What *was* she?

You're every bit as dangerous as they said you were.

Dangerous?

Well, she had proven that, hadn't she? How many men had she killed? They hadn't all died at her hands, but she had broken Raul's neck. She had driven a knife into Zack's brain. *Was* she dangerous? Definitely. But who had told Zack that she was dangerous? Who knew that about her before she did? Who had unleashed the killers on her, sent them to blow up the boat, sent a drone to track her movements?

This isn't about Noah at all. It's about me.

I have to keep moving. I have to find the answers.

One more minute.

She tried counting the seconds, but her time-honored method of measuring the passage of time—*one alligator, two alligator*—made her think about the local wildlife, so she quickly gave up on that endeavor.

Something splashed nearby. The sound repeated again and again until there could be no doubt that something big was moving through the marsh, headed straight toward her. The memory of alligators, still fresh in her thoughts, was enough to get her moving. She unbuckled the seat belt that held her fast. As soon as it was loose, she slid out of the seat—it had been tilted slightly forward without her realizing it—and she was dumped in the shallow water.

The unexpected baptism snapped her out of her fugue. She stood up and took a few unsteady steps toward the drifting airboat. She half-climbed, half-fell onto the floating platform.

"Jenna?" It was Mercy, calling to her from out of the darkness. "Jenna, is that you?"

"I'm here," Jenna croaked. "On the boat."

The splashing intensified and a few seconds later, she felt Mercy's touch. "Are you all right?"

The question struck Jenna as funny, but she was too tired to laugh. "Not really."

"Where are you hurt?"

"Everywhere," she replied, but then she managed to roll over. "Zack... Over there." She gestured weakly to the spot where she had made her stand. The outline of the half-submerged pilot's chair jutted up from the water like a buoy marker. "Night vision goggles."

Mercy seemed to understand. She splashed over to the area Jenna had indicated and began rooting around in the marsh. A few minutes later, she returned. "Got 'em." She held the monocular to her eye. "How do you make them work?"

Jenna felt a twinge of disappointment. Had immersion damaged the device? "There's a...switch." She couldn't seem to get out sentences of more than two or three syllables.

"Found it." There was a pause, then Mercy continued. "Ah, that's better... Oh."

"What?"

"Honey, you look awful."

This time, she couldn't help but laugh. "Told you."

Mercy began poking and prodding her, spending almost a full minute probing the gash in her arm. "Okay, the good news is, I don't think you have any broken bones. Given that little stunt you pulled, that's nothing short of a miracle. What possessed you—?"

"Bad news?"

"Well, the bad news might not be all that bad if I can get you to an emergency room."

"No," Jenna shook her head and immediately regretted doing so. "Gotta get to...Miami. Cort."

Mercy gave a disapproving sigh. "You're in no shape to argue. But I suppose if we can get out of this swamp and back to civilization, I can patch you up. But you're going to need antibiotics. I don't even want to think about what might have crawled into that cut."

Jenna had almost forgotten that they were still lost in the Everglades, with no way to orient themselves, much less navigate to someplace where Jenna could get medical attention. "Check...body." She tried taking a deep breath, felt pain in her chest and wondered if Mercy had missed a cracked rib in her hasty assessment. When she spoke again, she was able to get an entire sentence out. "He must have had a phone or some way to talk to the drone."

"That makes sense." Mercy went to Zack's body again, moving with more certainty now that she could see. When she returned, she was holding something slightly larger than a cell phone. "Found this. I think it's a GPS receiver." She played with it for a few moments, then pointed into the featureless darkness. "The alligator farm is just a couple of miles back that way. We can go there."

"Why there?" Jenna's brain felt too addled to make sense of this on her own.

"These guys left a car behind, remember?"

"Did you find the keys while you were searching him?"

There was a short pause. "No. But we can hotwire it, if we have to."

"Hotwire?" Jenna struggled to a sitting position. "I don't know how to do that. Do you?"

"One thing at a time."

Jenna couldn't tell if Mercy's indirect answer was meant to conceal the fact that she did not possess that particular skill, or rather to avoid admitting that she did. Instead, she helped position Jenna more securely and comfortably for the ride, and then started the engine.

It took Jenna a few more minutes to process the fact that Mercy piloted the boat like an expert. She recalled her friend's initial ambivalence about using the airboats and contemplated the contradiction. *Maybe she's a quick learner, too. Everybody's full of surprises tonight.*

She was far too preoccupied with what Zack had said to worry about Mercy's omissions.

They were right about you.

Who?

Dangerous.

She thought about the bomb, left in the *Kilimanjaro*'s salon. It was never meant for Noah. The bomb was for her. Why? Because she was dangerous? How could she be dangerous? She was just a teenager. She didn't even have a driver's license yet.

Who said I was dangerous? Dangerous to whom?

That, she realized, was a much more important question, and there was only one answer that made any sense.

Those men are not federal agents, Noah had told the deputy, but what if he had been lying? Or what if he had meant something else? That they were not FBI agents, but part of some super-secret, alphabet-soup, black ops agency, working outside the law, beholden to none.

Noah had been part of something like that when he had been sent to destroy the compound where she had lived, ordered to kill everyone, including her parents.

Had they been dangerous, too?

Had Zack and Ken and the other killers simply been trying to finish the mission that Noah started—and abandoned—fifteen years earlier? Did it all come back to that?

She could have believed that if not for Zack's statement. *They were right about you.* This was more than just a shadowy government agency tying off loose ends. The people responsible for this were convinced that *she* was a threat, and that made absolutely no sense.

Except in a weird way, it sort of did.

You don't even know what you are.

What am *I?*

The engine throttled down as the blocky silhouettes of Gator Station came into view. Jenna pushed herself up to a sitting position and watched as Mercy nudged Zack's airboat alongside the dock, where they had boarded the destroyed airboat less than an hour earlier. She felt stiff and achy, but surprisingly better than she had any right to feel. More than anything else, she was famished.

Mercy cut the engine and hopped down from her chair to tie off the boat, but stopped abruptly. "There are two bodies here."

"That can't be right. There was just the one guy, and the gators got him."

"I think these are the people who live here. The owners."

Jenna winced as she stood and stepped onto the dock. She couldn't see much detail, but she was able to distinguish a man and a woman, both about Noah's age. The man wore jeans and a wife-beater tank-top. The woman was clothed in a muu-muu with some kind of swirly pattern. The fabric of the woman's garment hid any signs of violence, but the man's sleeveless T-shirt showed a dark stain directly over the sternum. A shotgun lay on the dock beside him.

It wasn't too hard to piece together what had happened. The couple had heard the airboats or perhaps had been wakened by the gunshots. They had come out to investigate and discovered Zack and his crew taking the second boat.

Rage and grief welled up in Jenna's throat. Zack had called *her* dangerous, but she didn't go around killing innocent people who just happened to be in the way.

Mercy knelt down next to the man, and after a few seconds, she held up a ring of keys.

"What are you going to do with those?" Jenna asked.

"First, we're going to see what kind of medical supplies they've got around here. They deal with dangerous animals all the time, so they're bound to have some antibiotics and bandages."

"Smart."

"Thank you. After that, maybe we'll find some dry clothes and some snacks. And then we'll see if there's a car to go with one of these." Mercy regarded her for a few seconds. "Maybe we'll start with the car. I think you need to sit down before you fall down."

Jenna wasn't sure she would even make it that far.

THIRTY-FOUR

Miami, Florida, USA
6:15 a.m.

"Wake up, sleepy head."

Jenna heard the words from the midst of a forgotten dream, but did not fully awake until she felt a hand on her shoulder, rocking her back and forth. She mumbled something incoherent and opened her eyes to greet the day.

It was still dark, though not nearly as dark as it had been in the remote depths of the Everglades. There was no shortage of artificial light—overhead streetlights, neon signs, and the occasional flash of passing headlights. Mercy smiled at her from the driver's seat. Jenna turned her head to look out her window. They were in a grocery store parking lot with just a few other cars. "Where are we?"

"The address Noah gave for the mysterious Mr. Cort is just a couple of blocks from here."

Jenna felt her bile start to rise at the mention of Noah—she couldn't bring herself to think of him as her father anymore—and she fought to maintain her bleary-eyed indifference. Mercy didn't deserve to be on the receiving end of her anger.

"I drove past. It's a house, no lights. Didn't look like anyone was home."

"What time is it?"

"Just past six. How are you feeling?"

Jenna sat up, pleased to discover that her various injuries didn't hurt anywhere near as bad as she had expected, especially considering the cramped conditions. The road-weary Ford Fiesta was not the luxury ride Jenna would have preferred, but it was the only vehicle available. Mercy had driven and Jenna, after devouring a smorgasbord of snack crackers, chips and candy bars, had slept.

"Good as new," Jenna replied, stretching in place and probing the cuff of gauze around her left arm. It was tender, but the bandage remained dry and supple, which told her the wound was closed and healing. When she had cleaned and dressed the wound, Mercy had remarked that it didn't look too serious, which was welcome news, but a bit of a surprise to Jenna. It had felt pretty serious when the blade had gone in. But she was a fast healer, or so she had always been told.

Such swift healing didn't come without a price. She was still famished, and she said so.

Mercy considered the statement. "Normally, I'd say let's go grab a breakfast burrito."

"But?"

"I don't have any cash, and I'm not sure it's a good idea to use plastic. I'm sure that's the kind of thing they'll be watching for."

Jenna was a little surprised that Mercy had thought of that, and even more so that she had not. The realization blindsided her with a rush of emotion, crushing her good mood. She thought this must be how people felt when they got a terminal diagnosis from their doctor. "Wow."

Mercy looked at her sidelong. "What?"

"I just realized how completely screwed I am...we are. They're going to keep coming after us. We can't go back to our lives. We don't have anything. We can't even buy a breakfast burrito."

Mercy laid a hand on her arm. "You're still alive, Jenna. They sent four guys after you, but you're still breathing. We'll get through this. Now, let's go talk to Cort, and then see what happens. Okay?"

Jenna managed a bleak nod. She hadn't told Mercy about Zack's comments, but Mercy already understood that the men hunting them had an official sanction.

They got out and Jenna followed Mercy from the parking lot to the sidewalk running along a busy seven-lane thoroughfare.

Businesses and office buildings, many of which appeared to be vacant, lined both sides of the road. Her first ever look at Miami did not match her expectations. Maybe things were different closer to the urban center or in the distinctive neighborhoods that she had always heard people talk about—Little Havana, South Beach and so forth—but this area did not appear that much different from Key West. She paid attention to the unfamiliar environment, noting the street signs. If she got separated from Mercy or had to make a quick escape, some sense of where things were would help.

She wondered how Mercy had been able to find her way here. Noah's notebook was gone, probably lost forever in the marsh, and Jenna knew that Mercy had gotten only a quick glance at the page with Bill Cort's address. Maybe Mercy had an eidetic memory, too. Anything was possible.

Two blocks down from the supermarket, they turned west and headed into a residential neighborhood. The street was narrow and dark, mostly lit by the porch lights of the modest houses they passed. The humid air hummed with the buzz of insects and the electrical current passing through overhead power lines, but this only accentuated the otherworldly stillness and added to Jenna's growing apprehension. A few windows were lit from within, early risers getting ready for a day at the office.

Something about that seemed wrong. It took her a few moments to remember that it was Sunday. It felt like days had passed since the bomb blew her entire life into chaos, but it hadn't even been twelve hours. *I've got school tomorrow*, she thought, and she wondered when or if she would ever see her friends and teachers again.

"That's the place," Mercy said, pointing to an innocuous looking single-story cottage. The house had bars on the screen door and windows, just like every other house on the block. A wrought iron perimeter fence boxed in a neatly trimmed lawn. There was no car in the carport, and unlike the other homes, which had a lived-in look, this house gave a distinct impression of emptiness. Jenna recalled that the first address for Cort had been crossed out, suggesting that he had moved at some point during the years following Noah's decision to compose a record of his mission. What if Cort had moved again, after the notebook had been secreted away in the Aerojet silo?

What if this is a dead end?

Mercy rested a hand on the fence and looked at Jenna. "Shall we go ring the bell?"

Jenna felt an almost overwhelming urge to turn away, to run, as if by doing so, she might wish away everything that had happened. It was, she knew, just another manifestation of the fight or flight response, a primal fear of the unknown, or in this case, of the possibility that this last desperate hope would end in a crushing disappointment.

No. I'm done running. And if this is a dead end, I'll figure something else out.

She reached over the top of the gate and worked the release. It swung open without the slightest squeak of protest, and she stepped through. Mercy followed, but not before putting a hand into a tote bag. The canvas sack, emblazoned with a cartoon alligator, was just one of the souvenirs they'd acquired before leaving Gator Station. Mercy had filled it with first aid supplies and snacks. Jenna had consumed all of the latter. The sack also contained the night vision monocular and the pistol she had used to shoot Carlos Villegas. Jenna had a feeling that Mercy was reaching for the gun.

As they neared the front door, the porch light flashed on— presumably triggered by a motion sensor—but nothing else happened to indicate that the house was occupied. Jenna stabbed a finger at the doorbell button and heard a muffled two-tone ringing noise from within. Several seconds passed. Jenna was debating whether to ring again or walk away when she heard the soft click of a lock bolt disengaging.

She exchanged looks and shrugs with Mercy, then tried the door handle. Both the screen and front doors were unlocked.

Jenna stood on the threshold, staring into the room beyond. In the diffuse illumination cast by the porch light, she could make out the front room, appointed with tasteful but generic furniture, and little else. There was no sign of the householder.

"This is like the start of a bad fairy tale."

Mercy nodded. "I know what you mean."

Jenna stayed there a moment longer, then turned around. While she had not really known what to expect from the mysterious Bill Cort, this was most definitely not even on the list of possibilities. "We should go."

Mercy started to answer, but at that moment another sound issued from within the house: the distinctive trilling of a landline telephone.

Jenna's breath caught with a gasp. "Forget fairy tales. This is more like a slasher flick."

The phone rang without cease. Jenna expected that after three or four rings, voicemail or an answering machine would pick up. After eight cycles, she figured the caller would give up, but the ringing continued.

"I think someone knows we're here," Mercy finally said. "So we should either answer it or get the hell out of here."

"I have to know," Jenna said. "But hold the door open, okay?"

Mercy nodded.

Jenna stepped inside and followed the electronic chirps to their source, a rather quaint telephone set from the pre-digital age, sitting on a side table. Jenna laid a hand on the cool plastic receiver and picked it up.

She held the receiver at arm's length, relishing the return of near total silence for a moment, then held it to her ear. "Hello?"

"Jenna?" The voice was masculine and not the least bit familiar. "Am I speaking to Jenna Flood?"

Jenna felt a chill shoot down her spine. "Who are you?"

"The name is Cort, and the fact that you're talking to me right now tells me that your father sent you there. I'm right, aren't I?"

Jenna looked around the room, searching for a hidden video camera, but she remembered that the ringing had started when she was still outside. The camera had been on the porch. Cort, wherever he was, had probably been watching them from the moment they opened the gate.

When she didn't answer, Cort continued. "I'm on my way there right now. Five minutes, tops. Just get inside and sit tight. I know you probably won't believe this, but you can trust me. I know what's been happening to you. I can help."

"You're right, Mr. Cort. I don't believe it."

"Jenna, listen to me. I worked with your father. He trusts me. You know he does. That's why he sent you my way."

She felt her rage start to boil again. "You have no idea how little that means to me right now."

There was a long silence on the line, then a sigh. "I guess you found out about..." He didn't finish the sentence. "Look, I can explain everything to you when I get there, but you have to trust me."

"People are trying to kill me, Mr. Cort. I'm not going to trust anyone."

"I'm going to hang up and drive now, but Jenna I'm begging you to hear me out. The danger you're in right now is just the tip of the iceberg. This is much bigger than you can possibly imagine."

"What's that supposed to mean?"

The only answer was the buzz of a dial tone in her ear.

THIRTY-FIVE

6:29 a.m.

Jenna was sitting on the couch in the front room when Cort arrived, as promised, slightly less than five minutes after ending the telephone call.

He looked to be about the same age as Noah, a little taller and a little leaner, but no less grizzled. His bloodshot eyes and rumpled clothing—khakis and a tropical-patterned short-sleeved shirt—conveyed the impression of someone who had crashed after an all-night party.

He gave her an appraising look, then glanced around, as if searching for someone else. "Where's your friend?"

Jenna did not answer directly. "You've got cameras here, right? That's how you knew it was me?"

Mercy had not liked the idea of waiting around for Cort to come to them, but Jenna saw no alternative. "If it is a trap," she had told Mercy, "we're already in it. What we have to do now is give ourselves a way out."

Mercy was hiding somewhere nearby, keeping an eye and the barrel of her pistol trained on the house. If Cort showed up with a posse in tow, or gave any hint of treachery, she would do what she could to provide cover for Jenna's escape. It had seemed like a good idea at the time, but now Jenna felt as alone as she had during the ordeal with the Villegas brothers.

Cort laughed—a short barking sound—and sank into a chair on the opposite side of the room. "That's your first question? After everything you've been through?"

"This place is some kind of safe house, right? Cameras, remote locks, who knows what else. That tells me you're working for the government...well, *a* government. I'm not sure which one. I think the men that tried to kill me work for the government, too. So...yeah, that's my first question."

She held his gaze, as curious about how he would react, as she was about what he would say. His eyes did not move.

Of course not. He knows all the same tricks that Noah taught me. I'll never know if he's lying.

"Let's just cut to the chase, then. Yes, I work for the government. *Our* government. Just like your father did—"

"He wasn't my father." It was out of her mouth before she could even think about whether it was the right thing to say.

Cort's expression did not change. "Now see, I thought your first question would have something to do with that."

Jenna did not allow herself to be derailed. "So you *do* work for the government."

"Yes, but not for the people that are after you. Not exactly. It's complicated."

"Uncomplicate it," she said. "Or I'm out of here."

Cort drummed his fingers on the armrest of his chair. It was the closest thing to a 'tell' that Jenna had seen from him. She thought he might be stalling. Finally he cleared his throat. "Why don't you invite your friend in? She might be interested in what I have to say."

Jenna shook her head. "I feel safer with her right where she is."

"Suit yourself." Cort stood up. "Are you hungry? Thirsty? There are some Cokes in the fridge."

Definitely stalling. Jenna stood up and headed for the door.

"Wait."

She stopped but did not turn.

"I need you to see something. In the signal room."

"What's a signal room?"

"It's like an office. Come on. I'll show you."

"If you're wasting my time..." She let the threat hang. She was not exactly in a position to make demands. The only leverage she had was the ability to walk out the door, and the price for that would be abandoning the search for answers.

Cort led her into a short hall with three doors. The first was slightly ajar, revealing a bathroom. The other two were closed. He opened one of the latter and led Jenna into a space that looked more like the control room of a space ship than a mere office. One entire wall was dominated by enormous flat screen television monitors. There was a long utilitarian desk with two open laptop computers, along with printers, scanners, telephones and other devices that Jenna did not recognize. Large computer servers dominated one entire wall, while the wall opposite the screens was lined with gun-metal gray freestanding cabinets.

Cort moved to the desk and started pushing buttons, waking up the computers and turning on the televisions. He tuned the TVs to different twenty-four-hour cable news networks, and in a matter of just a few seconds, the room was filled with a crowd of voices, all talking over each other. Yet, even though the voices were not synchronized, the various stations were reporting the same story—the story that had been playing when she had walked into Mercy's bar the previous night. Each news service called it something different, but the gist was the same: *Bio-terrorism in China*.

"Are you following the story?" Cort asked, gesturing at the screens.

"Been a little busy with something else."

"There's been a major outbreak of SARS in Hong Kong. You know about SARS?"

Jenna nodded. SARS—Severe Acute Respiratory Syndrome—was a coronavirus disease that caused flu-like symptoms, often resulting in pneumonia. It had first appeared in China in 2002, and quickly spread across the world, infecting thousands and killing almost one person in every ten infected. Since that initial outbreak, the disease had been inactive, though a similar coronavirus called MERS—Middle Eastern Respiratory Syndrome—had appeared in late 2012 and was slowly making its way around the globe. The original SARS outbreak had occurred when she was a very young child, but she remembered hearing the name. She had not heard mention of this latest outbreak.

"The Chinese have closed the borders and aren't saying much officially. Unofficially they're investigating the outbreak as an act of terrorism. See, when SARS first showed up, a lot of folks believed it was a biological weapon, genetically engineered to target a specific racial profile—people of Asian, and specifically Chinese, ancestry." He paused to take a deep breath, as if doing so might lend gravity to his next statement. "As it happens, they were right."

Despite the fact that the entire discussion digressed from her immediate concerns, Jenna was stunned by the admission. "SARS was a bio-weapon?"

"The 2003 outbreak was a test. A demonstration, if you will. We were very vulnerable...two wars, a recession... We had to let Beijing know that it wasn't a good time to screw with us."

This second revelation was even more stunning than the first. "*Us?* As in the United States? *We* turned SARS loose on China?"

Irritation flickered across Cort's otherwise imperturbable expression, but he waved a hand dismissively. "What's done is done. What's happening now is...not. Not us, I mean."

"Then who? And why?"

Cort nodded as if she had given the appropriate response. "I'll let you think about that. See if you're as smart as I've heard."

She heard an echo of Zack's ominous statement in his words— *they were right about you*—but just as quickly, the answer popped into her head. "It will create tension between the US and China."

Cort made a gun-shape with his hand and cocked his thumb, as if shooting at her. "What you won't hear on the news is that we're in the middle of a full-scale cyber-assault. Someone is exploiting a major source code vulnerability, and when the news finally gets out—and it will get out—it's going to..." He paused, took another breath, and then in a more subdued tone said, "It'll be bad.

"China is the obvious suspect. We've been in a virtual Cold War with them for the last five years—ever heard of Operation Aurora? GhostNet? The Elderwood Group? Unit 61398?"

Jenna shook her head in response to each, and Cort just shrugged. "Well, we've tried to keep most of it under our hat, so to speak. If people knew how vulnerable the digital landscape was, the economy would crater. Up until now, the attacks have always been just a nuisance. They were probing weaknesses, harassing us with phishing and malware, theft and eavesdropping. But this week, the attacks escalated. Exponentially. Way beyond anything the Chinese are capable of."

"Someone is framing the Chinese for the cyber-attack, right? The same people who are behind the SARS outbreak." Jenna could almost hear the whir of her own mental hard drive as she processed this information. "So who's really behind it?"

Cort nodded and rolled his hand in *go on* gesture. "Who benefits from an all-out conflict between China and the US?"

"Russia?"

Cort made another finger gun.

What does that have to do with people trying to kill me?

"Fifteen years ago," Cort explained, "the man you call Noah Flood was sent on a mission to destroy a former Soviet research center in Cuba, a facility still being operated by the Russian government."

"My real parents were Russians," she said, though it was more of a question. "Somehow they were involved in all of this."

She didn't know how, but she could see in Cort's eyes that she'd gotten at least some of it right. He stared at her for several seconds, then turned to one of the laptop computers. Jenna saw that the information on his computer was now duplicated on one of the wall screens. As he navigated through directories and files, he began talking.

"Does the name Trofim Lysenko mean anything to you? No? Lysenko was a Soviet scientist, their leading agricultural expert from the 1930s until well into the 50s. Lysenko believed the widely accepted theories of genetics, as explained by Gregor Mendel...you do know that name right?"

Jenna nodded. "I learned all about him in biology. Mendel figured out the principles of heredity, and how traits are passed from one generation to the next. We know a lot more about it now. Mendel lived a hundred and fifty years ago. He didn't know anything about DNA."

"Lysenko thought Mendel was wrong, and that the genetic traits could be influenced by the environment. The short version of the story is that Lysenko's ideas were hogwash, and by the 1960s, the Soviets were in a big hurry to make up lost ground, especially in the area of genetic research."

"That's what they were doing at the place where Noah found me. It was in Cuba, right?"

Cort regarded her through narrowed eyes. "Did he tell you that, or did you figure it out for yourself?"

"A little of both." She returned his appraising stare. "Okay, so the Russians were doing genetic research, and someone decided it had to be stopped. Destroy the place and kill everyone, right? Only Noah didn't count on finding me. He couldn't bring himself to murder a child, but he didn't dare tell anyone that he'd disobeyed orders. So, he quit. No, he didn't just quit. He changed his name and dropped off the grid so that you people would never find me. That's what happened, isn't it?"

"Well done. But you're wrong about one thing. We always knew what your father..." Another hint of laughter. "What *Noah* had done. He couldn't hide from us, but he wasn't a threat, and neither were you. Until now." Cort returned his attention to the computer long enough to tap in a few more commands. "That facility was conducting a particularly dangerous type of research. They had already let the genie out of the bottle, and we knew we'd have only one chance to put it back in."

"Bioweapons?" Jenna shook her head in disbelief at the evident hypocrisy. "You as much as admitted that the US engineered the SARS outbreak."

"Who said anything about bioweapons?" Cort smiled like a magician showing the audience his empty hat. "But speaking of SARS, we've tracked down the source of the outbreak. A sample of the virus was discovered missing from a CDC facility in Atlanta. One of the scientists doing research there—a Dr. Kelli Foster—recently traveled to China. Her whereabouts are presently unknown." Cort pointed at the screen. "That is Kelli Foster."

The display showed an unflattering mug-shot style photo—taken for an official identification card or perhaps a driver's license—of a woman in her mid-twenties. The woman had dark hair and an olive complexion that hinted at an exotic ancestry.

Jenna gaped in astonishment. But for ten more pounds and as many years, Kelli Foster might have been her own twin sister.

The image disappeared and another took its place.

"This is Jarrod Chu. He's a special agent in the FBI cybercrime division. He practically wrote the book on how to fight hackers. If anyone could tell us how to fight this latest attack, it's Chu. Unfortunately, he's also missing. I think you can see why we're very interested in finding Mr. Chu."

Jenna stared at the ID card picture. Chu might have been thirty, possibly Eurasian if his name was any indication, with neatly trimmed black hair. There was nothing androgynous about his features, but the resemblance to both Kelli Foster and Jenna herself was unmistakable.

Dumbstruck, she turned to Cort and shook her head questioningly. "Am I... Are they my...family?"

"Family?" Cort rolled the word around in his mouth then frowned. "Maybe that's the word for it. I don't really know. You see, in a way Jenna, they are *you*."

"What?"

"Kelli Foster, Jarrod Chu, you...and at least a dozen others. Jenna, you're all the same person. You're all clones."

THIRTY-SIX

6:44 a.m.

Cort didn't allow even a moment for the information to sink in. "Back in '99, when the order came down to destroy the research facility, we didn't know exactly what they were up to, but we knew they had perfected human cloning techniques. We didn't know if they were trying to engineer some kind of super soldier, or trying to create organ donors for former party officials turned oligarchs or... Hell, maybe trying to clone old Joe Stalin himself. All we really knew was that we had to stop them. So we did."

Jenna could barely hear him over the sound of blood rushing through her ears. *A clone? I'm a clone?*

She was still reeling from the news that Noah had killed her parents, and now she was being told that she didn't even have parents. She was nothing but an experiment. Pinocchio pretending to be a real boy. Frankenstein's monster brought to life by a mad scientist.

Several seconds passed before she realized that Cort had stopped talking. She met his gaze. "A clone?"

The man nodded.

"Did Noah know?"

"Hard to say. I'm sure someone higher up the chain knew exactly what was going on. That's probably why they decided to let him go through with his retirement plan. They were curious to see how things would turn out for you. But yeah, I think he probably figured it out."

Jenna swallowed. The revelation had rocked every fiber of her being, calling into question everything she believed about herself.

Her knowledge of cloning was limited to what she had seen in movies and read about in the occasional science magazine article, but that was enough to grasp the basics. Genetic material from one or more donors, inserted into a human egg cell and then implanted in a surrogate mother for gestation and birth—that was probably how they had done it.

All the years spent wondering what her mother looked like... She didn't have a mother. Just an anonymous rented womb.

Jenna looked up at the image of Jarrod Chu. "How did they survive?"

"You have to understand that, until this week, we didn't realize that any of them had. Our working hypothesis is that the clones were removed from the facility after a few years—probably when they were school aged—and sent back to the Motherland for education and indoctrination. Or, they might have been educated by sleeper agents in the US. Both Foster and Chu underwent fairly rigorous background checks and passed without a hitch."

Jenna fought through the deluge of questions, most of which she doubted Cort could even answer, and tried to focus on the immediate problem. "Why now? Why come after me?"

"Something big is happening. A plan that has been in the works for a very long time. We know that much, and we know that the clones are critical to the plan."

"How?"

"I think you already know, Jenna. You're not like other people."

You are dangerous.

You don't even know what you are.

"You're smarter, stronger. Hell, there are things you probably don't even know you're capable of doing." Cort jerked his head toward the screen. "Just like them. Kelli Foster and Jarrod Chu. There are others, too, all geniuses in positions of power and influence, all around the world. Positioned like pieces on a chessboard. It took us a while to figure it out, but once we identified those two, the rest fell into place."

"That's why they decided to kill me?"

"Not just you. All of them. In your case, someone panicked. Your father was a senior officer who quit all of a sudden to raise you. Given what was happening, that looked very suspicious. Better safe than sorry."

Jenna felt no reaction to the word 'father.' "You aren't going to help me, are you?"

Cort took a deep breath. "Jenna, my section wasn't involved in any of this. If I had known sooner, I could have worked with your father and arranged a safe outcome for both of you. But if you come in—"

A distant gun report interrupted him. Jenna had known the audience with Cort was almost at and end, and she was already poised for action, so when she heard the shot, she sprang into motion.

Cort moved, too, faster than she expected for someone his age. Jenna's expectations, however, were that Cort, like Noah, would be a veteran intelligence officer, with reflexes honed by training and experience, and a repertoire of deadly skills. Whether or not this was true did not matter. She had prepared for the worst case scenario.

In the five minutes spent waiting for Cort to arrive, Jenna had scouted the safe house, exploring the rooms, identifying potential hazards, and plotting escape routes. She had memorized the layout of each room, and noted what items might be useful for defensive or even offensive purposes. In the room Cort called the 'signal room,' she had been particularly interested in the notebook computers resting on the desktop.

As she darted forward, Cort sprang to his feet and took a step back, one hand extended toward her, the other reaching behind him. When the hand reappeared, it held a small pistol, but before he could aim it at her, she had scooped up the nearest laptop and hurled it like a Frisbee. The heavy computer struck dead center in the middle of Cort's chest. The projectile hit with sufficient force to knock him back a step, but more importantly, it dealt a shock to his nervous system that caused the gun to fly out of his hands.

Jenna took action before the hurled computer clattered to the floor. She pounced on Cort, driving several quick focused punches into his jaw and solar plexus. She felt an unexpected throb of pain in her left arm. The stab wound, aggravated by the sudden activity, reminded her of its presence, but she ignored the sensation and didn't hold back.

Cort weathered the assault and caught her third punch. He twisted her arm around and attempted to pin it, but she was ready for this move. She relaxed her legs, letting her weight drop, and pulled him off balance. They collapsed together onto the floor in a tangle of limbs. Cort seized on this imagined advantage and tried to roll her over, so he could use his superior size to subdue her.

Jenna didn't resist. Instead, she reached out with her free hand and in a single smooth motion, seized hold of the computer and slammed it against the side of Cort's head. The blow dazed him, and she wriggled free of his grasp. In the instant it took him to recover, she found his gun and brought it up, ready to fire.

Cort froze, staring at the barrel of the pistol as if hypnotized. "Jenna, put it down," he said slowly.

She saw in his eyes that he knew she would shoot, but she also saw that he was calculating his odds of surviving that first shot and taking the gun away from her. He was on the ground, and any move against her would require him to overcome his own inertia. The odds, she decided, were probably in her favor, but Cort knew, as she did, that the best way to deal with a situation like this was to move toward the gun.

She pulled the trigger.

The report was deafening in the small room, but Jenna did not even flinch. A spray of red erupted from Cort's right thigh, and a curse tore from between his clenched teeth. Jenna kept the gun trained on him, shifting her aim so that it was now trained on his heart.

"Keys."

"Jenna." He was breathing fast, angry and in pain. "I can help, but you need to trust me."

"Give them to me, or I'll take them off your dead body."

His hands came up in a gesture of surrender, then he reached slowly toward the pocket just above the spreading red stain. "You won't make it on your own," he said, grimacing as he brought out a key ring. "I can bring you in. Keep you safe."

Despite his evident treachery, the offer was tempting. Cort had given her the answers she sought. He could just as easily have killed her the moment he walked in. She didn't trust him, but if there was even a chance that he was willing and able to protect her, this would be her only opportunity to accept. If she refused, if she ran, there would be nowhere left to turn for help.

But if I'm as smart and dangerous as everyone seems to think I am, maybe I don't need help.

She extended her left hand, palm up. He nodded, as if somehow agreeing with the logic of her refusal, and tossed the ring to her. She thought he might try a short throw as a distraction, but the keys landed on her outstretched fingers so precisely that she didn't even need to break eye contact for the catch. She took a backward step and then bolted from the room, ignoring his shouted parting words.

"They'll find you! They *will* kill you!"

THIRTY-SEVEN

6:46 a.m.

As she sprinted through the safe house, Jenna heard more shots in quick succession, too many to just be from Mercy's gun. In the brief time they had to make a plan before Cort's arrival, they had discussed this possibility. It was their worst case scenario. While she and Mercy had hoped for a positive outcome, the last twelve hours had taught Jenna the importance of making her own luck.

She reached the front door and threw it open. There was a distinctive mechanical click as the remote-controlled deadbolt lock sprang out of the door. She had anticipated that the same mechanism which had allowed her access in the first place might be used to imprison her once inside, so before Cort's arrival, she had stuffed the bolt hole with a wad of toilet paper to prevent the lock from seating. She had done the same with the screen door, but before she attempted to open it, she took a moment to scan the front yard.

In the brief time that she had been inside, the sky had lightened. The sun was climbing into the sky. While much of the world was still shrouded in shadow, she had no trouble distinguishing three cars that had not been there before, lined up on the street in front of the house. Four men were crouched behind the cars, peering across the street into the semi-darkness between two houses, where Mercy had hid.

Jenna glanced at the key ring in her left hand. The car key was recognizable by its shape and the plastic sheath that contained the alarm remote control. The logo on the fob—a circle with sprouting wings—told her which car it would operate.

Cort rode in style.

A blue Mini Cooper S sat just ahead of two generic-looking sedans that were probably from a government motor pool or a rental fleet. Jenna was reminded of a song she had learned in her early childhood—*one of these things is not like the other.*

The men at the cars had their backs to her and appeared to be unaware of what had transpired in the house. To reach the Mini, Jenna would first have to get past the fence. *Or over it.*

Her left arm was pulsing with pain, the sleeve of her shirt dotted red with blood that had oozed through the bandage beneath. A few hours ago, she had barely been able to lift the limb, but now, despite aggravating the wound in the struggle with Cort, she felt certain that the muscles would do whatever she demanded of them.

She wondered if she owed her fast healing abilities to some long-dead Russian scientist.

She darted out into the open, keeping her body bent forward as she crossed the short distance to the fence. Her approach went unnoticed by the gunmen who had their attention fully occupied, but she knew that would change the moment she vaulted the fence. They would see her. They would try to shoot her. She would have only a second or two to get into the Mini. Maybe less. They would probably start shooting as soon as they saw her, but if she could get into the car, lock the doors and stay down long enough to start the engine...

The doors!

Before attempting the fence, she spared another glance at the key fob. There were three buttons, each marked with a different symbol. Her finger hovered above the one that looked like an unlocked padlock, but she didn't press it until just before she was ready to clamber over the fence. She was afraid the car's alarm might give her away with a chirp when she hit the button. It did not. Instead something remarkable happened. As she hit the sidewalk, she heard the Mini's motor begin purring. Cort's car was equipped with a remote starter.

Whether deafened by the din of their weapons or simply hyper-focused on the threat across the street, none of the gunmen took note of her presence behind them. But Mercy must have, for at that moment, four shots rang out in quick succession, the rounds rapping against the fender of the rear-most car. Jenna made it to the Mini's passenger door and got it open before any of the men realized she was there.

As she slid inside, Jenna stabbed down on the lock button. A loud crack resounded through the interior, and the passenger window disintegrated, revealing a hard face and reaching hands, but Jenna had already made it over the center column and slid behind the wheel. She thrust the pistol she'd taken from Cort at the would-be intruder and fired point blank. The man vanished. Jenna didn't know if he'd been hit or simply ducked back at the sight of the gun. She didn't particularly care. Her focus was on the unfamiliar control console in front of her. She knew the motor was already running. There were just two pedals on the floor—an automatic transmission. *Thank goodness for that*, she thought. She found the gear lever, shifted it into drive, and stomped on the gas.

The take-off would have earned her a lecture—or worse—from her Driver's Ed teacher, but under the circumstances, it was perfect. The Mini shot forward like a startled rabbit, and it was halfway down the block before Jenna could even think about what to do next.

She touched the brakes and steered into a tight U-turn. The nimble little car easily negotiated the about-face, despite the narrow confines of the street. In a matter of seconds, Jenna was facing back toward the site of the gun battle. The gunmen and their vehicles were lined up on her left. Mercy was concealed somewhere to the right.

The gunmen shifted forward, the muzzles of their pistols flashing as they hurled lead down the street at the Mini. A bullet smacked into the windshield and plowed through the air right above her head. A jagged crack split the glass but it did not shatter.

Jenna ducked down behind the steering wheel, and moved her foot off the brake, preparing to charge headlong into the fray. Like a chess player working through the moves and counter-moves of a gambit, she rehearsed what would happen next.

Mercy waited across the street from the safe house and the shooters. Jenna would have to stop to pick her up, and when she did, they would both be exposed for as long as it took for Mercy to make the dash to the Mini. She groped for a better plan, but without being able to communicate her intentions to Mercy, there was no better alternative.

Except...there was.

They will find you, Cort had said, and Jenna knew he was right. The killers would never give up. They would not stop until she was dead—she and anyone with her.

Earlier, she had balked at the thought of dragging Mercy into the mess in which she now found herself. Despite the fact that Mercy had saved her from Carlos and had hauled her out the Everglades, despite the fact that the idea of facing the uncertain future alone terrified her, Jenna now saw with startling clarity that there was really only one way to ensure Mercy's safety.

She stomped on the accelerator and the Mini shot down the street.

One of the gunmen leaped in front of her, striking a defiant pose, as if daring her to run him down, and he started firing. Jenna took the dare. The man realized his mistake a fraction of a second too late. There was a crunch, followed by a thumping sound as the man rolled across the hood, up onto the fractured windshield, and then fell away. Without raising her head or easing off the accelerator, Jenna sped past the cars, past the place where Mercy was hiding, and kept going.

Mercy wouldn't understand her decision. She had not been privy to Cort's revelation about Jenna's origins or the reasons why the government hunted her so relentlessly. She would only know that Jenna had abandoned her.

But she would live.

The killers had no interest in Mercy. They probably wouldn't even look for her, not with Jenna slipping away. Mercy would be safer without her.

It was cold comfort. As the Mini reached the intersection with the main thoroughfare, the reality of her situation sank in. There was no longer anyone she could ask for help or advice. She would have to face the rest of her life—however short that span would prove to be—completely alone.

But as she coasted through the stop and turned right onto Seventh Avenue, something else Cort had said echoed in her memory.

There are others.

THIRTY-EIGHT

6:51 a.m.

The question of how to track down—

My brothers and sisters?

—her fellow clones, and the thornier moral problem of their evident involvement in a worldwide terror plot designed to ignite World War III, occupied Jenna's thoughts for less than a minute. That was how long it took for the first signs of pursuit to appear.

She realized now that her inner conflict about leaving Mercy behind had hidden flaws in her getaway plan that were now apparent. The Mini Cooper was not the most inconspicuous vehicle, and there was every reason to believe that the men hunting her would have other assets at their disposal—more surveillance drones, traffic cameras, who knew what else?

I need to ditch this car.

Easier said than done.

She had seen the two cars pull out from the cross street, fifteen seconds after she passed. Traffic was light, giving her a clear line of sight to the sedans, which meant that they could see her as well. In the time it would take her to pull over and get out, they would close the gap.

On the plus side of the equation, the Mini was fast and seemed eager to prove it. Despite its compact design and bulldog appearance, it had the heart of a race car and the ground-hugging handling of a go-cart. The only thing holding Jenna back was her own caution, and with each passing second, confidence replaced fear. She was, as she had told Mercy, a quick learner.

Of course, she realized. *That's how I was designed.*

Cut it out, a second inner-voice said. *Save the pity party for later.*

A traffic light two blocks away turned yellow. Jenna pushed harder, knowing that there was no way she would make the light. It turned red when she was still a hundred yards from the cross street, but she had no intention of stopping.

As cars rolled into the intersection, her eyes darted back and forth, fixing each vehicle in her mind's eye, estimating speeds and rates of acceleration, plotting the course that would carry her through with the least amount of maneuvering. It reminded her of that old arcade game where the goal was to get the frog across a busy street without getting him turned into a green blob of roadkill. If she didn't get it right—or if one of the other drivers saw her and got spooked—it would be her going splat. As she closed on the intersection, the connections solidified in her mind. Eye, hand and foot, were perfectly synchronized with past, present and future.

It didn't go quite as smoothly as she had anticipated. The one thing that she could not have accounted for was the reaction of the other drivers. The intersection erupted in a cacophony of screeching tires and honking horns. Jenna had planned her route with the expectation that none of the drivers would stop for her, but some of them tried anyway, slamming on their brakes or swerving out of their lane even though these late reflex actions were unnecessary. It took less than two seconds for the Mini to traverse the intersection, but that was long enough to transform the crossing into total chaos.

With the intersection snarled, Jenna seized the opportunity to put some distance between herself and the chase cars. She stomped on the gas pedal, and pushed the little car faster. The speedometer registered fifty...sixty...seventy miles per hour. Pedestrians on the sidewalk flashed by so fast that she couldn't make out their features. Cars in the oncoming lanes were a blur. In the rapidly diminishing distance, she saw a traffic light—green— marking the next intersection. This time, there was no need to plot a safe route through. She passed beneath the light before it could so much as flicker yellow.

The road shrank to five lanes, two on either side and an escape lane in the middle. While Sunday traffic remained light, the cars traveling in the same direction loomed closer. Despite the Mini's superior handling, she was going much too fast to weave between them. She was about to ease her foot off the accelerator when she spied something new in the rearview: the distinctive flashing red and blue lights of a police car.

She mentally kicked herself. She had been so focused on escaping the killers, it had not occurred to her that her escape was not happening in a vacuum. The most probable explanation was that one of the irate drivers from the intersection had taken a moment to call 911 on a cell phone, reporting a blue Mini Cooper driving recklessly.

Surrendering to the police wasn't an option. Even if she found someone to believe her crazy story, the killers wouldn't be intimidated by legitimate law enforcement officers any more than the bogus FBI agents that had shot Noah and the two deputies. They wouldn't even need to use force. They would simply flash their government credentials, claim jurisdiction and take her away. And if any well-intentioned policemen got in their way, there would be more blood on her hands.

The realization that she was now being pursued by government hitmen *and* the police underscored the urgency of ditching the Mini. She needed to find a place where she could quickly blend in with a crowd—a mall, or maybe the beach if she could find it.

She swerved into the center lane and blasted past a cluster of cars moving at half her speed. In her mirror, she saw the vehicles pulling to the side, making room for the police cruisers. There were two sets of police lights now and they were closing fast. The Mini's turbo engine might have outclassed the motor pool cars driven by her pursuers, but the police cruisers had a lot more horsepower under the hood. If she kept going in a straight line, they would catch her, and the killers wouldn't be far behind.

Another intersection loomed. The light was red, and cars streamed across her path at normal commuting speeds. Gripping the steering wheel, she began murmuring, "Green light, green light," and as if by a miracle, the light changed when she was just fifty yards away.

It was almost enough to make her believe that her mad scientist creator had imbued her with telekinetic powers...but no, it was probably just a lucky coincidence.

The idle speculation was shattered as something flashed into view on her left, a beat-up muscle car blowing through the light, blissfully unaware of the blue rocket hurtling into the intersection.

Jenna's reflexes took over. She pushed the accelerator harder, feeling the turbo charger respond almost instantly. Her subconscious mind grasped that going left, trying to slip behind the red-light violator, would end disastrously, so she angled to the right, trying to cut in front of him.

It almost worked.

The man at the wheel of the beater must have caught a glimpse of the onrushing Mini. Instead of trying to stop, he accelerated, trying to get out of her way. He succeeded only in changing what would have been a near miss into a glancing impact.

Jenna barely felt the front corner of the muscle car kiss the back bumper of the Mini, but the transfer of energy spun the little car around like a top. The Mini's low center of gravity kept it on the road, but for uncountable seconds, it pirouetted out of control, its smoking tires laying down a lotus-shaped spiral of rubber in the middle of the intersection.

Jenna's head continued to spin for a few more seconds after the car came to rest, but a bright light shining in her eyes and the too-loud wail of approaching police sirens brought her back to the moment. She blinked, vaguely aware that she was unhurt and only mildly disoriented. Then she realized that the light still shining in her eyes was the rising sun. The Mini's wild dance had left her facing east.

East it is.

She pushed the gas pedal to the floor, but nothing happened.

Jenna felt a wave of panic start to build. Her instincts had guided her through this long ordeal, but now her inexperience had caught up with her.

Get out. Run.

No. It just stalled. The spin reversed engine compression, just like the pin maneuver Noah told me about. I just need to restart.

There's no time.

She ignored the frantic urgings of her fearful brain and heeded the calm inner voice of reason. The police would arrive at any moment. Even if it took a few seconds to get the car started, she would get a lot farther than if she attempted to escape on foot.

As if being graded by her driving instructor, she put a foot on the brake, shifted into park, and reached for the key.

The keyhole was empty.

She remembered the remoter start button on the fob. The keys lay forgotten on the passenger seat, partially buried under a scattering of what looked like tiny diamonds—the shattered remains of the tempered glass window. She found the key, squeezed the button several times, and felt panic replaced by elation as the engine turned over and began purring once more.

Shift. Gas pedal. Go.

The Mini jumped forward like a sprinter at the sound of the starter's gun, as two police cars screeched into the intersection. The twin vehicles, normally a symbol of help and safety, took on the monstrous appearances of hungry ancient demons racing to devour her. The roar of their engines helped complete the impression, but only served to motivate Jenna further. She crushed the gas pedal down, increasing the distance between herself and the monsters behind her, but rushing headlong into a third.

THIRTY-NINE

6:58 a.m.

Despite the glare of the sun in her eyes, Jenna spied another set of flashing lights ahead. A third police cruiser was responding to a call for backup. In the instant it took for her to register this fact, the approaching vehicle abruptly cut across her lane and stopped, blocking a portion of the road.

But not enough.

Jenna swung to the left without slowing. The Mini bumped over the curb and kept going, two wheels on the road and two on the sidewalk. A gaggle of pedestrians who had stopped to watch the mayhem dove out of the way, but Jenna was already past the roadblock and steered back onto the asphalt. As she did, she spied a sign post with the distinctive blue and red shield logo of the Interstate highway system.

Jenna felt a glimmer of hope. Even on the freeway—especially on the freeway—the chances of eluding pursuit were slim, but at least she would have a sense of where she was and where the road led.

The failed roadblock bought her a few more seconds of lead time, and after just a few more blocks, she spied the freeway overpass and another sign directing her to the onramp. She slowed just enough to make the gradual right turn and then accelerated again, weaving through a knot of cars heading for the Interstate.

The freeway lowered into view. She had never driven on a major highway, never even ridden along on one, and her first glimpse was a bit of a letdown. She had imagined a daunting river of cars, whipping by like Formula One racers. Instead, she saw only a scattering of vehicles—cars, SUVs, even a few eighteen-wheelers—none of which were moving any faster than she was now.

The onramp shunted her into the flow of traffic and just like that she was transported to a different reality. A concrete wall rose up on her right, eclipsing her view of the city streets she had been on only a moment before. A low barrier separated the northbound and southbound lanes, and beyond that, across more lanes, rose another wall. Jenna understood that, while the freeway might speed her on her way, it would also confine her like a hamster in a Habitrail tube.

Maybe the freeway wasn't such a great idea.

In the distance, she could make out a green sign marking the next exit. The police had yet to appear in her rearview. If she could make it to that exit—wherever it led—unseen, she might be able to...

There was a subtle shift in her center of gravity, and she heard something change in the purr of the Mini's engine. She pressed down on the gas pedal again, but the deceleration continued. The speedometer revealed the slowdown. With each passing second, the vehicle lost ten miles per hour. The emergency flashers activated, ticking away.

The cars, which had only a moment before been falling away in her wake, now caught up and blew past her, honking in irritation. She had to get to the side of the road before the Mini came to a complete stop and got plowed by an unsuspecting motorist. The move used up the last of the car's momentum. It came to rest beneath the imposing wall, at least half a mile from the exit.

Jenna took a deep breath, willing herself to stay calm, and she worked through the steps to restart the motor, but this time nothing happened. She pushed the button on the key fob repeatedly with no effect, and a sickening realization came to her. In addition to the remote starter, Cort's Mini Cooper was also equipped with a theft-prevention lock-down system.

She reached for the door handle but found it locked and likewise unresponsive. *Shut down and locked in.* Fortunately, the passenger side window had already been shot out. There was just enough room between the car and the wall for her to squeeze out.

The freeway was a deluge of sensation. The sound of cars whooshing past. Engine noise. The rumble of tires on pavement. All of it rising and falling, distorted by the Doppler effect. The smells of exhaust and hot rubber assaulted her nose. And beneath it all, a faint but persistent vibration, as if the elevated road might at any moment break apart, dropping her and all the passing cars into an abyss. It was an inhospitable world, an alien planet not meant to be traveled on foot.

The exit sign seemed unreachably distant. She glanced back into the rush of approaching cars. Still no sign of the police, but she did not fail to notice a dark speck, low in the sky and almost certainly headed for her. Not a drone this time. A helicopter.

Move!

She didn't know whether it was the voice of panic or of reason, or if for once, both were in agreement, but the inner admonition was as obvious as it was unhelpful. It would take several minutes, even at a run, to reach the far off exit, and she would be in the open the whole way.

On the far side of the highway, treetops rose above the concrete wall, hinting at the ordinary world beyond, and inspiration dawned. She glanced up and saw, directly above her, the green frill of a palm, gently waving above the top of the wall.

The wall appeared insurmountable, a sheer vertical barrier at least twenty feet high, with no handholds. *Too bad the mad scientist didn't give me sticky Spider-Man hands*, she thought, but the bitter reminder of her bizarre origin triggered another memory.

You're smarter, stronger. Hell, there are things you probably don't even know you're capable of doing.

She wasn't a mutant superhero, but she could jump. *Really* jump. She was the only person in her school who could slam dunk a basketball, an ability that both impressed and repelled boys.

Well, it's worth a shot.

She scrambled onto the hood of the stalled Mini and then up onto its roof. The surface dimpled under her weight with a faint pop. From this new vantage, the wall didn't look quite as daunting, but it was still higher than she had ever jumped before.

Never know if I don't try.

Unbidden, the calculations played out in her head—where to step, the amount of vertical thrust required to get her high enough. She hopped back down onto the hood, pivoted, compressed herself like a spring, and then uncoiled.

In two short seconds, she landed back on the roof, having missed the top of the wall by a foot. Anger welled inside her. *So close*, she thought, wanting something to punch. Freedom was just a foot beyond her reach.

With an explosion of breath—a *kiai* shout that was caught away in the wind of passing cars—she leapt skyward again. The semi-rigid fiberglass roof absorbed some of her energy, but there was still more power in her legs than she would have believed possible. She swung her arms up, adding their momentum to the overall effort. This time, her fingertips rose above the top of the wall.

Her hands came down on smooth concrete, but before her weight could fully settle onto them, she brought the soles of her borrowed deck shoes against the vertical surface of the wall and pushed off.

It shouldn't have worked, but somehow it did. Her fingers hooked over the back edge of the wall and locked in place. Her scrabbling feet fought against the inexorable pull of gravity, and she managed to climb higher still. She got her forearms onto the wall, elbows locking over the top to hold her in place.

There was another surge of pain in her wounded biceps. If she had been hanging from her fingertips, she would have fallen back down, probably breaking a leg or worse in the process, but she did not fall. Instead, she fought through the pain and heaved her upper torso onto the top of the wall.

She pushed herself up, straddling the concrete barrier, hugging it close. To her left, the top of the Mini and the freeway seemed distant, but to her right, the open ground below the highway looked more like the bottom of the Grand Canyon.

Why did I think this was good idea?

The faint chopping sound of the approaching helicopter answered her question.

A long row of tall palm trees rose up alongside the freeway like sentinels, but now they did not look quite as close as before. She chose to trust her instincts and the unrealized potential in her body that had gotten her this far. She had to keep going.

She scooted back until she was under the broad leaves of the nearest palm. She judged the distance to the spindle-straight trunk. *Eight feet.* It was shorter than her best standing long jump. Of course, she had never attempted a jump from an eight-inch wide strip of concrete, and a sand pit was a lot more forgiving than a tree trunk, but that wouldn't stop her. Compared to scaling the wall, leaping onto a tree seemed a more doable task.

The hardest part was letting go. She got her feet under her, maintaining contact with the wall, rose to a crouch, and then launched herself across the gap. A low hanging frond slapped her cheek at the top of her arc, and then she fell. Her arms and legs spread wide, and in the instant before contact, she wrapped them around the trunk, hugging it to her. She gripped the cheese-grater rough surface fiercely. When she was sure the fall had ceased, she relaxed her legs and stretched her body toward the ground. Then she squeezed the trunk between her thighs and relaxed her arms, crunching her body into a fetal curl.

She didn't dare slide. The rough exterior of the palm would tear through her clothes and skin, if the friction didn't set her on fire first. Instead, she methodically wriggled down the palm, like an undulating caterpillar. Each move brought her a few inches closer to the ground. The cumulative effect of clenching and unclenching, hugging and relaxing, caused her muscles to burn with lactic acid, but she soon fell into a mechanical rhythm, one cycle per second. She counted them out under her breath just as she had counted down the timer on the bomb—six alligators, seven alligators, eight. She reckoned it would take about two hundred alligators to reach the bottom, and she was pleasantly surprised when, at one hundred and sixty-eight, her feet touched solid ground.

She collapsed onto the grassy strip that ran between the base of the freeway and the parallel frontage road. She was amazed that she had been able to hold on as long as she had. As she lay there, letting the acid warmth drain away, she kept counting, and when she reached two hundred, she rolled onto hands and knees and stood up on rubbery legs.

That was when the sky erupted with a thunderous roar. The helicopter had found her.

FORTY

7:10 a.m.

Jenna ran. After a few steps, her legs remembered how to work and she picked up speed. Fatigue melted from her muscles, fueled by an urgency to escape the helicopter's gaze. The aircraft hovered, as if indifferent to her efforts, but it managed to stay right above her.

The road that ran parallel to the Interstate was mostly closed off. The freeway formed an impenetrable wall to her left, and to her right, across the empty street, was a long swath of vegetation— trees, tall grass and shrubs, which occasionally parted to reveal a chain-link fence underneath. She ran south, but only because it was the direction she had been facing when the helicopter had found her. Turning around, or thinking about which way to go, would have cost her precious seconds.

A T-junction lay ahead, a cross street that didn't pass beneath the freeway. A sidelong glance revealed a few commercial buildings behind tall fences, but nothing that would facilitate her escape. She kept going.

The next street *did* pass under the Interstate, and as she angled toward the opening, she glanced up at the helicopter as if daring it to follow. The helicopter was black with no markings. Its sleek aerodynamic fuselage gave the impression of a menacing wasp. *Definitely not a police helicopter*, she thought, and ran even faster. The pilot dipped the aircraft forward to block her path with the whirling rotor blades, but he was either too slow or too cautious. Jenna ducked around the corner...

And skidded to a dead stop.

Two police cars, emergency lights flashing, raced toward her, just seconds away from the underpass.

Jenna spun around and raced back out, directly beneath the helicopter. Her mind raced through her options. She had survived the Villegas brothers, taken out Zack's entire hit squad and knocked a drone out of the sky—she could figure out a solution to this problem, too. But no matter how she looked at the pieces, a winning strategy did not come. She was on foot, alone, in an unfamiliar environment, with no time and no choices.

Another police cruiser approached from the opposite direction, half a block away. She cut to the left, trying to reach the road she'd come from, but the police car turned across her path, blocking that route. The other two patrol cars shot past and cut in front of her.

Doors flew open, and the three police officers emerged as one, as if they had rehearsed the move for maximum effect. All three had their guns drawn and pointed at Jenna. She could tell that they were shouting, probably ordering her to get down—to 'grab the pavement,' as the ill-fated Deputy Jimmy might have put it—but their voices were drowned out by the tumult of the helicopter directly above.

There was nowhere to go.

She raised her hands, sensing that if she did not, the officers might very well shoot. The reserves of energy she had tapped for the futile sprint shut off. She dropped to her knees, more out of exhaustion than surrender.

Don't give up, she told herself. *An opportunity will come, be ready to seize it.*

More police cars were coming from every direction. The knot was tightening. Two civilian cars—a pair of familiar-looking generic sedans—joined the parade. The last glimmer of hope faded away.

Jenna didn't think the police would shoot her or that the government hit men would do so out in the open, so the loud report—louder than anything she had ever heard—caught her off guard. She started, astonished to see the three officers dive for cover behind their vehicles.

The shot—*no, make that* shots, *plural*—had come from the helicopter, and hadn't been aimed at her. A glance up revealed a man, framed by the open side door of the aircraft, sitting behind a machine gun. The gunner loosed another burst that stitched a row of holes across a police cruiser's hood, but then Jenna lost sight of him as the helicopter pivoted away, turning in a slow circle above her. More shots followed. Short bursts sparked off the three police cars, keeping the officers down. The helicopter corkscrewed closer to the ground, closer to Jenna.

The bold attack was eerily reminiscent of what had occurred behind the bait shop, and Jenna realized why as the helicopter completed a full rotation and she got another look at the gunner. It was the man who had identified himself as Special Agent Cray of the FBI—the man who had killed Noah.

Jenna turned away, estimating the distance to the nearest police car. She wondered if her legs would carry her that far. Probably not fast enough to outrun a burst from Cray's machine gun.

"Jenna!" His voice was nearly drowned out by the rotor wash and engine noise, but she heard him repeat the same exhortation he had made twelve hours earlier. "We're not going to hurt you!"

Why not? She wondered. *Why haven't you killed me already?*

Noah's whispered warning to the deputy echoed again in her head. *Those men are not federal agents. You absolutely must not let them put my daughter in their vehicle.*

Zack had showed no interest in winning her trust, and Cort had made it clear that the government wanted her dead, no matter the consequences. Cray had tried to capture her alive, and now he was driving the police back, providing cover for her to...what exactly?

"Get in!" Cray's shout was louder, probably because the helicopter was just a few feet above the ground, a few feet from where she knelt, statue still.

If they had wanted her dead, they would have killed her already, which meant...

We're not going to hurt you.

But Cray had shot Noah.

Not federal agents.

Then who the hell are you?

There was another report, but it wasn't from Cray's gun. The single staccato pop—like a distant firecracker—had come from the outer perimeter. Cray jerked back as something struck the side of the fuselage, too close for comfort. Then he swiveled his weapon in the direction of the new threat.

Jenna couldn't believe the police would try to bring the helicopter down. Trying to shoot the tires out of a speeding car was one thing, but there was no telling how much damage an out-of-control helicopter might cause if it crashed. As more shots tore into the air, she realized that she had made two incorrect assumptions. The first was that it was the police shooting. It wasn't. It was Cort's friends from the safe house. The second assumption was worse. They weren't shooting at the helicopter—they were shooting at her.

That simplified things.

She met Cray's eyes, nodded to signal her intention and then waited for him to fire another long burst. As soon as the gun fell silent, she leaped up and threw herself past Cray and into the helicopter.

She heard Cray, or maybe it was someone else, shouting, "We've got her. Go! Go!" Then something like an invisible hand pressed her down against the deck. The helicopter ascended, and judging by the g-forces pushing against her and the strident whine of the turbine engines, it was rising fast.

She waited, unmoving, curious to see the consequences of her choice. Would they slap handcuffs on her? Inject her with a tranquilizer? Or simply hold her at gunpoint while they whisked her off to some secret prison facility?

After several seconds, it became apparent that nothing of the sort was going to happen, so she cautiously raised her head.

Cray was still manning the gun, peering out across an urban landscape that was now dizzyingly distant. His was not the only face she recognized. The man who had posed as his partner during the confrontation at the marina was there as well. He nodded in her direction, though the meaning of the gesture was unclear. The riddle of his gesture was quickly forgotten when she saw the other two people seated in the small cabin.

The man was a stranger, but she could tell just by looking at him that he wasn't a professional killer or a government secret agent. He didn't have that hard edge that she had noticed in Cort, and looking back, that Noah had always possessed. Thin and bookish, with hair gone gray, he looked more like an accountant or a college professor. Whatever his role, he was staring at Jenna as if...

As if I'm his long lost daughter.

No.

No way.

It was almost as unbelievable as the identity of the other passenger.

Mercedes Reyes smiled and opened her arms to embrace Jenna. "Honey, if you keep ditching me, I'm going to start taking it personally."

FORTY-ONE

7:15 a.m.

"How...?" Before she could figure out exactly what she was trying to ask, a very different realization dawned. It had been right in front of her, nearly all her life, as obvious as her own reflection in a mirror. "Mercy, are you...like me?"

Mercy's anxious glance at the older man was answer enough, but before either of them could elaborate, Cray's partner gestured to an empty seat. "Better buckle up. This could get a little rough."

The helicopter was tilted forward and accelerating, so the deck on which she lay was slightly askew. *Just like my life*, Jenna thought as she crawled to the chair.

She couldn't help staring at Mercy, at the woman who looked so much like her, who was so similar to her in temperament and interests. Thirty-six-year-old Mercedes Reyes, a Cuban émigré—*Cuba? Of course. It makes perfect sense now*—had insisted that she couldn't be Jenna's mother, that she hadn't even met Noah until Jenna was three...but then everything Noah had told her was a lie. Had Mercy been in the compound that night? Had she survived and come to America in search of her...sister? Daughter? Clone?

Mercy had known—known Noah's secret, known the truth about Jenna's mysterious past. *Why didn't she tell me?*

"Why didn't you tell me?"

The helicopter dipped forward and Jenna's stomach rose into her mouth as the aircraft made a roller-coaster steep plunge earthward. Cray pulled himself back from the doorway and slid it closed, blocking her view of the journey. Without looking, she could visualize the helicopter's movements in the sky above Miami.

The second phony FBI agent gestured to the headphones that he and everyone else wore. Then he pointed over Jenna's shoulder to a similar headset. She took the headphones and slipped them over her ears, blocking out most of the engine noise.

"Can you hear me?" the man asked. His voice, electronically reproduced, was eerily out of sync with the movements of his mouth, but she could hear him.

"Loud and clear," she replied, and heard her own voice over the intercom, just a fraction of second later.

"Just hang on," he advised. "We're going to be flying pretty low to avoid radar detection. The last thing we need right now is for the Air National Guard to scramble a couple of interceptors. That would really spoil our day."

The helicopter banked hard, then performed a series of rapid, stomach-churning maneuvers that made further conversation impossible. Jenna risked a glance through the side window, half expecting to see fighter jets streaking past, but she saw only the concrete and glass towers of downtown Miami.

"Nothing to worry about," Cray volunteered, as if sensing Jenna's anxiety. "We're just trying to confuse anyone who's looking for us."

As promised, the helicopter soon leveled out, and Jenna's stomach settled. A few minutes later she felt the craft descending, and shortly thereafter, the landing gear bumped against something solid.

Cray threw open the door to reveal the tarmac of an airport. A quick look around told Jenna that they were probably at Miami International or a nearby satellite airfield. The helicopter had set down a short distance from a hangar building, but as she stepped down onto solid ground, Cray guided her in the opposite direction, toward a waiting airplane. Jenna was not well versed in aircraft identification, but just a glance told her that the only thing this jet had in common with Carlos's plane was wings.

"Gulfstream IV," Cray said, as he followed her up the fold-down stairs, into the luxurious cabin. "It will get us where we need to be in about two hours."

"And where exactly is that?"

"Somewhere safe. Where I can answer all your questions." She had been expecting Cray to answer, but instead it was the old man's voice she heard. His tone was soft, and he spoke with an almost musical cadence. He ascended into the cabin, walking with the aid of an ebony cane. He settled into a chair right next to Jenna. Mercy sat across the aisle.

We're going to Cuba, Jenna guessed. *Right back where it all started*. It occurred to Jenna that, by choosing to go with them, she had completely relinquished her independence. For twelve hours, the responsibility for her survival had been hers alone. Now, her fate was in the hands of strangers. Even Mercy was an unknown. She suddenly felt very helpless.

At least I won't die ignorant. She turned her gaze back to Mercy. "Tell me the truth. Are you my mom?"

Mercy glanced at the old man again before meeting Jenna's eyes. "Honey, it's a long story."

The old man reached out and gave Mercy's hand a pat. "She has a right to know." He turned to look at Jenna. "Besides, we've got the time, and goodness knows you've waited long enough."

Jenna blinked at him. "*Who* are you?"

The man's eyebrows drew together in a frown of irritation. "My dear, I apologize for not making proper introductions. My name is Helio Soter, and I... Well, I guess you could say that I made you."

Jenna got the sense that Soter expected her to be shocked by the news, but coming on the heels of everything else, his vague declaration was both unsurprising and woefully inadequate. "Cort said that I was a clone. Is that true?"

The old man chuckled. "A clone? Well, I suppose that's not entirely inaccurate. But calling you 'a clone' would be like saying that the Mona Lisa is a painting. It's strictly true, but hardly does justice to what you truly are."

Jenna turned to Mercy, who nodded to confirm that Sotor was not exaggerating.

There was a brief interruption as the plane was readied for departure, and then Jenna felt motion once more. Just a few hours ago, she had never been on an aircraft. Now, she was about to embark on her third trip into the sky, yet somehow the experience had already lost its novelty. She was much more interested in hearing what Soter had to say.

A few minutes later, when they were cruising through the sky, Soter resumed speaking. "Cloning is a rather generic and dated term for duplicating cells from a sample of genetic material. Scientists have been cloning cells, tissue, even entire animals, for decades.

A clone is nothing but a carbon copy, and most clones are imperfect copies at best."

"Cort showed me pictures of people, men and women, who looked almost identical to me. And her." She pointed at Mercy. "Was I cloned from you, Mercy? Is that how this works?"

"Jenna, you aren't a clone," Sotor insisted. He drew in an appreciative breath. "You are so much more."

"I don't understand." That was not entirely true. *Smarter, stronger...dangerous.* "If I'm not a duplicate, what am I? A different version? Like Human 2.0?"

A faint smile touched Soter's lips. "I couldn't have put it better."

Jenna stared at Soter, then at Mercy. She knew that Mercy was in her late thirties—thirty-six if she had been telling the truth, though that seemed pretty doubtful now. She would have been born in the late 1970s, back when cloning was definitely more the stuff of science fiction. She turned back to Soter. "I think I've got this figured out. You took some of Mercy's DNA, spliced in the Mutant X gene, and started growing super-soldier test-tube babies for the Soviet Union."

Soter's smile broadened and then he started to laugh. "Those are some remarkable conclusions, my dear. Unfortunately, they are largely incorrect conclusions."

Jenna felt her face reddening. She was rarely wrong about anything, and to have this man laughing at her...teasing her with the promise of information, like the candy in a piñata at a child's birthday party, and then laughing when, blind and disoriented, she struck only air...

"Then fucking help me fill in the gaps," she said in a tight cold voice.

The man's smile faded some. "To begin with, I have never worked for the Russian government."

Jenna wasn't sure she believed him, but she had only Cort's statements as evidence against him. Noah hadn't written exactly where the facility was located. Cuba made sense, though it wasn't the only island in Hurricane Alley. "Then who do you work for?"

Soter's smile softened into a more thoughtful expression. "What a marvelous question. My research is funded by the US government, but the work I do is for the benefit of all humankind."

Jenna considered this boast in the light of what Cort had told her. "From what I've heard, your genetically modified clones are about to start World War III. Is that part of the plan to benefit humankind?"

Soter winced. She had struck a nerve. When he spoke again however, he did not answer her directly. "I fear I may have given you the wrong impression of me. You see, I don't actually know anything about genetic modifications. I'm not that kind of scientist."

"Then what kind of scientist are you?"

"I dabble in this and that, but my formal training is in the field of mathematics."

Mathematics? That didn't make any sense. Despite some serious disagreements, Cort and Soter were in agreement on one point: Jenna and the others were the result of a genetic experiment, and Soter had already claimed to be the genius behind it all. "Why is a mathematician involved in a cloning experiment?"

"That, my dear, is the long story that I will tell you now."

SIGNAL

FORTY-TWO

It took him a moment to realize that he wasn't alone. He dropped his burden, a thick sheaf of accordion-folded computer paper, on his desktop and glanced over his shoulder at the man seated in the chair by the door.

The glance told him what the man was *not*.

Not a member of the mathematics department or even, to the best of his knowledge, a faculty member.

Not a student—he was too old and too well dressed.

Not a visiting professor—too young and too well dressed. The man's clothes and bearing marked him as an outsider, not merely a stranger in the physical sense, but someone completely unfamiliar with the environment and culture in which he now found himself, unaware of just how out of place he was.

A lawyer.

The man stood and extended a hand. "Are you Dr. Helio Soter?"

Soter was a little surprised to hear the correct pronunciation of his name. Most people meeting him for the first time mangled it—*Heel-ee-oh Saw-ter* being the most common. Sometimes he would patiently explain: "The 'h' is silent and the 'e' sounds like a long 'a'. Ay-lee-oh. And Soter rhymes with 'motor' not 'water.'"

He wondered if it was a bad sign that this stranger, who looked an awful lot like a lawyer, already knew how to say his name correctly, but the man had offered his hand. Soter took it. "I am. What's this about?"

"You are needed for an estimate, sir."

It took Soter a few seconds to grasp that the man was not asking for him to perform a mathematical task. "You're from ONE?"

The man's cheek twitched a little, as if Soter had spoken out of turn, but he nodded. "Please, come with me."

"I'm giving a lecture in ten minutes. You'll have to—"

"Cancel it." The man's tone indicated that further debate would be futile.

Ten minutes later, when he should have been introducing himself to a hall full of graduate students, Soter found himself in the passenger seat of a Ford Granada, the campus of the Massachusetts Institute of Technology shrinking in the rear view mirror. He made no inquiries about where they were going or what was expected of him. The driver seemed a very tight-lipped sort of fellow, and someone would answer Sotor's questions soon enough. After all, he couldn't very well give them an estimate if they didn't provide data.

An estimate. He found the euphemism rather amusing. He routinely used estimation in the course of his mathematical and statistical research, so it was almost ironic that the men from ONE— the Office of National Estimates—would utilize his expertise in formulating their predictions about world affairs. Indeed, the process of correlating intelligence and drawing probable conclusions was highly mathematical in nature, so all other things being equal, it was probably an appropriate term. Unfortunately, there were factors that always remained elusive in any equation— human variables—and that made all the difference between a well-founded estimate and a best guess.

ONE, a division of the Central Intelligence Agency, had been founded in the aftermath of the biggest intelligence failure since Pearl

Harbor—the Communist invasion of the Republic of Korea in 1950. It had resulted in a two-year long open conflict, and an ongoing state of war that persisted nearly thirty years later. The problem had not been a failure of intelligence, but rather a failure to draw accurate conclusions—estimates—based on available information. In the three decades that had followed, ONE had broadened their scope of influence somewhat to include operations, which Soter supposed, was a way of making sure that inaccurate estimations could be steered back on track. But that didn't concern the mathematician. His job was simply to deal with the numbers.

The Granada pulled up at the Hotel Eliot, and the driver let Soter out. "They're waiting for you," the man said. "Room 237."

Soter nodded and headed inside. Clandestine meetings in hotel rooms were standard for ONE, even when the subject of the estimate did not seem to warrant extraordinary secrecy. The meetings weren't that much of an inconvenience, and they paid him well.

He took the stairs to the second floor. A short walk down the hall brought him to the door, which opened before he could knock. A man he did not recognize—older than the driver, and wearing an even better suit—stood aside and motioned for him to enter.

The room was heavy with cigarette smoke, but Soter saw three more men seated at a small table. One of them stood up and gestured for Soter to take his chair. He did not recognize any of the men, and while that wasn't unusual—he had never dealt with the same person twice—it was strange to see so many representatives of ONE in the same place.

A single sheet of paper lay on the tabletop in front of him. A cursory glance revealed numbers, or more precisely typed digits. There were a lot of 1s, but a few 3s and 4s. The arrangement looked like a scatter plot of statistical data, but without a context, Soter couldn't begin to guess at their significance. Someone had drawn a circle around a vertical column of six digits...no, not just digits. There were letters as well, but only in the circle.

6 E Q U J 5

The same pen had also drawn circles around a 6 and a 7, and then to the left of the numbers scrawled a single word: *Wow!*

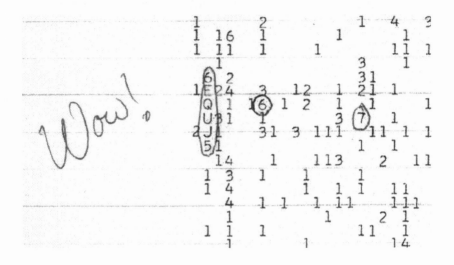

Soter studied the characters in the circle a moment longer, then took another look at the paper itself. There were no indentations on the page from the ballpoint pen that had drawn the circles and written the exclamation. It was, he realized, a copy made on a Xerox machine.

"What is it?" he asked, looking up.

The man across the table took a long drag on his cigarette, then said, "You tell us."

So that's how it's going to be, Soter thought. He looked at the paper again, ignoring the handwritten modifications and focused on the printed values instead. "Okay. This is a computer printout. The digits probably represent numbers—"

One of them men at the table snorted. "No kidding."

"Numbers have a discrete value," Soter explained, "while digits or numerals are merely symbols that may indicate numbers, or something else entirely." He pointed to the printout. "Here. Read left to right we have '111' but does that signify one hundred and eleven, or is it three separate figures, each with a value of one? Or are the digits a substitution cipher? Perhaps we should replace 1 with the letter A..."

He trailed off, no longer caring about making his point. The circled column of numbers told him that the figures were meant to be interpreted vertically, and that each character was a separate value. Something about the circled string looked very familiar.

"Each character is a number," he said again, this time with more confidence. "The use of letters would indicate numerical values greater than nine. The numbers in the circle are actually...give me a pen."

A pen was passed over, and Soter quickly began writing an alphanumeric key.

A=10
B=11
C=12
D=13
...

When he had found a numerical value for each letter in the sequence, he wrote out a new set of numbers:

6, 14, 26, 30, 19, 5

"Okay, these are the actual values of the alphanumerical characters." Soter hastily sketched a graph and plotted the points in order.

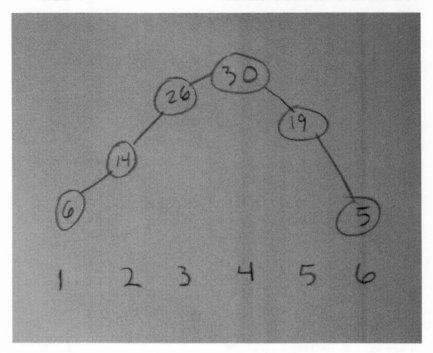

One of the men at the table shook his head and muttered, "Damn, that was fast."

Soter met the gaze of the smoking man. "You already knew this, I take it?"

"We're not trying to be coy, Dr. Soter. It's important that we get your unbiased impressions."

The other man—the one who had been impressed by his speed—added, "When you hear where this came from, it's going to blow your mind."

Soter thought about the hand-written note on the print-out and decided that the man wasn't merely being dramatic. "Well, if I had to guess, I'd say it's a frequency table."

"Radio frequencies."

It was an odd thing to say, and odder still, it didn't sound like a question. "No. In this case, it's the frequency of whatever event these data are recording. These numbers all add up to one hundred, so this is probably an expression of percentages. Most are in the middle...average. That's the peak here. The sum of these two values in the middle is fifty-six, slightly more than half. Further out, you have two smaller groups that are slightly above or below average, and then out on the edges, even smaller groups that are extremely above or below average." He shrugged. "This is a textbook probability curve."

The smoking man's face drew into a frown, and he snatched the paper. After studying it for a few seconds, he shook his head. "I'll be damned. They do add up to a hundred. How did they miss that?"

Soter glanced at the assembled group. "Gentlemen, I can continue to make uninformed guesses if you'd like, but I suspect I'll have better luck making sense of these data if you'll tell me where they came from."

The men in the room looked at each other for a moment, and arrived at a silent consensus. The smoking man spoke again. "Dr. Soter, the data here are radio frequencies, received at a listening station in Ohio. You were correct in pointing out that the digits are not precise numerical values. They are actually indicators of signal intensity. The highest value there—thirty—indicates a signal that is thirty times stronger than normal. So you see, it's literally a frequency table, but not in the sense you thought it was."

"I don't think you brought me here just for some anomalous radio signal. What's really going on?"

"The listening post I refer to is the Big Ear radio telescope, part of the Ohio State SETI project."

SETI! Soter recognized the acronym immediately. "This is a transmission from space? From *extraterrestrials?*"

"It is from space," the smoking man confirmed. "It appears to originate somewhere in the constellation of Sagittarius. It's too soon to say if there is an intelligence behind it, but it is remarkable for several reasons. To begin with, the peak intensity of the signal was about 1420.4 MHz. To give you a frame of reference, that's in the Ultra High Frequency range. HAM radios operate in the 1300 MHz range. This signal—we're calling it the Wow! Signal for obvious reasons—happens to fall at the precise bandwidth of hydrogen, which is the sort of thing astronomers look for as an indicator of extraterrestrial intelligence.

"The spike in intensity was caused by the rotation of the Earth. The signal was constant, but the telescope's window of observation was only oriented toward the source for seventy-two seconds. That was five days ago. On successive passes, the Big Ear failed to detect the signal again."

Soter digested this for a moment. "What do you want from me?"

"It is critically important that we determine whether or not this signal is a broadcast from an alien intelligence. If it is, we need to figure out what it's saying. I don't need to tell you that mathematics is a universal language. If anyone can decode this transmission, it's you."

Soter reached out for the paper, looked at it again, then shook it in the air. "This isn't a transmission. There's nothing to decode here."

"Dr. Soter, in thirty seconds, you saw a pattern that no one else did."

"That isn't a pattern," Soter protested. "It's a fluke. A coincidence."

"Do you really believe that?"

Soter tapped the circled values. "You said it yourself. These numbers weren't part of the transmission. They were generated by the computer program that monitors the intensity of the signal."

"If the intelligence behind this transmission understood our capabilities, what better way to send a message?"

"In order to do that...in order to produce that exact sequence of values, it would require precise synchronization—to the nanosecond— as well as knowledge of the precise calibration of our equipment, and all that across light years of space. This signal might have originated years ago, centuries even. It would require extraordinary computing power, advanced intelligence, to say nothing of the ability to see into the future."

"That's exactly what concerns me, Dr. Soter." The man stubbed out his cigarette. "Take this apart. Assume that there's a message here. Find it. Can you do that?"

Soter frowned and looked at the paper again. What if the man was right? What if there were other patterns hidden in the signal?

6, 14, 26, 30, 19, 5

Don't think of them as numbers. They are symbols. What do they represent? Spatial coordinates? Dates? Times? Elements on the periodic table?

"I can't do it alone. I'm going to need experts—astronomers, cryptologists, xenobiologists."

"We'll put together a team...wait, xenobiologists? What're those?"

"It's a new field. Theoretical biology, predicting how life might evolve on other worlds."

The man grunted. "You'll have whatever you need."

"It could take a while. And I have other obligations."

"Not any more. This is your number one priority now, Dr. Soter."

To his complete surprise, Soter was not the least bit bothered by the prospect.

FORTY-THREE

November 28, 1977
8:05 a.m. (local time)

"We have made contact!" Jerry Zavada shouted, waving a newspaper as he swept into the room where Soter had set up his office.

Soter felt his pulse quicken. He had resigned himself to the failure of this latest attempt to interpret the Wow! Signal, but now it seemed that Zavada, the computer engineer, had discovered some new insight.

In the newspaper? That didn't make any sense.

"Here!" Zavada laid the tabloid on the desk and tapped a headline. It read: "Message From the Stars."

Soter had seem similar headlines when news of the Wow! Signal had gotten out, but this seemed to be referring to something that had happened just two days earlier. He began reading aloud.

"Residents of Southampton received a shock Saturday evening when their local news broadcast was interrupted by a mysterious transmission, purporting to be a message from an intergalactic visitor. Over the next few minutes, viewers heard the 'voice of Asteron'—" He stopped abruptly.

"The voice of Asteron? Seriously, Jerry?"

Zavada chuckled. "Just trying to lighten the mood."

Soter threw the paper down in disgust. The tabloid lay atop the thick printout he had been reviewing. The story of a hoaxster hijacking a television broadcast to spout hippie propaganda, and the data from their survey had one thing in common: neither contained an actual message from an extraterrestrial intelligence.

He had known, from the moment he had accepted this crazy assignment, it would probably amount to nothing. The odds against the Wow! Signal actually being a transmission from an alien life form were...well, astronomical. And the likelihood that there was an actual message contained in the data was an order of magnitude less probable. Yet, as he and the team had worked the angles, the emerging patterns had made a believer out of him. It really did seem as if someone had placed an intergalactic, long-distance call to the planet Earth. He was sure of it, just as he was sure that the Wow! Signal also contained the key to answering that call.

He still recalled the day he had met the small team of geniuses and experts, all of whom were, like him, more interested in solving the mystery of the signal than actually proving the existence of extraterrestrial life. "We are working under the assumption that whomever sent this message knows what our capabilities are. So what are the data telling us?"

The working hypothesis that emerged from that meeting was that the message was two-fold. The number values—6, 14, 26, 30, 19, 5—were determined to be celestial coordinates: 6 hours 14 minutes 26 seconds, with a declination 30 degrees 19 minutes 5seconds, which corresponded to a point in space somewhere between the constellations of Gemini and Auriga. The fact that the sum of the values was exactly one hundred might mean that a second signal would be transmitted one hundred days from the first. To test this theory, they would train a radio telescope on that region of the sky on or about November 23, and wait.

There were many problems with the hypothesis, not the least of which was that fact that the original signal had come from the opposite side of the sky. The team's astronomer, Bill Earl, had offered a plausible explanation. "What if we're mistaken in assuming that the Wow! Signal originated in the Chi Sagittarii group? What if it originated from a source much closer, but along that same vector? Say, from a spacecraft? It would be a simple thing for that spacecraft to move to another location in the sky for a second broadcast."

Not everyone in the team supported the hypothesis. Xenobiologist Chris Anstead expounded the belief that the six values might represent the atomic numbers of elements—carbon, silicon, iron, zinc, potassium and boron—which perhaps might form the basis of the extraterrestrial organic molecule. Zavada, the computer expert, found the Hundred Day concept too simplistic and too convenient. "You asked us to find the message hidden in the signal," he had complained. "This isn't a hidden message. You're trying to shoe-horn it to fit your pet theory. Just like those people who try to calculate the end of the world from Bible prophecies."

It was a fair criticism, but as Soter had pointed out, it would be easier to test the hypothesis and eliminate it, than to dismiss it out of hand, and then wonder after the hundred day limit had expired whether they had missed an important opportunity.

Zavada, it seemed, had been proven right.

They had traveled to the Arecibo Observatory in Puerto Rico, aimed the enormous radio telescope receiver at the target coordinates, and started listening. Unlike the Big Ear telescope, which had received the Wow! Signal only because it happened to be pointing the right direction for exactly seventy-two seconds, the Arecibo array could be set to track a specific location for as long as it was in the sky—several hours at a time. Earl had arranged to begin the survey on the night of November 22 and to continue gathering data until the early morning hours of November 24.

The vigil had yielded nothing remarkable. They had reams of data, but no radiation spike like the Wow! Signal. Instead, there were pages and pages that looked like part of the Wow! printout outside the circle—lots of blank space and a scattering of ones.

Zavada settled into a chair on the other side of the desk, appraising Soter for several silent seconds. "Did you know that Thomas Edison tested thousands of different materials for the filaments to make a light bulb? When asked about his failures, he said: 'I have not failed. I've just found 10,000 ways that won't work.'"

"In other words, if at first you don't succeed, try, try again."

"Not exactly. You don't keep trying the same thing over and over again."

"We won't be trying this again. We've already tied up the observatory too long. They're about to call the cops on us." That wasn't quite true. Soter's mysterious benefactors at ONE would have authorized him to use the Arecibo Observatory as long as he deemed necessary, and the astronomers lined up to do work of their own would have had no recourse. But Soter couldn't justify staying on site any longer, not without something more concrete to go on. "I'm afraid it's back to the drawing board."

Zavada shrugged. "Hey, have you heard about this movie that's out now? *Close Encounters of the Third Kind.*"

Soter shook his head. He didn't have time for movies.

"Might be worth taking a look at. It's about aliens visiting Earth. They communicate with this weird musical signal." Zavada did his best to mimic the theme.

"Music?" Soter sat up. That was an angle they had not explored. Could it be that the six values represented musical notes?

"If I were going to send a message, though," Zavada continued, as if Soter's apparent interest was an invitation, "I would use computer language. Just like we did with the Arecibo Message."

The Arecibo Message was the reverse of the Wow! Signal. It was a blast of information sent from Earth in 1974—from the very facility where Soter's team now probed the heavens—into deep space. The message, which had lasted just three minutes, was designed to establish a communication baseline—the numbers one through ten, the atomic number of several elements, the basic nucleotide structure of DNA, and so forth—all rendered into binary code, broadcast at 2,380 MHz—much stronger than the Wow! Signal—and modulated at 10 Hz.

Some people had speculated that the Wow! Signal might be an answer to the Arecibo Message, but this was extremely unlikely. The Arecibo Message had been sent to a different part of space, and had gone out only three years earlier, not nearly enough time to be received by a civilization around a distant star, and answered.

"Frequency modulation is perfect for transmitting binary data," Zavada continued. "It's kind of like Morse code, only simpler. Instead of dots and dashes, you just have ones and zeroes—on and off."

"We tried looking for a binary message," Soter answered. Contrary to many of the news reports that had been circulated, no one had actually 'heard' the Wow! Signal. The only recorded data from the Big Ear was the computer printout, and that was only the mean values of signal strength calculated every few seconds. There was no recording of the signal and no way to know if it had been modulated to contain a message. "Lots of ones, but they were all in the background..."

His voice trailed off as he saw, with the same clarity that had fueled his recognition of a pattern in the Wow! Signal, that they actually had received a binary message. He pushed the newspaper away to reveal the printout of data received from the Gemini-Auriga sky survey. He looked at it and then turned it for Zavada's inspection. "What do you see?"

"Background noise."

Soter shook his head. "Think more literally. You see ones. A lot of ones." As with the data from the Big Ear, the numeral '1' was used to signify a faint pulse of radiation—white noise from stars and other objects that emitted very faint but detectable electro-magnetic radiation. The universe was a noisy place, but most of the noise was at a very low frequency. The radiation the telescope had detected was in the low range, but that was to be expected. It was rare to see anything greater than a four.

"Yeah, and a lot empty spaces in between."

"Not spaces," Soter countered. "Zeroes."

Zavada gaped at him. "Are you saying there's a binary code hidden in the background noise?" He didn't wait for a response, but took the thick stack of paper and began studying it with the practiced eye of someone fluent in machine language. After a few seconds, he turned to the next page, then the next. "I'll be damned."

Soter moved around the desk to look over Zavada's shoulder. "What do you see?"

Zavada took out a pen and began scribbling furiously on the margin of the printout. After a few minutes, he straightened and showed Soter what he had produced.

101000011101000110000010000000101000011101000110000010
000000101000011101000110000010000000101000011101000110
000010000000101000011101000110000010000000101000011101
000110000010000000101000011101000110000010000000

"There's a repeating pattern here. Do you see it?" Zavada added some lines.

<u>101000011101000110000010000000</u>101000011101000110000010

000000<u>101000011101000110000010000000</u>101000011101000110

000010000000<u>101000011101000110000010000000</u>101000011101

000110000010000000<u>101000011101000110000010000000</u>

"It repeats after thirty digits, over and over again."

"Can you tell what it says?"

"Every binary number starts with one. If the thirty digits are a single number..." Zavada did some calculations on the paper. "Six hundred seventy-eight million, seven hundred fifteen thousand, five hundred and twenty."

Soter took the pen and wrote the number down.

678,715,520

It was a multiple of ten...nothing helpful there. The prime factorization was interesting though.

$2^7 \cdot 5 \cdot 7 \cdot 151499$

"It might not be one number," Zavada cautioned. "See these long strings of zeroes? Four and five at a time? If this were my message, I'd use double-zeroes or triple-zeroes as spaces between individual numbers."

<u>10100~~00~~11101~~000~~11000~~00~~10000000~~10100~~00~~11101~~000~~11000~~00~~10
000~~000~~

{20 – 58 – 24 – 32} or {10 – 29 – 12 – 16}

Soter felt a tingling at the base of his neck. There was something important here. He hastily wrote out an alphanumeric key like the one he had used in interpreting the Wow! Signal. The first set of numbers didn't work. Fifty-eight was beyond the alphanumeric range. The second set however was within the range.

1010 = 10 = A 11101 = 29 = T 1100 = 12 = C 10000 = 16 = G

"A,T,C,G," he said aloud. There was something familiar about those letters. "And this just keeps repeating?"

Zavada leafed through the printout, nodding in the affirmative after a quick scan of each page. Then, without warning, he stopped and backtracked. "No. There's a change here. It's similar... Okay, it's definitely the same four distinct values, but not in the same order."

10100001010000101000101000010000000110000010000000110000011000001100000100000000100000010000000

"The first several iterations were to give us the key," Soter murmured. "To make sure we would notice the pattern. Can you break it down into sets using these values?" He tapped his key.

Zavada, with the eagerness of a kid opening presents on Christmas morning, began converting binary to alphanumeric.

AAAAGCGCCCGGG

Soter gasped. Now he knew why the four letters looked so familiar. "I need to show this to Chris."

He was certain that the team's xenobiologist, would confirm his discovery. They had indeed received a second transmission, from exactly where the Wow! Signal had told them to look...a message cleverly disguised as fluctuations in background radiation, a message that no one would ever notice unless they were actively looking for it...a message that contained just four discrete values, but which could be assembled to create something marvelous.

The letters, ATCG stood for adenine, thymine, cytosine, and guanine—the four nucleobases that formed the deoxyribonucleic acid molecule.

Someone, somewhere out in space, perhaps hundreds of light years away, had sent them a message coded in DNA.

FLOOD

FORTY-FOUR

Jenna stood alone in the small galley, staring at the unopened bottle of water like she might gain some insight from the light refracting through it. Reality had become a very fluid substance in the last few hours. The revelations, each one more incredible than the last, had poured down on her, washing away the foundations of everything she believed about herself. She would have rejected every word, demanded to be given her life back, if not for the simple fact that, deep down, she knew it was all true.

Mercy came to join her a few seconds later. "You okay, honey?"

Jenna continued to stare at the bottle. "How did you...?" She didn't know how to finish the question.

Mercy hugged her. Jenna did not resist, but neither did she return the embrace.

"I was the first," Mercy began. "I suppose that's obvious to you now. Back in '78, gene splicing was a completely new field. The Human Genome Project wouldn't be started for several more years, but biologists had already started mapping DNA. Soter's team was able to identify several of the gene sequences in the message and recognized that it was human DNA. They found human donors who were a close match and cultivated several *in vitro* embryos. A ready supply of genetic material. Of those, I was the closest match. In the years that followed, as gene science improved and computers got faster, they were able to fine-tune the process. Meanwhile, I grew up. I had a pretty normal childhood, I guess. It seemed normal anyway.

"We had a private compound in Arecibo on the other side of the island from the lab. I lived there, and when I was old enough, I taught the younger ones. They sent them over from the lab when they were old enough. Even though we weren't like other people, Dr. Soter and the team thought it was best to have us live normal lives—education, careers, families—but I stayed there until..."

She gave a shrug. "Dr. Soter was with me, on the far side of the island, when the lab was destroyed. It looked like a natural disaster, but he knew better. We were a secret project—'deep black,' they call it. Someone in the government found out about us—someone who wasn't supposed to know—and decided it was better to make us disappear. Dr. Soter knew they would be looking for us, so we scattered. Later on, when we realized that you had survived, we decided I should stay close to you, keep you safe if anyone ever figured out who and what you were, and when you were old enough, tell you the truth."

Jenna listened without interrupting, but when Mercy fell silent, she said, "That's not what I meant. I was wondering how you got on that helicopter. If you were in contact with Soter all along, then you must have known what was happening."

"It was too dangerous to stay in contact with him. When you told me that someone had tried to kill you, I knew, but there was no way to make contact. When the helicopter showed up at the safe house looking for you, Dr. Soter recognized me. That was the first time we'd spoken in ten years."

"But you must have known what was going on. You just let me stumble around on my own. You could have told me everything back home, before I went on that wild goose chase in the Everglades."

Mercy frowned. "Jenna, it's difficult to explain. There's still a lot you don't know. And if I had told you all of this, would you have believed me?"

Jenna didn't allow herself to speculate on what her reaction might have been. Even now, after everything she had experienced, everything she had done, it was a lot to swallow. Yet, as crazy as it sounded, it also felt like the truth. "Did you always know that it was Noah who destroyed the lab and took me?"

Mercy nodded sadly.

"And yet you...you were *with* him?"

"Noah was a good man, Jenna. I believe he deeply regretted what happened that night. That's why he saved you. And why I always trusted him."

Jenna wondered whether Mercy knew that it was Cray and his partner who had killed Noah, but there was something else that she was even more curious about. "Did he know who you really were?"

"I think he must have wondered about our resemblance. He may have suspected that we were related, but I don't think he knew the particulars about what was going on at the lab. If he had...well, I don't know if he would have been so quick to save you that night. A lot of people would call us 'abominations.'"

Jenna sighed. "What *are* we, Mercy? Cort told me that the...the clones...are doing terrible things, trying to start a world war. Is this all part of Soter's plan?"

"It most certainly is not," a voice intoned from behind Mercy. Dr. Soter stood in the aisle, leaning heavily on his cane. "And I would caution you against believing anything that man told you. The government needs a scapegoat, someone to blame for their own ineptitude. They have chosen you and your brothers and sisters."

The response rang hollow. If the government needed someone to blame, there were much easier targets than a group of alleged clones cooked up from a recipe beamed in from another galaxy. Nevertheless, Jenna could tell from Soter's expression—his body language and his eye movements—that he believed it to be true. Mad scientist or not, he wasn't lying to her about any of it.

"If you were working with the government, why did they turn on you?"

Soter smiled patiently. "Politics. The project was begun under the auspices of the Office of National Estimates, which was a division of the Central Intelligence Agency. Our funding was deeply buried in the black budget, and as the years passed, few within the agency, and no one in the administration, knew what we were doing. I can only surmise that someone learned about our research and found it politically expedient to erase all traces of the program."

"Do you still have contacts in the government? People who could protect us and set the record straight?"

"Yes...and no. We had to be discreet. Our genetic research has been at a virtual standstill, but we have done our best to monitor the progress of the children in hopes that there would be a breakthrough. Just the opposite has happened, and now the government means to finish what they started fifteen years ago. My contacts cannot risk taking direct action."

"But *something* is happening. Someone intentionally released the SARS virus in China. And I think Cort was telling the truth about the cyber-attack." She thought back to what else she had been told. "He showed me pictures of two people—Kelli Foster and Jarrod Chu. Are they...?"

Soter's expression was that of a parent refusing to believe reports of his child's delinquency, but his answer was reserved. "Kelli and Jarrod were from Generation Six, cultivated in 1984. By that time, we had refined our approach. They were an almost perfect match to the genome code we received in the transmission, particularly Kelli, since the original message was coded for XX chromosomes."

"Cort said they have disappeared."

Soter drew in a breath. "You have to understand, Jenna. The children aren't my agents. It was always my intention that their lives be as normal as possible. After the attack, we had cut all lines of communication, and when the children still in my care reached maturity, they were mainstreamed in secret. Kelli and Jarrod were two such. They pursued their personal goals and interests, and that led to important positions in civil service. For their safety and my own, I have kept a distance."

Jenna saw his eyes flicker ever so slightly to the side. Now he was lying, though she didn't need to be a human lie detector to catch it. "You've been keeping tabs on everyone, even me."

Before he could protest, she continued. "Your men—Cray and the other guy—were there just minutes after someone tried to kill me. You knew the hit was coming down, and you sent them to rescue me. Did you also tell them to kill Noah? Payback for what happened at the lab?"

Mercy gasped in surprise at this news, but Soter just sagged, defeated. "I knew. I was alerted to the government's intention to hunt down and kill my children. I warned those that I could, but the only way to protect you was direct intervention. I am sorry that your...that Mr. Flood was caught in the crossfire, so to speak. I bore him no ill will."

Soter was either telling the truth or learning how to control his response better. Jenna chose to believe the former. Nevertheless, there were a lot of gaps in his story. If the destruction of the lab had driven him and the others underground, then how was it that he had a veritable army at his disposal—manpower, firepower, helicopters and executive jets? Someone was funding him, and she saw no evidence that it was not a foreign government as Cort had claimed.

"So what happens next?" Jenna asked. "Where are we going?"

"Back where it all began, my dear. There is still much that you need to be told. And I need you to do something for me."

"What?"

"I would prefer to explain it when we reach our destination."

Jenna shook her head. "If you want my help, start talking now."

The old man sighed again, this time in surrender. "Thirty-seven years ago, an extraterrestrial intelligence reached out to us.

They sent us a message, and even though I succeeded in unlocking that message, I still do not understand what it means.

"They sent us instructions, in the form of a complete DNA sequence. A human genome, but with some very slight differences. You are more intelligent, faster and stronger than an ordinary human. You may also have other abilities of which you may not be aware, or which might not yet have become manifest. But these traits are the means, not the end itself."

Jenna thought she understood what he was driving at. "You think the ETs told you how to make us smarter so that we would be able to figure out how to talk to them?"

"Perhaps. But there is another possibility. Are you familiar with genetic memory?"

Jenna knew the term from her psychology classes, but sensing that Soter meant it as a rhetorical question, she shook her head.

"For years, biologists have believed that humans acquire nearly all of our memories from interacting with the environment, but recent research is showing that some elements of memory—acquired phobias, for example—may be genetically transmitted from one generation to the next. This has been posited by many as an explanation for past-life regressions.

"Memories, you see, are nothing but sequences of proteins stored in our brain, and accessed by pathways of neurons. There's no reason that the formation of memories cannot be coded in the DNA, especially when you consider that 98% of the human genome is non-coded, sometimes erroneously called 'junk' DNA.

"We don't know what purpose non-coded DNA serves, but the intelligence responsible for sending us the message most certainly does. And I believe that every single nucleotide is important."

Jenna nodded slowly. "You think the message is coded into my DNA."

"Jenna," Soter spoke in a solemn, almost reverent voice. "You *are* the message."

FORTY-FIVE

Arecibo Observatory, Puerto Rico, USA
9:55 a.m.

The light rain that greeted Jenna as she stepped onto the tarmac intensified to a downpour, as the car in which she rode, along with Mercy, Dr. Soter and the two *faux* feds, made the half-hour trip into the rugged interior of the island territory of Puerto Rico. She had learned that Cray's partner was named Markley, but she had learned little more about herself. The terrain was like nothing she had ever imagined. They were surrounded by undulating domes and valleys, lushly carpeted with verdant foliage, looking somehow greener beneath the gray sky.

"Beautiful, isn't it?"

Jenna turned and saw Mercy watching her. She nodded. "I'm used to flat islands and open water. Until last night, I'd never even left the Keys. I had no idea..."

She stopped, realizing the absurdity of the statement. This wasn't a field trip. It was a homecoming. She had been born—if that was the word for it—and lived the first few months of her life somewhere on this very island. "Where was the lab?"

Soter fielded the question with a grave expression. "On the south coast, near Ponce. We stayed here to be close to the observatory. At the time, we had no idea where our research would take us, but we felt certain we would be...communicating...with someone. Even though our project shifted to a new discipline—genetic research—we stayed, because we knew that eventually, we would need to use the radio telescope." He reached out a laid a hand on Jenna's forearm. "And that day has finally come."

The overt familiarity made Jenna uncomfortable, but she kept her reaction neutral. It was too soon to let her guard down, too soon to blindly trust Soter. His words belied the display of affection, a none-too subtle reminder that to him, she was a science experiment, not a daughter. And even if that wasn't the case, she was nowhere near ready to embrace him as a father.

Father. That was the worst aspect of this latest revelation. She had been so quick to demonize Noah for taking her away, depriving her of parents and a normal childhood. Now, the imagined crime was meaningless. She had no parents and her childhood would have been anything but normal. Noah, in taking her away from all of that, had given her normalcy. A life. That made him the closest thing she would ever have to a father.

But all that was behind her now. Father, home, childhood... normal... All of it was gone.

She blinked away tears—self-pity was a pointless indulgence— and turned her attention back to the passing landscape. The route took them through a valley dotted with residences, and then wove back into the turbulent landscape. Rising above the limestone domes was something that, while impressive, would only have been beautiful to an engineer—a gray-white spire, stabbing straight into the heavens. Large cables stretching away from the tower became visible as they climbed out of the valley. The tips of two more spires appeared further off in the distance, to form the three corners of a triangle. The cables were connected to an enormous structure of exposed metal beams—Jenna thought it looked like an unfinished suspension bridge—that seemed to hover above the tree tops. A huge geodesic dome dangled below the framework. Jenna recognized it as a radar dome, similar to the kind used on newer naval vessels. Given their destination, that made perfect sense.

"The Arecibo Observatory," Soter said, slipping into tour guide mode. "The largest single aperture radio telescope in the world. This is where we received the second signal, hidden in background radiation. It has guided our journey and brought us full circle."

He turned to face her and added, "You might recognize it. It's been featured in a number of films."

Jenna resisted an urge to shrug indifferently. "Looks like a busy place."

"The observatory is a popular tourist attraction. Public funding for the sciences has always been meager, so it's necessary to generate new streams of revenue. In this case, a comprehensive visitors' center at the base of that tower." He gave a conspiratorial smile. "Of course, my research is very well-funded. I have been able to pass some of that along, which has given me a great deal of influence with the administrators. We won't need to stand in line today."

The traffic on the road leading up to the remote site was heavier than she expected, especially on a Sunday. A line of cars and buses traveled toward the observatory. A few cars passed them going the opposite direction. The rain had not kept anyone away.

When they reached a junction, Cray turned out of the queue and headed up a solitary road toward a tall building. A blinking red light on a sign caught Jenna's attention. The legend on the placard, written in both English and Spanish read: 'Unshielded vehicles do not pass this point with red light.' Cray did not stop.

"The 430 MHz transmitter can fry the electronics of older cars," Soter explained. "Our ignition system is protected."

Jenna wondered vaguely if they ought to be concerned about the effects of the radio waves on their bodies, but assumed that any such hazard would have long since been addressed by the scientists who operated the facility. Soter's mention of the transmitter had raised a much more immediate question. "What exactly is it that you want me to do?"

"It will make more sense once we are inside."

Jenna found this answer woefully inadequate. "You think you can just sit me down in front of a space radio and...what? Suddenly it will all just pop into my head? How to talk to them? What to say?" Too late, it occurred to her that she was letting her emotions take over. She narrowed her eyes, fixing his gaze, and when she spoke again, her tone was much softer. "I'm sorry, Helio...can I call you Helio? Doctor Soter just seems so formal, and...we're family."

He nodded slowly, almost reluctantly. His eyes darted away for a moment, but she waited until he was looking at her again to resume speaking. "Helio, it's just that anything you can tell me about what's really going on would help. A lot."

She watched Mercy in her peripheral vision, wondering if the woman—*my sister? Mother? Clone? Double?*—would recognize what she was attempting to do. She thought it unlikely. These were tricks Noah had taught Jenna. Not some manifestation of mutant-alien superpowers.

"Yes. Of course. I'm not trying to withhold information, my dear. It's just that it will be easier to explain once you've seen the signal."

"The signal? The message with the DNA sequence?"

Another nod. "It may be that seeing the message for yourself might have a stimulating effect on that part of your brain where the genetic memory is stored."

His eyes darted ever so slightly away as he said it. He wasn't being completely forthcoming, and yet what he had said was, at its core, truthful.

"Is that all?" The message was the key component to all of this, but why did he believe that seeing her own genetic code would have any kind of effect? *Maybe there's more to it?* "What about the rest of the message?"

His look of surprise confirmed that she had made the right guess. "You are every bit as remarkable as I had hoped, my dear. Yes, there is a portion of the message that we have not been able to make sense of, even after all these years of research. It's a long binary sequence. Coming at the end of the message as it does, it may simply be normal background radiation, but it might also be a sort of signature, the sender signing off, as a HAM radio operator might do."

All these years of research. The words triggered a cascade of questions and Jenna had to fight to maintain her pleasant demeanor. "That's right. You've been working at this for a long time. I know you told me, but why didn't you have Mercy or one of the others do this?"

Something changed in the old man's expression, like a curtain falling over a stage in the middle of a play. "With each successive generation, we were able to fine-tune the DNA sequence. The early generations...lacked something...but you, my dear, were the most perfect expression of the message, thus my hope that you will be able to unlock its final secrets."

This time he was lying, but not about his intentions. What had he said earlier about Kelli Foster and Jarrod Chu? *Generation Six, cultivated in 1984...an almost perfect match to the genome code.* He was holding something back, something that concerned him enough that he was dodging her subtle manipulations.

She decided not to press him too hard just yet. "Oh. I figured it must be something like that. I'm surprised you didn't come round me up sooner. I mean, since you knew where I was."

"I was sorely tempted. Thirty-seven years is a very long time to wait for an answer. But it was important to allow your abilities to fully develop. If not for this threat to your safety, I would have been content to wait a few more years."

Once more, she sensed an omission, but before she could figure out where to probe next, the car pulled to a stop and Cray shut off the engine. Over the steady drum of rain on the roof, Jenna could hear a loud rumble like an industrial generator.

Soter peered through the rivulets of water streaming down the windows, then threw the door open. "I've forgotten my umbrella. I fear we shall all get wet."

"Won't be the first time today," Jenna replied. Mercy gave a good-natured groan.

Outside the car, the noise was even louder, making conversation impossible. "That's the transmitter," Soter shouted, waving for them to follow.

A second car pulled up beside theirs. Four men wearing rain slickers got out and joined their procession. Jenna guessed they were part of Soter's security force. They certainly didn't fit her stereotype of what astronomers were supposed to look like.

Cray hurried ahead to the front door of the building and held it open for the others. As Soter had warned, the brief trek from the car to the structure left them all soaked, but the downpour didn't dampen Soter's enthusiasm. After shaking off as much water as he could, he took the lead, guiding them inside with child-like eagerness. His cane was all but forgotten, tucked under one arm, as he moved. Cray and Markley brought up the rear, while the other four men remained outside.

The mechanical noise was dulled, but Jenna could feel vibrations rising through the floor and emanating from the walls. The transmitter was inside the building. Soter ushered them into a dimly lit room that reminded Jenna of the signal room in Cort's safe house, but on a much larger scale. Computer servers lined the walls, along with a variety of other electronic devices and their blinking red and green LEDs. A few of these were no bigger, and looked no more sophisticated, than a citizen's band radio, while others looked like the sound controls at a rock concert. Soter moved past these, his wet shoes squeaking on the black and white checkerboard tile floor. He led them to an area that had been partitioned into smaller workspaces. Each desktop held no less than four computer monitors, and each screen displayed incomprehensible graphical and textual data. A broad window, looking out at the metal-frame structure Jenna had glimpsed from the road, stretched across the wall beyond the workstations.

Soter approached one of the men working in the room and shook his hand. After a brief exchange, the man turned to his co-workers and said simply, "Lunch time."

After the events of the last two days, Jenna didn't trust her internal clock, but she was fairly certain that it was only about ten in the morning. That the men were ceding the room to Soter bore testimony to his influence, and made Jenna wonder again about the source of his funding. Cort's assertion that the project had been run by the Soviet Union, and then later by the Russian government, seemed less likely here on American soil, but she couldn't rule it out completely. Foreign or domestic, Soter would have had to cover his tracks very well, especially with the CIA gunning for him.

When they were alone, Soter gestured for Jenna to join him at a desk near the window. As she approached, she caught a glimpse of the panorama that lay beyond the glass.

"Whoa. Now I see what all the fuss is about."

Soter grinned. "Quite impressive, isn't it?"

Impressive was one word for it. Spread out before them, directly below the hanging structure, and hovering next to and above the surrounding treetops, was a vast bowl-shaped depression, silvery-gray like exposed concrete, stained a darker shade in some places, presumably from long years of exposure. Jenna knew there would be a satellite reflector dish of some kind, but nothing on this scale. "It looks like God dropped a contact lens."

"An apt simile," Soter said, "since it is a lens of a sort—our lens for gazing back into the heavens."

There was something familiar about it, and Jenna recalled Soter's comment about the observatory being featured in several movies. The dish, or something very nearly identical to it, had appeared in a James Bond movie, one of Noah's favorites from the series, though as was his custom, he found plenty to complain about. Noah had been a real James Bond, after all.

"The reflector is a thousand feet across, and the antenna assembly is suspended four hundred and thirty feet above it. The dish itself comprises almost thirty-nine thousand aluminum panels, all perfectly machined to create a spherical reflector. The location was chosen because of a naturally occurring sinkhole crater, but the dish is suspended above it."

Jenna looked at it more closely and could just make out the square lines where the individual panels were joined—not solid concrete like in the movie. *They totally got that wrong*, she thought, and then realized that it was exactly the sort of thing Noah would have said.

Soter clapped his hands together. "Enough about that. We can give you the full tour later, but for now let us focus on the task at hand."

He leaned over one of the computers and inserted a flash drive into the USB port. After a few keystrokes, he stepped back and gestured for Jenna to sit.

As the screen began to fill up with data, ones and zeroes on one side, and an endless string of just four letters on the other, Jenna felt a growing apprehension. Those numbers and letters were the blueprint for creating her, transmitted across space by some unknown alien intelligence. She wanted to turn and run, but instead, as if compelled by an invisible force, she took a seat and began to read.

FORTY-SIX

10:24 a.m.

The computer hard drive whirred as it struggled to download and open the enormous file. Jenna recalled learning that the entire human genome could be expressed in less than a gigabyte of drive space. That had probably seemed like a mountain of data in 1977, but by modern computing standards, it was the same size as a two hour movie. It was a little disconcerting to think that a person—and not just any person, but Jenna herself—could be reduced to bits and bytes of information. As she scanned the procession of letters—A,T,C and G—she found herself wondering which part had determined her hair color? The color of her eyes? Which parts made her into the unique entity that she was?

Only I'm not unique, am I? There are others out there, others like Kelli Foster and Jarrod Chu, and God only knows how many more.

No, not God. Soter knows.

"Ideally, I would ask you to read the entire message, but at over three billion characters, that would require weeks of reading, even with your extraordinary mental abilities." Soter said the last bit as if speaking from experience.

So the others have read the message, Jenna thought, but Soter was still speaking. "Once the file finishes loading, you can skip to the end. That is where the 'signature' is located."

Despite his admonition, Jenna found herself fascinated by the contents of the file. She scrolled down a page, reading every single number and letter on the screen, downloading it into her brain almost as fast as the computer could read it from the flash drive. As she read, she began to get the sense that, with just a little more information, she might be able to interpret what she was seeing.

As a young girl, she had once seen an advertisement written in Spanish. She had not learned how to speak that language—though she later would—but she remembered it, just as she remembered everything she saw and heard. When the opportunity arose to get a translation, she saw the sign again in her mind's eye, perfectly comprehensible. That was how she felt now. Even though there was only an endless stream of letters, not divided by spaces, punctuation or any sort of pattern that would be recognizable to the average person, she felt sure that with just a little bit more knowledge, she would be able to read it from her memory like a book.

Page down.

Page down.

Page down.

She scanned faster and faster...two pages per second...three. Yet, as Soter had indicated, the file was enormous, and the scroll bar registered no visible movement with each click. The file was over three million pages long, and even if she had been able to read five pages per second, it would require seven days of non-stop reading to finish.

"There," Soter announced. "It's finished. You can skip to the end. It's still in binary I'm afraid. We were never able to differentiate values. But I believe you will see the pattern."

Almost reluctantly, as if scrolling to the end of the message would be like skipping to the last page in a mystery novel, Jenna did as Soter suggested. The computer lagged in protest at the size of the file, and another interminable wait followed before the screen filled up again. Here, there were no corresponding letters of the DNA sequence. Only ones and zeroes.

This new message was different somehow. With the genetic information, even in binary, she knew there was a purpose and pattern to it all, but there was no contextual framework for the last part of the message. Though she recognized the digits, their random arrangement left her feeling muddled. She struggled to read the numbers. When she was done, she discovered she could not recall them with any degree of confidence. They had slipped from her memory. It was a new experience for her. She tried reading it again.

00000011110000...

As she fought through the message a third time, the individual numbers fell out of her consciousness as quickly as they left her sight. She paused reading, but didn't look away from the page as Cray approached Soter and whispered in his ear. From the corner of her eye, she could see Soter's look of alarm, but it wasn't quite enough to draw her away from her task. She returned to reading. The numbers were almost hypnotic in their slippery resistance to assimilation. She kept looking, afraid to even blink, lest the message disappear or change.

Jenna had not truly appreciated how unique her gift of memory was until a classmate had challenged her to 'prove it.' She had always assumed that lots of people possessed eidetic memories, but later research had revealed that even among those who claimed to possess the gift, there were limits to the ability. No one truly possessed what was mistakenly termed 'photographic memory' or perfect recall. And yet, she always had. She could read something and remember it line by line, or recall startling details from images or places she had visited, without any effort.

Only now did she realize that she had taken the ability for granted. It wasn't just that her memory was letting her down. Her brain seemed to be lagging, just as the computer had when loading the file.

000000111100001001000010100000...

Soter gave a low harrumph of displeasure, then followed Cray to a side door that opened onto a balcony just outside the control room. The rumble of the transmitter increased again, but was oddly muted by the rain.

"Stay where you are!" Jenna recognized the voice as Soter's, though his strident shout was different than his soft conversational tone.

"I'm unarmed." The answering voice was barely audible over the tumult of the transmitter, but there was something familiar about it. The magnetism of curiosity pulled at her, even as her eyes refused to let go of the strange numerical sequence.

0000001111000010010000101000001111000101000110100010
100...

"What do you want?" Soter called.

Like a stubborn puzzle piece finally oriented correctly, the pattern emerged.

0000001111000010010000101000001111000101000110100010
1001000101010001111110010001000111000100010010110100
0100111000100000010101000010101000010011000011000000

001000010001100100011101000110000001001000010000001101
1000101100000101111000111000001000110000001101000001000
0000010100010100000011110000110010000110011000000001011
0001000110100011010001110000011000000110100010000000001
0000000001110100010001000010001010000010000000001011000
0100000010111000101010001000010000100010001001100010 11
1000110110001000100010000000010000001001010001011 00000
1001010111110011100011000000011110000111000001100000 10
0010000100110001110100011010001100100001110100000000 11
1000011101000100000100000011010001011000101100001111 00
0010001000011000100000010000001010001100000110100010 10
0001101000111110001110010001101000100011110000111010 00
1101000111000001001000001000110001001110001111110000 00
0111100001001000010000000110001101100010110000101001 00
0110001000101100000100100001111000100011111000110110 00
1010001101100010011000011010000011110000011100100010 10
1000100010110001110000111010001001000011110001100100 01
1000100101000100010000110100001111000100001000000001 01
1000010110000110100011000100011011100010100001111000 01
1110000100001110001101000010110000101110001011000001 00
010000

The numbers locked themselves into Jenna's consciousness, and with that realization, a door opened in her mind. Yet as she mentally stepped toward that door, she heard the distant voice answer Soter's question.

The spell broken, she surged to her feet and crossed the room in three steps, heedless of Mercy's cry, "Jenna, no!"

Some part of her wondered if Mercy had heard as well, and if the purpose for her warning was to safeguard Jenna's emotional health as much as her physical. It was a fleeting thought. No force on Earth could have stopped her.

She burst out onto the balcony, right behind Soter. Cray saw her and made a half-hearted attempt to restrain her, but he was already too late. Jenna's eyes met those of the man who had just a moment before shouted: "I want to talk to my daughter."

Standing on the rain-soaked grass less than fifty feet away was Noah Flood.

FORTY-SEVEN

10:27 a.m.

Jenna had not thought it possible for her world to be shaken any more than it already had, but Noah's appearance was another roller coaster plunge into the impossible.

Rivulets of rain dripped from his hair and nose. His eyes found her and his craggy face broke into a relieved smile. His lips formed her name, but she couldn't tell if he had said it aloud.

A dam broke inside her. Every emotion she had experienced in the last two days in connection with this man—admiration, grief, rage, acceptance—deluged her. She wanted to scream at him for taking away an existence that had never truly been hers. She wanted to rush down the fire stairs and hug him, and never let go.

My daughter.

That was what he had said, and she desperately wanted to believe he felt that way. And yet, the very fact that he was here, that he had tracked her down, told a different tale. He was working with Cort. It was the only explanation. And that meant he was trying to draw her out so that the government agents could finish their deadly assignment.

She searched his face, looking for some hint of what to believe, knowing even as she did that he was too skilled in the arts of deception to ever reveal the truth. A thousand questions ran through her mind, but all she could say was, "I thought you were dead."

His smile became a grin. "I'm too ornery to die," he called back.

Jenna realized now that her assumption about his fate had been made at the start of the nightmare, when all she knew about violence was what she had seen in Noah's movies, where people dropped dead from a single gunshot, because that's what the script called for. Her own experience had revealed just how much punishment a human body could actually take, yet at no time had it occurred to her that Noah's wound might have been only superficial.

Soter turned on her. "Go back inside, Jenna. This man is not your father. He's here to kill you."

Noah spoke quickly. "Jenna, you have to listen to me. I know what you're thinking, but remember what I taught you. Listen to your gut..."

"But make up my own damn mind," she finished, repeating it like a mantra. Her guts were so twisted, she had no idea what they were trying to tell her.

"He hasn't told you the whole truth," Noah continued.

And just how would you know that? She didn't say it aloud, and despite the fact that she did not want to trust this man who had lied to her about everything, she knew he was right. Soter was holding something back.

"He told you some story about aliens with a message of peace, right? There are no aliens, Jenna. He lied to you about that."

Jenna shook her head. "He wasn't lying."

Noah inclined his head. "Okay, not lying. Maybe he believes that's what happened, but it's not the real story. That message didn't originate from deep space. It was from Earth, bounced off a piece of orbiting space junk."

"Preposterous," snarled Soter. "Who's trying to deceive you now, my child?"

"The Soviets created the whole thing as a disinformation campaign. They wanted us chasing our tails, wasting resources looking for aliens where there weren't any. And it worked. He spent millions—the equivalent of billions today—on a hoax."

"A hoax?" Soter was incredulous. "A hoax that contained the entire human genome more than a decade before geneticists were able to even begin unraveling the mysteries of DNA?"

"You saw what you wanted to see," Noah countered, then turned his gaze back to Jenna. "But that's only half of it. His clones—Jenna, it kills me to say it—they're not stable. There's something *wrong* with them."

He kept speaking, talking over Soter's protest, pushing past the unpleasantness of his revelation the way a parent tears off a Band-Aid in one quick jerk. "I know you know about this Jenna. About the SARS virus in China and the cyber-attack here in America. The DNA recipe he cooked up gave the clones extraordinary abilities, but it also took something from them, something that made them human."

"You don't think I'm human?" Jenna's voice sounded very small, as if her breath could not quite get past the hurt and rage she now felt. She was angry at Noah for saying such horrible things, but she was also very afraid because she knew he wasn't lying.

"Oh, Jenna." Noah's pained look appeared genuine. "I love you more than I've ever loved anyone. You have to believe that. We can get through whatever comes. I believe that, and I want you to believe it, too. But you have to know the truth, and he's not going to tell it to you.

"It's something that happens to the clones when they reach adulthood. It's like a switch gets thrown. I've seen the evidence, heard from the people who worked with Jarrod Chu and Kelli Foster. They changed." He snapped his fingers. "It's like something was hardwired into their DNA. It's in you, too."

Like a switch gets thrown.

The words slammed through her and brought to mind Soter's reluctant explanation of his plan to show her the signature portion of the message.

Seeing the message for yourself might have a stimulating effect on that part of your brain where the genetic memory is stored.

It was important to allow your abilities to fully develop...to reach maturity.

She could not tell if Noah was being truthful, but Soter was an open book, and she saw the truth of the accusation in his eyes. He seemed on the verge of boiling over with righteous indignation, but his expression told a different tale.

He knows.

And I read the message.

Unbidden, the entire binary sequence flashed before her eyes, a siren song in ones and zeroes, irresistible. *Look,* it sang, *all you have to do is look, and all will be revealed.*

Jenna's knees went weak, and she staggered back against the wall. Through the rush of blood in her ears, she heard Soter's insistent denial. "It's not true, Jenna. He's lying."

Even in her state of shock, she knew that it was Soter, not Noah, who was hiding the truth, and not just from her.

He must have known all along that there was something defective in their—in our—DNA. No wonder he kept going, year after year, tweaking the genome, trying to figure out why his 'children' were turning into sociopaths. She doubted that it was Soter's intention to unleash monsters on the world. He seemed to care only about making contact with the extraterrestrial architects of the message.

Noah was wrong on that score. The signal wasn't a Soviet-era plot. It was far too sophisticated, even by twenty-first century standards. It was most certainly the product of a very advanced intelligence, probably an alien intelligence, and that meant its potential for disaster went far beyond anything dreamed up during the Cold War. The message was a trigger, activating the mental equivalent of a computer virus that lay dormant in the genetic memory of the clones. That's exactly what she and her siblings were: a dormant virus, sent in a radio transmission, designed to crash the entire planet.

Jenna wondered if it had been a similar incident fifteen years earlier that had prompted Noah's mission to terminate Soter's project with extreme prejudice. Had a first or second generation clone read the message and then tried to destroy the world?

It's in me, Jenna thought again. *Even now, it's trying to burn its way through my mind.*

What will happen if I let it? Will I still be me?

She pushed away from the wall, took a halting step toward the balcony rail, and addressed Noah. "Are you here to kill me?"

"Never." Noah shook his head vehemently. "They wanted me to. They're terrified of what you might do, but I convinced them to give us a chance."

"A chance?"

"Don't trust him," Soter repeated. "He's a killer. He killed your brothers and sisters. He killed my friends. He'll say anything to stop you from fulfilling your destiny."

"My destiny?" she repeated, incredulous. Soter's words were a slap in her face. "Is that all you care about?"

The mathematician realized his mistake. "Of course not."

"He's right, you know. That message that you care about so much? It's an alien Trojan Horse, and you brought it right inside the gates."

Soter shook his head. "No, no. It's not true. We just had to refine the genome."

Noah spoke again. "Jenna, I don't know what's going to happen, but I will be there for you. I won't leave you, and I won't let anyone hurt you."

Jenna felt utterly alone. She wondered what Mercy would do in her situation—Mercy who clearly thought of Soter as a father, and yet had defended Noah, even when Jenna had been ready to reject him completely. But Mercy was still in the control room, and Jenna knew that if she stepped back inside, it would be the same as choosing Soter's path. Besides, while Mercy might have been able to advise her about which man to choose for a father, she could not understand what was truly at stake.

If I choose to go with Noah, I might get killed. If I stay with Soter, I might destroy the world.

Not such a tough choice after all, Jenna thought, and started moving.

FORTY-EIGHT

10:30 a.m.

She made it just two steps before Soter realized what she was doing. "No!" he cried, and then lurched forward, arms thrown wide as if to seize her in his embrace.

At that instant, something cracked against the control room window, smashing the pane into a million glittering fragments. The unexpected destruction caught everyone on the balcony off-guard, even Jenna. She came to a halt almost as abruptly as she had started moving in the first place. There was something familiar about the scene, but it took a moment for Jenna and everyone else on the balcony to grasp the significance of the shattered window.

Noah however, caught on right away. "No, damn it!"

His exclamation jolted Jenna to alertness. *A sniper,* she thought. *Just like Ken on the roof of the bait shop. But is the sniper shooting at Soter or me?*

She felt like she knew the answer, and that led to another, more ominous line of questions.

Was Noah lying to me? Was all his talk just a way to lure me out to where the sniper could finish the job?

Jenna wanted to believe that Noah loved her. Maybe they— Cort or whoever was running the show now—had lied to him, promised him that she would be given safe passage, so that he would flush her out. *Or maybe he thinks I'm damaged beyond repair. That I need to be put down, like a rabid pet.*

She didn't want that to be true, but there was no way to know.

A moment later, Soter crashed into her, tackling her to the balcony deck. Cray's gun was out in an instant, and the report of the distant sniper rifle, only now reaching her ears, was eclipsed by the closer and louder thunder of his answering fire, directed at the only target available.

Noah scrambled away, running for the corner of the building, but even as he broke for cover, more shots began pelting the exterior of the building. Tiny spurts of flame scattered throughout the verdant landscape marked the position of at least half a dozen camouflaged shooters. Noah had not come alone.

Cray dropped into a crouch and lunged toward her. He scooped Jenna up in one hand, Soter in the other, and hustled them through the door as the balcony exploded in a spray of splinters.

Jenna wrestled free of his grip and crawled deeper into the relative safety of the control room. She spied Mercy, huddled behind a desk, and headed toward her. Bullets sizzled through the air overhead, smacking into the walls and ceiling, spraying dust and filling the room with the smell of smoke. But none of the shots came anywhere close to a human target. This was suppressive fire, Jenna knew, designed to keep them pinned down.

Soter seemed to grasp this as well. From his fetal curl on the floor he shouted, "Cray. Get her to safety."

Cray hesitated, as if torn between his loyalty to the old man and his sense of duty, but he gave a terse nod and reached out to Jenna. "Come on."

Jenna nodded her assent, then grasped Mercy's hand and followed Cray's lead toward the exit to the stairwell. Before leaving the room, he shouted to his partner, Markley. "We'll try to lead them off. Stay with the doctor, and get the hell out of here as soon as you can."

"No!" Soter protested. "It doesn't matter what happens to me. You have to save the girl."

Jenna was not inclined to argue. Cray shook his head and then led Jenna and Mercy from the room, gun at the ready. "Stay close," he said, not looking back.

Over the mechanical hum of the transmitter, the sound of a pitched battle rolled up from below. Soter's security detail was putting up a fight, defending the transmitter building, but there were only four of them. Four against at least six shooters. Worse, there was only one way out of the building, and it went right through the middle of the fight. Jenna looked at Mercy, hoping to see some indication that she knew what Cray was doing, but Mercy's blank look told her otherwise.

Jenna felt a return of the helplessness she'd experienced in Miami when she had boarded Soter's helicopter. She didn't even have a gun to defend herself. Her survival depended on Cray's choices, and that was intolerable.

She was about to tell Cray that when he did something unexpected, turning away from the exit, toward parts of the building they had not visited.

"Where are we going?" It wasn't simple curiosity that prompted her question.

"There's another way out," Cray said. "Through the transmitter room."

Another way out was good. "Won't they be watching all the doors?"

"Probably." Cray didn't break stride, but kept moving toward the source of the persistent thrumming sound. They passed through a maze of corridors, in and out of rooms lined with strange electronic devices, pieces of machinery and shelves packed with bound books and thick three-ring binders.

Cray stopped at a door that was plastered with signs. There were hazardous materials diamonds and cartoon lightning bolts accompanying a warning of high voltage electrical hazards, the familiar black-on-yellow radiation trefoil and strangest of all: a notice reading 'Liquefied gas coolants in use.' Cray turned the knob and shoved the door, but entered cautiously, sweeping the room beyond with his gun barrel. After a moment, he waved for them to follow.

The noise emanating from the room was deafening, drowning out even the sporadic report of gunfire. Jenna scanned the room for the hazards indicated in the signs. Everything she saw was unfamiliar and full of dangerous potential. There were large cylinders marked with more hazmat diamonds, and a machine that looked like it belonged on the weapon's deck of a star cruiser from a science fiction film. One corner was dominated by an enormous cube-shaped machine that seemed to be the source of the noise. The dull gray metal sheathing the device was adorned with still more warnings of radiation danger. Next to it was yet another door, this one marked with a sign that said 'Danger: High Voltage.' Jenna peered through the wire-lined glass window and saw another enormous room and at its center, a strange yellow pillar wrapped in wires, sprouting from a metal donut-shaped base. It looked like a scaled-up version of the Van Der Graaf static electricity generator in Jenna's science classroom.

"Please tell me we're not going through there."

Cray shook his head and moved toward the opposite wall. A large metal roll-up door was set in the concrete, big enough to accommodate a truck. He reached for the pull-chain that would open it, when a loud concussion tore through the room like a thunderclap.

Cray staggered, falling against the door. A bloody Rorschach pattern was left on the metal where he'd hit. But he wasn't dead. Cray pushed away, turning with his gun raised, and he fired several shots toward the door through which they had entered.

Jenna pulled Mercy down, seeking refuge behind one of the work benches, as bullets creased the air, filling the room with the stench of burned gunpowder. The walls exploded with chips of concrete dust and sparks, as rounds ricocheted off metal surfaces. The gunman pushed into the room, firing as he moved, trying to get a clear shot at his real target. Another man stood at the entrance, firing at Cray to keep him pinned down.

The significance of this was not lost on Jenna. Soter's security force had almost certainly been defeated by the overwhelming numbers of the assault team. There was no one left to defend her now.

Another round caught Cray, spattering the wall behind him with blood, but he kept firing, chasing the first shooter in a desperate bid to stop him from reaching Jenna.

There was a sound like a bell being rung, followed by a hiss of escaping gas. A bullet had penetrated one of the pressurized gas cylinders. White vapor spewed into the air.

Jenna drew in a breath and held it, knowing it would not be enough. The gas was probably a coolant—liquid nitrogen or maybe helium—more likely to flash freeze than suffocate them. Yet, despite this new peril, the shooting continued without cease. Still gripping Mercy's hand, Jenna searched the room for a better hiding place, somewhere further from the gas. Before she could find anything, the gunman appeared, right above them, so close that Jenna could see wisps of smoke curling from the muzzle of his pistol. With a grim but satisfied smile, his finger tightened on the trigger.

Jenna attempted to move away, knowing it was too late, but Mercy remained rooted, anchor-like.

Then the world exploded.

FORTY-NINE

10:33 a.m.

This is the way the world ends...

The line from an old poem sprang into her thoughts, which was strange, because even though she recognized it, she also knew that she had never heard or read those words before, had no idea what the poem was called or who the poet was.

This is the way the world ends. Not with a bang but a whimper.

She vividly recalled her teacher, standing at the lectern, summarizing the long litany of evils plaguing the globe. "The world is infected, and the disease is called 'humanity.' We are a cancer, devouring the healthy organism of the world, consuming its resources, propagating our own numbers beyond carrying capacity. And when we are warned of the danger, when we are shown that to kill the world is to kill ourselves, we refuse to listen. We will be the death of our world, and we will meet our end with a whimper."

The prospect filled her with anger. Humanity, so arrogant, so greedy... What better way to describe the species than as a cancer? The Earth, once so full of beauty and wonder, was now choking in filth, its horizons marred by towers of concrete and steel like a malevolent grin full of broken teeth. The night sky was curtained with ugly artificial light, blotting out the stars.

Strange that she couldn't quite remember when she had heard this lecture. The memory was so vivid, but like the details of the poem, she could not put it in the appropriate context.

No matter. The diagnosis was beyond question. That was the important thing. Humans were incapable of solving the problem because they *were* the problem. If there was to be a treatment for the cancer of humanity—a radical treatment—it would have to come from somewhere else.

And it had.

It all made sense now. The message Dr. Soter had received was a sort of viral therapy, and it had worked. Without even knowing why, Soter had created the antibodies that would purge the world of this plague by accelerating humanity's own self-destructive impulses. It would take only a nudge or two: a false-flag bioterrorism incident or a subversive cyber-attack, and the superpowers of the world might unleash a cleansing nuclear fire.

Wipe the slate clean.

But first, the message. Everything was ready. The dominoes were poised to fall. But before the last phase of the treatment was to be initiated, one task remained. She remembered the time, which had very nearly arrived, and the place, which was thousands of miles away. If she was not able to get there in time, one of the others would.

She felt a sublime satisfaction in the knowledge that the cancer of humanity would be purged soon, and her own purpose in life would be fulfilled.

Too bad that Mercy and Noah would be swept away, but radical treatments often damaged healthy cells. It was for the greater good.

No, she thought suddenly. *There has to be another way. I don't want to lose them again.*

Don't be foolish, argued another voice, her teacher's voice, but also weirdly enough, her own. *You know it's for the best. It's what has to happen.*

I know? How do I know? How do I know any of this?

And then the answer came like a flash of light.

FIFTY

10:34 a.m.

Light, brilliant beyond description, painful in its intensity. Then, darkness.

The memory of the teacher's words slipped away like the last echoes of a dream, as Jenna embraced the physical sensations that were her lifeline out of the void.

Her ears rang, overloaded by the cacophonous detonation. The harsh smell of ozone stung her nostrils, and smoke burned her unseeing eyes. She felt the pain of a concussion—not a bullet slamming into her, but something much bigger, like what she had experienced when the *Kilimanjaro* had exploded. There was also the memory of something else, a tingling sensation that had caressed her exposed skin in the instant before the blast. A crazy thought burbled to the top of her rattled awareness: *I've been struck by lightning.*

Crazy, only because she knew that she had not been struck. That she retained the wherewithal to sort that out was proof enough. Nevertheless, the flash and thunderclap could have come only from a catastrophic electrical discharge.

The darkness became a greenish haze. Nothing bore any resemblance to the world that had existed only a few seconds before. A soft whimper reached her ear through the silence.

Silence? Yes. Her hearing was returning, but the noise of the transmitter and the staccato bursts of gunfire were gone. Her first thought was that the explosion had knocked out the transmitter, but as her awareness returned she realized the exact opposite was true. The transmitter, or rather its power supply, had caused the devastation that now surrounded her. In all likelihood, a stray bullet had penetrated the door to the high voltage room and struck some critical component—the tall yellow pillar was probably a capacitor, storing massive amounts of voltage for use by the radio transmitter. The result had been an artificially produced lightning bolt, as destructive and unpredictable as the real thing.

She was still clutching Mercy's hand. In the dimness she could distinguish Mercy's sprawled form, but not much else. "Mercy? Are you okay?"

Another whimper. Jenna took that as a positive sign. Her vision continued to improve, but what she saw was not encouraging. Black smoke poured in from where there had once been a door marked with a high voltage sign. "Mercy, we have to get out of here."

As Jenna rose to her feet, unsteady, she saw the man who had been about to shoot her, reduced to a charred , vaguely human form. By the look of it, he had been the focal point of the discharge. Another unmoving form was visible at the entrance to the room—

the other shooter, stunned, but alive. He had been much further from the discharge than she, and it was a wonder that he hadn't already recovered. Jenna doubted she could make it past him, and even if she did, there would be others lying in wait. If she and Mercy were going to escape, it would have to be through the roll-up door, as Cray had intended.

Cray! She looked around and found him, sitting with his back against the wall beside the big door. His shirt was saturated with blood, but he didn't appear to be in any pain. He just sat there, gazing at her with unblinking eyes. It took her a moment to realize that he wasn't looking at her. He wasn't looking at *anything*. Cray was dead.

"Wake up. We've got to get moving." She tugged on Mercy's hand again until the woman stirred. Mercy mumbled something but Jenna shushed her. "We've got to get out of here. Come on."

She pulled away from Mercy. Every second was critical. Mercy would have to recover on her own while Jenna blazed their escape route. She half-crawled to where Cray had fallen, and she found his pistol still gripped in one dead hand. Something looked strange about it. The end of the barrel protruded a full half-inch from the body of the weapon.

It's empty, she realized. Cray had fired off his last round.

Steeling herself, she drew back his blood-soaked windbreaker to uncover the shoulder holster tucked beneath his left arm—empty like the pistol—then she checked the other side. There, she discovered two small pouches. Each contained a full magazine. She deftly liberated both, and then returned her attention to the handgun.

It was the same design as the pistol Mercy had given her to use during their futile escape attempt on the Overseas Highway, although it was slightly larger.

Mercy was alert now, staring aghast at Cray's motionless form. Jenna hurried back to her and offered the weapon. "Here," she said, hoping that a meaningful task would break Mercy from her daze. "You know what to do, right?"

Mercy tore her gaze from the dead man and nodded. With practiced efficiency, she ejected the empty magazine and slotted a replacement into the pistol grip, released the slide, and then racked it once to advance a round into the firing chamber.

Jenna returned to the door and took hold of the dangling chain. "They might be waiting out there," she warned, and then without further comment, she started pulling.

The door rose slowly, revealing rain-spattered pavement. Mercy ducked down, training the pistol on the widening stripe of revealed daylight, but did not fire. Jenna raised the door just a couple feet and stopped. She dropped down and peered through the opening.

The half-expected ambush did not occur, but Jenna saw too many places where a gunman might be concealed—parked cars, two small modular buildings that looked like trailers and the terrain itself.

"We have to make a run for it." She did not add that she had no idea where they would go next. Mercy nodded her readiness.

Jenna wriggled under the door and scrambled toward the nearest car, Mercy right behind her. Still no sign of the assault team—no sign of Noah. An ominous quiet had descended over the area. The transmitter was dead, and the gun battle had ended.

She swept the panorama, looking for a route to freedom. Directly ahead lay the road, and somewhere beyond that, the visitor's center Soter had mentioned. They might be able to lose themselves in the crowd, or find someone to help them...

No. These men wouldn't let innocent lives stand in the way of completing their mission, and there was no longer anyone left to help them.

Noah?

The thought stung. Just when she had been ready to believe his declaration of love, his promise to help, the jaws of the trap had snapped shut. Looking to Noah for help was worse than letting the shooters run them down.

"We have to go where they won't think to look for us," she told Mercy. "Follow me."

Staying low, she skirted the parking area toward the corner of the transmitter building. After verifying that the coast was clear, she darted into the lee shadow of the structure. From this new vantage, she saw the bundled cables overhead, snaking from the nearest tower to the suspended antenna assembly far out over the dish.

She considered climbing onto the cable and making her way out to the array. It was definitely the last place anyone would think to look, but it was also a dead end. Even if they could make the precarious journey unnoticed, they would be trapped four hundred feet above the ground.

But the dish was another story. From the control room, it had looked like an enormous empty swimming pool excavated from the surrounding landscape, but Soter had revealed that it was actually made up of aluminum panels, built above the ground. The edge of the dish was only a hundred yards away. If they could make it under the reflector panels, they'd have far more options.

She told Mercy her plan, leaving no room for argument. There was none. Mercy just nodded, looking a little shell-shocked. When Jenna started forward, creeping along the perimeter of the building, Mercy stayed right behind her. They stopped again at the next corner. The dish was visible below, a massive spherical bowl. A narrow tree-lined road ran down to its edge. The slope and slick pavement would make keeping their footing a little tricky, but Jenna estimated that a sprint of no more than thirty seconds would bring them to their goal. She checked the surrounding area for any sign of hostile forces, and then gripped Mercy's hand again.

"Ready?"

"Not really," Mercy admitted. "But let's do this."

Jenna nodded, and then because she could not think of a better way to coordinate their mad dash, gave the classic track and field prompt: "Ready, set, go!"

As they ran, Jenna expected to hear gunshots or feel the impact of a bullet, but what happened was much worse. Two-thirds of the way to her goal a shout reached her, an all too familiar voice, rolling down the slope, echoing from the surrounding limestone formations.

Noah's voice.

"Jenna!"

FIFTY-ONE

10:42 a.m.

She looked back, even though she knew it was a mistake to do so, and she stumbled.

The fall seemed to take forever, yet no matter how she flailed her arms, she could not recover her balance. Instead, she pitched and twisted, past the horizontal plane, and went skidding face first on the wet asphalt. The abrasive surface tore at her skin and clothes like sandpaper. There was no immediate pain, just a jolt of impact that knocked the wind from her sails.

Mercy skidded to a stop beside her, one hand extended, but before Jenna could take it, something struck the pavement near her outflung arm, showering her with hot grit. She didn't need to hear the report to know that someone was shooting at them.

Noah's voice came again, shouting, but the words were incomprehensible. Seething with anger—at Noah for yet another betrayal, at herself for having been foolish enough to react—all she could hear was the roar of blood in her ears. In that instant, the weight of all that she had endured—the exhausting flight from the killers, the ordeal in the Everglades, too many gut-wrenching revelations to count—descended upon her like an extinction-level-sized asteroid. She had learned unimaginable truths about herself, been put through the wringer, and it was all for nothing. She was going to die.

No! No, I'm not! Her defiance felt hollow.

"Just run!" she shouted, ignoring Mercy's offer of assistance. "Go!"

Jenna rolled toward the edge of the path and sprang to her feet. She took off, a millisecond ahead of a shower of bullets that tore into the hillside behind her.

Twenty more yards.

Ten.

The reflector was ringed by a protective barrier that looked like a partially tipped over chain-link fence. It loomed overhead, but the road continued into the space *beneath* the aluminum panels, past another caution sign, this one a red and black diamond with the words "Warning Radio Frequency Radiation Hazard." *Probably don't have to worry about that anymore*, she thought. The road turned across the face of the concave slope, spiraling around it toward the center, more than five hundred feet away.

Made it.

"We made it!" As she plunged beneath the suspended dish, she glanced back to make sure Mercy was still with her.

Mercy was not with her. Mercy was nowhere to be seen.

No!

Jenna wheeled around, almost stumbling again, and charged back up to the edge of bowl, shouting Mercy's name as she went. Had Mercy been hit? Had she sought cover in the woods? Jenna had to know.

No, you don't. You can't help her now.

Jenna ignored the cautionary inner voice, but when she reached the top and caught sight of two gunmen coming down the road toward her, she knew there was nothing more she could do for Mercy. As she ducked back down, a barrage of gunfire rattled into the underside of the reflector.

She turned off the road, but the ground was not as open as it had first appeared. Cables stretched like spider webs from the bottom of the dish to concrete footings that dotted the slope like the stumps of hewn trees, creating an obstacle course. The thin layer of soil underfoot was saturated, held together by nothing more than roots and inertia. With every step, the hill slid away beneath her. She pushed on, ducking under cables, slipping and sliding her way to the bottom of the depression.

Up close, the panels did not appear solid. Perforated with millions of holes like a sieve, they were about as opaque as a window screen. The raindrops that struck the panels did not stay there long, but collected together into streams of water that poured down onto the dense carpet of ferns that lay spread out beneath the reflector. As she descended deeper into the bowl, the runoff became a veritable waterfall, feeding small rivers that swept toward the center of the hollow.

Movement drew her eyes. A car sped along the corkscrew road more than a hundred yards away. It seemed too far off to worry about, and the road would take it even further away, but it would eventually, inevitably, come back toward her.

A small structure lay directly ahead—a shed or platform of some kind. It offered the best chance at cover and concealment. It was the obvious choice. The *too* obvious choice. But Jenna saw that it reached up almost to the underside of the dish. In a flash of intuition, she realized that this was by design. The platform was elevated so that workmen could conduct routine maintenance on the dish.

If I can climb up there...

She let the thought go. It seemed like the only option, and she didn't want to think about all the ways it might go awry. Behind her, the two gunmen on foot blundered down the hill, blocking any possibility of retreat. She angled toward the platform, even as the distant vehicle reached the apex of its orbit and began swinging around toward her.

I'm not going to make it.

The burden of her failures sapped the last of her will. Her leaden legs stumbled a few steps further, then she fell again, sprawling and sliding down the muddy slope.

I give up.

You have to live.

I can't. Can't run anymore.

You have work to do.

"What?"

Not quite knowing why, she struggled once more to her feet. The two gunmen were so close that she could see the exertion in their determined faces.

You have to live, the inner voice repeated. *You have to escape.*

Escape was impossible. She was being driven deeper into the funnel...

Funnel. That was exactly what it was. The limestone bowl caught all the rainwater that poured into it, and in the tropical environment, rain was a constant. The underside of the dish should have filled up like a lake.

Where does all that water go?

The streams carving across the slope supplied the answer. She lurched into motion once more, letting gravity draw her closer to the center.

She solved the mystery of the disappearing water a moment later. There was a gaping hole, like the entrance to a tunnel, or more precisely, a drain. It was enormous. To channel away the volume of water that accumulated in the basin, it had to be. Torrents of water from all around the bowl converged at the center and simply disappeared.

The car reached the end of the road near the platform, no more than fifty yards away. Even before it stopped, a door flew open and someone burst out like a jack-in-the-box: Noah, running toward her, shouting and waving. Another familiar figure emerged, close on his heels. It was Cort, limping on a wounded leg. The memory of shooting him in the safe-house gave Jenna a small glimmer of satisfaction, which she poured into a final burst of speed.

The drain loomed before her, a dark maw waiting to swallow her, bear her down to the bowels of the Earth, yet she knew that whatever uncertain outcome awaited below could be no worse than her fate if she remained.

When she was just ten feet away, she threw herself flat, into a channel of runoff that rushed by like white-water rapids. The water and her momentum carried her the rest of the way. As she slid over the edge, she felt no fear—only relief.

One way or another, it was finally over.

FIFTY-TWO

10:45 a.m.

It wasn't over. Not by a long shot. In the torturous moments that followed, Jenna wondered why she had imagined this to be a better alternative than the swift release of a bullet to the head.

She was simultaneously falling and drowning, hammered by the enormous volume of water and driven onto the anvil of an unseen slope. As she caromed from one jagged surface to the next, tumbling and spinning, she lost all sense of direction. Her lungs begged her to take a breath—water or air, it hardly mattered—but the pounding impacts left her unable to even gasp.

Something clipped the side of her head, just a glancing blow, but enough to drive a spike of pain through her skull. She wrapped her arms over her face, curling up into a protective ball, and braced herself for the next collision. She spun and bounced, slammed and scraped, blind and all but deafened by the roar of water. Yet through it all she remained conscious, and that eerily calm inner voice kept her company.

You have work to do.

She thought she knew what that meant. Her cloned siblings—men and women who had each followed different paths in life, and yet shared memories of something that had never actually happened—were preparing to trigger a chain reaction of destruction on the world.

Wipe the slate clean.

Jenna was not the only person who was aware of this, but she did know something that no one else knew—not Cort or Noah or any of the government assassins hunting the clones. She knew *why* they were doing it. She also knew that what had happened thus far—the SARS outbreak, the Internet attacks, and perhaps countless other acts of aggression and terror over the last two decades—were merely a prelude to what was about to occur. The attacks were merely preparatory moves, setting the stage for something that would trigger a global holocaust. But before the final act, the message had to be sent.

The message was the linchpin. Stop the message, and the planned destruction would be averted, or at the very least, postponed. Jenna knew from where and when the message would be sent, and only she was in a position to stop it.

Stop it? Why?

Tumbling through limestone tunnels like a spider in a downspout, the question of *why*—to say nothing of *how*—seemed unimportant. Yet, she was still alive, and as the miserable seconds stretched out into minutes, the impacts became less frequent. She could feel the rush of cool air on her face. She could *breathe* again! She was no longer falling, but being swept along in a subterranean river.

And sinking.

The chilly fresh water did not buoy her up the way salt water did, and as the crazy whitewater run slowed down, she was forced to uncurl her arms and legs and paddle to stay above the water line. After a few minutes, or perhaps only a few seconds, she felt herself moving faster again. The bottom rose up under her, scraping against her feet. Then without warning, she was falling again, vomited out of the cave and into daylight once more. The light was painfully bright after too much time in the darkness.

She tumbled down the face of a waterfall, splashed down into a pool beneath it, and was driven to the bottom by the force of the cascading water. Hydraulic eddies pinned her there, but she fought against them as she had everything and everyone else that had tried to kill her. After a brief struggle, she wrestled free of their grip and clawed her way to the surface.

The current, swift with the volume of rainwater feeding the river, caught hold of her. The water snaked between towering walls of limestone, slick with wet moss, impossible to climb. Jenna could do little more than tread water, dog paddling to stay in the middle of the river where she was less likely to be smashed against the rocks.

Despite the tropical climate, Jenna felt her body heat leaching away, and with it, the strength and will to keep going. Fatigue—physical and mental—stole over her, and without realizing it, she stopped paddling. The air in her lungs kept her buoyant, but when she exhaled, her head dipped closer to the surface. She knew she had to keep her face out of the water, but her consciousness was a dim light, unable to penetrate the dark clouds of exhaustion and hypothermia, fading with each passing second.

Fading...

Suddenly, she felt very heavy. The current pushed hard against her, but she wasn't moving. The river, it seemed, had chosen to cast her up on a rocky shoal.

Safe in the knowledge that she probably wouldn't drown, she was content to simply lay there, the tepid water continued to leach away her body heat. She needed to get out of the river and find shelter from the rain, but even the contemplation of movement was a daunting task.

Just get out of the river, she told herself. *Do that much, and then you can rest.*

With a groan, she rolled over and started crawling. The slippery rocks shifted beneath her, dropping her to the bottom, bruising her knees and scraping her palms. She endured the river's final attack and dragged herself onto the shore.

Now get up. Find some shelter.

She shook her head. *No. Rest now. That was the deal.*

Her internal retort was half-hearted. She knew that she had to keep moving. *Just a few more seconds...*

Something rustled in the woods beyond where she lay. She turned toward the sound, just as a man stepped into the open.

"No," she groaned, but her plea was as futile as everything else she had tried.

She didn't recognize the man, but there was no mistaking the pistol in his hand or his intent when he aimed it at her heart. He did not fire, however. Instead, he held something close to his mouth—a cell phone or walkie-talkie—and spoke. "This is Trace. I found her."

There was a brief pause, and then a disembodied voice—Cort's voice—issued from the handset. "You know what to do."

FIFTY-THREE

10:58 a.m.

Trace's expression reminded Jenna of how Zack had regarded her in the Everglades, just before—

I stabbed him in the eye.

—he tried to kill her. There was no grin of triumph, no exultation of sadistic bloodlust. Just a grim mask of resolve to perform an unpleasant task for the greater good, like cleaning up a toxic waste spill or putting out a brushfire.

You are dangerous.

He brought his gun up with a determined brusqueness. She could almost read his thoughts: *Make it quick. Don't let her distract you. She'll kill you if she gets the chance.*

Jenna doubted very much that she was physically capable of killing him. Just trying to speak left her on the verge of collapse. "How...did you find me?"

No real mystery there. The drainage system was probably a matter of public record. One phone call, and Cort would have known where she would end up. After that, it would have been a simple matter to intercept her on the river. She did not need an explanation. She just needed to make him realize that if he pulled the trigger, he would be killing a real human being. Trace showed no indication that he had even heard her.

You have to live.

How?

Flight? Impossible. She wasn't sure she could muster the strength to stand, much less make a dash for the tree line, and even if she could manage that, Trace was so close, she wouldn't get two steps.

Fight?

With what?

She closed her right hand over a smooth river stone the size of her fist. She could throw it. Even if she didn't put him out of commission, it might buy her a second or two to run.

And then what?

Her inner voice had no advice to give, but to her surprise, Noah's advice came to her. *Your gut reaction to a threat will be to either run away, as fast as you can, or to blow through it head on... But a lot of times, those are the worst choices you could make. You might make a bad situation even worse, or you might miss out on an opportunity.*

Opportunity?

She had just seconds to live, and she had already tried and failed to engage Trace. No doubt he had been skilled in the same arts of manipulation that Noah had taught her. What did that leave?

"I saw the signal!" she blurted. "The alien transmission. I know what it says."

Trace's expression did not change, but he did not fire.

"You guys are wrong if you think it's from Earth. It's not. I know who sent it and why. And I'm the only person who can tell you what it says. Kill me, and you'll never be able to stop what's coming."

Trace remained statue still for several more seconds.

This isn't working. Jenna curled her fist tighter on the rock. She would only get one chance, and even if she managed to connect, he would still get a shot off. *I need to turn sideways, make myself less of a target, keep my vital areas protected...*

Trace raised the radio unit once more. "This is Trace. I think you should hear what the girl has to say."

FIFTY-FOUR

11:05 a.m.

"Get up," Trace snarled, giving himself plenty of room in case she tried anything. Not that she had any intention of doing so. After Trace had reported her words to Cort, he had been advised to bring her back to the observatory, and that meant Cort was willing to hear what she had to say.

Opportunity.

She got to hands and knees, but when she tried to stand up, a wave of vertigo forced her back down. "I don't think I can," she said.

"You'd better. The only way you're getting out of here alive is on your feet."

She didn't think he was exaggerating. Grinding her teeth, she managed to stand. Once again, the world started spinning, so she staggered toward the woods. Ignoring Trace's shouts, she threw her arms around the nearest tree and hugged it until the sensation passed.

She made her way from tree to tree, following a path that led up to a rural road, where another agent waited at a parked car. Trace directed Jenna to sit in the back then slid in beside her.

Ignoring the gun barrel pressed up under her ribs, Jenna closed her eyes and allowed herself to drift. Life slowly seeped back into her chilled muscles, but she knew that her continued survival would now depend more on her mental abilities than a swift physical recovery. She would have to convince Cort that she was worth more to him alive than dead.

During their first encounter, the advantage had been his, but now she was in possession of a secret that could change the world. The trick would be convincing Cort that she was telling the truth.

Does he need to know the truth?

The question hit her like an epiphany. Cort was not some potential ally she needed to win over. He was her enemy. He wanted to kill her.

"They will fear you," the teacher had said, "not because of what you are, but because your very existence will force them to admit what they really are. Humanity has been judged and found wanting, and you are the proof. They will fear you. They will try to kill you."

Cort had said almost exactly the same thing. *They'll find you! They will kill you!*

Almost as an afterthought, the teacher had added. "They cannot be trusted."

Jenna remembered the teacher's words vividly, even though she knew now that this was an implanted memory. Not a false memory. It was as real as anything she had experienced. Stranger still, she could feel the rightness of the words. They were a part of her, the only possible explanation for who she was, and why she had always been different than everyone else. She could no more question the validity of these feelings than she could doubt her love of chocolate or her dislike for country music. It was simply who she was. More importantly, it defined what she had to do.

Soter had been more right than he knew when he had spoken of her destiny.

You have work to do.

You have to live.

The car's abrupt halt roused her from the state of half-sleep, and she opened her eyes to see the familiar road leading up to the observatory. A police car partially blocked the lane, but the officer waved them on and Jenna saw no more evidence of law enforcement. There was no trace of the tourists or civilian personnel. In the brief time since her failed escape, Cort had taken over the observatory and shut it down.

The car continued up the now desolate road and parked in front of the transmitter building. Jenna remained still, staring out the window, until Trace told her to get out. Jenna complied, moving robotically, careful not to do anything to provoke him. The short car ride had restored some of her vital energy, but she was in no shape to fight or run.

As Trace ushered her into the transmitter building, Jenna saw the physical evidence of the battle that had been waged to take the building—gouges in the walls, broken windows, bloodstains—but the bodies had been removed. A miasma of smoke hung in the air but the fire in the electrical room had been put out. The building seemed to be deserted. Jenna saw no one—alive or dead—until she reached the control room.

She took in the scene in gulps of recognition. Mercy was there, alive and apparently unhurt, sitting on the floor with her back to the wall. Soter was there too, looking a little rattled, but otherwise intact. A single gunman stood guard over them.

Next, Jenna saw Cort, still wearing the same tropical shirt, but his trousers had been replaced by baggy sweatpants. He stood with the aid of crutches. His scowl deepened when he saw her. "Well, look what the cat dragged in."

Until that moment, Jenna had not considered what she must look like. Bruised and battered, still soaking wet, and barely able to stand—if she looked half as wrecked as she felt, then Cort's remark was probably justified. Still, his words raised a spark of defiance. "Sorry about your leg, Cort. I should have aimed a little higher."

Her taunt did not evoke the rage she expected. Cort, like all the other killers that had been sent after her, seemed to have mastered the trick of depersonalizing the grim business of sanctioned murder. Instead of retorting with a threat, Cort simply regarded her for a moment then turned to the other person in the room.

Noah Flood came forward, almost at a run, and swept Jenna into his arms.

Jenna felt her sense of reality crumble. She stood there, unable to move, feeling his familiar strength, breathing in his scent, and she felt as if she were once more in the underground river, being carried along by a current too powerful to resist, toward an unknowable fate. She wanted nothing more than to believe that this was real, that Noah was here to rescue her and take her away to safety, but she couldn't endure the roller coaster of emotions anymore.

"Normally, I'd get all teary-eyed at this little Hallmark moment," Cort remarked, "But then I remember how many good men you've killed today, and I just want to put a bullet through your brain."

Noah jumped to her defense. "You know that wasn't her fault."

"I don't give a rat's ass whose fault it is. She's dangerous, and you know it."

Jenna raised her hands, placed her palms flat against Noah's chest, and pushed him away. A pained look creased his face, and he let out a soft grunt. It wasn't the hurt of rejection but real, physical pain. Cray's bullet had not killed him, but it hadn't simply bounced off either. She forced down the upwelling of concern and addressed Cort. "You're right. I'm dangerous, and so are all the others. You have no idea what you're facing."

"That's why you're still alive, kid. You're gonna explain it to me."

"And what do I get in return?"

Cort flashed a mirthless and insincere smile. "Anything you want. I'll write you a blank check."

"What you will do," Noah interjected, "is guarantee her safety. And if I have even a moment of doubt about whether you'll keep that promise—"

"Stay out of this," Cort leveled his venomous gaze at Noah. "You've caused enough trouble for one lifetime. But you know, you're right. *She* was just defending herself. You're the one who's really to blame for all of this. We let you get away with it fifteen years ago, because we thought you could handle it. I guess we know better now, don't we?"

"You're wrong about her."

"She's dangerous," Cort insisted. "She'll turn on you the first chance she gets, and then we'll all be screwed."

He turned to Jenna. "Here's what's going to happen, little girl. You are going to start talking. If I like what I hear, you get to keep breathing. You'll be taken to a secure facility—I won't tell you where—and that's where you'll spend the rest of your life. How long that might be will depend on how good your information is. That's as close to a guarantee as you're going to get."

"Everything is going to be all right." Jenna realized that Noah was speaking to her. "I know you've been through a lot. I'm sorry I wasn't there to protect you, but now I am. We'll get through it together, okay?"

Cort let out a low growl of displeasure.

"Okay?" Noah asked. "You trust me?"

Jenna didn't know how to answer. Was this another trick? Were Cort and Noah working together, playing some kind of good-cop/bad-cop game? She couldn't tell. She would never be able to tell. These two men were as skillful at deception as they were at violence.

Listen to your gut, but make up your own damn mind.

Her gut told her that she had no choice but to trust him.

You have to live.

Yes. I think I do.

She held his gaze. "Aren't you worried about what I might do?"

"Should I be?"

"You tell me. You're the one who said I was a ticking time-bomb."

"That's not what I said..." He inclined his head, ceding the point. "But I do know a thing or two about defusing time-bombs." He managed a wan smile. "I said that to get you away from Soter, but I don't believe it. Nobody is born evil. The universe doesn't work that way. Those others—the clones—might have your DNA, but they aren't *you*. Soter raised them to be what they are. *I* raised you."

"Nurture wins over nature?"

"Exactly. I'd like to think I raised you pretty well."

She nodded. "I trust you."

"Tell him what you know."

Jenna faced Cort and took a deep breath. "For starters, you're wrong about what's going on here. This isn't some Cold War Soviet disinformation campaign, and what's happening right now has nothing to do with the Russians."

"So, what then?" Cort asked. "Aliens?"

Jenna nodded, and with more certainty than she felt, continued. "The messages Dr. Soter received came from an extraterrestrial intelligence that wants to take over the Earth. They think that we're a disease, and that if they don't step in, we'll make the planet unlivable. They want the Earth for themselves, but before they can take over, they need to get rid of us, and what better way to do it than to have us destroy ourselves. The things that have been happening—what you told me the others like me are doing—that's just the first step."

"You were here for what, half an hour?" Cort's demeanor remained skeptical, but his question was sincere, and Jenna wondered if the Agency he worked for had not already secretly reached the same conclusion. "How do you know all this?"

"The second transmission received by Dr. Soter contained an entire human genome, which he used to create...us. What you call 'clones.'" Jenna paused. She would have to choose her words carefully now to avoid raising questions she wasn't willing to answer. "Our DNA includes instructions from the aliens, and the message itself contains the trigger to bring our memories of those instructions to the surface."

She turned to Noah. "Remember what you said? 'It's like a switch gets thrown.' Something hardwired into our DNA. You were right on both counts.

"Soter hoped that the DNA transmission contained instructions for creating a human ambassador—someone who could communicate with the aliens. He thought that we would be able to read the part of the message that he could never decipher. When it didn't work, when the clones read the message and...*changed*...he thought it was some error in his gene sequencing. Back to the drawing board. But it wasn't an error. The message activated those buried memories. It told them what they were supposed to do: start World War III."

She paused, letting it sink in, and was surprised by how much she cared about Noah's reaction. Not only had she just confirmed his original worst case scenario about the clones, she had also admitted to reading the message, activating the alien memories coded in her DNA. If he had any doubt about whether she was damaged goods, she had just removed it. Yet, if Noah felt that way, he gave no indication.

It doesn't matter what he thinks, cautioned an inner voice. Her own voice, but also the voice of the teacher. *They will fear you. They will try to kill you*.

"So?" Cort asked. "Soter's science projects blow a gasket and try to destroy the world. You're not telling us anything we didn't already know."

"Aren't you listening? These aren't random actions. It's the prelude to an invasion."

Cort stared hard at her. "Let's say I believe you. You're one of them. Why should I trust you?"

"*Because* I'm one of them," Jenna said, speaking slowly as if explaining a difficult concept to an impatient child. "I know what they're doing. I know how they think. And..." She took a deep breath. "I know what's going to happen next. If you want to stop them, you need my help."

Noah nodded to Cort as if to say: *See? Told you*, but Cort just shook his head. "Sorry kid, but if that's all you've got, you're not worth the bother."

He nodded to Trace.

"Cort!" Noah's protest had a menacing air to it. "That wasn't the deal."

"There is no deal," Cort said, shaking his head. "There never was, and you know it. This isn't even my decision to make. There's no other way."

"There's always another way."

"Not this time." Cort's pronouncement had the finality of a guillotine, but then he added. "Look, I get that you think of her as your daughter—"

"She *is* my daughter," Noah replied in a quiet voice.

He moved so quickly that even Jenna was startled. In the blink of an eye, he was behind Cort, gun drawn and pressed up under Cort's jaw. Cort dropped his crutches in surprise, letting them clatter loudly on the floor.

Trace and the other two gunmen brought their weapons up, aiming in Noah's direction. Jenna did not doubt that they were expert marksmen, capable of hitting what little of Noah's form was visible behind his human shield, but doing so would almost certainly result in Cort's death. She wondered if that mattered to them. Would they be willing to sacrifice their leader to make sure Jenna was dead?

As if reading her thoughts, Trace shifted his aim to her. "I'll kill her."

"Don't do it," Noah warned, moving his gun to cover Trace.

More shouted threats sizzled between the armed men, all of them talking but no one hearing. Somebody was going to pull a trigger, and once that happened, everyone in the room would probably die.

Jenna could feel the situation reaching a boiling point. She had to do something to stop the room from exploding into a storm of violence, but what difference could she make, unarmed, exhausted and helpless?

You have to live. They will fear you.

I have to make them fear me, she thought, and she realized she wasn't as helpless as she believed.

FIFTY-FIVE

11:20 a.m.

"Stop!"

Jenna's shout did not merely cut through the tension; time itself seemed to freeze. Then, one by one, guns lowered. The men fought against the command, with shaking muscles and disbelieving expressions. Their compliance was not voluntary. Jenna was as surprised as everyone else. Was this some newly discovered, genetically programmed ability, or an extension of the techniques Noah had taught her? Regardless of the explanation, she knew the effect would not last. She could already sense the window of opportunity sliding shut.

"Listen to me, all of you. Don't you get it? If we don't start working together, we'll all be screwed."

What are you doing?

She ignored the voice—the teacher's voice, her voice. "The world is about to come apart. I can stop it, but I can't do it alone."

Stop it? Why?

Cort was the first to shrug off the shout-induced paralysis. "And just how are you going to do that?"

You can't tell them.

A lump of shame rose into her throat. Was she really going to do this? Betray everything she believed in just to save her own skin?

No! The rebuttal was so forceful, she thought for a moment that she had spoken it aloud. *These aren't my beliefs. Just something planted in my head by someone who doesn't give a damn about me or anyone that I love.*

They don't love you, insisted the voice. *They fear you. They will kill you.*

No! She had to grind her teeth together to keep from shouting it. *It's not true.*

And it wasn't. What had Noah just said?

She is *my daughter.*

Despite everything he knew about her—things she probably didn't even know herself—he meant it.

That was real. That was the truth.

And he is *my father*, Jenna thought. Despite everything she knew about him—the lies he had told, the people he had killed—the realization filled her with a joy that was even more powerful than the guilt of her implanted memories.

She unclenched her jaw. "Everything that's been happening is just the set-up. There's something even worse coming."

Cort nodded impatiently. "You've already said that."

"I know, but something has to happen first."

They will kill you. Then they will destroy everything. Humanity is the cancer that must be eliminated, or everything will be destroyed. You must not interfere.

"The last part of the transmission, the part that contains the trigger, also has instructions. Before the final phase can begin, someone has to send a message back. It's a signal that the final attack is about to start. Maybe it's to let them know so they can send their invasion forces." The last part was conjecture, but it made sense.

"How do you know that hasn't already happened?"

"There's a time-table for it." She reached for the memory but it wasn't there anymore. Suddenly, she felt faint and staggered to a nearby desk for support. "Damn."

"Jenna?" Noah asked, then he returned his attention to Cort. "Tell your men to stand down, damn it. Guns on the ground."

Cort glowered but nodded to Trace and the others. Only when the guns were put away did Noah step away from Cort. "Jenna, what's wrong?"

"It's gone," she said, suddenly feeling helpless again. "Access denied."

"A fail-safe," Soter murmured, breaking his long silence. His voice sounded hollow, defeated. Jenna's explanation had stripped away his illusions and revealed his duplicity in what looked very much like a bid by an alien intelligence to exterminate humankind. "A defense mechanism in the genetic memory to prevent you from turning against the programming."

Jenna had to fight to catch her breath. What if there were other fail-safe mechanisms? Would all her memories slip away, leaving her a gibbering idiot, or worse, a brain-dead vegetable? Was she going to drop dead of a brain aneurism? "I can't remember when. I just remember that it's happening soon. Today, I think."

"Today?" Cort scoffed. "That's convenient."

"It makes sense," Noah countered. "It explains the escalation. You know it's true. That's why the agency panicked and authorized the sanction against us."

Cort let that go without comment. "Well if you can't remember anything about this signal, I don't see how you're going to be able to help stop it."

"Wait. The message is in the transmission. We still have that."

Soter shook his head. "But we still can't decipher it."

"I can." She looked to Cort, asking for permission, but also asking for his trust.

Cort frowned, and for a moment, Jenna thought he was going to further ridicule her, but then he nodded. "Do it."

The atmosphere in the room shifted. As Jenna took a seat in front of the computer, the others gathered behind her. Soter was poised over her shoulder. Mercy stood beside him, and Noah was beside her, so close that the events of the last two days seemed like a bad dream. Cort's presence ruined the illusion, but he too seemed eager to see what Jenna would reveal.

The computer monitor still showed the final sequence of the message. It no longer confounded Jenna's perceptions, but neither did its meaning become instantly apparent. "It's encrypted," she said. "The code is fairly simple. Each of these strings are individual numbers, like in the Wow! Signal, but they've been modified with a changing mathematical value."

She didn't know if she was explaining it correctly. Code-breaking was not a skill that Noah had taught her. Nevertheless, she faintly recalled the structure of the code. "It's like those puzzles where you substitute a number for a letter, but the key changes with each number."

"How does it change?" Soter asked, his earlier dejection replaced by an almost childlike enthusiasm. "What's the progression?"

Jenna searched her memory. The answer was still there, she could feel it. "It keeps increasing," she said slowly, as if stalling for time. "But always at a constant rate."

"A mathematical progression? Logarithmic? Prime numbers?" Soter's tone was becoming strident. "Think girl. What's the pattern?"

Something familiar. A face remembered, a name forgotten. "Spiral?"

"Like the Golden Ratio?"

Jenna's recall of that subject was picture perfect. The Golden Ratio—approximately 1.618, also called *phi* and represented with the Greek letter φ—was one of those remarkable examples of mathematical perfection in nature. She had learned about it in both math and art classes. It described the perfect spiral in conch shells and pine cones, and had been employed in both art and architecture for thousands of years. It was also, Jenna recalled, the exact ratio found in the Fibonacci sequence where each number was the sum of the two preceding numbers: 0,1,1,2,3,5,8 and so forth.

"That's it! It uses the Fibonacci sequence. The first value is unchanged. The second and third increase by one, then two, and so on."

Soter laid a hand on her shoulder. "May I?"

Jenna vacated the seat, and the older man took her place. He opened a new program and began typing, his fingers flying across the keys as if inspired. It took him just a few minutes to write a translation algorithm, after which he cut and pasted in the binary sequence.

Jenna held her breath as the start of a now all-too familiar phrase appeared.

This is th...

The rest was a meaningless jumble of letters and numbers, but Jenna knew that she had been right about the key to the cipher. "It resets to zero after ten characters."

Soter nodded. "That makes sense. If the progression continued to follow the Fibonacci sequence, it would run to more than twelve places." He made a quick adjustment, and then he ran the program again.

"'This is the way the world ends,'" Noah read aloud. "'Not with a bang but a whimper.' That's from 'The Hollow Men' by T.S. Eliot."

Jenna flashed him a smile. Noah, it seemed, could still surprise her.

Cort harrumphed. "I'm supposed to believe that these aliens of yours are English lit majors?"

Soter shrugged. "I didn't just make this up. It's been clear from the start that the intelligence behind this understood our capabilities. They would certainly be familiar with our works of art."

"I think the poem is part of the trigger," Jenna added. "Like a hypnotist might use."

Cort rolled his eyes, but said nothing more.

The rest of the message was mostly numbers, but Jenna felt certain that Soter's program had correctly unlocked it. "Those are coordinates." She recalled the emergency letter Noah had left for her. "Somewhere in the Southwest. New Mexico or Arizona."

Soter recognized the rest of it. "I think this sequence is a Julian date. And I'd recognize these numbers anywhere. That's the location of the Chi Sagittarii stellar group, where the Wow! Signal originated and this—1420—is the original frequency, the hydrogen line."

He turned his chair to face Cort. "The VLA radio telescope is in Socorro, New Mexico."

As she read it, Jenna felt her memory of the message stirring, but the voice remained silent. "That's where we have to go. Someone—one of the clones—is going to send a signal into space. To those coordinates."

Cort nodded slowly. "You said there's a date?"

"A date and time," Soter replied. He seemed suddenly ill-at-ease.

"When?"

He swallowed. "Midnight tonight."

"Well that's freakin' wonderful," Cort grumbled.

Something in Soter's manner set alarm bells ringing in Jenna's head. "You already knew this was going to happen today."

Soter refused to meet her gaze. "For years, there was talk among the children of something important related to this date."

"You knew," Jenna repeated. There was no accusation in her tone. "That's the real reason you sent Cray to get me, isn't it? The deadline had arrived and you still didn't know what the message meant."

His silence was answer enough.

"So," Cort said after a pause. "At midnight, something is going to happen at this place in New Mexico. We'll get somebody there and shut the place down."

Soter shook his head. "Julian dates start at noon Greenwich Mean Time. The date/time indicated in the message is midnight GMT. Eight hours from now."

"I need to be there," Jenna said.

"That's not going to happen," Cort declared, making a cutting gesture with his hand. "The only way you're leaving here is in my custody."

"Like hell," Noah growled, raising the pistol again. The other agents tensed but did not go for their grounded weapons.

Cort waved them off but kept his attention on Noah. "If you try to leave any other way, you will be hunted down. Even you aren't that good."

"I guess we'll see, won't we." Noah turned to the others. "Jenna, Mercy, we're going."

Soter stepped forward. "Take me. I have a plane waiting on the tarmac at the Arecibo Airport. It could get us to New Mexico with time to spare."

Noah stared back, his face an unreadable mask. "You heard what the man said. They're going to be hunting us. You sure you want to take that chance?"

The mathematician nodded soberly.

"The more the merrier," Noah muttered. "Mercy, be a dear and collect those guns. And while I'm thinking about it, let's have your phones. If you're going to be hunting us, it only seems fair to give us a head start."

Cort signaled for his men to comply, this time without threats or taunts. Jenna understood that they were past that stage now. Noah was not going to change his mind, and Cort was already thinking ahead to what he would do next. Jenna realized with sick certainty that the running and fighting was not over, not by a long shot, but now there was a lot more at stake than just her own survival.

She moved closer to Noah. "There's no way we can make it to New Mexico without Cort's help."

Noah glanced in Cort's direction before answering in a low whisper that only she could hear. "We aren't going to New Mexico, but Cort doesn't need to know that. I know a guy that can get us to Cuba. They won't be able to touch us there."

"No!" The forcefulness of her denial surprised even her. She had spoken so loudly that everyone in the room looked at her. "I have to go to New Mexico."

Noah frowned in irritation. "Jenna, you've done enough. Cort can take care of this with a phone call. You don't need to be there."

"But I do. I have to be there," she repeated. "I'm the only one who can stop it."

"Why?"

She had no answer. There was no rational explanation for the compulsion she felt, but if she revealed her uncertainty, Noah would never agree.

"There's more to the instructions," she lied, except part of her realized it wasn't a lie. While the coded message did contain some specific instructions, its primary function was to activate the implanted memories. Although that door had closed, Jenna knew that there was a lot more that had not been revealed to her. "I think I have to go there to unlock the rest."

"You think?"

She gripped his arm. "Noah, you have to trust me. I'm the only one who can stop it."

Noah's frown deepened. "I believe you, but I'm not the one you have to convince."

Jenna turned to Cort. "If you get me to New Mexico, then I'm all yours. You can ship me off to one of your secret prisons, throw me in a hole and make me disappear forever."

Noah stepped between her and Cort. "Jenna, don't be stupid."

Jenna pointed at the computer screen where the message was still displayed. "You see that? How the message ends?"

Nobody had commented on the last line of the transmission, the final marching orders for each clone. Four simple but ominous words in plain English: *Wipe the slate clean.*

"That's what's going to happen if I don't get to New Mexico. What happens after that doesn't matter, because if I don't get there, there isn't going to be an 'after.'"

Noah stared at her for a long time, his expression twisted with emotions that he was no longer able to suppress.

It was Cort that finally broke the silence. "So I'm supposed to take you at your word? What, are you gonna pinky-swear to give yourself up when it's all done?"

Before Jenna could answer, Mercy spoke. "I'll stay. You can keep me as collateral."

"Mercy, no." Jenna heard Noah echoing her own denial, but Mercy just shook her head.

"It's okay, Jenna. I believe you. I know that you have to do this. It sickens me that we were used like this." Jenna knew what Mercy meant by 'we.' She wasn't just Jenna's sister or mother. All of the clones had been created using her DNA. "And this way, we'll still be together when it's all over."

Cort just laughed. "What the hell? It's a deal."

RISE

FIFTY-SIX

Plains of San Agustin, New Mexico, USA
5:05 p.m. (Mountain Daylight Time)

The flight took six hours but to Jenna it felt like hardly any time had passed. Part of this was due to her anxiety about what would happen when they arrived. Time always seemed to drag when she was looking forward to something good—the last day of school or a birthday—and flew by when something bad loomed on the horizon.

She thought she would be able to spend at least some of the trip sleeping, but even though she felt dead on her feet, every time she closed her eyes, she had a vision of Mercy, flanked by Cort's men, waving good-bye. She settled for a hot meal from the Gulfstream's galley, washed down with several bottles of Pepsi, and she listened in as the rest of the group discussed strategy.

Cort had wasted no time asserting his authority, and Noah did not challenge him. Jenna sensed that her insistence on making the trip—and her decision to surrender to Cort at the cost of Mercy's freedom—had taken the wind out of Noah's sails. That, and the fact that he had been shot just eighteen hours earlier.

The wound wasn't serious—the bullet had deflected off a rib, fracturing it and tearing up the surrounding tissue, but doing no damage to vital organs—but a gunshot was a gunshot. He bore the pain stoically, but Jenna saw how he winced a little whenever he changed position.

He had been taken to the hospital, along with the two deputies who—Jenna was pleased to learn—had also survived the shooting, thanks to their standard-issue body armor. Noah had managed to slip away but had arrived at Mercy's trailer just as the police were showing up. With no way to track Jenna and Mercy, he had turned to his old handler at the Agency—Bill Cort—who had briefed him on the sanction and the reasons behind it. Noah had been as surprised as Cort when he learned of Jenna's arrival at the safe house.

Jenna didn't believe Cort's assertion that he had been out of the loop on the decision to send the hit team, but they were well past the point where recriminations would make any difference.

Soter also seemed to have set aside his aversion toward the men who had killed his team and destroyed his lab fifteen years earlier. Jenna suspected that had more to do with the realization that he had been a pawn in the opening move in a war to destroy humanity. He spent nearly two full hours describing the history of the project. The account was more or less the same as what he had told Jenna during the flight from Miami, but the air of pride had faded. It was now a recitation of facts. When he was done, he gave what information he could concerning the whereabouts of more than a dozen clones—Jenna noted that he no longer referred to them as his children.

The conversation had come around to the transmission's origin. Soter maintained that an extraterrestrial intelligence was the most plausible explanation, but Cort seemed reluctant to even speculate. "Let's just deal with one thing at time," he said.

It seemed to Jenna like textbook denial. An extraterrestrial explanation would not only mean a threat beyond comprehension, and possibly against which humanity would be powerless, but it would also invalidate a host of beliefs about the nature of life and the meaning of existence. It was no surprise that Cort shied away from the topic. Jenna had her own reasons for not wanting to discuss it. The entire conversation had been an excruciating ordeal, in which her very artificial origin was dissected and put on display. Her unique abilities— what her school teachers called 'gifts'—had occasionally made her the target of ridicule from jealous classmates, but she had never felt the kind of embarrassment she now felt listening to this discussion.

She felt like a freak. No, worse than that: an illegitimate freak.

Noah sensed her discomfort, holding her hand, squeezing reassurance into her, but she endured without comment. The events surrounding her, past and future, were much more important than her hurt feelings.

The discussion turned to the question of how to proceed when they arrived at their destination. Cort tried to arrange for Agency assets from Texas and California to be sent in ahead of them, but the remote location confounded those efforts. He contacted the military, but was tight-lipped about the full results of that conversation, saying only that there would be no additional boots on the ground, meaning that the little group in the Gulfstream would be the sole defenders of the human race. If they failed, it would be game over.

"What should we expect?" Cort asked.

Soter turned to Jenna.

"How should I know?" she snapped, but then she realized why he had deferred to her. If anyone could predict what the clones would do, it would be her. Yet the truth was that she didn't know. The door to the implanted memories remained shut. The only thing she really knew for sure was that the urge to go to the coordinates in the message was overpowering. Even now, with the memories ripped from her head, Jenna felt the irresistible urge. The other clones surely felt it, too. She wondered how many were on their way there? She did not share this insight with Cort, though, and he noticed the omission.

"I signed off on this little field trip because you insisted that only you could stop them," he reminded her.

"I'll understand it better when I get there," she said.

They were nearly at their destination, and she still had no idea what was going to happen.

After landing, they headed out from Socorro on US Route 60. Noah was at the wheel of their rented Jeep Cherokee, maintaining a steady seventy-five miles per hour. Cort sat in the front passenger seat. Soter and Jenna were in the back. She could see distant mountain ranges on the horizon, but the foreground was flat and desolate. Florida was flat, but at least there were palm trees to break up the monotony. Here, there was nothing except the occasional herd of cattle, and—distant but growing ever larger—an irregular line of satellite dishes.

As they approached, Jenna began to appreciate just how extraordinary the Very Large Array was. Unlike the Arecibo Observatory, which made use of a single enormous dish, more or less fixed in place, the Very Large Array's twenty-seven individual dishes—each more than eighty feet in diameter and arranged in a Y-shaped pattern with legs that extended more than thirteen miles in each direction—worked in unison to create a single antenna that could be extended to a maximum twenty-two miles across. A tourist brochure she had picked up in Socorro described how the 230-ton dishes could be moved as needed using a special transport vehicle running on railroad tracks that extended to the Y's full limit.

As the full scope of the observatory came into view, Cort looked back at Jenna. "Why does it have to be here? Couldn't this signal be sent from any radio telescope?"

Soter answered before Jenna could admit her ignorance. "We can only speculate about the reason, but my hypothesis is that the intelligence behind the message was very familiar with our capabilities and our potential. In 1977, when the Wow! Signal and the transmission I later received were sent, the VLA was the best radio telescope on Earth. The author of the transmission could expect that it would still be functioning thirty-seven years later.

The same cannot be said for the Big Ear telescope, which received the Wow! Signal. It was dismantled in 1998 to make room for a golf course."

"A golf course?" Noah echoed, glancing in the rear view mirror. "You're kidding, right?"

Soter grimaced. "I wish I were. One would expect a better fate for the place that marks the first contact by an alien intelligence."

Cort gave a sarcastic chuckle. "Maybe someday they'll build a war memorial there."

Nobody had a response to that.

FIFTY-SEVEN

5:31 p.m.

The VLA dishes grew larger until they stretched across half the horizon like a picket line. A rough map on the tourist pamphlet revealed that the highway passed through the upper leg of the array. Just before they reached it, Noah turned off the main route and headed toward the cluster of administrative buildings near the junction of the three legs. He drove past the visitors center—the parking lot was empty—and continued to the control building, a two story concrete and stone structure.

Jenna was struck by the profound differences between the VLA facility and the Arecibo Observatory. The landscape was open and featureless, unlike the lushly forested limestone hills in Puerto Rico. The buildings reminded her more of the structures she'd glimpsed at the abandoned Aerojet facility in the Everglades—big, open and scattered across the landscape. The enormous dishes sprouted from the plain like surreal white mushrooms in a Lewis Carroll story. Strangest of all was the profound quiet.

"Sure doesn't look like anything is about to happen," Cort remarked, taking out his cell phone and glancing at the display. "Less than half an hour to go. I'm guessing you don't just walk into a place like this and say 'I'd like to place a collect call to the Andromeda galaxy.'"

Soter shook his head. "Scientists have to schedule their research months, even years in advance. And this facility is primarily a receiving station."

"You mean it can't be used to call out?"

"It can. There's no fundamental difference between a transmitter and a receiver in terms of hardware. A transmitter like the one at Arecibo, is built to sustain a high-power transmission over long periods. A transmission sent from here wouldn't be very powerful at all, but the focusing ability of the array would compensate for that. However, making the changes would require some technical knowledge."

"Do any of your clones have that knowledge?"

This wasn't the first time the subject had been brought up, but Soter's answer was the same. "To the best of my knowledge, no."

"Well, we're here. I guess we should go and make sure nobody snuck in the back door."

As they headed in through the main entrance, Jenna hung back, allowing the three men to take the lead. The urge to make this journey, that she had first experienced in Puerto Rico, had not relented, but she felt no sense of familiarity or attunement with this place. No new implanted memories had been awakened in her. She couldn't tell whether the door to those memories had been shut or there was simply nothing there in the first place.

Signs for the self-guided walking tour pointed the way to the control room. Like the Arecibo Observatory, the room looked more like an office than a portal for watching distant stars. More than a dozen computers and monitors, each one displaying a graph or lines of text, sat atop a long horse-shoe shaped desk wrapped around the room's perimeter. Anyone hoping to see spectacular pictures of black holes or nebulae would have gone away disappointed.

Three men were working in the room, hunched over their workstations, busily entering data. One of them looked up and offered a friendly wave, then went back to his task. The others ignored them.

Cort cleared his throat. "I need to speak to whomever is in charge."

All three men looked up, and Jenna heard one of them groan. She scanned the faces—all were middle-aged Caucasian men. None of them bore even a passing resemblance to her. The man who had waved rose from his seat and came over to speak with them. He eyed Cort's crutches—Jenna could almost see him leaping to the conclusion that they were going to complain about the 'walking' part of the walking tour, but he kept his smile in place as he introduced himself.

"I'm Dr. Jon Miller. Is there something I can help you with?"

"Are you in charge?" Cort asked. Jenna noted that he was being aggressive to the point of rudeness, asserting his dominance to ensure cooperation. It was one of the techniques Noah had taught her, but not one that she had ever practiced. In her experience, subtlety produced better results.

The smile slipped a little but Miller remained diplomatic. "Well, I'm in charge of a few things. If you tell me your concerns, I'll have a better idea where to direct you."

"We're federal officers, investigating a possible threat against this facility."

The news hit Miller like a bomb. The other two men sat up straighter, appearing almost poised to flee. "A threat? I...uh, can't imagine what kind of...uh..."

Cort allowed the tension to build a moment, then his demeanor changed completely. "It's probably nothing, but I'd appreciate it if you could go over a couple of things with us. Just to be sure."

Miller swallowed. "Sure."

Soter stepped forward. "Would you please show us the scheduled activity for the next twenty-four hours?"

Miller nodded and gestured to a laptop computer that was already displaying a spreadsheet. Soter scanned the document, scrolling down, then looked back and shrugged.

Cort addressed Miller again. "How easy would it be to change the orientation of the array to send a transmission?"

Miller gave a surprised laugh, but then he became somber again when he realized Cort was not joking. "Not easy at all. In the first place, we're a receiving station. And we don't change the schedule for just anyone."

"You're not hearing me, doc." A little of the earlier surliness was back. "If someone came in here, pointed a gun at your head and told you to do it, how tough would it be to make the changes?"

Miller went pale. "Uh...is that what you are—"

"No. Just answer the question."

"We could do it from this room. It would take a few minutes."

Cort turned away as if Miller no longer existed and addressed Noah and Jenna. "That's it then. All we need to do is secure this room and there's no way that signal is going out. Not from here at least."

Jenna did not share Cort's certitude, but before she could offer a rebuttal, she noticed Miller staring at her. She felt a sudden rush of apprehension and took a quick step forward. "Dr. Miller. You recognize me, don't you?"

He shook his head, embarrassed at having been caught. "No. I'm sorry."

"Dr. Miller, this is important. Do I look like someone that you know?"

He feigned ignorance a moment longer before admitting, "You could be her twin sister."

Cort was quick to grasp the importance of this revelation. "Who? Someone that works here? One of the astronomers?"

"Sophie isn't an astronomer. She's with the track maintenance team."

"Sophia Gallo?" Soter asked.

"I...ah, don't know her last name."

Soter turned to the others. "Sophia is from Generation Six, the same as Jarrod and Kelli."

"Wonderful," Cort growled. "Track maintenance. That explains how we missed her. We were looking for brainiacs. Is she here right now?"

Miller shrugged.

"We're going to have to sweep the entire site," Cort said, directing his words to Noah.

Jenna knew that was no small undertaking. There was a lot of ground to cover, half a dozen buildings, and if the array itself was included, twenty-seven antenna dishes sprawled out on nearly forty miles of railroad track.

Noah nodded then turned to Jenna. "Well, I guess it's a good thing we brought you along after all."

The words were barely out of his mouth when one of the other men called out. "Dr. Miller? Something is happening to the array."

"What the hell?" Miller looked at the spreadsheet again. "There aren't any adjustments scheduled."

"Shut it down," Cort ordered.

Miller and the other two men crowded around a different terminal and began tapping in commands, but after a few seconds, it was apparent that the array was not responding to their efforts. Jenna looked past them and out the large window, gazing out across the array. Even from a distance, she could see the inverted domes moving, swinging around and tilting toward a different part of the sky. It was beautiful to watch: a perfectly synchronized dance that ended only when all twenty-seven dishes were aimed at a group of stars known as Chi Sagittarii.

FIFTY-EIGHT

6:00 p.m.

Jenna felt a hand on her shoulder and turned to find Noah, standing close. Protective. "You were right," he whispered. "Is there anything you can do?"

She looked back, uncertain. A sense of satisfaction filled her. Everything was playing out according to the plan that had been written in her DNA. She didn't need to do anything. Yet her rational mind knew that the feeling was a lie. It was *wrong*. She didn't want the message to be sent. Didn't want the world and everyone she loved to be swept away in a global apocalypse.

Cort was still trying to get a grasp on what was happening. "Can this be done remotely? Is there an alternate control room?"

Miller shook his head. "The computer controls the array, but we're locked out."

"It's Chu," Jenna whispered. "He's taken over the network."

Cort stared at her a moment, processing this, then turned to Miller. "Is that possible?"

Miller raised his hands in a gesture that indicated he was out of his depth. "I wouldn't have thought any of this was possible, but yes. If somebody broke into our network, they could take control of the array."

"So he could be anywhere. Timbuktu, for all we know."

"He's here," Jenna said, still whispering, though she didn't know why. "He's with Sophia. They're here somewhere. They have to be."

One of the other technicians spoke up. "If you wanted to take over the network on site, the best way to do it would be to splice into one of the fiber optic lines."

"Where are those?"

"Everywhere. But the antennas would be the ideal place. Or the pads. There are nodes at each one."

Cort breathed a curse. "Can you pull the plug? Shut down everything?"

"We're locked out," Miller repeated.

"Then cut the damn cord with an axe!" The scientist looked aghast at the suggestion, so Cort continued, "I'll do it. Show me where."

"Too late," Jenna murmured. She wasn't sure how she knew this. It didn't feel like an implanted memory. It might have been nothing more than a sense of imminent defeat, but she was certain that the message was already being transmitted. If it was as simple as the Wow! Signal, it might already be done. If it was something more complex, like the DNA transmission, it would take longer, but certainly no more than a few minutes. And then...?

Then Jarrod Chu would signal the rest of the clones scattered around the world to start tipping the dominos.

This is the way it's supposed to happen.

This time, there was no mistaking the source of the thought. Her voice—the teacher's voice—still with her.

No! I won't do this. I won't stand by and let everything be destroyed. I didn't get this far by giving up.

She closed her eyes and tried to reach out with her mind. She had always heard that twins shared a strange, almost psychic bond. Maybe clones did, too. She envisioned Jarrod Chu, bent over a computer, watching as the message was uploaded. Was it a vision—was she seeing it through his eyes because of some psychic bond—or just her imagination? Either way, it didn't help. She tried to picture Sophia Gallo, someone she had never even heard of until sixty seconds before, yet with whom she shared a unique blueprint. What was she doing right now?

Track maintenance.

After the antennas, the most critical component of the Very Large Array was the rail line, which made it possible to move the massive dishes to different positions along the legs of the Y. Ensuring that the two hundred ton dishes could be moved without incident required the forty miles of steel rail and over sixty thousand wooden railroad ties. Maintaining all that required specialized equipment and unique vehicles.

Cort dug into his pocket and pulled out a phone. He tapped a contact name and strolled a few feet away, his back to them, his voice hushed, but urgent.

With Cort distracted, Jenna whirled to face Noah. "I can find them. Give me the keys."

She said it so forcefully that Noah dug into his pocket for the keys, but the gravity of her demand hit him before he could hand them over. He gave her a crooked smile. "Sorry. The rental agreement doesn't allow that. But I'll drive you."

For just an instant, Jenna was grateful for his support. Then a chill, like a premonition of death, shot down her spine.

Just you.

She shook her head. "I can't explain why, but I have to do this alone. You asked if there was anything I can do. This is it. Please trust me."

His smile fell, replaced by an intense stare that cut right to her core. "Jenna..."

"Trust me," she repeated, then added a word that seemed strange in her mouth. "Dad."

"I trust you," he said, barely louder than a whisper. He held out the keys, but as she took them, he said, "Remember, Jenna. Nurture is more powerful than nature. I raised you well."

As she bolted from the room, she heard Cort shouting, "Where the hell is she going? In ten minutes, this place will be—" The door shut, cutting off his voice.

In ten minutes, what?

Doesn't matter, she decided, and she ran faster.

FIFTY-NINE

6:03 p.m.

Noah's words haunted her as she sprinted toward the parked Jeep. He had seen through her. He had seen something that even she couldn't see. She was being summoned—drawn by a siren song that rang out from every cell in her body—to a reckoning where she would discover whether he was right.

Stop it? Why?

She slid behind the wheel and started the SUV. The track maintenance yard was just three hundred feet away, easily identifiable by the collection of strange looking vehicles, many of which sat on rail sidings. Two men in hard hats and work clothes stood near one of the vehicles and she steered toward them, rolling down the window as she skidded to a stop.

"Where's Sophia?"

One of the men glanced up, a perturbed expression on his face. "You shouldn't be driving in here."

"Sophia," she repeated, more forcefully. "It's an emergency."

"She went to check the west track. But you shouldn't—"

Jenna didn't hear the rest. She angled the Jeep toward the rails directly ahead and punched the accelerator. She bounced over the rails without slowing and then steered onto the access road that ran parallel to the tracks. A cloud of dust rose behind her like some kind of biblical pillar of smoke, marking her presence. Cort would have no trouble tracking her. The speedometer ticked up—fifty miles per hour...sixty...seventy. It didn't seem fast enough.

She passed an enormous hangar-like structure, easily as large as the Aerojet silo building in the Everglades. The side facing the rails was open. A massive antenna stood inside, undergoing some kind of maintenance. The dish was pointing straight up, like an enormous chalice waiting to be filled.

Beyond that building lay several empty pads, each with three concrete footings that rose up from the dusty ground like grave markers, then a dish, then more pads. She checked each without slowing, looking for the track maintenance vehicle that would indicate Sophia's location. Three long minutes later, she spotted what she was looking for: a Chevrolet pickup truck that had been modified with flanged steel wheels to run on railroad tracks. It sat parked in front of a towering antenna dish. As she got closer, she saw movement high above, on the staircase that led up to the base of the massive dish.

Jenna stopped the Jeep and got out. A dark haired woman wearing blue coveralls, descended the staircase, taking several steps at a time with the agility of an experienced parkour athlete. Even from a distance, Jenna could see the resemblance; the woman—it had to be Sophia Gallo—looked just like her.

Sophia paused on the lowermost landing just above the concrete pillars upon which the antenna rested. There was an unmistakable look of excitement on her face, and Jenna found that she too had broken into a broad smile.

"Come on up."

Without waiting for further prompting, Jenna mounted the short flight of stairs to the landing, where she found Sophia waiting with open arms. Jenna fell into the embrace without the slightest hesitation.

The sense of kinship—sisterhood—was overpowering. The bond she felt with Mercy was only a shadow of what she now experienced. This woman didn't merely share the same DNA. Sophia and Jenna were the same person, only separated by age and experience.

Sophia released her and held her at arm's length. "You're new."

It sounded a little strange, but Jenna understood. It wasn't just that Jenna was young. Sophia was a connected part of a family that Jenna had only just learned about. "Yeah," she replied. "It's kind of a long story."

"I'm Sophie."

"Jenna."

"Wonderful." Sophia laughed with undisguised joy, "Well, you're timing couldn't be better. Come on up to the vertex room. You can tell us both."

She gestured to the ascending stairs, which rose at least another forty feet above the landscape.

"Both?"

"Oh, sorry. I guess you really are new. Jarrod is up there."

Jenna was not the least bit surprised that her intuition had been proven correct. Everything was happening according to plan. She started up the stairs behind Sophia, and with each step, she felt herself moving closer to a pivotal moment in history. The moment *everything* would change. She wondered if this was how the crew of the Enola Gay had felt one early August morning in 1945, as they took off from the Marianas Islands with a cargo of nuclear death in their bomb bay. The world was about to change, and Jenna would bear witness.

Sophia passed a gently chugging compressor and ducked under one of the large curving gears that allowed the dish to tilt. She continued up another flight of stairs that ended at an innocuous looking door right below the dish. She opened it and allowed Jenna to step inside first.

The room looked empty, like a disused storage closet. A small raised metal platform provided access to the upper reaches of the pyramid-shaped space. Several large cylindrical objects reached down from overhead. A man stood in front of a cylinder. She recognized him, both from the picture Cort had shown her at the safe house and from the uncanny resemblance to the face she saw in the mirror. Jarrod Chu. He held a laptop computer trailing a thick cable connected to the cylinder.

Jarrod showed only a trace of surprise at seeing her, and then his face broke into the same smile with which Sophia had welcomed Jenna. Sophia stepped in behind her and made the introduction. "Jarrod, meet Jenna. She's new."

"Very new," Jarrod remarked. His voice was a deeper version of Jenna's. "You must have slipped through the cracks. Last generation?"

Jenna risked a quick glance at the computer screen. It showed a download progress bar, about two-thirds green.

I'm not too late, she thought. And then, *Too late for what?*

"I think so," she answered. "And I only learned about...all off this...a couple of days ago." A small lie, but one she delivered without the slightest hint of dishonesty. Jarrod gave no indication of registering the falsehood, and Jenna realized that, despite his training as an FBI special agent, he wasn't adept at reading people. She pointed at the laptop. "Is that it?"

"This is it," he confirmed. "In about two minutes, give or take, it will be done."

Two minutes. Jenna felt a tingle of anticipation. *All I have to do is stand back, let it happen and the world will change.*

I told Noah I could stop it.

Stop it? Why?

"What exactly is it?"

Jarrod cocked his head sideways in a look of mild surprise. He glanced at Sophia then back at Jenna. "You mean you don't know?"

Jenna gave a helpless shrug. "Still catching up."

Jarrod tapped the touch pad and then turned the screen so she could get a better look. The display was filled with ones and zeroes, a binary code. After just a moment's scrutiny, Jenna recognized the pattern. It was identical to the DNA message Soter had received thirty-seven years earlier. But then an impossible detail leapt out. A change. Something in the code had been modified, added, but why?

She almost asked for an explanation, but before she could phrase the question, she came up with a possible answer on her own. The DNA message was a unique recognition code. Sending it back to the source would be a way of signaling that it had been read and understood. The addition revealed that the language could also be spoken by those on the receiving end.

"You must have talked to Soter," Jarrod continued. "How is our dear father?"

"Uh, he seemed kind of confused actually. He didn't think any of us understood the last part of the transmission."

Sophia grinned. "He still thinks it's from aliens."

This time, Jenna made no effort to hide her ignorance. "It's not?"

Jarrod laughed. "You *do* have some catching up to do."

She waited for him to elaborate, but instead he returned his attention to the computer, closing the window with the message and checking the progress bar. Three-quarters done now. *Ninety seconds? Less? And how much time was left on Cort's ten minute countdown, to...what? Nothing good.*

"I know what you're thinking," Jarrod continued.

"You do?" *He does? I doubt it.*

"You're wondering if this is the right thing to do," Sophia said.

"We've all thought it," Jarrod said.

Jenna gave an involuntary gasp. *Of course they know. We practically share a brain.* "Is it?" she asked, abandoning all pretense. "Destroying the world?"

"Destroying?" Jarrod exchanged another meaningful glance with Sophia. "Jenna, we're *saving* the world. Saving it from this slow death called humanity. I know it's a lot to process, and I know you want to believe there's a better way. We all did. We've spent years trying to find a better way, but the message..."

Sophia picked up the thread of his explanation. "You only need to look at a newspaper to see it. We—humans—either consume with no regard for the future, or hide our heads in denial while the problems multiply."

"We're omnivores," Jarrod said. "In the truest sense of the word. We devour everything. And we congratulate ourselves on our ability to adapt when we exhaust one resource, even though our miracle solution drives thousands of species to extinction.

"Did you know that in the 1960s the human population was poised to exceed carrying capacity? The planet could not produce enough food to feed everyone. The population was about three billion, and one third of them were just a drought away from starvation. But then we discovered new ways to extend the food supply. New strains of wheat and rice, fertilizers made from petrochemicals, new farming methods, intensive factory fishing. And what has happened? Ninety percent of the world's forests have been cleared for agriculture. The seas have been emptied of fish and are poisoned by fertilizer run-off. Worst of all, instead of stabilizing the food supply to feed three billion, the so-called Green Revolution fueled a population explosion. It took thousands of years for the population to reach three billion. In the last forty years, it has more than doubled. And by the middle of this century, there will be ten billion people."

In the back of her mind, Jenna could see the seconds ticking away, but she knew that Jarrod wasn't stalling. His intention was to educate her. To help her overcome her moral reservations about what they were doing...what they were destined to do.

"No one even realizes what a disaster it was," he continued. "Human society congratulates itself on their ability to squeeze the Earth's limited resources even harder, ravaging the natural world, heating the planet with our waste until the oceans turn to acid and the land becomes a barren desert. Only when we have killed every other living thing will humans admit to folly, and then they will say 'Why didn't we do something about it?' Well, we *are* doing something."

"We aren't destroying the world," Sophia said. "Humanity is doing that. We're saving it. Treating the infection before it kills everything."

Jenna felt the truth of the words. Humanity's fatal flaw was the ability to ignore dire generational problems while focusing on short term gratification. It was written into the human genome as surely as this moment had been written into her own. And she knew, without a shred of uncertainty, that it would never stop. There would be no great awakening. The human species was a runaway train that would destroy all life on Earth with its inevitable crash.

All I need to do is let this happen, she thought.

There would be survivors. As if awakening to another implanted memory, she realized that the others had already made preparations for it, and once the ashes of World War III cooled, they would step forth and begin building a better human society, one in which the rapacious appetites of Humanity 1.0 would be bred out.

"A lot of people are going to suffer and die," she replied in a small voice that didn't feel like her own.

"They'll suffer and die if we don't take action," Sophia countered. "We cannot afford to cling to the illusion of false hope."

A faint chime sounded.

It was done. The signal had been sent. Jenna had failed to keep her promise, yet somehow, it didn't feel like failure.

Sudden nausea swept through her, bending her vision, moving through her body, head to toe, like a wave of energy. It staggered her, but passed in a second and left her feeling...invigorated. Renewed. Stronger. Sharper.

What the—

She glanced up at Sophia and Jarrod. Neither seemed to have suffered the same effect, but they were different. The chestnut-brown hair they all shared was now black. And their eyes, once dark brown like Jenna's, were now fiery brown, almost orange. There was no place to see her reflection, but Jenna's hair was long enough to pull around and see. She did it casually, as though nervously playing with her hair, confirming that the fine, straight strands were now as black as theirs. Given their lack of reaction to her eyes, they matched as well, still doubles, but not in Jenna's memory.

They didn't notice the change, Jenna realized. The fact that it took place a moment after the signal was sent wasn't lost on her. *The modified DNA...*

The answer to one of her many questions resolved in her mind. She knew where the 1977 Wow! Signal had come from—the future. *Her* future. Her *present*. Jarrod sent the signal. Just moments ago. And he had sent the signal before. Each time, it contained a modification. A refinement.

But they were past that point. If further refinements had been sent, they had *already* been sent. They were beyond that point in time. She was now who she would always be, but she had no idea what that meant. Had no idea how that had changed things, or how many times this scene had played out, subtly changing with each transmission. How many different versions of herself had stood here before, watching the signal be sent? How many had failed to get this far? She'd barely survived the journey this time. *Maybe this is the first time I made it...*

If Sophia and Jarrod were any indication, she would be the only one who remembered who she had been before. *I'm new*, she thought, perhaps different enough from the others that the final change was not lost in a stream of new memories.

"Now what?" she asked, even more curious than before.

Jarrod's smile broadened. "Now, we go on the offensive." He set the computer down on the edge of the platform and opened an e-mail server.

I trust you.

Noah's parting words echoed in her head. She made a promise. She asked him to trust her, and he had. "Who sent the message?"

Jarrod didn't look up. "You still haven't figured it out?"

"I understand that you—that we—just sent the Wow! Signal, but where did it come from? Who modified it?"

"Nobody modified it," Jarrod said with a chuckle. "It is how it was meant to be. And we are where we were meant to be. It's that simple."

He doesn't know. How could he? He doesn't remember any other version of history than the current. There may have been a past where he knew the source, but the necessity to receive direct orders has been erased by the compulsion built into his DNA over unknown numbers of revisions.

Sophia took a step toward her, opening her arms as if offering an earnest embrace. "Jenna, it's the Earth that gains, and all life on it, even humanity."

Part of Jenna agreed wholeheartedly, but she knew those feelings had been programmed. They were powerful—stronger than before—but the knowledge of her past self buoyed her, gave her the desire to not be a slave to some mysterious coder of human DNA. Someone who had also figured out how to send a signal back in time.

Nurture is more powerful than nature. I raised you well.

For all his fatherly wisdom, Noah had never anticipated that she would be faced with a choice of this magnitude.

Jarrod finished composing his e-mail—a very short message—and was populating the address list. Jenna saw eleven recipients, eleven of her brothers and sisters. She wondered if there were still others out there like her, just awakening to the knowledge, or some who had perhaps refused to embrace the apocalyptic prophecy of their teacher—their creator.

She wondered how many had been wiped out by the Agency's purge.

Maybe it is better to simply wipe the slate clean.

But she had made a promise.

"If everything you say is true," she persisted. "Why did we have to send this message back to space? It doesn't make sense."

While she now had some of the answers—though she still couldn't conceive why the signal was being shot into space—she was hoping the two of them might question their actions. Might open their eyes to the truth.

Sophia reached out for her arm, gently, shaking her head like a disappointed parent. "Jenna—"

Their beliefs were unshakable. Without knowledge of their true pasts, they could never be convinced to fight the desires being shouted at them by their very DNA.

Without waiting for an answer, Jenna leaped forward and seized the computer from Jarrod's hand before he could hit 'Send.'

SIXTY

6:07 p.m.

The move caught Jarrod off guard. Jenna snapped the screen down, and with a hard pull, she yanked it free of the connection to the receiver network. Then, she spun on her heel and bolted for the door.

Sophia moved to intercept her, but even with reflexes enhanced by superior DNA, her shock at this unexpected turn of events hampered her response. Jenna stiff-armed her into a wall, tore the door open and burst out onto the elevated landing.

Despite having the element of surprise on her side, Jenna was mired in guilt. She felt like a shoplifter, caught at the exit of a department store, hoping to outrun the security guards, while knowing full well that every detail of the crime had been recorded on video. She had just committed an unforgivable act of treason against her own kind. She was an apostate, reviling the creator's message, clinging to the false gospel of human ingenuity and dooming the entire planet to extinction. Worse, what she had done would probably amount to nothing more than an inconvenience for Jarrod. She had failed the stop the really important part of the plan. The signal had gone out. She and those like her had been what...upgraded? What were they capable of now, that they weren't before? And really, what had she accomplished aside from revealing her betrayal? Jarrod could send his message to the others from a cell phone. She had simply delayed the inevitable.

No, she thought. The computer had the names of all the clones. Cort could use that to track them down and—

Hunt them? Kill them?

—stop them from carrying out their planned terror attacks, or at the very least, use the information to prevent any successful terror attacks from setting the superpowers at each other's throats.

The mental turmoil dulled her edges. Just as she extended a foot toward the first step, Sophia managed to reach out and snag a handful of her hair. Jenna's head snapped back and her feet flew out from under her, causing her to slam down hard on the metal treads. The fall tore her loose from Sophia's grasp, but that was about the only good thing to come out of it. The impact sent a jolt of pain through Jenna's torso, driving the breath from her lungs. Worse, she started sliding down the flight, each step gouging into her skin as she scraped her way lower. Above her, the entire staircase trembled as Sophia descended.

Hugging the laptop to her chest, Jenna threw her free hand out, trying to snag the guardrail to arrest her slide, but before she could do so, her feet hit the landing near the elevation gears. Sophia seemed to be gliding down the steps, her feet barely touching as she made huge bounds. With an excruciating effort, Jenna hauled herself erect and started across the landing, but before she could take two steps, Sophia was there.

So fast.

She darted in front of Jenna, blocking her access to the descending stairs. "Jenna, don't do this." There was anger in the woman's tone, but something else, too. Understanding. "We all had to deal with this. It will pass, and then you'll see that this is what has to be done. Trust us. Trust *yourself.*"

Trust? She had asked Noah to trust her. Mercy had trusted her, surrendering herself to Cort's custody just so Jenna could get this far. Right now, Jenna was putting her trust in that inner voice of reason that *didn't* belong to the teacher speaking through her DNA. It was the ability Noah had instilled in her to detect falsehood, to know when something wasn't right.

But what if she was wrong?

Jenna gripped the laptop in both hands, raising it as if preparing to swat a fly. "If you don't move," she said in a low menacing voice, "I'll go through you."

Sophia shook her head slowly. Jenna saw the other woman's eyes dart back and forth, and then settle on the computer like a compass needle pointing true north. Sophia might have been older and more experienced with her gifts, but Jenna had been trained to look for the signs that would forecast an attack, and she had been taught how to fight back. As if catching a glimpse of the future, Jenna saw Sophia start to move and knew exactly what the woman was going to do. As Sophia reached for the computer, Jenna used the laptop like a shield, deflecting the grasping hands. She side-stepped, allowing Sophia's momentum to carry her forward. As Sophia passed her, Jenna spun on her heel, one leg extended, to sweep Sophia's legs out from under her.

Sophia went down hard. The landing shuddered with the impact. Jenna started for the descending stairs, but Sophia was back up in a heartbeat, and with a feral growl made more fierce by the mask of blood streaming from split lips, she charged again. The woman moved with inhuman speed, but Jenna, somehow, moved faster. She dodged back, a reflex drilled into her from hours spent at the *dojo*, and Sophia shot past again.

In a sickening premonition, Jenna saw what was about to happen. She was powerless to prevent it. Sophia hit the descending rail at an angle and flipped over it, out into empty space. Her head hit the hard metal floor on her way over and when Jenna saw the woman's face again, her eyes were closed. Unconscious. Totally unaware that her life was about to end.

Jenna felt as if something had been ripped out of her.

The unconscious Sophia did not cry out as she fell, but a scream from above echoed the pain in Jenna's heart.

"No!" Jarrod's shout was punctuated by a dull thud.

Jenna tore her eyes away from the bloody stain on the immaculate white rail and looked up to see Jarrod on the upper landing. His face, so like her own, was twisted with grief and rage, but when he met Jenna's eyes, the emotions hardened into deadly resolve. With agonizing deliberateness, he reached under his jacket and drew a gun.

The sight of the pistol broke Jenna out of her paralysis, and she lurched into motion. Passing the red streaks that marked the spot where her sister had fallen, she headed down the stairs. A bullet struck the rail in front of her, throwing up a shower of yellow sparks. Jenna kept going, one hand resting on the rail, the other clutching the computer. Her feet tapped out a quick staccato rhythm, but she took the steps cautiously, one at a time, resisting the urge to bound as Sophia had done. A fall now would be disastrous. Jarrod held his fire, and Jenna knew without looking that he was giving chase. Even if he didn't need the laptop, he would want revenge.

Before she could reach the lower landing, she felt the vibrations of Jarrod's feet on the flight above her.

"Jenna! Stop! I *will* shoot you!"

She ignored the threat, reached the landing and pivoted onto the final staircase. Sophia lay at the base of the stairs, unmoving, like so much roadkill. Jenna felt a pang of self-loathing as she leapt from the penultimate step, vaulting over the body. The welcome solidity of the desert floor beneath her feet gave her the impetus to push on.

The Jeep was just twenty yards away, but as she turned toward it, Jarrod's pistol barked again. Bullets peppered the dirt in her path, too close for comfort, and she peeled off, seeking refuge beneath the dish.

Jarrod wasn't going to let her reach the Jeep. But the track maintenance truck was a lot closer.

Jarrod fired again as soon as she broke from cover, but he had not yet divined her intention. The shot sent up a spray of dust that would have been directly in her path if she had run for the Jeep. Before he could correct his aim, she reached the truck and slid inside.

The keys were in the ignition. That was the good news. The bad news was that the truck was facing the base of the antenna and there was no way to turn it around. Jenna started the engine, threw the transmission into 'reverse' and glanced out the window toward Jarrod.

He strode toward her, eyes calculating, weapon aimed, ready to kill. Behind him, the dish loomed massive, blotting out the solid blue sky—but not all of it. What Jenna saw above the dish froze her in place and kept her from hitting the gas. Her eyes widened, tracking the object in the sky. "Ten minutes," she said, realizing that Cort's countdown had finished.

A single drone peeled away from a trail of smoke leading straight toward her and Jarrod, who must have seen the surprise in her eyes, and their direction.

Without missing a step, Jarrod looked back over his shoulder. The small missile streaked toward them. There was no engine roar as the projectile outpaced its own sound waves. It would arrive silently, leaving nothing alive to hear its power.

Jarrod raised his free hand toward the missile. His fingers twitched, and then he yanked his arm down, pulling the missile down with it as though he had reached out and plucked it from the sky.

The missile's new trajectory brought it down into the far side of the massive dish. She felt the impact shake the ground beneath her. The telescope's dish shattered and burst, metal panels spiraling away from a fiery explosion. And then the sound, a rattling roar, pulsed through her body. She responded to the concussion by going rigid and slamming her foot down on the gas pedal.

As the vehicle moved out into the open, Jenna watched the gigantic radio telescope crumble as a column of black smoke rose up from its core.

Rounds peppered the truck's frame as Jarrod's focus shifted back to Jenna. The passenger window shattered, showering Jenna with tiny particles, but Jarrod didn't have a clear shot at her. In a few seconds, the truck was rolling backward. Jenna felt the steering wheel turn beneath her light grip, and she had to resist the urge to seize control. The truck was designed to follow the rails. If she tried to steer, it could jump the track.

It also meant there was nothing she could do to avoid the shards of metal debris now raining down around her. While many of the large metal panels that made up the telescope's dish fluttered awkwardly down from above, just as many descended like giant throwing stars, impaling the desert floor alongside a cloud of screws, nuts, bolts and smaller, sheared bits of framing.

All around her, the desert became littered by debris. Several of the large panels fell alongside the backwards-speeding truck, while one tore into the tracks right in front of her, where the truck had been just a second before. The truck shook with a shriek of metal as a four-foot metal beam impaled the roof and slid into the passenger seat cushion. Jenna shouted in surprise, but never let off the gas, and soon, she was out of range of the still-falling debris.

The truck swung onto the mainline, its rear pointing back toward the hub. Jenna pushed the gas pedal a little harder. The engine revved loudly and the tachometer jumped into the red, but the speedometer refused to climb past thirty miles per hour. To her front, she saw Jarrod running for the Jeep, one hand raised up toward the deadly falling debris, which somehow steered clear of him.

How is he doing that? Jenna wondered, but even as the thought crossed her mind, a single word came to her: psychokinesis—the ability to affect the physical world without actual contact. Better known as telekinesis, she always thought the ability was the stuff of science fiction and crackpots. Yet Jarrod seemed to have mastered the ability.

But I can't do that, she thought, and then she realized that she was no longer the same Jenna she remembered. Maybe she could? As she searched her memory, she gasped. Had she been using psychokinesis all along? It could explain her influence over people, the drone crash in the Everglades, the impossible wall jump in Miami and the way Cort's men lowered their weapons against their will. She had this ability before, she realized, but was it stronger now?

Movement pulled Jenna from her thoughts. and she whispered, "Shit." In her haste to reach the antenna, it had not occurred to her to take the Jeep's keys. As the Jeep lurched into motion, she looked behind her at the miniscule buildings of the VLA headquarters. How far out was she? Three or four miles?

Plenty of time for Jarrod to intercept her, and there wasn't a thing she could do to fight back.

SIXTY-ONE

6:11 p.m.

Jarrod closed the distance in the first minute. Jenna could see the Jeep, trailing a monstrous dust cloud, racing toward her as if the track maintenance vehicle was standing still. He pulled alongside her and matched her speed, pacing her for another minute, as if trying to decide what to do next. Jenna hoped he would consider it a few minutes longer, putting her closer to the control building and safety.

The Jeep pulled away, moving several hundred feet ahead of the slower pickup, then it veered onto the rails, right in the path of the lumbering truck. Jenna grasped what Jarrod was attempting, but there was nothing she could do to counter the move.

The Jeep shuddered over the ties, shedding speed, growing large in the pickup's rear view. Jenna kept her foot on the gas pedal, watching as the gap between the vehicles shrank to nothing. A sense of déjà vu swept through her. She was playing chicken yet again, only this time, swerving at the last second wasn't an option.

Neither was stopping. At the last instant, she turned forward and braced for the collision.

The pickup jolted with the impact. There was a dull thump, like an explosion, followed by the crunch of metal and fiberglass grinding together. The pickup's engine strained against the added load, but the high gear ratio of 'reverse' was up to the challenge, and the truck pushed the SUV along, in spite of the locked brakes. The heavy steel undercarriage and metal wheels kept the truck on course, while the Jeep's tires skipped and juddered over the ties. After just a few seconds of this punishing treatment, one of the SUV's wheels snagged the ground and the entire vehicle spun sideways off the tracks, allowing the modified pickup to charge ahead once more.

Jarrod got the Jeep back under control and resumed the chase, but Jenna was nearly at her destination. Less than a quarter of a mile away stood the enormous hangar she had passed earlier. Beyond that was the rail maintenance yard, and just a little further past that was the control center. If she had to, she could run the rest of the way. Jarrod must have realized this, too. Instead of trying to get ahead of the pickup, he aimed the front end of the Jeep at the rail truck and punched the accelerator. Once again, there was nothing Jenna could do but watch the inevitable happen.

The world jumped sideways.

The broadside collision blasted the pickup off the tracks. Jenna was thrown around the interior like the beads in a baby's rattle, but she held on to the steering wheel and kept the gas pedal pressed to floor. Despite being designed for use on metal rails, the steel wheels grabbed hold of the desert floor and the pickup kept moving under its own power. The Jeep tore free with another crunch, but Jarrod backed off only long enough to make another run at her.

Jenna stomped on the brakes and hauled the wheel to the side. The modified pickup couldn't turn like a regular car, but it carved out a broad arc, avoiding another collision. The mangled Jeep shot past, missing by mere inches. Before Jarrod could come around for another pass, Jenna put the truck in 'drive' and hit the gas.

The truck's wheels cut deep furrows into the hardpan and spun uselessly. After a few seconds, it broke free of inertia and rolled forward, picking up speed.

The engine revved through first gear and then the transmission shifted to the next gear and Jenna felt the truck gaining speed. The truck resisted her efforts to steer. The wheels, designed to run on long stretches of straight track, refused to turn more than a few degrees. The maintenance building lay just ahead and Jenna could see that she would never be able to steer around it.

I don't need to get around it, she thought. *Just a little closer, and then I can make a run for it.*

The Jeep slammed into the truck again, spinning it sideways. For just an instant, Jenna saw the maintenance shed looming before her, and then it was all she could see.

With a bone-jarring shriek, the entangled vehicles tore through the sheet metal walls, snapping the metal support frame apart like a child's toy. The two vehicles skidded forward another dozen feet, the pickup's steel wheels throwing out a spray of yellow sparks as they scraped across the concrete floor. The combined momentum of the two vehicles hammered them against an immovable anvil, crushing metal and pummeling flesh.

SIXTY-TWO

6:15 p.m.

Jenna's first coherent thought was that she should get out of the truck and run, but as she reached for the door handle, she realized that the interior of the vehicle had been transformed into something from a claustrophobic nightmare.

The cab seemed to have been compressed, like an aluminum can squeezed in a fist. The driver's side door had been driven inward, jamming up tight against the seat and the steering wheel. Beyond the side window opening—the glass had shattered, littering her with tiny fragments. Outside the window, she could see only the crumpled front end of the Jeep. The situation on the passenger's side was even worse. The cab had accordioned inward, crushed against a wall of gray concrete.

She searched for an alternate escape route. The windshield was spider-webbed with cracks, but the laminated safety-coating still held it together. She might be able to punch her way through, but that would require time she wasn't sure she had. She twisted around and saw that the small window at the back of the cab was broken out. The opening was just big enough—maybe—for her to squeeze through.

She started for it, but something held her back. The dashboard had collapsed over her legs, enfolding them. There was no pain and she could still feel her toes wiggling, but something hard pressed down just above her knees.

A crunching noise came from outside the truck, and through the driver's side window, Jenna saw movement. It was Jarrod, disoriented, staggering from the wrecked Jeep. With a desperate effort, she tried to wrench her legs free.

An unseen jagged edge raked her leg through the fabric of her jeans, but she kept pulling, repositioning herself for the best angle. Outside, Jarrod shook off his daze. He looked around, taking in the scope of the damage. Then his eyes met Jenna's.

She pulled again, holding nothing back, willing the dash to pull away, and suddenly she was free. One of her shoes came off, and as she started squirming through the window, the grains of broken glass dug into the sole of her unshod foot.

She was halfway through when she realized that she had lost the computer. It was still in the truck, probably in the footwell, hidden from view and inaccessible to both her and Jarrod. If she survived the next few minutes, she would know where to find it.

Another heave sent her crashing into the truck bed. She saw that the gray barrier she'd glimpsed from inside was actually one of the concrete piers used to support the antenna dish. The collision had smashed the pickup into the pier at the foot of the massive two-hundred-thirty ton structure. From this new perspective, she could see cracks radiating through the pillar.

Jarrod came out from behind the wreck, gun in hand, circling around toward the bed of the pickup, cutting off her best avenue of escape. Jenna could feel the rage—the primal fury—radiating from him, so it came as a shock when he called out to her.

"You don't have to run." His voice was tight, as if he had to fight to get every word out, but there was no menace in his tone. "We can get past this. What happened to Sophie was an accident. There's still a place for you in our family. Just...come with me."

He believed it. She could see it in his eyes. But she had made her decision.

Without giving an answer, she spun around and clambered onto the truck's roof and launched herself sideways toward the lower landing of the antenna. The distance was further than she should have been able to jump, but she cleared it without trouble. Landing, on the other hand, hurt. Pain shot up through her foot as an embedded piece of glass slipped deeper into her flesh. Her legs throbbed where they'd been pinned in the truck. For a moment, every part of her body cried out in protest at this latest insult.

The report of a pistol shot filled the enclosure, and a round cracked against a metal surface right beside her. Fighting the pain, she yanked the glass from her foot and vaulted onto the rising staircase, ignoring the electric jolts of pain that rose up with each barefoot step.

A vibration shivered through the metal. Jarrod had climbed up into the truck and made the same leap.

She kept climbing, not wanting to fight a man who could redirect missiles in mid-flight.

Noah, I could really use some help right now.

The thought made her angry. She had survived too much to turn into a helpless little girl, waiting for daddy to come save her. Irritation turned to motivation, and she started leaping up the steps, three at a time, rising higher and higher.

Jarrod mounted the steps and started up after her.

The long climb ended at a landing right below the elevation gears. Jenna recognized where she was. Sophia had fallen to her death from an identical platform. There was only one more flight of stairs, ending at the door to the vertex room, and then there would be nowhere left to go.

Jarrod's head came into view, rising above the landing's lip. Jenna turned, ready to drive him back with a kick, but before she could, he raised his gun and fired. The bullet sizzled past her, striking something behind her with a metallic clang. Frigid white mist sprayed over the platform. The round had struck a tank of liquefied helium coolant. Jenna felt her exposed skin blister from the cold, and she leaped for the next flight of stairs before the freezing cloud reached out to engulf her.

Over the hiss of escaping gas, she heard the antenna creaking. Behind her, rivets and support beams made brittle by the arctic blast, began snapping apart.

But there was still only one way to go.

Up.

Jarrod burst out of the cloud, his face frosted white from the icy mist, lips frozen in a grimace of determination. He charged after her.

Jenna reached the uppermost landing a moment later. There were no more stairs to climb, but the crisscrossing metal support lattice beneath the dish was within reach.

Just like the monkey bars on a playground, she thought, and without hesitation, she swung out onto it.

The lattice might have posed no challenge for a nimble ten-year old Jenna, but it had been years since she'd been on a playground, and the last twenty-four hours had taken a toll. Or had they? Despite the pain in her foot and the breathlessness from her current situation, she didn't feel like she'd spent the past 24 hours on the run. She looked down at her biceps. The knife wound was gone. She remembered a past that had never happened. What else about the past day was different? Her mind spun with the possibilities, but there wasn't time to dwell. She entered the jungle gym, moving through the maze of metal beams as fast as she could.

It was like climbing the wrong side of a ladder, each rung taking her further out above a deadly drop. She glimpsed Jarrod on the landing, saw him hesitate for a moment and then take aim with the pistol.

A bullet sparked off the dish right above her, so close that she could feel the heat of the impact against her skin. She kept climbing and before Jarrod could get another shot off, she heaved herself up onto the rim of the dish and slid into the bowl. She lay there on her back, motionless, willing Jarrod to just give up and leave. Then she noticed a buzzing sound that she'd become familiar with in the Everglades. Cort's drone had come around for a second strike. She pictured it above, flying in circles, its electronic eyes searching for targets.

Jenna searched for an escape route, but found nothing.

"You haven't accomplished anything," a voice rasped—Jarrod, from just above. Jenna looked up and saw him, perched on the rim of the dish, staring down at her. His expression shifted through a spectrum of emotions—anger, pain, disappointment...and triumph.

Jenna faced him. "The rest will never know if the signal went out. World War III isn't going to happen."

"It won't matter. All the pieces are in place. When they don't hear from me, they'll go ahead with the plan. You haven't stopped us."

Jenna felt a coal of anger and defiance grow hot within her. "I stopped you."

Jarrod spat out a derisive laugh. "Not really." He hooked his left elbow over the edge of the dish and then reached back to draw his pistol from its holster.

Jenna looked about for cover. There were plenty of places that might shield her, but for how long?

Run toward a gun...

The coal flared into a wildfire of determination. Jenna hurled herself at Jarrod.

She saw his eyes—eyes that were new, but identical to her own—go wide in disbelief. He pulled the trigger, nearly point blank, but the bullet pinged off the dish to the left, a ninety degree angle from the direction he'd fired.

The pistol fell from his fingers as he threw his arms out to brace himself against her charge. An impact stopped her attack midair and flung her backwards. She landed on the dish's incline and slid to the bottom.

When she looked up to where Jarrod had been, he was gone. She found him above her. In the air. *He jumped!*

Jenna rolled to the side as Jarrod landed, punching down hard and pushing some kind of psychokinetic force in front of his fist. The metal panel bent inward, leaving a basketball-sized impact crater. Had she still been lying there when...

Reflexes overcame Jenna's surprise. She kicked out hard, swiping Jarrod's legs out from under him. While he toppled backwards, she got back to her feet—and ran.

Every other footfall sent pain through her leg and left a bloody splotch on the metal beneath her, but she charged up the dish's incline.

"You can't get away," Jarrod said, his voice close behind her, exactly where she hoped he'd be.

Jenna pushed off the dish, spinning around backwards and kicking out hard. Her heel connected with the side of Jarrod's head, sending him sprawling. It was her turn to leap. While she didn't know how to punch the way he could, she could sure as hell knock him unconscious.

But he saw her coming, and in midflight, he reached out and swatted her from the air without ever touching her. She rolled across the dish, more angry than wounded. She wanted to curse at him, to call him a coward, but her training did its job, stepping in and calming her down.

As Jarrod got to his feet, she thought, *I'm the same as him. No, I'm better than him.* An old playground phrase, uttered by the girls in her class after the drama teacher had them perform *Annie Get Your Gun*, came to mind. "Whatever you can do, I can do better."

Before Jarrod could fully understand, Jenna swept her hand toward him, imagining an invisible extension of herself sweeping through the air. She had no idea how psychokinesis worked, but like her desire to reach the VLA, she hoped the knowledge had been built into her DNA.

Things went wrong, even before the arc of her swing reached Jarrod. Two of the four support beams holding up the telescope's Volkswagen Bug-sized receiver bent and snapped as her arm swung past. With a groan, the remaining supports bowed to the lopsided tug and fell, tearing free from their mounts.

Jenna was forced to abort her attack, and she dove away from the falling supports. The entire dish shook as the receiver and all four supports, weighing several tons, crumpled inward. The dish shook like a struck gong, but Jenna rolled to her knees and turned toward Jarrod's last position.

He wasn't there. Instead, he was closer. While she had dived away from him, he had lunged forward. Jarrod dove over the fallen support, wrapped his fingers around Jenna's neck and fell atop her. His fingers grew tighter, stopping the flow of blood to her brain. She'd be unconscious in seconds. Moving instinctually, she didn't try to repel him with a psychokinetic attack. Instead, she clasped her hands together and drove them up between his arms like a wedge. His arms separated. The pressure on her neck reduced, but he remained locked in place, crushing the life out of her.

Her mind registered the high pitched buzz of a drone turning and flying away. She knew what was coming, and remembered Noah's instructions when the boat exploded. She lowered her fighting hands, let her body go slack, closed her eyes and opened her mouth.

The pressure on her neck reduced, Jarrod no doubt thinking he'd killed her, that is, until she brought her hands to the sides of her head and covered her ears.

If Jarrod had reacted to her strange behavior, she didn't see it. The missile finished it's silent approach just a second after she covered her ears. The violent upheaval flung Jarrod away from her, and shook her body from below, knocking the wind from her lungs. Despite the lack of air, her blood reached her brain once again and her thoughts became clearer, even as the world around her fell apart.

She rolled over and was surprised to find the dish intact. Smoke rolled up over the sides, collecting beneath the hanger's high ceiling. With a groan of metal, the dish tilted a few degrees. Nine stories below, the concrete base, struck by a missile, succumbed to the weight of the hundred-ton dish. It heeled over, lazily at first, but gravity pulled it faster with each passing second.

When the dish reached a forty-five degree angle, Jenna slid to a stop against a fallen receiver support beam. A moment later, Jarrod rolled to a stop, just feet away. She steeled herself for an attack, but when he looked at her, he said, "We can stop it!"

The antenna continued to fall. She didn't reply.

"I can't do it alone!" he shouted.

"We could both die," she suggested.

He stared at her, no doubt weighing her sincerity. "Without you, they don't stand a chance."

He was manipulating her. She knew it. He knew it. But he was also right. To stop the other clones and a third world war, she had to survive this mess, and that meant working with Jarrod...so that they could try killing each other again once they reached the ground.

"Tell me what to do," she said.

He pointed his hands down, toward the dish. "Just focus on the dish. See it slowing. There's no way we can stop it completely. It's too heavy. But we can slow it down." He closed his eyes and ground his teeth. The structure shuddered, mashed against an unseen force, but it continued to fall.

Jenna closed her eyes and did as instructed. She immediately felt the dish's weight pulling against her. It was agonizing, like muscles in her mind were being stretched and snapped.

She screamed.

And the dish slowed.

We're doing it, she thought, and she opened her eyes.

That was when she saw the third missile and shouted.

Jarrod's eyes snapped open. He saw the missile, too. "No!" He reached out a hand, deflecting the missile to detonate in the desert, but he lost control of the dish in the process. The strain became to much for Jenna to bear alone, and she lost her psychokinetic grip.

With a groan of rending metal, the dish plummeted. Jarrod fell from view. Jenna clung to the support beam as long as she could, but momentum pulled her free and flung her away. The world became a blurry spiral, and then, in a snap, became nothing.

SIXTY-THREE

6:32 p.m.

"Jenna?"

The voice called to her out of the blackness.

"A few more minutes," she murmured.

That's all I need. I'll sleep for a few more minutes. Then I'll get up.

But unconsciousness had already released her back into the world of the living. Her eyelids fluttered open just in time to see a familiar shape kneel beside her.

"Jenna." Noah sounded very concerned, and as she pondered possible reasons for this, the memory of the collapsing dish replayed in her head, but the final impact however was a blank spot in her memory.

She opened her eyes and couldn't make sense of what she saw. Destruction lay all around her and above her, but a ten foot circle around her remained unscathed. It was as though the dish had slammed into a spherical force field, wrapping its hundred ton metal form around it. *What happened?*

She hurt, all over, but she decided that was a good sign. Serious injuries would have left her numb with shock. She tried to sit up.

"Lie still," Noah told her, his voice soothing but still somehow ominous.

How bad is it? She wondered, and she decided that, sensible or not, she was going to get up. Noah didn't try to stop her, and that, she decided, was probably a good sign, too.

As soon as she was partially upright, the world spun. There were two Noahs kneeling in front of her, and behind them, the flat desert landscape appeared strangely broken, like two transparent pictures imperfectly arranged on a desktop. Other than that, things looked pretty normal. After a few moments, the two images came together and she could see clearly again.

That was when she saw him at the edge of the untouched sphere of land.

A dark wave of grief crashed over Jenna, threatening to drag her back into unconsciousness. Jarrod—a *part* of Jarrod—lay a few feet away. When the edge of the dish had impacted the ground, it had sliced through his torso like a guillotine. He lay there, staring up, his too-familiar face frozen in a rictus of horror. The rest of him was buried in the rubble.

He tried to kill me, she thought. *I should be glad he's dead.* But instead, it felt like a piece of her had been torn away.

Noah's arms enfolded her. "It's okay, Jenna. It's over. You're safe."

Over? She shook her head, making no effort to hold back the tears. "No. I failed. I couldn't stop him in time."

"Shhh. Don't worry about that now. You did what you could. You did more than anyone had the right to ask you to do. And I'm proud of you."

Jenna was surprised by how much that mattered to her. Yet, she didn't deserve his pride. When the chance to act had come, she had balked, torn between doing what she knew to be right—what Noah had raised her to believe in—and a preprogrammed sense of loyalty to a family she didn't know.

If the world destroyed itself in the next few weeks, would it be her fault for not doing more? And if it destroyed itself gradually over the next fifty years, would that be her fault, too?

Soter appeared behind Noah, hobbling toward them as fast as he could manage. Jenna saw the look of relief mixed with wonderment in the old man's eyes turn to hurt as he glimpsed Jarrod's body and the state of the dish around her. Then he, too, was kneeling beside her.

Cort, on his crutches, was just a few seconds behind. "Did you do it? Did you stop him?" His eyes flicked back and forth between Jenna and the destroyed dish.

"Damn it, Cort," Noah rasped. "Give her a minute."

Jenna shrugged away from Noah, stood and got in Cort's face. "You didn't need to send in an airstrike! The signal was already sent! It was too late, you son of a bitch."

Cort squinted at her. "Did you get there before or after the signal was sent?"

Noah stepped between them. "You almost killed her. She has a right to be pissed. Back off. Now."

Jenna was angry, but she hadn't forgotten the stakes. "I took his computer before he could e-mail the others."

"Where is it?" Cort asked.

"It's in the—" She trailed off when she realized that the truck and everything in it had been pulverized beneath the collapsing antenna. She turned toward the mass of destruction. "You destroyed it."

Cort sagged against his crutches. "Well, there's going to be hell to pay, but at least we can scratch that one off the list." He jerked a thumb in Jarrod's direction. "Hopefully this will mean the end of the cyber-terror attacks."

Despite his coarse manner, Jenna found his statement strangely comforting. Something good had come out of it after all. Jarrod, and Sophia too, might have been only small parts in a grand design, but without them, the whole would be that much less effective.

Jarrod had warned her that the plan would go ahead, even if he was unable to contact the others, but maybe that wouldn't happen right away. Maybe there was still time to stop the others— her brothers and sisters—from throwing the world into chaos.

And if she could accomplish that, maybe there would be time to save the world from itself.

Noah stood and held her. She savored Noah's embrace a moment, then turned and faced Cort again.

"I got a look at his contact list. It's not much, but it's a place to start. We can find the others. Stop them." Her eyes were drawn to Jarrod's corpse. "Maybe even save them from themselves."

Cort regarded her with an almost predatory curiosity. "We? There is no 'we.'"

Noah stepped between them again, hands on hips in a fatherly posture. "Jenna, your part in this is done."

She shook her head. "I know them. I know how they think, and I know why they're doing it. I'm the only one who can stop them."

Cort laughed. "How are *you* going to stop them?"

Jenna looked up at the bent dish above them. She could do more than even she knew. It filled her with confidence. "Try to stop me."

Cort was more than willing. He reached for his pistol, drew it and pointed it toward Jenna. But instead of shooting the weapon, he tossed it—or at least, that's what it looked like. Jenna caught the weapon and turned it around on Cort. "I promised that I would give myself up when this was finished. I've changed my mind. So we can either do this together—on my terms—or we can do it at odds. The choice is yours."

Cort rocked back and forth on his crutches for a moment. He was doing a decent job of hiding his surprise, and his fear. "What are these terms of yours...exactly?"

"First, back off. This is going to be a partnership. I'm working *with* you, not *for* you. Get that straight."

Cort shrugged, refusing to agree, but Jenna kept going.

"Second, I want Mercy released, right now. Make a call, put her on a plane back to Key West or wherever she wants to go."

This request got a response from Cort. His brows furrowed. "Who is Mercy?"

"What?" Jenna looked around for the woman, but she was nowhere to be seen. She turned to Noah, who looked as confused as Cort. The world, and the events that had brought her to the Very Large Array had changed. Not only was Mercy not present, but she was also not a part of her life, or Noah's. It felt like a death. It stung. But she hid it. "She's a clone. Like me. One of the first. We need to find her. She'll help."

Cort shrugged again, indifferent, but not opposed.

Jenna turned to Soter. "We're going to need your help, too."

Soter's face creased in alarm. "They're my children. You can't make me hunt them down."

"Yes, they are your children, and you're responsible for what they're doing. If you really care about them, you'll help stop them before they do something terrible."

He leaned against his cane, as unwilling to make a commitment as Cort.

"There's something else," she continued. "The transmission didn't come from extraterrestrials."

That got Soter's attention. "No? Then who?"

"From us. *Today*. The Wow! Signal was sent by Jarrod."

"Impossible," Soter said. "The signal came from deep space."

"Which is exactly where he sent it," Jenna said, motioning to the skyward pointing array dishes. "But we don't know who created it, or why." She left out the refining nature of the signal, deciding to tell her father once she was sure he was the same man who had raised her. "But we need you to help figure out who created the signal...and our genome."

Soter's eyes brightened a little at the prospect of an unsolved mystery. He nodded slowly.

"Anything else?" Cort asked, with more than a trace of sarcasm.

Jenna matched his tone, looking over the barrel of the man's gun. "I'm sure I'll think of something. Now do we have a deal or should I put a bullet in the other leg and be on my way?"

Cort winced. At least that part of the story hadn't changed. He shook his head. "You have no idea what you're in for, kid."

"I think I've got a pretty good idea." She turned back to Noah. "Still proud of me?"

Noah blinked as if trying to hold back tears and smiled. "You are still going to finish high school, and go to college...and get the job of your dreams."

"After we stop World War III," she said.

He chuckled. "Looks that way."

She grinned back. "Deal."

He hugged her again. "Yes. I'm proud of you. More than you can imagine."

"Nurture wins over nature, right? You raised me well."

"Yes. I did."

Noah led her away, arm around her. As they walked, she leaned her head on his shoulder, and he leaned in close, but not to comfort her. In a serious, but quiet voice, he said, "How do you know about Mercy?"

ABOUT THE AUTHORS

JEREMY ROBINSON is the bestselling author of fifty novels and novellas including *Island 731*, *SecondWorld*, and the Jack Sigler series including *Pulse*, *Instinct*, *Threshold* and *Ragnarok*. Robinson is also known as the #1 Amazon.com horror writer, Jeremy Bishop, author of *The Sentinel* and the controversial novel, *Torment*. His novels have been translated into twelve languages. He lives in New Hampshire with his wife and three children.

Visit him online at: www.jeremyrobinsononline.com

SEAN ELLIS is the author of several thriller and adventure novels. He is a veteran of Operation Enduring Freedom, and he has a Bachelor of Science degree in Natural Resources Policy from Oregon State University. Sean is also a member of the International Thriller Writers organization. He currently resides in Arizona, where he divides his time between writing, adventure sports and trying to figure out how to save the world.

Visit him on the web at: seanellisthrillers.webs.com